WHO HOLDS T

A NOVEL BY

WHO HOLDS THE POWER?

A NOVEL BY FURIOUS

BY

FURIOUS

www.bookstandpublishing.com

Published by
Bookstand Publishing
Morgan Hill, CA 95037
3707_1

ISBN 978-1-61863-340-8

Printed in the United States of America

DEDICATION

This book is dedicated to the Ivan in all of us.

A NOTE TO THE READER

Who Holds The Power? is a work of fiction. Names, characters, places, and incidents either are the product of the author's imagination or are used fictitiously, and any resemblance to actual persons, living or dead, events or locales is entirely coincidental.

"Respect yourself and others will respect you."

- Confucius.

1

MONDAY, FEBRUARY 13, 1989

It is about 10am when Ivan Thompson gets out of bed. Stepping out of the shower he dries himself off and slips into his black and white Adidas jumpsuit. Throwing on his Nike cross trainers, he quietly makes his way towards the door.

Before Ivan is able to let himself out, another door to his left opens. His mother who is in her room watching the Oprah Winfrey show quickly comes out when she heard his footsteps. "Well look who'sup." She says smiling. "Good morning and happy birthday."

"Thanks Mom." Ivan responds. He has just turned thirteen. Reaching into the pocket of her blue robe, she hands him two envelopes. The first envelope he opens a card signed by both his mother as well as his father. His two older siblings, Jennifer and Simon has also followed suit. Their names are also listed. Ripping open the second envelope, he finds two new bills inside. A fifty and a hundred. Kissing his mom, Ivan places the money into his wallet. "So what are you going to do today old man?" She asks. Oh I see that you have jokes! Ivan thought. "I don't know." He answers.

"It's more than likely that Rizzo, Andrea, Denise, and myself will probably go down to the Treasure Chest, see a movie and take a carriage ride along the lakefront."

"That sounds nice." Says his mother. "Well have fun baby, and be careful." "I have no choice." Ivan replies. He now grabs his duffel bag.

Putting on his leather overcoat, Ivan is now situated in the hallway. A small coat rack is located near the stairwell. The latter of course not only leads to the front porch, but also to his grandmother's apartment. Ivan and his parents along with his brother Simon all lives on the second floor. Their building is a well-kept red and white two flat.

Located on Chicago's west side, the structure stands at 3429 W. Lexington Street. Ivan's grandmother is the owner.

Located also on the westernmost corner near Homan Avenue, the fire engine red dwelling is flanked along a tree lined side street, surrounded by well-preserved greystones, a Minuteman gas station, and the Eisenhower expressway. Just two blocks to the north, a rapid transit line known as the West-Northwest route exists. Located in the median between four lanes of traffic, two trains are now seen calling for passengers.

(Most notably at its Kedzie and Homan station) Bethany Hospital is seen in the distance just one block further.

Just two blocks south lies a vacant unused complex. Displaying a backdrop of office buildings, a warehouse, other industrial hubs, a larger corporate tower, and a commercial center, during its heyday this colossal building was once the central headquarters for Sears and Roebuck Company. Although Sears has now moved into what is dubbed as the world's tallest building in 1974, its flagship store, survives another decade.

Its Homan Avenue store closed in the fall of 1984.

Ivan is very mature young man for his age. Although he is only thirteen, he is highly intelligent, handsome, and a born diplomat. He's extremely fluent in Spanish, French, and now studies Chinese. In reference to his school curriculum, Ivan has excelled in every major subject with the exception of Math. However, despite his difficulties pertaining to the latter, the determined youngster has done all but fail.

Having been physically obese previously, Ivan has suddenly transformed into that of a natural born athlete. Running and jogging seven days a week, he also lifts weights at the YMCA, and not to mention that Ivan also, is a student of the martial arts. The weather outside is both windy as well as chilly, with perhaps a mild pinch of warmth as Ivan steps onto the front porch. As the sun beams directly above him, he inhales the smog consisting of namely fumes from nearby vehicles, freshly cut grass, and marijuana.

The origin of the smell employed by the cannabis alone comes from a red Chevy Blazer. Situated across the street, many gray clouds of smoke began emerging from the partially opened windows. Next comes the laughter followed by the sound of continuous puffing. Finally, the coughs of enjoyment. Puff. Puff. Pass. And then of course rotate.

Ignoring the potheads in the modern-day Mystery Machine, Ivan begins his journey towards the end of the block. Continuing east, he goes left on Kedzie Avenue and proceeds north. Walking five blocks, he reaches the corner of Jackson Boulevard.

Overlooking a recently rebuilt bus garage to his right is his favorite eatery Jimmie G's. Going inside, he enters the lobby and places his order. Once his order is placed, Ivan takes a seat in what is now the dining area. Prior to the eatery's renovation, this particular room was once a meat locker. Located just three blocks from his house on Arthington Street is the West Metropolitan YMCA. Its not because of his unbroken English, his physical features, nor is it about his larger IQ that causes resentment from most of his peers. Perhaps Ivan's only crime is that he chooses to be one thing, and one thing only.

Himself. Ivan, unlike most of his peers doesn't look for trouble. In fact, Ivan is the exact opposite. He is always respectful, honest, and most of all, he's very kind. And like most young men coming of age, he is also curious about girls. In fact, Ivan also like them. But however unlike that of his fellow peers, he does not chose to go through great lengths as to grope or to fondle them up.

Ivan in his own rite has chosen to be a gentleman. He believes in striking up general conversations with girls, getting to know them, asking them out, and perhaps an innocent game of tag in between. Others who has known him throughout the years, namely those closer to him, believes that it is these particular qualities that has rendered him a target.

Others have gone through great lengths as to call him a "nerd" and a "faggot" because of his lack of aggression when it comes to girls. To the rest, Ivan is just a virgin.

Furthermore because of his failure to kneel before his peers, Ivan is therefore declared "too soft." On a regular basis namely from kindergarten to the present day, Ivan has been beaten, bullied, and to add insult to injury… Blackmailed.

But however, perhaps the worst cases of scenario for which he has dubbed as his own personal labyrinth, began following his enrollment into the fourth grade. Besides being persecuted by most of his fellow classmates, two of Ivan's former teachers Mrs. Reid and Mrs. Armstrong had even bigger plans. Although his G.P.A. was far superior to that of the other students, the sadistic, mean spirited queen bee duo instead, failed him anyway.

And as a result of their heartless actions, Ivan spends the following year repeating the fourth grade. Now situated in the boys' locker room at the YMCA, Ivan closes his eyes and begins to meditate. Minutes later, the youngster opens his eyes. Slowly rising to his feet Ivan walks into the bathroom. Facing himself in the mirror, he bows his head.

"Its going to be a new day." He said to himself.

Gymnasium A

In this room, there are over a dozen people. Many are adolescents some preteens. On the basketball courts, boys between the ages of twelve and seventeen compete against one another while the girls sit on the bleachers and watch.

The rap song entitled "Gangsta Gangsta" by N.W.A. echoes throughout the sound system.

Gymnasium B

In this room, Ivan and one of his longtime friends Charles Davis joined by two other young men as well as a female are all busy practicing their free throws. The two other young boys are close affiliates representing Charles. They attend the newly opened Andrew Jackson Language Academy located downtown. Furthermore, these two young men are exchange students from Africa. Given their overall height and as well as their reach (although minors), one can easily mistake for them as varsity players. The young lady who is the shortest in the group is eleven-year-old Nicole Sanders. Better known as "Nikki", the southern-born princess is truly every boy's dream. With a light brown caramel complexion, long curly hair (shoulder length) and beautiful hazel eyes, Nikki also has the figure of what is believed to be the body of a "goddess." As the most recent arrival to the neighborhood, namely on Ivan's block, Nikki lives only with her mother Paula Sanders. Mrs. Sanders, twenty-nine-years-old is employed by First Chicago Bank.

After spending two hours on the court thus perfecting their playing techniques, sweating profusely, Ivan and his friends are all convinced that they've done well and therefore, calls it quits . Wiping off the excess sweat from their bodies with towels they borrowed from the recreation office; the young party of five is now walking down a brightly lit corridor. The corridor itself immediately returns them to both the first gym as well as the locker rooms. But however upon their journey, comes eight boys. The first five are clad in typical street attire. Designer jumpsuits , baseball caps, and well-polished sneakers. This particular unit of hoods is among the first to block the group's path. The second opposing group dons T-shirts, football jerseys, and jeans. Just like that of their friends, they too wear sneakers.

It is not obvious that the other three youths are acting as "backup." Each of these self-proclaimed "gangsters" or in street slang "gangtas" employs every height. Tall, medium, and short. The leader of course, is also the shortest as well as the heaviest.

He is seventeen-year-old-Henry Jackson. Better known as "Hannibal", the junior gang leader is a high school dropout and without a doubt, he is the oldest member of the group. About four feet to nine inches tall, Hannibal dons a black leather outfit (pants, turtleneck, and jacket), white designer sneakers (presumably Adidas) and a huge gold chain. The latter employed what looks like the continent of Africa.

The two lanky young men whose apparel matches that of their boss is none other than his lieutenants "Mookie" and "Ice Pick." Of course their real names are Michael Mitchell and Isaac Pitman. These infamous threesomes are key leaders of one of the most powerful gangs in the city. The 24th Ward Mafia. The so-called three "wise" men, who has often terrorized Ivan, suddenly has a position for him. On the account of his newly discovered talents, Hannibal himself feels as though Ivan can be quite useful in closing business deals, forging truces, and his favorite: Engaging his rivals.

But after being harassed on a regular basis whenever it is by Hannibal himself or his subordinates, and don't forget about his own cousin's betrayal, Ivan gives the gang general a "no thanks." As he now faces his opposition, Ivan takes note of the first five standing before him. It is quite obvious that these boys are "new jacks." Or more specifically, new members. "So what's up man?" Hannibal grins. Producing a brush from his pocket, he brushes his waves. "Its yo last chance." Ice Pick adds as he attempts to fondle Nikki. Nikki immediately slaps him. At this point the two exchange students Moussa and Akeem are now nervous. But however, at the very same time this duo remains fearless, still focused, and prepared for battle.

Even though he himself wishes to punish them, Charles urges them to remain calm. “Let’s go!” Ivan snaps. Without warning, Ivan catches Hannibal off guard. Executing a solid palm strike to his face, the dumbfounded leader loses his footing as he staggers backwards. Landing flat on his ass upon impact, Hannibal then hits his head onto the hardwood floor. “Mothafucka!” He cries. Trying to get up as quickly as he can, like one who has had one too many, the embarrassed leader now staggers his way towards the bleachers. Finally plopping down, Hannibal catches his breath.

Charles, Moussa, and Akeem followed by Nikki has each began to position themselves against the foot soldiers as Ivan throws up his right hand. This fight is his. Ice Pick who is now seated next to Hannibal, and Mookie snaps his fingers, and gives an order. Ivan, at this point is in a Taichi stance. Of course it doesn’t take a rocket scientist to realize, that this young man is ready for battle. “Whoop his ass!” Ice Pick shouts. “Hell yeah!” Mookie further instigates.

Maintaining his fighting stance, Ivan is positioned at a forty-five degree angle. With his hands up, and his knees bent, the first of Hannibal’s members attempts to mix it up with Ivan as he works his boxing skills. Throwing a left jab, a right cross, and then a left hook, Ivan immediately parries and then blocks every punch.

Focused on his breathing while dancing, Ivan comes back with a faster and a much powerful left jab, a right cross, and a devastating left hook. Now delivering a right uppercut, his first opponent falls to the floor. Seconds later, a right cut over his eye appears. Upon hitting the floor on impact, the hood trainee is now unconscious.

A second opposing team member charges after Ivan with his hands up, and attempts to employ his boxing skills. Parrying, and blocking, Ivan dodges to his left and then to his right. Bobbing and then weaving (both left and right), the more advanced fighter delivers his shots. Striking both of the other boy’s ribs, Ivan comes across with an upper cut. Executing a right cross and then a left hook, the young Ivan “The Terrible” sends another right cross. Within seconds the youngster’s lip is now busted. Shortly thereafter, it became visibly bloody. But however the carnage doesn’t stop there.

Still determined, the second youth keeps it moving. But yet as Ivan continues to block, parry and even hit his opponents’ hands, now employing his own Muy Thai fighting techniques, Ivan begins snapping unbearable kicks, knees, and pulverizing punches.

Now dazed and disoriented, the much taller thug now has a swollen eye. As Ivan summons a left elbow and then a right across the second trainee's face, an explosion of blood and saliva appears. Following through with two more, Ivan then aligns the side of his right foot. Taking it to his opponent's shin, the victor to be snaps a left roundhouse.

As a powerful right dropkick aligns to his chin, for this hoodlum in training, his world also goes black. Staggering and slipping, the youngster falls and hits his head.

The other three tries a different approach. Upon seeking to wear down their opposition, these freshman hoods will too suffer the same fate. As they try to attack him all at once, Ivan snaps two roundhouse kicks followed by one elbow. Perhaps the next attempt carried out by the fourth enemy appears to show at least some promise.

Demonstrating what appears to be Karate almost has Ivan's interest. This would-be special opponent employs all of the basics. Including Kata. The shorter youngster with a shiny baldhead surprisingly wears the traditional ghee and dons what appeared to be a black belt. Mookie and Ice Pick smiles and shakes hands with Hannibal.

But, however, before "Danny" can even land the first blow, Ivan quickly attacks him. As he delivers a spinning crescent kick to his face, the comic relief fighter knocks himself unconscious. Crashing into the wall head first, he begins to slide. At this point the youngster appears like that of a homeless person. Slumped over and of course sleeping.

At this point, the three wise men are no longer smiling.

Situated on the opposite side of the gym are Ivan's friends. Unlike the three-gang leaders, they cheer and they clap. When word had gotten out about Ivan's brutal assault against the 24's, at least half of the entire building; youths, teens, and adults all rushes in to witness what is believed to be, the battle of the decade.

Now engaging his fifth opponent, Ivan snaps two crescent kicks (both in and out), and follows up with two ax kicks. Taking flight, the newly skilled fighter delivers a stunning and powerful flying roundhouse. As the blood and saliva becomes visible, the medium built youngster turns his head to the right and then falls. Face down. The entire gym, this time cheers for Ivan. As three more of Hannibal's minions enter the room, Ivan doubles it up. Snapping the sole of his left foot into the first, he then executes a double sidekick, blanketing both the stomach; followed by the head of another. Delivering a spinning hook kick to the head of the third, a fourth rushes in and catches a left front kick.

As the number of 24's continues to grow, so does Ivan's momentum. Following up with a spinning rear leg foot sweep, he summons a hip toss to another. Elbowing another mindless youth, Ivan then takes both fists and employs two strokes to the sternums of two others. Returning to his fighting stance, the young victor bows his head. The three-gang

leaders meanwhile frown and nod their heads in disbelief. "This shit ain't over yet nigga!" Hannibal says. He now gets up. "Yeah, yo ass might have won the victory, but you ain't win the war bitch!" As his fallen opposition cries out and moans in agony, Ivan begins to smile. Ice Pick on the other hand, becomes nervous. In the center of his jeans, a huge wet spot appears. Five minutes later, a team of building security guards walks in.

Shortly thereafter, their supervisor a tall well-dressed gentleman comes in behind them. "Okay everybody." He begins. "The shows over break it up." The head captain, a strong muscular figure walks over to Ivan's group. "Are you guys alright?" He asks. "Yes sir." Ivan responds. "We saw you on the camera." The captain explains. "Man, you looked good out there." "Thanks." Ivan says politely. The man nods his head. "I didn't know you had it you." He says looking surprised. "Neither did I." Ivan replies.

Although Hannibal, Mookie, and Ice Pick have already left, many of their fellow brothers have not. As they remain laid out some unconscious, others moaning in pain, the guards slowly began helping them up. Now back on their feet, the youngsters are escorted out.

By 6pm, the sun now begins its descent into the western suburbs. A bright full moon joined by a delegation of twinkling stars takes its place. One by one each of the city's streetlamps began coming to life. Around this time the temperature also drops, as Ivan stands on the corner of Madison Street near Hamlin Boulevard. Situated in front of a building that once housed a movie theater, is now the home of a bowling alley.

For decades, this particular area was amongst the most vibrant and the most prosperous. Having survived the Great Depression, two global wars, and racial shifts, the community known, as Garfield Park would eventually give way to another change.

In response to the assassination of Martin Luther King in 1968, a full-scale riot breaks out. In the aftermath, dozens of stores were leveled. Although a few have risen from the ashes, many of them did not. Today, only a modest fraction of these shops still exist. They are joined by newer fixtures such as Sports City, T.K. Tops And Bottoms, M.P. Flea Market, Service Optical, George's Music Room, and last but not least Luigi's Pizza.

Even though the overall community is predominately black, the majority of its business owners are not. With the exceptions of George's Music Room and The Cascade Bowling Alley, many of the other stores are either Arab or Korean owned. Ivan's uncle owns the Cascade. Having spent the last fifteen minutes on this now bright corner, Ivan checks his watch. The time is now 6:30. Five minutes later, a red Plymouth Voyager pulls up. A center door slides open. The driver was Linda Wallace, Rizzo Harrison's grandmother. Rolling down the windows, the not so bad looking forty something smiles and then waves. "Hello Ivan." She says. "Hello Ms. Harrison." Ivan answers back. "How are you?" "And happy birthday." "Thanks Mrs. H." Ms. Harrison then kisses her grandson's best friend. While Rizzo himself rides shotgun, his friends Andrea Dupont, Denise Wilson, and Charles Davis are also seen. They are seated both in the middle as well as the rear. "I can't remain in this spot for long." Rizzo's grandmother explains.

As soon as Riz and the others steps out, Ms Harrison begins to drive off. "Well you guys have a good time." She says. "And please stay out of trouble." "I think we're good for it." Rizzo assures his grandmother. "Yeah, you'd better be." She grins. "For your sake especially." Waving once more, the not so elderly woman heads back east.

Cascade Bowl

The normal business hours for this establishment are often from nine in the morning until ten in the evening during the week. On both

Friday's and Saturday's, the hours are therefore expanded. Instead of closing at ten in the evening as he normally does, Sam will later make his announcement at exactly twelve midnight. But however, given that it is a special occasion (in reference to his nephew's birthday), the prominent business owner has decided to close his doors at 6pm.

Amongst tonight's guest are none other than Rizzo, Denise, Andrea, and Charles. Others included Charles's friends Moussa Tsvangirai and Akeem Opolot. Also in attendance is Ivan's dream girl Nicole Sanders. Some of his friendly acquaintances from his martial arts class are seen, as well as others from the neighborhood "Y."

On the family side besides his Uncle Sam, would be who else? His parents. For the duration of the evening, each guest including the birthday boy himself is given unlimited access to each working lane. At this time, Ivan is now seated amongst friends and family as he happily accepts his gifts. The smells in the room consist of Connie's Pizza and Harold's chicken. Situated near a set of lockers and the fire exit is Kenneth Davis, Charlie's brother. Ken is doing what he is paid to do. DJ.

To many of his friends and classmates who know him at Providence St. Mel (a catholic high school also in this neighborhood), Kenneth is better known as "DJ. Killer watt." Everyone is having a good time here. No complaints. Just clean fun.

When Charles told everyone how Ivan single handedly fought off the gang members who tried to harass them, the others all put their glasses together. The partygoers' preferred drink: Welch's grape juice. They toasted to the man of the hour himself. Who immediately blushes shortly thereafter. "For as long as I've been knowing Ivan." Charles began. "I never would have expected for him to go off like that." He pours what is left of the juice into his glass. Mr. And Mrs. Thompson looks at one other and smiles.

"Me neither." Says Nikki. "He's always been the silent type." Glancing over at the young man, she smiles flirtatiously. "It was like a scene from Bruce Lee's Fist of Fury." Moussa added. "He was really tough." Akeem Says. "There have been rumors flying around the school about Ivan working out, and he was getting stronger." "Even faster." Rizzo explains. Sitting before all of his best friends, and his parents, the birthday boy is still speechless. As everyone now began to eat, Ivan's brother Simon and his girlfriend Elizabeth arrive. The pair grabs some plates and began piling on chicken.

"So what's the good word?" He says to the others. "And happy birthday again." Simon then tells his brother. Ivan nods with satisfaction. "Your brother here got into a fight at the Y with some of Hannibal's henchmen." Mrs. Thompson explains to her oldest son. Devouring a slice of pizza, she then reaches over for a can of Coke.

Perhaps what impressed Mrs. Thompson wasn't the fact that her youngest son made mincemeat of Hannibal's hoods, it was the fact that he had met two key benchmarks. One Ivan has stood his ground like he never has before. He stood up for himself. And two, Ivan also stood up for his friends, and he fought for them. Unconditionally.

As for Simon, the story has once again rang a bell. "You know now that you've mentioned it mom, Gerald did tell me something about an ugly fight breaking out at the Y earlier." He began. "But I never would have thought Ivan was involved." "Not to mention mopping the floor with almost twenty dudes." "Ivan ain't got the heart to even to fight one person." "I'm telling you Simon man, he did." Kenneth tells him. Taking a break from working his tables, He grabs four slices of pizza and pours himself a can of Fanta.

"Charles was there with him." "Heck the whole neighborhood is talking about it."

"I got sick and tired of them." Ivan tells his brother. "Picking on me almost day after day." "Even night after night." "This confrontation was warranted." Rizzo tells the others. "Which part of going too far did they not comprehend?" Charles asks.

"I guess they did." Simon shrugs. He's not going to ruin my day. Ivan thought as he now thinks about his dream girl. Elizabeth who was somewhat embarrassed by Simon's gesture, sighs and then smiles once more. "Well congratulations man." Simon tells Ivan. He smiles and shakes his hand. "About time."

Taking what is left of his food, Kenneth/D.J. Killer watt now returns to his tables. Putting his headphones back on, he grabs some vinyl and mixes it up once more. At this point, Ivan hears some of his favorite songs. Among them is the latest from a group called Inner City. The track is entitled "Big Fun." As soon as he hears the sound of Paris's voice, the lead female singer, Ivan quickly rises. "How bout it Ms. Sanders?" He says in reference to Nikki. "A dance for the road." Ivan reaches out to extend a hand.

"Anything for you Mr. Thompson." Nikki flirts. "Ooooooooooh." The others all taunted. Ivan laughs. "Y'all need to quit. Taking Nikki by the hand, he leads her to the center of the room. This feels so good! He thought to himself. First I fight multiple thugs. In the end, I emerge as the winner. Its my birthday. And not only do I have a party. I'm here dancing with my actual dream girl! Considering we're just mere good friends.

As he now dances with Nikki, Ivan looks briefly at the ceiling and then back to his partner. This was his day. His evening. His beginning.

2

The next day at Jens Jensen Scholastic, a prominent elementary school where both Ivan and Nikki are enrolled, things are basically no different that of any other day. As the pair ventures beyond the central gates, they now enter the westernmost playground. Upon entry, many girls are seen. They are jumping rope, performing splits , dancing to house music, and even playing volleyball. The boys on the other hand are seen playing football, basketball, and playing cards. Others, particularly those within the older crowds are seen. A group of four, they are all taking part in what appears to be a "rap battle." The remainder (both boys and girls alike), are seen just socializing, hanging out, and moving about. Before Ivan and Nikki decide to play, the likely couple to be has taken the liberty of leaving their personal belongings inside. Although they could have left their backpacks and their jackets on the fence like that of the other students, they instead chose an alternative.

Built in 1961, the school was named for a prominent Danish-born architect. In classrooms throughout the entire complex, there are no lockers. The only correspondents consist of miniature wooden closets. Inside of these individual compartments lies a network of only six hooks. A single shelf corresponds among these six hooks.

Gymnasium/Auditorium

On the basketball court, Donnie Nicholson, Ronald Cox, Kendrick Watts, Yusef James and Morris Parker joins Ivan and Nikki. These six young men all play on the school's basketball team. The Jaguars. Fred Bosworth is their coach.

When tryouts began in early September, both Ivan and Nikki participate. But in the end, neither of them makes the cut. Those who did believed it was still unfair. For many months, it was speculation that Bosworth rejected Ivan because of his height.

For Nikki, it was because of her gender. In the team's twenty-six year history, not one female player has ever made the roster. The glass ceiling has yet to be broken.

At this time, both Ivan and Nikki partners up. On their team there's Donnie, the current captain, against Ronald, Kendrick, and Yusef. Morris, who is seated on the bench, decides to play next. The temperature outside is now sixty-four degrees as Donnie on the inside, tosses the ball into the air. The tip-off begins.

As the players began spreading out while working both courts at once, the six young, but yet competitive athletes all hustle. Jumping, reaching up and thus blocking the other player's opposition it is indeed a game. Employing the balls of his feet for the fourth consistent time, Ivan takes flight, jumps up and successfully clenches the ball.

Despite being stalked by Kendrick who now attempts to block him, Ivan summons the Wilson, jumps up and makes contact with the rim. Ronald and Yusef try to stop Ivan as he too goes airborne. But in the end, the relentless duo fails. Crashing head on like two locomotives, both athletes quickly fall. Ivan showing his true sportsmanship helps the players to their feet and keeps it moving. The score meanwhile is two to nothing.

Recovering briefly from his soreness, Yusef hustles for a tie. Bouncing the ball continuously between his legs, he dances; he spins, and even fakes out Donnie and Ivan.

Now attempting a lay-up, the confident player returns to the court of his home team. But however before Yusef can jump up and make his shot, Nikki parries the ball clean out of his hand. From where she now stands, Nikki jumps up from the balls of her feet and makes her shot. Quietly, the ball swishes through the net. Three points.

Even though the game is just getting started, Donnie, Ivan and Nikki are already having fun. They now have a total of five points. "Check." Says Donnie as he grins and bounces the Wilson towards Kendrick. Kendrick shakes his head and, then sighs.

"What's wrong Ken?" "You ain't get no nookies last night?" Donnie continues to ride his fellow teammate. "You ain't eat yo Wheaties this morning?" "Nigga what's up?"

The other players quickly began laughing. Kendrick smiles and gives Donnie the finger. Shortly thereafter, Kendrick bounces the ball back.

Scrambling about the two courts once again as players from both teams hustle, reaches up and then blocks, the ball is now in Donnie's court. As all three players Ron, Yusef, and Kendrick attempt to stick their defense, the slightly taller and larger captain, motions for Ivan and Nikki to spread out further. As the two hopefuls take heed to his advice, so does Yusef and Ronald. Meanwhile as the opposing captain stalks Donnie himself, his two players proceed to ride Ivan and Nikki.

As the four rival decoys continue to reach up and block one another, Ivan once more emerges from the pack. Jumping up, he clenches the ball and returns to the floor.

Landing feet first, both Yusef and Ronald waits . Surprisingly, Ivan looks at them and then laughs. In his mind given how his friends are persistent in reference to sticking defense, in his mind Ivan likens them to the villains Heaven and Earth. Perhaps if one doesn't know, it is a classic martial arts film starring Jackie Chan.

As Yusef tries to hit Ivan high by jumping up in front of him, Ronald attempts the opposite. He hits him low. Now trying to parry the ball away, He fails. Ivan ducks, bounces the ball once and does a quick left turn. Spinning off to the right, he fakes out Yusef once more and dances. Dribbling the ball between his legs while performing this motion on Ronald, the pair somehow becomes weary allowing Ivan to retain his wind.

Sounding as though they are out of shape, Yusef and Ronald still goes after him. Breathing heavily and wiping away sweat as they attempt to employ their defense, Ivan ascends to the air for another lay-up. Although he makes his shot, he is still fouled by Yusef. However due to the fact that he still succeeds in making the actual shot, Ivan instead refuses to call.

With the ball now in Kendrick's court (the opposing captain), Kendrick himself passes the Wilson over to Yusef who then hands it Ronald. As soon as he gets it, Ron takes off.

Bouncing the Wilson, he now begins his footwork. Employing a series of crosses, spins, and sudden quick turns the point guard now ducks and then dodges both Ivan and Donnie. But however, this time they would not give up. From the time Ronald receives the ball from his captain up until the time he's greeted by Ivan and Donnie once more, the fired up athlete continues to mix it up. Bouncing the Wilson repeatedly between his legs, he continues to fake out the now relentless pair.

Sweating profusely Ronald is weary, tired, and perhaps somewhat confused. Meanwhile as Ivan and Donnie continues their collective defense against the embattled team player, Ronald himself somehow soldiers on. At this point, Ivan and Donnie are now unshakable. Still ducking, spinning, and dodging, Ronald finally loses them.

By this time, he is now reaches the center court. Attempting to make another jump shot comes another surprise. As Ronald takes flight with the Wilson in hand, Nikki also jumps up. Intercepting his would be jump shot for the second time; she steals the ball and dribbles her way back to the other side. Now pursed by Kendrick and Yusef, their combined efforts are yet still useless. Nikki's agility is virtually impeccable.

From where she stands, Nicole jumps and then leaps. Kendrick and Yusef on the other hand, are much too late. As the ball is summoned by both of her palms, it circles the rim first before ultimately falling through. Having flopped through the net, the Wilson falls and hits the floor. The beautiful but deadly princess for the second time delivers.

Thanks to Nicole's additional three, the team now has a ten-point lead.

Kendrick and Yusef, both whom are six feet although impressed are still dumbfounded. Donnie on the other hand is both impressed as well as shocked. Facing Nikki, he laughs. "Damn girl." He begins teasing her. "What did you eat this morning?" She smiles and then giggles.

Moving towards the rim, Ivan is again stalked by Yusef and Ronald. Throwing out their arms and jumping up over the five foot five youngster (who actually carries the most muscle), Ivan turns to the left and to the right. Bouncing the ball between his legs, he crosses; he spins, and then dances. Bouncing the Wilson between his own legs, Ivan sends the ball between Yusef's legs turns and then spins to reclaim it.

Bouncing the ball as he now returns to the court, Yusef and Ronald goes after him, but once again they're too late. Kendrick tries to block his path, but he too lucks out. Spinning left and then right around the embattled captain, Ivan takes it to the hole.

He executes another dunk. Shortly thereafter, Kendrick and his team call a time out.

In the end even though Kendrick's team managed to give Donnie's one hell of a fight, the latter of course; still prevails. The score is thirty-two to twenty eight.

"Good game y'all." Donnie says to everyone. The players all shake hands.

"Yeah, word up." Yusef added. He gives both Ivan as well as Nikki some dap for the second time. "Where in the hell have you two been?" He says facing them.

As they turned to face one another, Ivan and Nikki then laughs.

"He, he, my ass." Ronald chuckles. "The two of y'all should've been on this team!"

"I've gotta agree with Ron." Kendrick nods. "You two are JUST what we need." "Personally, I think that Bosworth was full of shit for not pickin' y'all to begin with." Donnie snaps. "In all the years I've been playin' with Ivan on the court, he's always had

some ugly assed defense." "He was always a strong Mothafucka." "Even when he was husky." The others nod their heads in agreement. Even Morris Parker who still sits on the bench. "Now there is something new to the equation." Says Kendrick.

"Not only does Ivan have the strength." He begins. "But he's now got the speed as well as the reach." Ronald finishes. "And don't forget the wind." Says Donnie.

"And if he's got the reach, that means that his ass can dunk." The Captain concludes.

"Something we have just witnessed." Yusef smiles. "And he does the shit so well too!"

"You had me, Kendrick, and Ron feelin' salty on the court this morning." Ivan smiles.

"Courtesy of the new me." He says. "No shit." Donnie nods. "And now you young lady." Kendrick begins. He now turns to Nikki. "You might be the shortest player, but yet you still have a ugly reach." "Even the most tallest player is no match for you." "But the story gets better." Donnie continues on. At this point, they are now seated; drying themselves off. "You shoot some crazy three pointers." "And one more thing." Yusef comes back. He turns to Ivan and Donnie. "That strategy was brutal as hell." He then gives them a pound. "I couldn't have thought of a better one myself." "Y'all made me work for mine." "Y'all rode me until I got to center court, and I thought I faked y'all out."

"Word, they were smart with theirs." Says Ronald. "I shake you two off, turn around to make a jump shot, and get caught by beautiful but deadly here." Yusef speaks in reference to Nikki. Once again, Nicole smiles. The others laugh. "Nikki got you good man." Donnie reminds him. Don then pats Yusef on the shoulder. "She jumped up and slapped it clean out of my hand." "Twice!" "And none of us could touch her." Kendrick says shaking his head. "Nikki was moving out like ol' girl off of Small Wonder."

"You fixed it where she would be able to come in, catch me off guard, and stick me." Ronald further catches on. "But before y'all could, you had to wear me down first."

"That was cleaver." "But anyway." Donnie concludes. "We all think that the both of y'all can really do some damage." He reminds Ivan and Nikki. "As far as the two of you trying out for the team again next fall, why not?" "Seriously, I think you'll make it."

"We'll see." Says Ivan. "Time will tell." Nikki adds.

"And by the way, we heard about your exhibition at the Y yesterday." Donnie says to Ivan. He looks at his ex-rival and smiles. "Goddamn." Yusef chuckles. He laughs and then shakes his head. "An entire gang of mothafuckas." "Ivan?" "And I thought that shit just happened on T.V." "It never pays to keep picking on people." Yusef joins in.

"Especially when they ain't never did shit to you." Nodding their heads, the others agree. "How long you have been practicing man?" Ronald asks Ivan.

"About a good year now." Ivan tells him. "That's cool." Says the others.

Now getting up, the group now prepares for another game. Ivan on the other hand, decides to run some laps. Taking his place is a well-rested Morris Parker.

"POWER UP!!!" Says Kendrick as roasts his fellow teammate.

Morris himself as well as the others all began laughing.

Room 403

Located on the fourth and final floor, this room houses roughly twenty students as well as two teachers. Based on their previous Iowa test scores and their current comprehension levels, the students are placed into to separate groups. Sharon Holmes, the head teacher has worked for the school board for over seventeen years. Her credentials includes working with kindergarteners, both grade and middle school students and in recent years teenagers. It has only been a year since Mrs. Holmes began working at Jensen.

At thirty-nine years old she is very attractive, full figured, and quite healthy. Her features hint that perhaps she enjoys cooking as well. Although well embraced by both her students as well as her fellow colleagues, Mrs. Holmes is still zero tolerant when it comes to nonsense. She treats her students as though they are her very own.

Meanwhile as for her own children, they are all grown up and attending college. Also divorced and single, Mrs. Holmes enjoys playing the piano, and surprisingly the veteran scholar also has a remarkable singing voice. Unlike most of her colleagues up to date, Mrs. Holmes is truly the young people's advocate. The sixth grade class, for which she currently teaches, sits at a strong intermediate level.

Amongst her prized students are of course Ivan and Nikki. Her assistant is Vearline Cobbs. Mrs. Cobbs unlike her fellow co-worker and friend is married with an eight-year-old son (attending the very same school) as well as a nephew whose age is comparable.

During her first season at the school, the thirty-seven-year-old teacher has worked as a substitute before ultimately filling her current position. Her predecessor was Ivan's uncle Rocky Thompson, his father's brother. Rocky like Mrs. Holmes was a long time employee of the Board. In January, he left to teach at Howard University.

For the past three years Mrs. Cobbs has seen this school as her second home. And like her partner in crime, she too loves children. She oversees the other group.

Later in the afternoon sometime after lunch, Mrs. Holmes leads Ivan and his fellow classmates out of the cafeteria-library. Returning to their classroom, the proud teacher and her students quickly reclaim their seats. For one young man in particular, it is now game time. In commemoration to Black History Month, the school each year hosts a series of special events. Among them is a trivia contest, which consist of four rounds.

To be a contestant, one must be extremely knowledgeable in reference to people, historical events, as well as a variation of timelines. In the end, Mrs. Holmes chose Ivan.

Since the contest first began three years ago, Ivan has always wanted to participate.

However his previous teachers rejects him because they believed he was "overqualified." Perhaps it was ironic due to the fact that those responsible, later flunks him. Three years later, Ivan's boat has arrived. With the building's central air still out of service (namely due to current season), and furthermore in response to the sudden spring-like temperatures Mrs. Holmes allows her students to open the windows.

For the next ten to fifth teen minutes, she allows her students to mingle. Now situated in the adjoining prep room with his eyes closed, Ivan meditates. Surrounded by office supplies, a mini refrigerator, and a coffee maker, Ivan considers this room to be his own personal thinking tank. Fifteen minutes later, there is a knock at the door.

"Who is it?" He asks. "Its Mrs. Holmes baby." "Mrs. Cobbs and myself wanted to ask you something." Sure, I'm all ears." He smiles. As he re-enters the classroom, his fellow students began to quiet down. Now facing their champion to be, Ivan has their full attention. "Is this your first time competing in the contest?" Mrs. Cobbs asks.

Parking her thin, but round frame on the edge of her desk, she crosses her legs. "Yes, it is." Ivan says proudly. "However, I can't lie to you." "I' am little nervous." And he is.

"Why are you just now participating?" Mrs. Holmes asks him. "Because my former teachers were idiots." He explains. "I bet they were." She replies. Ivan chuckles. As for his fellow classmates, many of them laugh. "All jokes aside." "Just like each and everyone of you, I can see a great deal of potential in Mr. Ivan here as well."

"He's equally gifted." "And nobody, and I do mean nobody." "Can tell you otherwise."

Mrs. Holmes not only tells this to Ivan, but she also tells the rest of her class. "Well anyway." The heavier woman rises from her desk. "Its time for a little shadowboxing."

As soon as Ivan returns to his seat, Nikki and Andrea then greets him. The two young ladies, who sit on opposite sides gives him a brief pat. Meanwhile, while the majority of his other fellow classmates look on, the frowning faces, the irritable sighs, and last but not least; the excessive mumbles appear. Shortly thereafter comes a series of boos.

Moreover, to add additional coals to this burning fire comes one ignorant taunt.

"Nerd!" Curtis Hawkins shouts. Mrs. Holmes at this point becomes furious. "Have you all lost your minds?" She asks. "Were gonna act civilized." "And by the way Curtis."

"You can get your nerdy ass out of my class." Now appearing angry, Curtis gets up and walks toward the door. In a fit of rage, he slams the door behind him.

Gymnasium/Auditorium

Situated on the easternmost stage are the three contestants. Besides Ivan, there is Justine Thomas from room 405 and Tyree Clark from room 404. Lauren Delaney, the school's guidance counselor acts as the hostess. Given her overall features, many have likened her to Anna Marie Johnson.

She recently co-starred with Ernest Thomas from what was obviously a spin-off from the T.V. sitcom "What's Happening" entitled "What's Happening Now." Amongst the judges is Karen Jamison, the assistant principal, Shelia West, the music teacher, and Daniel Peters, The history and social studies teacher. They are all seated on the opposite stage overlooking the west playground. Adam Rothstein, the principal is situated inside the coach's office. From a large glass window, the thin white haired gentleman looks on. The time is now 1:40 and the first round comes to a close.

As the sound of roaring "L" trains echoes through the walls from the outside, cheers, claps, and applauses on the other hand gives way to the inside. Ivan and Justine are virtually neck and neck with twenty points each. Tyree, meanwhile scores twelve.

In the second round, the topic is now sports. "What female runner overcomes Polio and competes in the 1964 Olympics?" Ivan abruptly sounds his buzzer.

"Wilma Rudolph." He answers. He is obviously on a roll. Perhaps one reason for which the game has been so intense from the initial round (namely between Ivan and Justine) is because Ivan unlike that of his competitors has sharper reflexes. "Very good." Says Mrs.

Delaney. Justine sighs. Although Tyree is further behind, he yet still soldiers on.

Mrs. Delaney clad in a silky red dress and matching pumps, proceed to drill the group once again. "For his failure to enlist in the military in response to the Vietnam War, this young athlete is stripped of his boxing license in 1967." "Who is he?" Before Justine could even think about it, Ivan quickly taps his buzzer. "Muhammad Ali." He says.

The bell sounds. Three times. Damn! Justine mumbles. "Who was the first black major league empire to play for a major team in 1966?" Mrs. Delaney asks.

In the beginning even Ivan himself is uncertain. As he closes his eyes briefly and meditates, Justine bites her nails. Tyree on the other hand, pleads to the fifth.

Just one second before the clock runs out, Ivan now answers. "Emmett Ashford."

For the second time, the bell rings three times.

By the time the forth and final round ends, it is now 3:00. Although most of the students are long gone, a small congregation is still present at this time. They occupy several classrooms on the forth floor. Aided by a few dedicated teachers, it appears to be what is known as an "After school Reading" program. Funded by the school board just three years prior, the program was invoked for students in grades four through sixth.

Its sole purpose was to assist the students in therefore improving their comprehension as well as having a little fun in between. The program has shown great promise with a ninety percent success rate. Outside of the complex, the last of three remaining school buses finally depart. As for this year's Know Your Heritage and Your History Contest, Ivan emerges as the key victor. As he collects his first place trophy, he shakes hands with Justine and then hugs her. While she collects a trophy for second place, Tyree last but not least takes home third. He gives Ivan a firm handshake. In return, Ivan gives him a pound.

Exiting the building through the main entrance, Ivan continues west on Harrison Street. Carrying his military sized duffel bag, he is suddenly confronted by six boys.

Approaching him from the Albany pedestrian bridge (stretching over the Eisenhower expressway) the group quickly surrounds him. Ivan shakes his head. "You know Curt, we can't continue to meet like this." He says to the leader. Ivan then smiles at his followers who at this point began grinning. Their leader on the other hand is not. He is apparently pissed. His name is Curtis Hawkins. Curtis, who was banished by Mrs. Holmes earlier, has recently gone from being the class clown to the class bully.

The motive behind such an act has yet to be determined. Since the second grade, Curtis has always a reputation for making people laugh. Each and every since year since the fourth grade, Curtis has been the star participant in the annual school talent show.

His stage act as usual consisted of comedy, skits , and parody songs. And each and year since his initial debut, Curtis has always won first place. Often times during lunch, he would often have his peers, namely those who sat at his table practically in tears.

Among them was Ivan, his newest adversary and his former classmate Rizzo Harrison. Given his overall physique, the fourteen year old actually looked more like an ex-youth con as opposed to a comedian. At 6'-2" Curtis has a fudge brown complexion, gorilla-like features and a well-muscled frame. His attire consists of a black skullcap, a matching turtleneck sweater, jeans, and top of the line sneakers.

With nearly every boy acting as his loyal slave, Ivan is now number one on his shit list. Many believe that Curtis resents Ivan, because Ivan himself would never bow down.

Even though Ivan is no Ritchie Rich, others argue that Curtis is envious namely because of his wealth. The obviously troubled youth is the oldest of three children. He has a brother who's only his junior by one year named Desmond, and a younger sister named Michelle. Michelle, who is ten years old, attends a private school.

Curtis never knew who his father was. He had walked out on his mother just six months before he was born. Situated on the corner of Kedzie Avenue near Lake Street, lies a dilapidated two flat. With a tavern on the first floor and the Lake Street "L" roaring above it, this is where Carrie Hawkins and her children lives. She works full time serving tables at a Baker's Square Restaurant located in west suburban Oak Park.

“That ain’t funny.” He snarls. Unfazed and yet still fearless, Ivan nods his head.

“What’s the matter Curtis?” “Did you get booed off of Amateur Night?”

“Sad Man Sims chase you off the stage?” Smiling once more, everybody including Desmond begins to laugh. “What the fuck y’all laughing at?” Curtis ask the others.

He then walks up and slaps Desmond. As shame and humiliation begins its course, the younger brother is ready to cry. The others are no longer laughing.

“Get this Mothafucka.” Curtis now gives the order. Shoving Ivan to the side, another boy snatches off his baseball cap. Leaning against the fence with his arms folded, the comedian-turned bully looks on at his disciples. As Malik Allen dances around like that of a loon, sporting Ivan’s hat, the angry lion emerges.

With his knees now bent and his arms in a chamber, his fist corresponds to what appears to be an upward position. As Ivan maintains his Kenpo stance, Curtis meanwhile begins to mock him. Singing Carl Douglas’s “Kung Fu Fighting, the others join in.

Everybody loves Kung Fu Fighting!
Huuuhaaaa!
Those Kicks were fast as lightning!
Huuuhaaaa!

As the five youths (minus their leader) quickly rushes in, Ivan fights fire with fire. Quickly blocking all of their kicks and punches, He comes back with his own fancy footwork. Delivering kicks, punches, sweeps, and massive takedowns, it is not a pleasant sight. Within seconds, they all fall to the pavement. By this time, traffic along west Harrison Street remains light. Only four to six cars are spotted, followed by a Cta bus. Stopping to collect passengers in front of Area Four (the police station), the Loop bound number seven then takes off. Across the street, several employees from the Chicago Tag Company are now the sole spectators. Now taking their cigarette break, they are in for another treat. As more youths cross the Albany Bridge from the north, and enters the school grounds, Curtis summons them over.

With six more advancing towards him, Ivan braces himself. As the first fighter attempts to box him, he delivers first a jab, a cross, and then a left hook.

Coming back twice as hard, Ivan dances, bobs, and then weaves. Now parrying consistently, he blocks and then dodges. Attacking in areas where the youngster is more susceptible, Ivan snaps a left jab, a right cross, and delivers a left hook. As a right uppercut summons his chin, Ivan then follows up with a spinning back fist.

Within seconds two bruises are formed. Leaning back with palms facing up, Ivan kicks out his right leg and plants it directly into his stomach. Coughing and wheezing for air, the boy extends out his arm. "Stop, alright man I quit!" He pleads.

Changing stances, Ivan executes a left crescent kick and then a right. Snapping a double front leg sidekick, the latter connects first to his opponent's abdomen and then to his face. Turning his body, he employs a spinning hook kick and then a rear leg double sidekick. Pivoting and changing stances, Ivan goes into hyper mode.

At a rapid pace, Ivan snaps as many as twenty sidekicks (face to stomach), and then a final hook kick to the back of the youth's head. This unfortunate fellow is knocked out long before he hits the pavement. The next hood smacks himself across the head repeatedly. Pretending as though he's a bull, he charges his way towards Ivan.

But before he is able to tackle his opposition, the short heavyset fellow is quickly immobilized. As soon as Ivan delivers first an ax kick and then a front, comes the darkness. The heavyset thug is out. Giving another rival a hook slash roundhouse combination, Ivan spins and jumps. Returning to his fighting stance, Ivan snaps a left inside crescent kick and knocks out his forth opponent. Spinning once more with his hands up, Ivan comes around once more and gives his fifth opponent more of the same.

In all, twelve youths are quickly disposed. No prisoners taken. Now more frustrated than ever, Curtis kicks away at the fence. His brother Desmond who is the first to go down suddenly wakes up. Curtis grabs him and pushes him toward Ivan.

"Go down a second time, and I'm fuckin you up." Curtis warns him. "Now let's do this." Who does this guy think he is? Ivan asks himself. This is not really like him!

With his hands up, a more petrified Desmond accepts his rematch. “You don’t have to do this Des.” Ivan pleads. “I understand Curt is your brother, I can respect that.”

“But you’re not his bitch.” “He doesn’t own you.” As Desmond begins to dance, the tall but thinner sibling throws a series of punches. In response, Ivan dodges, and then bobs and weaves. Now blocking, Ivan gives Desmond a right knee and then turns his body upward (Counterclockwise). Returning to the ground feeling twice as sore, Desmond moans. One knockout is efficient. Ivan tells himself. He then helps Desmond to his feet. “Be yourself.” He tells him. Having agreed with his brother’s newfound rival, Desmond nods and then takes off. “Sleep with one eye open tonight nigga.” Curtis says to his brother (now walking off). “I told yo ass.” “Be ready when I get home.”

Right about now, Curtis isn’t the only one heated up. Malik Allen, who danced around like a loon with Ivan’s hat earlier, now wants a piece of the action. Taking off his LA. Raiders jacket, he attempts to use it as a weapon. “Fool, you ain’t nobody!” He snarls.

“That wasn’t what your mother told me last night.” Ivan responds.

Employing his cat-like reflexes, Ivan grabs his jacket and forces Malik to his knees. At this point, Ivan nearly chokes Malik to death. His fudge brown complexion becomes red. Seconds later his skin turns purple. Freeing his latter opponent, Ivan once again shows mercy. During the initial battle, two heavyset twins later joined Curtis as his fellow spectators. After nearly destroying Malik, the two youths Lester and Leon Carter cracks their knuckles and remove their jackets.

As Lester tries to attack Ivan from behind, Ivan, in response employs his right hand to block the bigger man’s left jab. This particular block, which corresponds to a circular motion, is known as a “Poon Kiu.” Attempting to throw a right cross, Ivan’s left hand

blocks Lester’s punch by the employment of another “Poon Kiu.” Meaning at this time, Lester’s hand, his right is also trapped.

Upon turning his right hand into a “Dragon Claw”, Ivan steps forward. Tripping the tall and chunky youth with his right foot, Ivan’s Dragon Claw now makes contact with his opponent. As a result, Lester’s face is smashed. The oldest Carter twin screams.

“You punk mothafucka!” He shouts. Holding his face in agony, Lester shakes his head and then rises once more. Attempting to throw another series of blows, Ivan quickly blocks them away. Now parrying, Ivan snaps a left jab into his opponent's throat.

Delivering a left into his abdomen followed by a right, Ivan places Lester into a headlock. With his left knee bent upward, Ivan pivots his right leg and snaps the sole of his left foot dead into his rival's face. Lester is out. "Well Leon, its just you and me now." Ivan says to his brother. Removing his jacket, he then rolls up his sleeves.

"Bring it on G." Leon says. Both youths are now dancing. Closing in for a brief submission move, Ivan actually misses and becomes trapped in a chokehold. Leon then employs a bear hug. Curtis meanwhile is laughing. "Yeah, what's up now Bruce?" Leon taunts. He then applies more leverage. Ivan's face turns red. While in pain, he also becomes lightheaded. "Hell yeah, that's right!" Malik cheers him on. "Strangle the shit outta him!" Ivan although still in pain, is even more aggravated.

The Tag Company employees meanwhile are now cheering for him. Some of them even placed bets.

With every ounce of strength in his newly muscled body, Ivan finally breaks free.

Delivering a dragon claw to his face and then a "She Xing", a snake hand to his throat, Leon „s breathing is now labored. As he struggles to catch his breath, the fat boy is suddenly dumbfounded. Attempting to hit Ivan with a left jab, Ivan quickly counters.

Bending his knees, Ivan uses his left leg to create a "stealing stance." By doing this, Ivan blocks Leon's left leg and grabs his wrist. Now squeezing away at Leon's chin and his jaw, he now executes a "Tiger Claw." Pulling his opponents arms in towards him, Ivan plants his left leg onto his stomach. As he now lies on his back, Ivan sends the younger twin airborne. Crash landing onto the pavement, Leon is out.

The cheers are no more. Curtis and Ivan at this point are now face to face.

"Have you had enough King Kong?" Ivan asked the head youngster.

"Fuck you!" Curtis snarls. "Suit yourself Curtis." Ivan says. He shakes his head with uttermost of disdain. "Like I told your brother, it doesn't have to end this way."

Now prepared to fight, both young men began to square away. But however before anyone of them could land one blow, a marked police car comes into view.

"We can continue this tomorrow." Ivan tells his adversary. "Alright, bet." Curtis responds. Although the officer behind the wheel didn't see them, both Ivan and Curtis still have an understanding. Their common philosophy, live today fight tomorrow.

Picking up his duffel bag, and then his hat, Ivan retreats south on Albany Avenue. Curtis and Malik follows suit. Scooping up their boys, they retreat to the north.

Wallace Residence

On the first floor of Mrs. Wallace's brown and white two flat, Ivan and Rizzo are sitting at the dining room table. Quietly finishing their homework, the sound of a cricket suddenly plagues the room. "Man, stop that!" Rizzo laughs. He shakes his head and

points at Ivan. "How in the hell do you do that?" "I've been trying to ask myself the same question." Ivan chuckles. "It is kind of quiet around here." Rizzo finally agrees.

Entering the living room, he collects two tapes. Activating his grandmother's stereo, he pops in N.W.A. "Now that's more like it." Says Ivan. Smiling and nodding, both boys resume their studies.

Eazy-E: You're about to witness the strength of street Knowledge…

Ice Cube: I'm comin Straight Outta Compton, Compton

Following the sound of sirens, Ice Cube now says these words:

If something happens in South Central Los Angeles
Nothing happens
Its just another nigga dead

Straight Outta Compton
Crazy mothafucka named Ice Cube
From the gang called Niggaz With Attitudes

"You know man, that's the song." Rizzo began. He gives Ivan a pound shortly thereafter. Their homework is now complete. Having known each other for only three years, it seems as though Ivan and Rizzo has known each other since pre-school.

The relationship, for which they have, actually mirrors that of blood brothers. Rizzo, who is Ivan's junior by only two years, skipped two grades early on. He is also an honors student. And like Ivan, Rizzo speaks more than one language. Just two inches shorter than Ivan, Rizzo has a chiseled frame and a lighter brown complexion. Sporting a tall fade haircut, Riz enjoys art, boxing, swimming, and even skateboarding.

Unlike his partner in crime, Rizzo is quite the mathematician. His grandmother, a registered nurse often looks after Rizzo and his younger brothers during the day.

His mother works as a travel agent. She is employed at O'Hare Airport. Annie Harrison Campbell, twenty-nine wanted nothing but the best for her boys. Feeling as though her oldest (namely Rizzo) was too smart to attend Jensen, she eventually pulls him out and places him into Wicker Park Prep, an elite magnet school.

Putting away their textbooks, Ivan and Rizzo goes into the living room. Turning on the television, Rizzo then activates his N.E.S (Nintendo Entertainment System). Inserting a newly bought game pack, entitled River City Ransom, they began to play.

"Riz, man you're not gonna believe this." Ivan began. His eyes are still glued to the colorful screen. They defeat two bosses under what looks like a bridge.

"Who's messing with you now?" Rizzo asked Ivan. "I had a confrontation with Curtis today." "Straight up?" Rizzo's eyes are also glued to the large screen. "Curtis?"

"Yeah I remember him." "He was funny." Rizzo began to reminisce. "He used to have all of us rolling at lunchtime." "Well, not anymore." Ivan responds with disdain.

"He's getting really ugly." "How so?" Riz asks. "Its like he's gone from being the class clown to the class bully." Ivan explains. "Curtis has punked out almost every boy in the school." "If not that, just our class alone." "He's probably having some personal

problems or something." "That wouldn't be a surprise." Rizzo responds. "Why is he challenging me?" Ivan asked his best friend. "Only God knows."

"And then there's Malik." "Playing house servant." "He of course, jumps on the bandwagon." "Malik?" Says Rizzo. He was apparently surprised. "Ass kisser."

"Didn't Myra try to pick a fight with him the year before last?" "The same Myra who got her head busted?" "Yep." Answers Ivan. "It was in the library." "Damn, it was like Jezebel versus Jason." Rizzo laughs. "That was bogus." He says. "It all started when Myra said something about Malik's mother, and Malik of course summons a chair to her head." "He was suspended for two and a half weeks." "His mom had to cover her medical bills." "Myra had at least four stitches." Suddenly the doorbell rings. "Pause the game." Rizzo tells his friend. "I'll be right back." "No Problem man." Ivan replies.

"Go right ahead." Upon entering the hallway, Rizzo answers the door. It is his aunt Keisha. Jokingly ignoring her nephew, she barges in and greets Ivan. Now heading to her room, Keisha continues to stare. She obviously liked what she saw.

A sophomore at Lane Technical High School, Keisha is Rizzo's youngest aunt. At fifth teen, she is short, and has a round shape. Her skin tone favors that of dark chocolate.

Something for which Ivan had also liked. As Keisha enters her mom's house, she wears a red spandex body shirt (revealing some cleavage) as well as a pair of Lee's. The latter of course reveals her thickness. She is Ms. Wallace's only daughter.

"He is such a gump." Ivan says to Rizzo. "He even treats Des like his own personal cellblock bitch." "If I don't stand up to this guy Riz." "Who will?" "Gotta express yourself Ivan." "From the looks of it." Ivan began. "I'll have my chance."

"I made mincemeat out of all of his boys today." Ivan continues on. "Sending people after me left and right." Rizzo nods his head as he hears Ivan's story. "Rizzo, it was no laughing matter." "They went down quick!" All of twelve of them." Rizzo begins to laugh like a loon shortly thereafter. "Malik talking shit, and I ended up nearly killing him out there." "Where was this?" Rizzo asked. "Outside of the western playground." Ivan answers. "Tried to whoop on me with his jacket and I ended up nearly choking him to death." With his own jacket." "Eventually him and Curtis will get the message."

"They tried to jump me." "I bet they felt salty." Rizzo replies. "Hell yeah, especially Curtis." "I spared Desmond though." "Even though I knocked him out the first time, I later helped him up, dusted him off and sent him on his way." "Besides, he had a much bigger problem." "Eventually Curtis and me were face to face, ready to throw down... "But what happened?" Rizzo asked Ivan in suspense. "The boss battle was postponed." Ivan chuckles. "We both saw a police car, feared that the cops would see us and we parted our separate ways." "Anyway we agreed to pick up from where we left off tomorrow after school." "Just me and him." "You should have been there Riz."

"It was such a wonderful site." Ivan concludes. His voice mimics that of a serial murderer. Calm. Collective. And last but not least cunning. "Whatever Ted Bundy." Rizzo roasts. They are now at the final stage of the game.

The scenario takes place in a high school. Upon completion, the boys will have to do battle with a boss named Slick. Once Slick is defeated, the school will no longer be under siege. "You just watch yourself out there tomorrow." Rizzo tells Ivan. Obviously concerned. "I'll always have your back." "Likewise." Ivan gives his friend a pound.

Having disengaged the final boss, Ivan and Rizzo prevail. They finished the game. As the credits began to roll, Ivan replaces the game pack while Riz changes the cassettes.

"So its Valentine's Day." Rizzo began. "What are your plans?" "I'm taking Nikki out this evening." Ivan tells him. "That's cool." Riz replies. "You?"

Now sitting in the living room, the boys sip on bottles of Sunny Delight as they listen another new group. The latter is known as "A Tribe Called Quest." Fresh out of New York, their debut is entitled "People's Distinctive Travels and Rhythms." "I've got this date from a girl at my school named Teresa." "And as a reminder, I need to give her a call right now." Rizzo says. Reaching for the phone, he dials the young lady's number.

Ivan meanwhile checks his watch. The time is five twenty two.

Earlier this week, Ivan's parents and Nikki's mom had met privately at their home to discuss their children, who has recently become further acquainted with one another since Ivan's coming out. In other words Ivan's coming out in reference to his flawless victory against Hannibal's hoods, his stronger commitment to his books, his improving grades, and other recent achievements. Nikki like Rizzo his also Ivan's junior by two years.

And like Rizzo, Nikki who is only his junior by two months has also skipped two grades. Although she has yet to master a foreign language, Nikki's performance in her studies is comparable. On the day of his birthday following his celebrations at the Cascade, Ivan later asked his dream girl out. Although Nikki accepts, the pair still had to consult with their parents. After an hour-long discussion at the Thompson house a day later, an agreement was reached. Perhaps this meeting was appropriate due in mainly in part, that neither of their children were sixteen. Which was of course the legal age.

Sanders Residence

Sitting in her room, Nikki faces a mirror overlooking her dresser. Removing her net, her hair now extends. From her shoulders down to the rump, it is all hers. All natural.

He's got to give me at least a ten. She says to herself. Smiling and giggling, Nicole suddenly sees her mom. Standing in the doorway, Mrs. Sanders now steps forward.

"I'm sure he will." She says. Posing in the mirror, Mrs. Sanders and Nikki began to laugh. By all accounts, they are indeed mother and daughter. The resemblance between them is almost dangerously striking. Ivan, who is now seen in Nikki's doorway, teases them both. "Why didn't you tell me you had a twin sister Nikki?" At this point, Mrs. Sanders and Nikki are now blushing. "Boy, you better stop." They both reply.

Throughout the one story cottage frame, smells of potpourri, spaghetti, garlic bread and Italian Sausages. In the dining room, plates, forks, and knives are neatly laid out on the table. In the center are two unlit candles. Near the stereo system are six albums. Among them there's Sybil: Don't Make Me Over, Baby Come To Me: Regina Belle, Spend The Night by the Isley Brothers, My Fantasy by Teddy Riley, Its No Crime from Babyface, and Bobby Brown's Every Little Step. "And what are you up to Mrs. Sanders?" Ivan asks. He teases her briefly. Nikki taps his arm. "You're going to get it." She then grabs his hand. "Have fun you guys." Mrs. Sanders tells them.

"And because its a school night, I need you guys back here no later than ten."

"Understand?" "Yes, maam." "Yes, Mrs. Sanders."

Kissing them both on the cheek, Mrs. Sanders walks them to the door. With her daughter and Ivan now gone, the single mother now has five hours to herself. Reaching for the cordless phone, she confirms her date.

Outside the temperature is forty-nine degrees as Ivan and Nikki tours Saint Louis Avenue. Before reaching the corner of Harrison Street, they cross an alley. In the alley itself is a drug transaction. A young man who is at least eighteen is spotted. His clients are four slightly older males. All white and presumably in their early twenties, they are obviously here to make a purchase. Sitting in a gold BMW, the driver accepts what appears to be a gram of rock. In exchange, the driver hands the young man two large bills. As Ivan and Nikki walks by, they ignore both the buyers as well as the lone dealer.

"Maryland huh?" Ivan began. Although he initially paid no attention to the vehicle or it occupants, he had yet still managed to recollect where the car had been registered.

"From the clothes that they are wearing as well as their body language, they would have to be under a lot of pressure to come this far." Nikki began. "Maybe they had been hitting the books too hard, and were yet still pessimistic about making their grades."

Little did they know, perhaps it was a coincidence that these young men were in fact college students. Although the driver was more of a visitor from his respective state, the other three occupants were in fact students attending UIC. "But its still no excuse." Ivan says as he looks ahead. He then nods. "You're right." Nikki responds.

"You would actually lose more of your focus." "Its a guaranteed dead end." Ivan reminds her. "Hello?" "Thank you!" Nikki says with greater satisfaction.

Walking east along Harrison, they now reach Homan Avenue. Crossing the bridge, Ivan and Nikki are now at the Eisenhower Expressway. In the median once again is the Congress "L", also known as the West-Northwest route. The entire line and its stations opened for service in June of 1958. It made history as the first rapid transit line in the country (and possibly the world) to run along a major highway.

Its west terminal is Desplaines Avenue, located in a western suburb known as Forest Park. Going east, it runs downtown and terminates at O'Hare International Airport.

Upon entry at the Homan entrance to the Kedzie and Homan stop, Ivan and Nikki ignores the now closed agent's booth. Walking down the ramp, and onto to the platform, they then take a seat. Activating the heat lamps, Ivan and Nikki began to warm up.

"Considering that I'm no longer down south, where its usually hot." Nikki began.

"And although I've experienced my winter here in Chicago last year." "What I'm experiencing now is really something new." Ivan nods his head as he continues to listen.

"Spring in the middle of winter?" His date shakes her head. "Trust me Nikki, its nothing new." Ivan assures her. "Even though I was born here." The two sat under a windbreak consisting of clear plexiglass. "Perhaps the most recent time for which this city has ever experienced such weather was when I was born." Ivan adds.

"According to my parents, they said it was about sixty five degrees when they brought me home." "Hotter than it is today." "Pneumonia central." "Last week, even the forecasters brought it up." "Only Chicago would have some of the strangest weather in the world." Nikki says. For the duration of the conversation, Nikki did not take her eyes off of Ivan. Not once. It seems as though she has met someone new.

On the brightly lit platform, six other people join them. "Are you okay?" Ivan asked Nikki. For one moment, her hazel eyes became glassy. "Yes, I' am." She shakes it off. Nicole is almost in a trance. Fifteen minutes later, their train arrives.

The four-car unit employs the most recent generation of rail cars. The Budd 2600's series, which is only seven years old, is clad in its Spirit of Chicago attire. Its color scheme is actually a forerunner dating back to the bicentennial. The latter was formerly called The Spirit of "76." The adopted scheme is red, white, and navy blue.

Delivered between 1982 and as recently 1987, these particular cars have sliding doors and are handicapped accessible. Its adjoining brothers are the Budd 2200's.

Manufactured in Philadelphia, these cars were delivered to Chicago in 1969. Consisting of stainless steel silver, they employ "blinker type" (folding doors) and are fire resistant. Ivan and Nikki are now on board. "Western Avenue is the next stop." Says the conductor. They are seated in the first car. Among some of the local points of interest to be seen, is a supermarket dubbed "Down Home", Horan Park, and the Area Four Police Headquarters. Crossing the Albany underpass is Jensen Academy, the Harrison Courts housing complex and a factory. "Did you watch the NBA all star game Sunday?" Nikki asked. "No, I actually missed it." Says Ivan. "Too ill." He explains.

"But Donnie later told me it was the East that prevailed." Ivan concludes. "Do you think that's its possible for the Bulls to make it to the playoffs?" Nikki asked. Ivan pauses briefly before responding. "Well maybe." "It is a strong possibility." "How?" Nikki asked him. "Mainly because Jordan, Pippen, and Cartwright in particular have been giving it their all this year." Upon reaching the Western Stop, the conductor enters from the second car to collect their fares. Peering out of their window to the left is the Rockwell Gardens housing projects. Some of its units hide in the shadow of a full moon as the dark purple sky looks on. To the right, a multitude of well-kept homes are seen.

At this point several passengers are now complaining. An odor brought on by a homeless man now snoring in the back of the first car, becomes unbearable.

However when Ivan and Nikki boarded, the odor became obsolete. They both wore special fragrances. "Damn." Says another passenger. "Is this Chicago or Paris?" Some of the others laugh. "Some body really smells good." "This train at first used to stank." Says a young female passenger. "Maybe I should ride with them to the end." "Whoever it is." "Shit." "Is that cologne?" A third passenger asks. "Perfume?"

Leaving the Racine Station, the train now passes through other points of interest. Among them is the UIC Pavilion, and several Industrial turned lofts. The city skyline also becomes visible. Traveling under the Morgan Street Bridge, the train now stops at "U of I Halsted." Calling for passengers at the Renown University of Illinois campus as well as nearby Greek town, this train departs. As the eastbound O'Hare Congress passes a westbound Douglas train, the train crosses the Halsted Street underpass and descends into a portal.

Michigan Avenue & Adams Street (Downtown)

Situated in front of the Art Institute, which is now closed for the evening, Nikki sits patiently on a bench. Meanwhile Ivan her date, flags down a taxi. Like the true gentleman he is, Ivan opens the door. "Thank you." She smiled. "No problem." He responds.

On the bustling Magnificent Mile, traffic is at a standstill. An accident near Wacker Drive has occurred. A Ford Escort and a

Lamborghini are the sole casualties. Ivan suggest for the driver to instead take Lake Shore Drive.

Giordano's Pizza

Located in on the corner of Rush and Superior Streets in the upscale Gold Coast Community, this establishment is best known for its world famous deep dish. Because Ivan and Nikki knew about the possible half hour wait, and also due to their curfew they instead arrive here first. "Let me guess." Says the waitress as she greets the two minors.

"Non smoking yes?" "Absolutely." Ivan smiled. "You're very good." Nikki responds. Also impressed. "What a surprise." Ivan then tells his date. "We didn't have to wait at all." "That's definitely a sign that somebody's looking out for us tonight." "You have such a lovely accent." Nikki tells the waitress. "Where are you from?" She asks.

"Belize." The short waitress replies. "And thank you." Now seated, Ivan and Nikki take up their menus. "I'll be just one moment." Says the young woman.

"And by the way, my name is Brenda." Ivan and Nikki happily nodded. "So what would you guys like to drink?" "I'll have a Coke." Ivan answers. "I'll have a pink lemonade." Nikki replies. "No problem." Brenda tells them both. Having answered their initial request, the seemingly twenty something waitress returns to the front of the lobby.

"This is such a surprise." Nikki began facing her first date. With their decision already made, the two now put their menus away. "Where did you come from?" She says jokingly. Ivan, now pouring the both of them a glass of water looks at her and laughs.

"Thank you." She tells him. "Its like I'm getting to know you all over again."

"I have never known you to be such an aggressive fighter, and suddenly become so handsome." Nikki then rubs both of Ivan's powerful arms. "But yet, you're still sweet, you're intelligent, and you still have a big heart." "And that's what I've always loved about you Ivan." "You're nothing like the other boys in school." "And in conclusion, the entire neighborhood goes without saying." About fifteen minutes later, Brenda the waitress returns with their drinks. "So are you ready to order?" She then asks.

"Yes, please." Says Ivan. "We'll have the medium stuffed sausage and cheese and two garden salads." "Sounds good." The waitress responds. "It will be ready in fifth teen to thirty minutes." "Thank you." They both reply. Collecting their menus, the cheerful but laid back waitress returns to the front. "I think we played a good game today." Ivan began. "What do you think Nicole?" "We certainly did." Nikki says with the uttermost of satisfaction. "I think we turned more heads than the Exorcist." Ivan who is sipping his drink although laughs, holds it in. He averts the disaster of spitting up his Coke.

"The next time, turn your head." Says Nikki as she begins to laugh herself. "Well Donnie seems to think to think so, and so does the rest of the team." Ivan added.

"You've heard Ron this morning." He reminds Nikki. "Where have we been?" "And according to Yusef, we should have been made the team." As Nikki listens, she slowly sips her drink. "Personally I think that the reason why Bos has rejected us." Ivan continues on. "Is because he's still trapped in the old school." "Besides him being gender bias, I also believe that Bosworth is still under the notion that taller is always better."

"So what do you think that the chances are of the two of us being drafted next fall?" Nikki asked. "Its possible." Says Ivan. "Although it will be our last year before we

graduate, we could still win a few games." "And whatever high school or high schools we attend, we could always pick up from where we left off for the next four years Atleast." "True." Says Nikki. The two have now finished their drinks.

"What are your goals for the future Nikki?" Ivan asked. Nikki smiled. "Well given that my plans could always change." She began. "One possibility is me becoming a doctor and studying medicine so far." "Law is another likely avenue." "You actually favor more of a prosecutor or a DA." Ivan smiled back. "My mom actually told me that." Nikki chuckles. "What about you?" She asks. "You seem to be more into politics." Ivan's date responds. "I' am, as a matter of fact." Ivan nods his head. "I can see you either being a governor or a president." Nikki says, as she peers into his dark brown eyes.

"If it were up to me right now, I would send thousands of troops into South Africa." Ivan began. "With the help of my allies and other African states if necessary, F.W. De Klerk would be finished." "No more Apartheid." Obviously impressed with what she's hearing, Nikki smiles once more and gives Ivan a nod. "Once he's been removed from power, he would then stand trial." "Not only before the people of South Africa itself, but also the World Court." "That would be good." Says Nikki. She agrees with him.

Exactly thirty minutes later, the waitress returns with their order. "Good, the food is finally here." Ivan began. As they are now being served, refills on the drinks in all, the pair began to dig in.

Water Tower Place

Located on the northernmost end of Michigan Avenue, this marble trimmed building was built in 1975 by Urban Retail Properties. The tower section is a 74 –story 859-foot (262) reinforced concrete slab, faced with gray marble, and is the eighth tallest building in the city. In the U.S. alone, it is the twenty-six tallest. When built, it was the tallest reinforced concrete structure in the world. It contains an award winning Ritz-Carlton hotel, and luxury condominiums. There is also office space on the top floor containing a highly successful, atrium-style retail mall that shines on the magnificent mile.

The mall itself has eight levels of shops. On the eighth floor alone, there are over a hundred shops including department stores such as Lord and Taylor and Marshall Fields.

First run cinemas occupy the second and ground floors followed by several restaurants. They are all arranged around a stunning chrome-and glass atrium with glass elevators. It was even one of the first vertical malls in the world.

And last but not least, from the Michigan lobby along the escalators are fountains. They in part, also carry coins. Just to the north of Chestnut Street is the famous John Hancock Center. To the north of Chicago Avenue is lies a historical pumping station and a tourist center. A small park and the original water tower cover the west, and in between facing the marble complex lies a series of other retail shops. Among them are Crate and Barrel, I-Magnin, The Sharper Image, Waldenbooks, and Bloomingdale's.

Cineplex Odeon, which leases two theatres in the building (Four screens on the second level and four on the ground namely Chestnut Street), Ivan and Nikki now enters the latter. They buy two tickets for the Fly: The Return. Starring Eric Stolz and Daphne Zuniga, the movie is a sequel to a previous film from two years earlier.

As the lights in the auditorium began to fade and the screen comes to life, Ivan and Nikki already seated began cuddling up.

3

After two weeks of what Nikki called "spring in the middle of winter" has now come to an end. Old Man Winter is back. And this time its personal.

The entire Chicago region (including northwest Indiana and southern Wisconsin) is covered in snow. Park lagoons throughout the city are now pleasing to the eyes of those who ice skate. Although they appear solid, they are advised by local officials to cease and desist. The latter is due mainly in part to shallow ice and the potential dangers that follow.

Thompson Residence, Saturday

Repeatedly sucking in wind and sweating profusely, Ivan shadowboxes in the basement of his grandmother's apartment. Throwing kicks, punches, and blocks from the stairwell in the front to the laundry room in the rear; Ivan pursues and disengages his phantom opposition. Now jumping up, Ivan kicks the lights. But however with all intents and purposes, his misses the latter by one inch. Returning to his stance the young student bows his head. Situated in the room directly above him is his cousin Doug.

Initially sound asleep; the not so distinguished guest wakes up. Descending down the stairs, Doug takes note of Ivan who is now meditating. Fifth teen minutes later, he slowly emerges. Bowing his head before the lights, Ivan completes his workout. "Is that really you Ivan?" Says Doug, surprised by his cousin's new physique. Stretching and yawning, he then rubs his eyes. "You looking good man." "Thanks." Ivan responds with mild disdain. Finding a chair, Doug sits down. "Going to the gym?" He asked.

Once again reluctant to answer, Ivan nods his head. He is not happy to see his cousin. From their days in Kindergarten up until fourth grade, Ivan and Doug were almost like brothers. Douglas Cartier Sr, who has another son and a daughter from a previous marriage in Mississippi, later marries Helen Tyson here in Chicago. Helen, who already had a two-year-old daughter from a previous relationship, later gives birth to two sons.

Leonardo and Douglas Jr. Not too long after Junior's fourth birthday, the elder Douglas and his second wife later separates.

Almost a decade later, the whereabouts of "Big Doug" remains unknown. It was rumored that he moved to Canada. As time passed, Doug who is only Ivan's senior by two days later joins a gang. On the other hand, his brother Leo who is three years older becomes a thief. Despite Doug's father being out of the picture, his mother, Doug Jr himself, and his brother remained in Lawndale for eight years.

The Cartier house was a three-story greystone situated just one block west of the Thompson's. It stood on the corner of Lexington near Central Park Avenue. Both Ivan and Doug not only attended the same school, but they practically hung out, played video games, traded baseball cards, comic books, laughed and so on. They were nearly inseparable. But however when Henry "Hannibal" Jackson took interest in Douglas and recruited him, all of those good times suddenly became bad. The good Doug that Ivan once knew was no more. Doug who later became "Doughboy" because he knew how to make money (selling drugs) eventually sold Ivan out. On numerous occasions whenever Hannibal or his fellow hoods confronted Ivan, Doug on the other hand would do virtually nothing. It was as though he never existed. When his brother Simon learned of this, it became nothing more but music to his ears.

Simon, who is four years older, has long history of animosity toward his brethren. On a regular basis, he too blackmails Ivan. He bullies him; He extorts, and humiliates. Even when Ivan was overweight, Simon teased him. Insisting that he had "tities." Despite Doug's involvement with Hannibal, his sworn rival, Simon became closer to his youngest cousin. And together, the pair began to double team Ivan. A year ago just two days before thanksgiving, Mr. And Mrs. Thompson had a fallen out with Doug's mother. Both Doug and Leo at this point were out of control. On that very same day, in the bathtub of their home, Ivan attempts to drown himself. When Mr. And Mrs. Thompson learned of Simon's evil pact with Doug, they nearly killed him. As for their youngest son, he required a full year of therapy.

On the following weekend without warning, Doug, Leo, and his mother gathered all of their worldly possessions. Loading them on to a U-Haul, they left for Milwaukee. Having recollected such painful memories, Ivan becomes furious. Without warning, he attacks. Doug has no time to react. Rushing toward him Ivan yanks his cousin out of his chair. Snapping knee after knee into his abdomen, Ivan snaps first his left elbow and then a right. Doug's face is quickly bruised. Employing a left roundhouse, Ivan turns his head, spins and snaps another. As his left Nike makes contact with Doug's head and face for the second time, Ivan changes his stance. With his hands up, Ivan crosses one leg behind the other and delivers a right sidekick. At this point, Doug is against the wall. Literally.

With Doug's back against the cold concrete, Ivan maintains his left foot as it presses against his windpipe. Pulling down on his cousin's left arm, he applies additional leverage. Doug coughs and then gasps. "You son of a bitch!" Ivan thunders. "You've got a lot of nerve to bring your ass back here!" Doug's battered face turns from a lighter brown to a darker red. He screams in agony. "You have no idea of what you've done!" Ivan continues his assault. "Like you give a damn!" Giving his estranged cousin a hip toss, the dumbfounded and possibly horrified Douglas hits the hardened cement floor.

"You traitorous bastard!" "Get up!" Honoring his cousin's request, Doug slowly rises. "So what do you have to say for yourself Benedict Arnold?" "What have I ever done to you?" "And they say blood is thicker than water." "I beg to differ."

Although still in pain, Doug manages to stand. Ivan on the other hand resumes his fighting stance. "You sold me out!" He further snaps. Ivan then employs a dropkick. Despite his cousin's skin which is already black and blue at this point, the blood and sweat still surfaces. "Your own cousin!" "And yet, you are still shameless." At this time, Doug actually does feel guilty. He is ashamed. But most of all, this so-called gangster who has often commanded respect is now reduced to a defenseless coward.

His ego has been crushed; Doug's ability to fight back is reduced to mere swinging. Now crawling away as a means of retreating, Doug knows that he is no match for his powerfully built cousin. As he continues to crawl, Ivan slowly stalks him. As his eyes beam down upon his, Ivan can sense his fear. Having reached the steps, Doug grabs onto the handrail. Now sitting on the steps, Doug is now in a fetal position. (Curled up).

At 10:00 in the morning, both apartments are now empty. Mr. And Mrs. Thompson had gone shopping while Simon went to work at Burger King. To avoid unwanted attention, Ivan creates a diversion. Turning on the stereo, he cranks up the volume. As for his grandmother, there is no need to worry. She left for church an hour ago.

In other words, he can finish the job. "Come on, let me give you a hand." Ivan taunts him. Helping Doug to his feet, Ivan delivers a right jab to his throat. "Breathe." He tells his cousin. Doug's breathing remains labored as he coughs and pants.

All around the entire basement from the storage area to the laundry room, and then back to the recreation room, Ivan continues to mix it up with the young man he once saw as his cousin. Hammering him with a powerful left jab, a right cross, and hooking combinations Doug now has a black eye. Executing countless uppercuts across his stomach and chin, Ivan gives him a palm strike to the face. In the middle of the recreation room lies a glass table. Getting up for the fifth time although staggering, Doug finally pleads for his life. "Mercy." He whispers. "What mercy did you have on me?" Ivan asked.

Looking on with his bloodied nose, his black eye, and his bruised up face, Doug is unable to answer. "I thought so." Ivan shakes his head. Delivering a spinning crescent kick, Doug's tall, but thin frame falls through the table. Upon impact, the glass shatters.

Shutting off the radio, Ivan kills the lights. Grabbing his tank top, Ivan heads upstairs.

Not bad for a workout. He thought.

Downtown (Randolph Street and Wabash Avenue)

In this area, the vehicles operated by the Streets and Sanitation crews are numerous as these employees work diligently to rid the streets of the snow and the ice that plagues their corridors.

Chicago Public Library/Cultural Center

Situated on the fourth floor of what is known central branch of all operations, Ivan and Nikki combs the entire floor, in search of good books. At the very end of the room, the

two bookworms are now seated. From where they sat, one can get a glimpse of Garland Court, another Crate and Barrel furniture store, Heinemann's Bakery, and a Stuart's Clothing Shop. In this picture, the Loop Elevated is also seen. The latter, being in service since 1897 summons a pair of modern day 2600's. The two-car unit employs a Ravenswood "All Stops" train on what is the outer loop.

Opening their books, Ivan and Nikki began to browse. "So what did you find Ivan?" Nikki asks. He points out all of his literature. "The Black Angels and Uneasy Money." His closest friend slash neighbor nods her head. "They sound good." She says.

"What about you?" Ivan asked. "The Graveyard Shift and Fire Song." Nikki tells him. Ivan happily nods. "I never knew you liked Stephen King." He says. Nikki smiled.

"You never asked me apple head." She replies. "I've read a few of his novels also." The librarian in charge, a heavyset grayish woman puts a finger to her mouth.

"Oh, I'm terribly sorry." Ivan whispers. Obviously they were a bit loud. "Like Pet Sematary, Carrie, and Christine." Reaching into her purse, Nikki grabs her reading glasses. "Of course you realize that almost all of his novels were either already, or will soon become movies." Nikki informs him. But yet, Ivan himself already knows.

"With in a few months, Pet Sematary will come out." He responds. "In fact, next spring." "I'll be looking forward to seeing it." Nicole tells him. "You're obviously familiar with Clive Barker then?" Ivan assumes. "Yes, I do." Nikki abruptly replies.

His assumption is correct. "I strongly believe that Barker is King's protégé." She then tells him. Feeling a sudden draft, Ivan slips back into his sweater. "And speaking of movies." He began. "They say that eighty nine is going to be the year of the sequels."

"And why is that?" Nikki asks. "Because most of them being released, will be nothing more but follow ups." He explains. "So far, there's Ghostbusters 2, Star Trek 5: The Final Frontier, and Lethal Weapon 2." Having understood his case, Nikki nods her head.

"And this just to name a few." Her friend further breaks it down.

"I recall my parents two days ago, telling me about the horror films of back in the day." Ivan now shares with Nikki. At this point she briefly takes off her glasses.

With her mouth placed on one of the temples, she continues to listen. "We were comparing them to the films of today." He added. "The films of today are really funny." Nikki tells him. Throughout their conversation as she looks into his eyes, let alone besides listening, she can also smile. It isn't obvious that she now adores him.

"Take Robert Englund's, A Nightmare On Elm Street for example." Ivan points out.

"Thank you." Nikki buttons her sweater. The room is still chilly.

Chinatown (Armour Square)

Located just three miles south of Downtown, this area is the home to much of the city's Chinese-American population. It is a city within a city. Looking to escape the anti-Chinese violence that had broken out on the west coast, the first Chinese arrived in Chicago after 1869 when the First Transcontinental Railroad was completed. By the late 1800's, twenty-five percent of the city's six hundred Chinese residents settled along Clark Street between Van Buren and Harrison Streets Downtown.

Faced with increasing rent prices, the Chinese living in this area began moving south into the current area. The On Leong Merchants Association who, in 1912 had a building constructed along 22nd Street, now Cermak, led this exodus. At the time, this building

housed 15 stores, 30 apartments, and the Association's headquarters. While the building's design was typical of that period, it featured Chinese accents such as tile trim adorned with dragons. In the 1920's,Chinese community leaders secured approximately 50 ten- year leases on properties in this then newly developing Chinatown.

Because of severe racial discrimination, these leases needed to be secured by an intermediary, H.O. Stone Company. Jim Moy, then-director of the On Leong Merchant Association, then decided that a Chinese-style building should be constructed as a strong visual announcement of the Chinese community's new presence in the area.

With no Chinese-born architects in Chicago at the time, Chicago-born architects Christian S. Michaelsen and Sigurd A. Roanstad were asked to design the new On Leong Merchants

Association Building in spring, 1926. After studying texts on Chinese architecture, Michaelsen and Roanstad's final design was an example of "Orientalism", a western architect's interpretation of Chinese or other Asian architectural forms.

When the building opened in 1928, the On Leong Association used it as an immigrant assistance center that housed various meeting halls, a school, a shrine, and the Associations offices. It was often referred to as Chinatown's "City Hall."

To this day, the community is still a bustling and vibrant thoroughfare. Its overall population stands at roughly 6,899. But yet its still growing. A group of local business leaders has recently purchased 32 acres of property north of Archer Avenue from Santa Fe Railway. This hints the construction of new businesses as well new housing in the years to come. Even a new park along the riverfront is being considered.

Furthermore this neighborhood is the home to a number of banks, restaurants, gift shops, and grocery stores. Medicine stores (both herbal and modern) as well as a number of services that cater to those who are who are interested in Chinese culture. It is the community hub for Chinese people throughout the Chicago region, a business center for Chinese in the Midwest and a tourist destination for tourist and locals alike.

Exiting a southbound Lake and Dan Ryan train at the Cermak-Chinatown Station, Ivan descends down an escalator towards the street level.

Jing Wu Institute

Located on the corner of Wentworth and Archer Avenues, the school is housed in a wide two-story green and white structure. A large chimney occupies the roof. Many warehouses and other industrial buildings join it. They rest along the southern branch of the Chicago River. Walking back one block east of Cermak Road, Ivan enters the building. Now in the main lobby, he greets the receptionist. "Hi Sandy, how are you today?" Situated at her desk, the woman, a short and thin thirty something is obviously doing what appears to be paperwork. Dressed casually she wears make up, which actually brings out her natural tone. Her hair meanwhile, is tied up in a long brown ponytail.

"Fine as usual." She smiled. "And what about you?" "Well given that you asked, I guess its safe to say, I feel much better." Ivan smiled back. The woman blushes.

Buzzing him in through a glass door, he enters a large corridor with overhead track lighting. A variation of artwork and exotic plants covers the walls. On the first and second floors, are a total of fourteen rooms. An administration office and a fitness center, occupies the basement. Yao Hung Chow founded this school forty years ago.

Arriving in Chicago from Shanghai, China in 1949, Mr. Chow originally opened the school in a small storefront just one block away. To meet the needs of a growing number of students both Chinese and non-Chinese, Mr. Chow relocated the school to its current location at 2100 S. Wentworth in September of 1964. The sounds of loud kiais are heard up and down the halls. Opening the door to studio 114, at the end of the hall, Ivan discovers a class already in session. Although the instructors specialize in fighting arts such as Taichi, Kung Fu, and Choy Li Fut, many other disciplines are also taught.

Now clad in his traditional uniform, with an orange sash, Ivan is now seated amongst the other students. Within his own group, the teens, Ivan now cheers for what appears to be a children's class. Separating the adolescents as well as the visitors from the opposite side lies an opening covered by two floor mats. In the middle, there are two pupils. A boy and a girl, both seven years old. Wearing their protective gear, they spar.

Practicing what is obviously Tae Kwan Do, six other preteens are seated near a set of pull up bars. They too are in good spirits as they support their fellow classmates.

Among them is their scorekeeper and referee. A young man named Mark Choi. Dancing around on the mats, both practitioners continued to block and parry each other's attacks. Discovering two openings, the little boy snaps two kicks. The first that he delivers makes direct contact with her abs, the second her face. Falling instantly, the girl lands on her buttocks. The boy scores two points. His fellow student: One.

By showing good sportsmanship, the young man helps the young lady to her feet. "Good job Chris." Ivan applauds. "Come on Cathy, you can do it!" He then tells the other student. Bowing once more, the two students began their next round. As Christopher Head attempts to throw two jabs and a hook, Cathy Estes quickly blocks and then parries.

Coming back with a vengeance, She counters by way of landing her own combos. This round is declared a draw. By this time, both students have gone six rounds. These two combatants are the last to review their techniques. "Good job guys." Mark shakes their hands. Shaking hands, both pupils bow once more. Taking a brief glimpse, Mark stands in the center of the room. Checking his watch, he motions for his students to line up. Like well-disciplined soldiers, they obeyed his command. Now in their resting positions, the younger students all bow. Shortly thereafter, this group is dismissed.

Walking up to Mark, Ivan himself greets him. "What's up Mark?" He gives his Sifu a pound (a handshake). "Its been a great day Ivan, I can't complain." "What about you man?" "Pretty good, thanks." "Did you enjoy my party Monday?" Ivan asked his mentor.

"Most definitely, you know that I was more than happy to be there." Mark happily nods. "Thirteen huh?" Ivan nodded. "I remember when I was thirteen."

"You're a good guy Ivan, your parents tell me." "I knew you were from the day I first trained you." "That's why I gave you the nickname Gold Lion." "Because you have a heart of gold and the strength of a lion." "I understand that you're making some remarkable strides, and not just here alone." "Keep up the good work, and continue to be yourself." "Oh, I plan on it." Ivan says with great confidence. "I know you will."

Among Ivan's beloved teachers is twenty-year-old Marcus Steven Choi. To his family and closest friends, he is simply known as Mark. The youngest of three children, Mark is a second-generation American-born citizen. His grandparents immigrated to Oakland, California from Hong Kong in 1947. His parents, who represented the first generation, came to Chicago from Oakland in 1968. Mark was born the following year on March 1, 1969. A law student at DePaul University, he lives in on the city's near north side. A master in Choy Li Fut, a Shaolin form of Kung Fu, Mark also teaches Tae Kwan Do to preteens three days a week and is also an expert in Kendo, a Japanese form of fencing. In his black bag next to him is a gold leather case, and inside, a stainless steel Katana. To Ivan he too is like a brother.

On Thursday evenings, Ivan is also participates in his advanced Wing Chun course. "Where's your lady friend?" Mark asked his prized student. Reaching into his bag, Mark summons a bottle of Gatorade. "Who Nikki?" Says Ivan, he faces his junior mentor and began to smile. "Oh, she couldn't make it." "She had to attend her Violin class this afternoon." Five minutes later, the instructor for the 4:00 Teens Class enters the room.

"You'd better get ready." Mark suggests. "Right." Says Ivan. He gives him a pound.

"Zai jian."(Goodbye) As usual, Ivan is the first to line up before his instructor. The others quickly follow suit. The gentleman teaching today's class is a Mr. Lei Ho Leung. Mr. Leung, a prominent art collector, and the owner of an antique shop is also a grandmaster. He has competed many tournaments throughout the world for over a quarter of a century. And to this very day, the forty-nine year old married father of two remains undefeated. Mr. Leung is a master of Kung Fu, Taichi, Jeet Kune Do and Kali.

The latter art is a Filipino form of stick fighting. "Ni hao ma?"(How are you?) He asks Ivan. "Hen hao."(Fine) Ivan replies. "How is everyone today?" The short Beijing native now asked the rest of the class." "Great sir." His students all responded.

Before the youthful looking senior began to spread his knowledge among the masses, he first commands his disciples to do a series of warm up drills, such as push-ups, jumping jacks, and stretching. Inside of this well insulated studio, the students spend at least one full hour practicing and taking turns on the Wing Chun dummies.

Amongst his best four, namely in the teens class alone, to began his demonstration, Mr. Leung summons Ivan to go first. Bowing before his Sifu, Ivan approaches one of the dummies. Taking a deep breath, he first inhales and then exhales. At the blink of an eye, Ivan goes to work. Parrying, blocking, and punching with an unspeakable burst of energy, Ivan employs both of his legs for kicking not only the dummy's wooden legs, but also its shins followed by the abdomen. Parrying and then blocking, Ivan next targets a jab to the stomach. Parrying and blocking for the third time already, he punches up.

There has often been other days in class for which Ivan has employed too much leg power to the dummies, causing them literally to collapse. As he proceeds to engage the wooden opponent, Mr. Leung closely monitors his speed. Peering at his stopwatch, the other students also look on. On the stereo system, the rap song “Step Into the A.M.” by Third Base is heard. By this time as he breaths in and out, beads of sweat began to trickle.

Ivan has reached his top speed. Peering at his stopwatch once more, Mr. Leung presses the button. “Time.” He says. Ivan stops and faces his mentor. Bowing his head, he returns to his group. “Very good.” Mr. Leung tells him. “Fifty nine seconds.” Impressed by his new record, Ivan’s fellow classmates began to applaud.

“You’re looking really good Ivan.” Says one of his fellow classmates. Her name is Linda Lau. Like Ivan, she too is among the top four. “Thanks.” He says to her as he returns to his seat. The two shake hands shortly thereafter. It is now her turn.

Bowing her head before her teacher, Linda goes to work. Maintaining her speed, unlike Ivan, the petite young lady has to work twice as hard. Mainly because her goal is of course based on form. Blocking, kicking, parrying and then punching away at the

dummy, Linda first employs what would have been a crane hand to someone’s throat, and then a tiger claw. Kicking away at the wooden shins and knees, Mr. Leung calls it. “Time.” “Good job.” Says the grandmaster. “One minute and a second.” The others applaud. “You looked Marvelous Linda.” Ivan says. The two shake hands once more.

“Thanks Ivan.” Linda smiled. Returning to her seat, Thomas Wang rises.

To his all of his closest friends, family members, and even his teachers in the elementary school he attends, he is simply referred to as “Tommy.” Like both Ivan and Linda, Tommy is number three. Cracking his knuckles, he utilizes the same combinations. But however unlike Linda before him, Tommy employs only snake hands. Breathing in through his lungs and then out, the creative young student makes actual hissing sounds following each strike. Still seated among his peers, Ivan produces a small notebook from his duffel bag. “Time.” Says Mr. Leung. “One minute and two seconds.”

“Very good.” The others applaud Tommy as well. Both Ivan and Linda give Tommy a high five. “You the man Tommy.” Ivan commends him. The mildly husky young man, whose height is comparable, looks at Ivan and smiles. “Naw, you the man.” He says.

"You know just like that old film, The Five Deadly Venoms?" Ivan began. Linda chuckles. "Oh man!" Tommy pointed to him. "We're more like the Four Deadly."

"There's me, there's you, Linda, and Diego." "The early years." Linda laughs. "One of the new students will eventually join us, and become the fifth." She concludes.

"That could work." Ivan nods. The fourth and final student in this particular group is Diego Rodrigo Salazar. Diego, who is Ivan's junior by one week, is also a student in traditional western-style boxing. A sixth generation American-born citizen, Diego is next to the youngest of five children. The lean, but well toned youngster was born into a family of boxers. His great grand parents immigrated to Texas from Tijuana, Mexico in the early 1900's. Like Diego himself and his siblings, his parents were also born here.

In the city of Chicago. Diego like Ivan has also been at the school for a year. His rank is comparable to that of his fellow brother. By way of expanding his son's horizons, Diego Senior supports his idea to enroll in the school. He and Ivan are also close. Last but not least, least but not last; it is now his turn. As the short Mexican-American rises to his feet, both Ivan as well as Tommy gives him a pound. Bowing before his teacher, Diego takes it to the dummy. Parrying with his right, Diego punches at a would-be right jaw. Parrying both left and right with lightning speed, Diego hits the dummy's sternum.

Zipping through the makeshift figure before him, the sweaty youth pushes the arms upward and summons a right blow to the chest. As his right arm returns to the chamber, Diego dispatches a left Tiger Claw. The latter grips the dummy's throat.

Mr. Leung checks his stopwatch. "Time." Bowing once again, Diego returns to his seat. "One minute, excellent." Says the ageless master. The others also praise Diego.

Upon completion of this drill, Master Leung begins to employ another exercise. In this drill he demonstrates to his pupils firsthand, the Wing Chun in a no holds barred street fight. In this drill there's Ivan and Linda. Linda, who charges her way toward Ivan, summons a series of kicks and punches. As Ivan commences to block and parry all of her attacks, he finds several openings. For every opening he finds, Ivan connects the dots, but yet he aborts his strikes by a mere inch. A mere inch, which could either result in injury to his opponent, or worse:

Death. Still in his fighting stance, Ivan now has Linda cornered. Her facial features, a work of beauty has been spared once more. The sole of his left foot misses the latter by one inch. Her brown eyes widened.

Having removed his foot although it never touched Linda's face, the pair shakes hands and of course, bows to one another. Immediately thereafter, Tommy and Diego are dispatched. Both young men at this point are equally agile. While Tommy rushes in punching, kicking, and throwing flying spinning crescents, Diego on the other hand sends out front kicks (left and right), roundhouses, spinning hook kicks, and a drop kick.

Already, Ivan directs them both at once with consistent blocks and parries. Given that they all wore cups, Ivan then takes the liberty of cutting down Tommy with a left punch to his groin. As Diego meanwhile attempts to immobilize Ivan with consistent kicks, Gold Lion fights fire with fire. Ivan uses his own legs to block Diego's and snaps a left back fist. After helping his fellow students up, Ivan shakes hands and bows his head. Not too long thereafter, Master Leung summons a loud gong. Lining up before their Sifu once more, they are dismissed.

Uptown

During the nineteenth century, this particular area was only sparsely settled. Today it is one of the most densest and most ethnically diverse residential areas in Chicago. German and Swedish immigrants operated scattered farms. The Cedar Lawn in 1869, Buena Park in 1860, and Edgewater in 1887. Developments in what was then Lakeview Township brought middle-income and wealthy residents into the area.

Land spectator John Lewis Cochran's (1857-1923) Edgewater set a building pattern for the area that fostered a broader mix of classes. Along the lakefront he favored mansions, but west of Evanston Avenue, (now Broadway) he encourage multifamily housing. Cochran convinced the Chicago, Milwaukee, &St. Paul Railroad to stop at Bryn Mawr Avenue and two decades later, was instrumental in the building of the Northwestern Elevated Railroad Company tracks near his developments. These routes made the community one of the city's most populous residential centers.

A commercial boom at the turn of the century ushered in the days of glamour. To compete with the Downtown/Loop area and Woodlawn on the south side, the Central Uptown Association promoted the area's shopping and recreational opportunities with the images of New York City. The main thoroughfare became of course Broadway Avenue and the area; Uptown Loren Millers department store (later Goldblatt's) anchored the shopping district. Revelers visited the Aragon Ballroom (1926), the Riviera Theater (1919), the Uptown Theater (1925), and the Marine Room of the Tony Edgewater Beach Hotel. (1916) Thousands of worshippers flocked to the People's Church and tuned their radio's to hear the sermons of Unitarian Minister Preston Bradley. For a decade (1907-1917), Essanay Studios made the neighborhood the heart of the American film industry.

Luxury apartment buildings and hotels appeared along Winthrop and Kenmore Avenues. But however during the Great Depression, the extension of Lake Shore Drive made it possible for shoppers to bypass the area for places further north.

During the housing crisis of World War II, the large rooms of luxury apartments along the Winthrop-Kenmore corridor seemed ideal for conversion into profitable smaller accommodations. Some landlords neglected their property or did not require long-term

leases or security deposits , which made Uptown accessible to recent migrants and Chicago's poor. In the 1950's, whites from Appalachia, Japanese-Americans, from California and Native Americans from Wisconsin, Minnesota, and Oklahoma occupied the neighborhood's affordable, but yet deteriorating housing.

To add insult to injury in addition to the decaying housing stock, the State of Illinois released mental health patients into the area's smaller apartments and halfway houses.

The changes in the area's economy, population, and housing stock drew the attention of residents, business owners, community organizers, and public officials. Long time residents and commercial institutions created the Uptown Chicago Commission, which successfully sought designation as a conservation area in 1966. The federal government made the area a Model Cities Area. New residents joined the community's organization, including Jobs or Income now, sponsored by the Students for a Democratic Society; Slim Coleman's Heart of Uptown Coalition; and the Uptown Hull House's Organization of The Northeast. Wary of the land clearance that had accompanied urban renewal in Hyde Park and Lincoln Park, they wanted to improve local conditions while keeping the neighborhood within the means of the poor. They protested the Building of Truman College in 1976, which displaced several hundred residents.

Dozen of social service organizations opened to serve the needs of Uptown's diverse poor. Decades later the neighborhood continues to attract Immigrants from Central America, Asia, Africa, and the Middle East. Residents here who wished to distance themselves from its image of poverty and blight discovered a new way to protect their interests; they changed the public identification of their neighborhoods. Residents of the northern half rediscovered the name "Edgewater." As recently as nine years ago, the residents achieved recognition as a distinct community area.

Rainbow Skating Rink

For almost three decades since the 1960's, this establishment has been a popular skating rink for mostly teens and young adults. Situated in Buena Park, an area within the greater Uptown neighborhood, the building sits near the corner of Clark Street and Lawrence Avenue. Surrounded by other commercial establishments, the complex is also among many historic homes, both single and multi-family, followed by a wide spectrum of well-preserved mansions. Graceland Cemetery sits across the street.

The latter is typical of those that reflect Queen Victoria's reconception of the early 19th century "graveyard." Instead of poorly maintained headstones, and bodies buried on top of each other, on an ungenerous parcel of land; the cemetery became a pastoral landscaped park dotted with memorial markers, with room left over for picnics, a common usage of cemeteries. Ossian Cole Simmonds designed the landscape architecture for Graceland. Built and founded in 1860, many of the tombs here are of great architectural or of great artistic interest, including Ivan's favorites the Getty Tomb, the Martin Ryerson Mausoleum, (both designed by architect Louis Sullivan, who is also buried within these plots), and the Schoenhofen Pyramid Mausoleum. The industrialist George Pullman who was buried here at night, in a lead coffin within an elaborately reinforced steel-and concrete vault to prevent his body from being exhumed or desecrated by angry labor activists.

Along with its other famous residents, this park-like cemetery is notable for two statues by sculptor Lorado Taft, Eternal Silence for the Graves family plot and the Crusader that marks Victor Lawson's final resting place. Graceland is one of three notable 19th century cemeteries, which were previously, well outside the city limits ; including the other two being Rosehill (further north), and Oak Woods (south of Hyde Park), which includes a major monument to the Confederate Civil War dead.

In conclusion, in addition to the larger ones mentioned above, directly to the south of this land is the German Protestant Wunder's Cemetery (divided by a fence), established in 1851. Also Saint Boniface is four blocks north of Graceland circa Clark and Lawrence. To the east end, the walls to the entire cemetery are topped off with barbed wire.

Situated at the latter end of the 119 acres is the Howard "L." Also known as the North-South Route, a six car train is summoned to its nearby Sheridan stop.

It has been a full hour and a half since Ivan and his friends arrived. Upon entry, the group each rented a pair of skates, took it to the floor, played video games, and returned to the floor a second time. Two hours later, the group takes twenty. Bypassing the other skaters on the crowded floor, they finally succeed. Among the five including Ivan himself, there's Rizzo Harrison, Denise Wilson, Andrea DuPont, and Charles Davis.

At this point, they are all in the café section. "Man, its packed in here tonight." Rizzo began, as he observes the establishment. "You can say that again." Ivan backs him.

"Maybe during the summer, you would expect for it to be this crowded, but not on a winter night such as this one." He continues on. "But we're here." Denise reminds them.

She chuckles. "Hey Benson, get me something to eat." Andrea roasts Ivan. Ivan grins, and nods. "Hell naw girl, I ain't your butler." He snaps back laughing.

"Why don't you take yo sweet ass to the snack bar and do it yourself." "Ouch!" The others reply. Smiling and then blushing, Andrea taps Ivan's arm. Hard. "Such harsh language." Rizzo teases him. "You know, Ivan does have a point Andie." Charles says to Andrea. Jokingly, he takes note of his friends blossoming figure and then chuckles.

In response, Andrea smiles and gives him the finger. "Whatever." She says. Denise pats her on the shoulder and then smiles. "I envy you." She says. "I'll be lucky to eventually have a body like yours." "Anyway, Ivan treated us last week." Denise continues on. "Let me get this one." "And by the way, where's Nikki tonight?" She then asks. "She's attending her cousin's birthday party." Ivan explains. Andrea smiled.

"If I didn't know any better, I'd say she likes you." She tells him plainly. By way of agreeing with their friend, the others nod. "You guys would make a great couple."

"We first took note at your party last Monday." Charles explained.

"When you asked her to dance with you, did she hesitate to take your hand?"

"No, she didn't." Ivan answers. "She wasn't playing with me." "As a matter of fact, I think that her mind was already made up." Ivan concludes. "Long before the party."

The others nodded happily once again. "Doesn't she play the violin?" Rizzo asks.

"Yes, she does." Ivan responds. "Christy plays the clarinet herself." Rizzo replies.

"So what." Andrea roasts. "You know what?" Riz faces her. "I'm tired of you!" He playfully snaps back. Grabbing her long stringy ponytail, he tugs away. "RIZZO!" "Stop!" "Ok!" Andrea pleads, now laughing. "Yeah, I thought so." Rizzo grins.

He releases her. "So is anybody going out for the talent show this year?" She then asks. "For the first time, I might." Says Ivan. The others are appalled by his answer.

"What do you have in mind?" Andrea asks. "Rap." Says Ivan. "Really?" She asks once more. "Seriously?" "Stop playing!" Andrea says. She is not yet convinced.

"Straight up, he's really good, Andrea." Rizzo assures her. "I've been knowing Ivan since Kindergarten." Charles added. "He ain't playin." "I've battled with him from time to time, and trust me." Rizzo jumps back in. "He gets better and better."

"Would you like to hear sample of my work?" Ivan finally asked her. Andrea nods. "Riz and me will entertain you now." "The two of us will have a battle." Rizzo begins to break it down. "You can tells us what you think when we're done." "Word?"

"Bet." Says Andrea "Let's do this." Riz tells Ivan. Ivan himself shakes his head.

Look at Ivan
Who's truly unforgettable
Cause he smells bad
He's known as Ivan "The Terrible"
And if you get in my way
I'll cancel you out like a bad sitcom by you making friends with my AK
Falling victim to my slay
Yo momma's like Houdini turning more tricks like "That's Incredible"
Cause she's real flexible and you're perishable
I crack heads like eggs that's incredibly edible
Any last words because your time is up
The jokes on you
Now you're here to face the inevitable

Appearing as though she is turned on, Andrea claps. "I like that." She says. Ivan laughs with Rizzo. "Man, its like that tonight?" He asked him. Rizzo shakes his head.

"Its like that." He replies. "Word." Says the both of them. Their response was in unison. Andrea, along with Charles both began to chuckle. Ivan takes to the floor.

Well its round two
I thought you knew
You being the man of the hour?
Hell no! That stuff ain't true
I'll beat you like a drum
Turning you black and blue
Your rhymes are so gay
They sound like Nancy Drew
I'm like Salmonella
My rhymes will contaminate ya

And laminate ya
Like a bad case of Hemorrhoids
I'll straight inflamminate ya
You wanna wave the white flag?
Beg for mercy?
Don't even bother!
I'll leave you incapacitated
Left to die
In the Mojave Desert
Like your absent minded father!
With no knowledge or criticism
You definitely have no virtue
This is your final warning!
Surrender now!
Or I'll hurt you

Andrea and Charles applauded. "Go Ivan!" "Go Rizzo!" Both boys rose from their seats to shake hands and embrace each other. "Hey Kid and Play." Denise roasts them. She finally returns from the snack bar. "The food is paid for." She tells the others. "You still have to get it yourselves." "Thanks." Says Charles. "Did you know that Ivan could rap?" Andrea asked Denise. "I do now." She responds. "I heard like, his last few verses about leaving Riz to die in the desert like." "Like his father or something." Denise is equally appalled. "Let alone that was on my way back over here."

"You're just coming out of hiding completely aren't you?" She then asks. "Jesus Christ!" "Boy, you've got some ugly talent." "You ain't lying." Says Rizzo. "You've already won the talent show." Andrea added. "As far as I'm concerned. "He really should try out for it." Denise insists. "In that particular category, Ivan will violate whoever dares to cross him." Getting up from the table, the entire group heads for the snack bar.

4

THOMPSON RESIDENCE (THE PREVIOUS SATURDAY)

Hours later after Mr. And Mrs. Thompson returns from their normal weekend errands and among them grocery shopping, they finally enter their building. At this time their youngest son Ivan is still out and about in reference to his usual weekend haunts, namely the Cultural Center and his martial arts class. Simon, their oldest son is still at work. And the landlady also a relative, remains unavailable.

As Franklin Thompson brings in the remaining groceries, his wife Marie of nearly twenty years began stocking both the pantry as well as the kitchen cabinets, followed by the refrigerator. Not too long after Mr. Thompson returns with the remaining items, Mrs. Thompson gathers all of the family laundry. While Mr. Thompson stores the remnants into the pantry, his wife gathers her first basket and takes it downstairs.

Walking through her mom's apartment, she makes a left and goes through the unmade guest room. Unlocking the trap door, she begins her descent. Flicking on the lights, Mr. Thompson reaches the recreation room. Upon entry, she spots her nephews body.

It is face down on what had been a glass table. The latter is both cracked and severely damaged. Beneath Doug's body (although he is not dead), is a small puddle of blood.

Upon her initial discovery, Mrs. Thompson is already in shock. Putting her left hand over her mouth, she instantly froze. Dropping the basket with the clothes still inside, she screams for her husband. "Frank!!!" As her scream echoes throughout the ventilation system, Mr. Thompson quickly reacts. Retreating for their bedroom, the ex-Marine and former Vietnam vet procures a lockbox from the closet. Inside, is a well polished 9mm.

Picking the lock instantly, he summons the recently bought handgun. Removing the safety, Mr. Thompson cocks the hammer. Now strapped, the aging athlete takes off.

Dashing down two flights of stairs in record time, Mr. Thompson quickly catches his breath. "What's wrong baby?" He asks his wife. "Damn!" He says, jumping up. He too spots his battered nephew. Doug is still laid out before the both of them. Checking his pulse comes a sigh of relief. "He's still with us Marie." Mr. Thompson announces.

Feeling relieved, Mrs. Thompson sighed and plops down on the couch. Taking note of Doug, she nods her head. She is both sad and disgusted. "You wait down here, I'm gonna have a look around." Mr. Thompson suggests. As she bears a faint smile at this point, Mrs. Thompson shakes her head. Still brandishing his weapon, the head of the house now returns to the upstairs. Canvassing the entire first floor room by room as well as under tables, beds, under couches, and even the kitchen sink, Mr. Thompson then circles the building's exterior. Nothing. And with that, he returns to the basement. By then Doug is cradled in his wife's arms. The badly beaten youngster moans in pain.

"As far as I can tell." Mr. Thompson began. "It looks like nobody broke in." Putting the safety to his gun back on, he tucks it away into his holster. "What happened down here?" Mr. Thompson asked. "Don't try to get up by yourself man." He tells his nephew. "We'll help you up." Douglas moans and coughs. Along with his black eye, blue skin, and puffed up features for the effect, even his vocals are strained. His nose continues to bleed.

"Help me get him up." Mr. Thompson requests. Helping Doug to his feet, his uncle and his aunt places him on the couch. As he began to lie down, Mrs. Thompson places a pillow under his head. "Ivan." Doug's voice struggled. "Ivan jumped me."

Mr. And Mrs. Thompson turned and faced each other. "We've should have known." Says Mrs. Thompson. "But we'll have plenty of time to confront him." Her husband says showing only mild disdain. "Right now, we need to get this boy to a doctor." "Don't bother calling 911." "I'll take him to Northwestern myself." Mrs. Thompson nodded. "And baby if you can, clean this up." "I'll take Leon Spinks here to the emergency room, get em fixed up, and buy him a Greyhound ticket, because he's leaving tomorrow."

"Its time for him to go." "Right, we've got to keep these two separate." Mrs. Thompson agrees. "And while I'm at it, I'll be at Aronson too." Her husband also announces. "I gotta replace this table." "Your mother will be back in about two hours."

"And we don't want to worry her to death." "You've got that right." Mrs. Thompson chuckles. Mr. And Mrs. Thompson turned to their nephew. "My mother will already be at church by the time you take him to the bus terminal." "I'll call Helen this evening."

"Why you've hooked up with Hannibal, we'll talk about that some other time." Says his uncle. Right now, I'm taking you to the doctor." Helping Doug to his feet, Mr. Thompson slowly walks him toward the back. "The car's in the garage." He explains.

Returning from his martial arts class, still clad in his uniform Ivan enters the front door. Sitting in the living room are his parents. The couple is watching what appears to the movie "Bloodsport." Obviously, they were thinking about their youngest son as he came in. "How you doing son?" His father began. Mr. Thompson's voice was actually pleasant. "How was practice this afternoon?" Mrs. Thompson asked. For the first time, Ivan is not nervous. "It was really nice." Both of his parents happily nodded.

"Baby, can we talk with you for a moment?" Mrs. Thompson asks. Bearing a faint smile, Ivan shows them to the dining room table.

Around six-thirty on that very same evening, Simon returns home from work. Entering his bedroom to change out of his uniform, and into his street clothes, he walks over to his dresser. Looking down, he finds a white envelope. Producing a letter opener, he examines the contents. Among them is a snapshot of their cousin Doug. He is of course badly bruised and beaten. Face down in a small puddle of blood just the way their

parents had found him earlier, Simon suddenly looks ill. Along with this disturbing photo is a short letter. It reads: NEVER AGAIN. Throwing the contents onto the floor, the Cain-like sibling now holds his stomach. Gripping the back of his pants, Simon retreats to the bathroom.

As it is later revealed, Ivan's parents were all BUT angry with him. In fact, a part of them felt as though Doug had it coming, to so suddenly return home as though nothing happened. Many of those within his circles perceived it as a "well-deserved ass whooping." To others, it was simply poetic justice. But however, not even poetic justice came cheap. Despite his warranted dilemma, Ivan's parents were still displeased by his actions that not only them cost them a new table, but they also ended up paying Doug's medical expenses. Ivan was allowed to hang out with his friends for one last evening before being placed under house arrest the following day.

The following Sunday morning, Doug boards the Greyhound and returns to Milwaukee. He was never seen again. In the wake of the conflict between north and south, Ivan and Simon both declare a truce. The in-house family feud is over.

Monday, April 11, 1989(Spring Break)

On a warm and pleasant afternoon, Ivan and his friends are out at North Riverside Park Mall. Roughly ten miles west of Downtown Chicago, this mall attracts customers throughout all of western Cook County. Located in its namesake village, it sits on the corner of Cermak Road and Harlem Avenue. From the time of its founding, North Riverside have had few connections with the property on which the mall itself is located.

Once the domain of the Potawatomi, the forested land was purchased by a trapping and real estate firm in 1835. David A. Gage, treasurer of the city of Chicago, purchased approximately 16,00 acres along Harlem Avenue for his country estate. When Gage left office and the city treasury was found short of money, this property was turned over to the city of Chicago. Part of this land was used for the Cook County Home for Boys and later a tuberculosis sanitarium. For approximately one hundred years, the village grew to the west, near the Des Plaines River. By 1900, onion farmers had settled in the area between Gage's former property and Des Plaines Avenue. Members of the Holiness Association (many of whom were Chicago businessmen) used the properties for summer retreats. They even built homes between the Des Plaines Avenue and the river.

At the time of its incorporation in 1923, the Des Plaines River formed the western boundary of the village. The river in its forested setting brought in recreational and retirement opportunities, including the Optimates Canoe Club (founded in 1893). By 1926 the size of North Riverside doubled with the annexation of land west of the Des Plaines River. Residential construction boomed in the years after World War II as new residents many of whom were of Eastern European decent, moved into the new brick single-family homes. With manufacturing jobs available in other nearby western suburbs, the population has already peaked in just twenty years alone.

North Riverside Mall

Built in two phases beginning in the early 1960's(North Riverside Plaza shopping center) and (North Riverside Park Mall in 1975) this complex have brought in more commercial activity to this otherwise quiet area. These particular properties have been rendered invaluable; they now pay for over half of the village's operating expenses, making this far western suburb itself an affordable place to live.

Across the street in the neighboring village of Berwyn lies another strip mall. Known as the "Harlem-Cermak Shopping Center", a Mc Donald's restaurant sits on the southeast corner. And next to it, is a large metal pole. And on it there are as many as fifth teen cars. Stacked on top of one another, this is believed to be a sculpture of some sort.

The Downtown Chicago skyline is still seen, even beyond its western borders.

Meanwhile back in the main complex, there are many shoppers. Representing all walks, Ivan and his friends are still among them. Those among his cabinet like Rizzo, Charles, Denise and Andrea, Nikki as well as Lazarus also join them. As this time, they all split up into two different groups. "Within one hour, we will all meet back at the main entrance." Ivan tells the rest of the group. The rest of the group nods. While Riz, Charlie, and Laz remain with Ivan, Andrea and Denise join Nicole. While the girls proceed down the west corridor surrounded by flagship clothing, designer jewelry shops, and shoe stores (both domestic and imported), Ivan and the boys walk into a nearby Sam

Goody. The latter sits near the food court, opposite the main entrance. "Why don't we check out the Rap section?" Ivan suggests. Nodding their heads in agreement, Charlie, Laz, and Riz all follows his lead. Walking toward the back beyond the Gospel, R&B, and Alternative Rock, the group now approaches the Rap section.

"Do any of y'all know that Cube left N.W.A?" Lazarus asks. Beforehand, the others had already began browsing through titles as well as hearing a few samples when he made the announcement. "Yeah, as a matter of fact." Ivan began; he returns his headphones to their rightful station. "I read the story in yesterday's Sun Times."

"They have also been criticized by the FBI." Rizzo added. He sighed and shook his head. "Why is that?" Charles asks. "If I'm not mistaken, it could be because of their most recent song, my favorite "Fuck The Police." Ivan answers. "It was said that the FBI issued them threatening letters once, now that you've mentioned it." Charles remembers.

"Because they were like planning to do a concert in either Detroit or Sacramento."

"It was more than likely Sacramento." Says Ivan. "It has to be." "Because Sacramento is a largely Republican town." "Mostly Christian, well off, and of course mostly white even though there is some diversity, most of their views lean to the far right."

"That's true." Rizzo nods his head. "A lot of them do claim to be Christians." "And we all know that's bullshit." Charles snaps calmly. He grins and then chuckles. "You ain't never lied man." Lazarus shakes his head. "They the dirtiest of elected officials, and the biggest hypocrites." "You have a lot of their parents rejecting Rap music, and preaching against it." Rizzo began, he thunders. "While at the same time, you have their children in places like Denver, Sacramento, and others like it." "Behind their backs, secretly buying tapes and CD's, going to concerts, and even buying the T-shirts." "I'm quite sure they use

slang just like we do, behind closed doors." Rizzo concludes. "Maybe more than we do." "And its not such a bad idea for people in general, black, white, and so on; to free their minds and explore their horizons." "Keep in mind, this is nineteen eighty-nine, not fifty nine." Having heard his case, Ivan and the others all nod in agreement.

"As it later turned out, NWA pushed forward, arrived in Sacramento and performed anyway." Ivan began, briefly clearing his throat. "Almost immediately after the show, the police arrested them. "Within one hour, they posted bail." Rizzo chuckled. "I bet the cops themselves were pissed." He says. "I'm sure they were." Ivan responds. He smiled and shook his head. "Damn." Charles began chuckling. "Free speech can sometimes be a bitch." He says. "Rumor has it, that it was some politician trying to run for mayor, around the very same time NWA showed up." Laz began to explain. He was fronting to the people, swearing up and down he hated Rap." "Using Rap music as a scapegoat for all they recent woes, and vowing to do this and vowing to do that if he's elected, and shit like that." "That was bogus." Rizzo says with disdain. "So basically it was a cheap shot?" Ivan asks. "Just to win a few votes?" "Word." Says Lazarus. "In other words, whoever this guy is, I take it that he lost." Ivan chuckles. "I couldn't remember who this guys was to save my own ass, but eventually it'll come back to me." Lazarus concludes.

"Anyway, according to Ice Cube's interview with The Cut, Cube had suspected that Eazy and his manager Jerry Heller were skimming money off of the group's album profits ." Ivan began to point out. "More like double dipping." Rizzo added.

"Taking like fifty percent of everything that the rest of the group makes, and hoarding the funds for themselves." The others nod in agreement. "That's really fucked up." Says Lazarus. Still shocked to hear the most recent news from Ivan, he shakes his head.

"Of all the other members, I've always believed that Cube was the mastermind." Rizzo responds. "He actually wrote most of the songs for the group, Boyz-N-The Hood, Dopeman, and Gangsta, Gangsta just to name a few." The others nodded once more.

"Can I help you guys with something?" A store employee asks. The young man seemingly in his late teens to early twenties, appears to be both Liberian and Hmong.

"We're fine sir, thank you." Ivan says. He is greatly impressed. The tall but slender employee smiled. "No problem." He tells the group. Shortly thereafter, he returns to the stockroom. "Not only did he finish high school." Ivan continues on, he now canvassed the aisle. The others followed his lead. "But he's already in college as we speak."

“Straight up?” Rizzo asks. Ivan nods. “Man, he definitely going somewhere” Charles responds. “He’s gonna go solo.” Lazarus says to the others. “Believe what I tell you.”

“About a year from now, Cube will have his own group.” “He’s too talented.”

By this time, the others have already chosen their items. It is now down to Ivan himself. He picks up the most recent CD from Miami’s Too Live Crew. Its entitled, “Nasty As They Wanna be.” “I’ve been looking everywhere for this one.” Ivan says.

“George’s didn’t even carry it, and neither did Barney’s by the house.”

He now examines the contents on the back of the cover. “What did you pick up Charlie?” Ivan asks. “Public Enemy.” The husky youth tells him, he happily nodded.

“Fear of A Black Planet.” “That’s cool.” “What about you Riz?” “Geto Boys and De La Soul.” “I picked up the Jungle Brothers.” Lazarus added. He holds up his prize.

“It looks like we have chosen wisely.” Says Ivan. He is jokingly calm. Rizzo laughs.

“Just like the Grail Knight in the Last Crusade.” He began. “He told ol’boy to choose wisely, as he drank from one of the sacred cups.” “And did he choose wisely?” “Hell naw!” Charles chuckles. “Donovan died.” “Dude turned into a skeleton right away.” Lazarus also laughs. “Then you had Indiana Jones and that nazi assed doctor looking salty and shit.” “The Grail Knight, like he was trying not to laugh, told them he chose poorly.” “Everybody was cracking up real hard in the show.” He concludes.

Carrying their items to the front register, the boys summon their wallets.

As they proceed down the westernmost corridor of this large complex, the group observes a multitude of stores such as Carson Pirie Scott, M.C. Sporting Goods, Chess King, The Gap, Banana Republic, Wilson’s Leather, T.J.Maxx, Kay Bee toys, Dimensions and Fashions, a GNC Health shop, and a London Fog Outlet Store. All which are located on the ground level. Others even include JC. Penny, World Foot Locker, and Frederick’s. Passing a Mrs. Field’s cookie shop, the boys venture past a large construction area. Toronto-based Cineplex Odeon has recently acquired this space to build a new multiplex. Set to be completed in 1990, the latter will employ as many as 17,29 seats and more than likely house as many as six cinemas. Several other storefronts are also being refurbished. Besides what appears to be an ongoing renovation of this mall, upon completion other new tenants will follow. Having reached the far west end, the group now enters Montgomery Ward. Its consumer electronics division known as "Electronic Avenue", is located on the lower level. Ivan and the others arrive here.

"I need to hang out here more often with y'all." Says Lazarus. He observes the scenery around him, and then smiled. The youngest member of the group (just recently turned eleven) takes note of several girls nearby. Situated in a checkout line nearest the pedestrian lobby, they carry an assortment of garments. These particular young females were actually well within the boy's age racket. As the colorful young ladies pay the cashier, Ivan, Riz, Charles, and Lazarus are yet still browsing at the video game systems.

Having paid for their merchandise, the four girls (all of whom are unknown at this point) are now prepared to leave. As they exit the store, one of them appears as though they had left something, suddenly glances back. Upon her discovery, the short but mildly heavyset female spots Ivan and the boys. Staring at the leader for duration of her visit, the full figured female has made her decision. Tapping her friends, they all stop and look. By this time Ivan and the boys have finally made their purchases. As they finally walk towards the checkout line, the girls remain situated in the mall's lobby.

To make it seem less obvious, they stop at nearby photo shop. Shortly after making their purchases, Ivan and his entourage follows suit. While the girls all pose for several photo opts, Ivan's group also enters the shop. Looking around, they study the price ranges posted above the service counter. "How can I help you today?" One of the employees asks. "Give us one second please." Ivan says happily. "Sure, take your time." The burly, middle-aged gentleman insists. For a moment, Ivan and the others convene a brief meeting.

After doing a series of poses, Ivan, and Rizzo as well as Charles and Lazarus, all collects a number. As they wait for their pictures to develop, they finally catch up to the young ladies who were here before them. Like that of the proceeding group, they are also waiting. With their numbers in hand, the girls are situated in the center of the store.

Looking on, they catch a glimpse of colorful pictures of mostly people and their families and even their pets. Some are individual photos as well as black and white snapshots. Simon himself, Ivan's brother is a photography major at his high school.

"You know, even though my brother is such an ass, he still has raw talent." Ivan himself, tells the young lady. At this point, the sound of his voice nearly startles her.

Damn! She thought, now catching her breath. Ivan smiled. "I'm sorry, if I scared you." He says. The girl blushed. "Oh, that's okay." She replies. The young lady began to smile. "Have you girls been waiting long?" Ivan asks. "No, not really." The young lady tells them. "You actually showed up at the right time." Rizzo added. "Usually around midday, the business here is rather slow." "Ivan breaks it down to the girls.

"Especially with it being lunchtime, and so on." The seemingly cultured young ladies all began to smile. "Do you come here often?" They asked. "About every other week." Ivan tells them. The girls all nod in agreement. Shortly thereafter, the strikingly handsome young man introduces himself. "By the way, my name is Ivan."

Extending out his right hand, the young lady accepts it. Charles and Laz also introduce themselves. Rizzo takes their lead. "Catalina." "That's really a beautiful name."

"Why, thank you." The girl says. The young lady now known as Catalina really was quite a looker. She's the full figured female who initially spotted him. About maybe two inches shorter than Ivan, Catalina has a beautiful dark complexion, long shoulder length hair, and light brown eyes. Her attire consists of a white (V-neck) cotton sweater, a chain that bears her name, a short mini skirt, and a pair of black sandals. The latter, a recent fashion trend is employed by one open toe. A single strap at the end covers the heels.

Among her friends is a taller, but thin young lady named Rhonda. Clad in a long sleeved shirt and black stretch pants, she wears a pair of white sneakers. As a long bang covers her forehead in the front, a long ponytail on the other hand, covers the back.

Her skin tone favors that of a lighter bronze, while the eyes (of course) consists of a natural brown. The third young lady whose height is smacked in the middle, her name is Felicia. Clad in a yellow sundress and white sandals, the opposite color of Catalina's, she sported a bob hairstyle and hoop earrings. Unlike that of the other girls, Felicia wore make up. Her figure unlike that of both Catalina's as well as Rhonda's, Felicia actually had more curves. Her skin tone, for which Ivan had favored, is two shades darker.

Shaking their heads in agreement, Ivan and his friends faced one another and began to smile. "So where do you all live?" Ivan asks. "In the city?" "In the suburbs?" "We live in the suburbs." Catalina answers him. "Out here technically, just two villages over." Felicia added. "Forest Park just off the expressway." Rhonda helps them out. "What about you guys?" She asked the boys. "We're in the city." Rizzo answers. She nodded. "What part?" "On the west side." Rizzo tells her. "You don't seem like it." Felicia smiled.

"But it doesn't matter." Catalina grinned. "We still like you anyway." She says. Both Felicia and Rhonda giggled. And they did. For about the next half hour as they continued to wait for their pictures, the two groups mingled, laughed, and examined some the other portraits .

Collecting their pictures at the front counter, the two groups return to the lobby.

Shortly before going their separate ways, they all exchange phone numbers. "Its been a pleasure speaking with you." Ivan tells Catalina. Taking her hand, which smells of perfume, he kisses it. "If you all prefer to stay in touch." Rizzo began smiling.

"You're welcomed to give us a call." Also facing them, Charles and Laz gave a nod.

"There's no pressure." Ivan assures them. Felicia and Rhonda give each other a high five. "Man, listen to us." Ivan chuckles. "Straight up." Rizzo shakes his head.

"We sound like two ambulance chasing attorneys." The girls laugh in response.

Still speechless, presumably by Ivan's gesture, Catalina's blushes once more.

Two minutes later, another young lady enters the lobby from the Cermak entrance. Bearing a slight resemblance to the love-stricken young lady, she was initially with the group but was suddenly called away. It was obviously her sister, or perhaps a cousin.

However, as the unknown young lady attempts to approach them, she suddenly slips and falls. "Connie, are you all right?" Catalina asked her. As Felicia and Rhonda rush to her aid, Lazarus and a mall guard are actually the ones to help her to her feet. "Yeah, thanks." The girl says.

Spotting her purse, Laz also picks it up. From the moment she is back on her feet, the youngest member in the group hands it back to her. "Thanks." She tells him.

He smiled and gave a nod. "Take this." The young lady began. Handing him a piece of torn paper, she thanks the guard also. "Is mom here?" Catalina asked the young lady.

"Yeah, she's waiting outside in the car." The girl responds. The others nodded.

"We've gotta go." Says the leader of the group. "You have our phone numbers."

As the four females (including Catalina's sister Connie) began to leave, Ivan and his group followed suit. They return to the main entrance to meet Nikki and the others.

South Shore (near Lake Michigan)

Situated nine miles southeast of downtown, a 1939 description of this neighborhood stated that it was predominately middle class and upper middle class. But yet, as far as socially it didn't register. The physical characteristics of this south side neighborhood are visibly antiquated. Though the class gap among its residents has run at times quite wide, for most of its history South Shore has been a strong middle class enclave.

The area, bounded by 67th and 79th Streets to the north and south and by Stony Island to the east and west, was mostly swampland in the 1850's when Ferdinand Rohn, a German truck farmer, utilized trails along the area's high ground to transport his goods to Chicago. Before the community came to be known as South Shore in the 1920's, it was a collection of settlements in southern Hyde Park Township. The names of these settlements---Essex, Bryn Mawr, Parkside, Cheltenham Beach, and Windsor Park---indicate British heritage of the Illinois Central Railroad (now Metra) and steel mill workers who had come to inhabit them. Most of these settlements were already in place when the Illinois Central built the South Kenwood Station in 1881 at what is now

71st and Jeffrey Boulevard. As with many south side communities, the two events that sparked commercial and residential development were annexations into the city of Chicago in 1889. And second, the World's Columbian Exposition in 1893. The location of the fair in nearby Jackson Park prompted the sale of land and building lots and subsequently a housing explosion. White Protestants fled neighboring Washington Park as immigrants and African-Americans moved there. In 1905 these former residents of Washington Park built the Jackson Park Highlands, an exclusive residential community ensconced within South Shore. In 1906 they established the South Shore Country Club, a posh 67-acre lakeside playground, which excluded blacks and Jews.

A housing boom in the 1920's generated not only a large increase in the area's population, but also greater diversity among its residents and in housing stock.

Between 1920 and 1930 the population of South Shore jumped from 31,832 to 78,755. Many of these new residents were Irish, Swedish, German, and Jewish and had followed the native white protestants from Washington Park to live in South Shore's high rises, single family homes, and apartment houses. Institutions built here during these years reflected the community's growing diversity. By 1940 South Shore contained 15 Protestant churches, 4 Roman Catholic churches, and 4 Jewish synagogues.

As African-American families moved to South Shore in the 1950's, white residents became more concerned about the neighborhood's stability. The South Shore Commission initiated a program they called "managed integration," designed to check the physical decline of the community and to achieve racial balance. The initiative was largely unsuccessful on both counts. Although commercial decline did coincide with an increase in the African-American population (69 percent in 1970 and 95 percent by 1980), it had more to do with "redlining" and commercial disinvestments.

In the early 1970's, collaboration between the Renewal Effort Service Corporation (RESCORP) and the Illinois Housing Development Authority resulted in two rehabilitation programs called "New Vistas," When in 1973 the South Shore Bank attempted to relocate downtown, the Federal Comptroller of the Currency denied their petition to move under pressure from local activists. These very same activists became the bank's new management team the following year. The bank's reinvestment in South Shore is now imminent.

Within the next two decades, this area is expected to reemerge as a strong middle-class African-American community. Already the commercial strips on 71st and 75th Streets, are welcoming new businesses, with a shopping plaza on the corner of 71st and Jeffrey.

The Chicago Park District purchased the waning South Shore Country Club in 1972. The latter is now a Cultural Center. Three years ago, the new Regal Theater opened on 79th Street. Even in 1989, the neighborhood still doesn't socially register. South Shore remains an ideal destination for anyone who desires a congenial middle class community.

Rainbow Beach Park

Established by the city's park district at the beginning of the century, this land of recreation is bounded by South Shore Drive to the west, Lake Michigan to the east, and 75th Street to the north. To the south, its border lies along 79th Street.

The existing USS (United States Steel) South Works Plant is seen in the distance. During the late 1960's, after serving his country in Vietnam, a young Franklin Thompson (Ivan's father) who was then twenty-one actually used to work here! For many years prior to his son's return, his father, a veteran in the Korean War had also been employed.

For a short time, Frank and his dad actually worked at the mill side by side.

As the creatures of the air, namely the pigeons and the seagulls travel high above the waters; swooping down repetitiously they collect their daily trout. Along the southernmost shoreline, hundreds or maybe dozens swim and bathe. Others are resting in the sand, children running and playing, some are building sand castles and then some.

Working diligently to insure their safety, are of course the lifeguards. Being alert, observant, professional, and dedicated is their job. Nothing more. Nothing less.

Inside the recreation center which in part hasn't aged very well, houses an office, two locker rooms (namely for the life guards), a first aid center, two public phones, and last but not least, two restrooms.

Scribbled on the walls of the men's bathroom are gang symbols, drawings of genitals; male and female followed by countless obscenities.

Ironically, there's even a mock phone number. Spray-painted in bold red letters, it reads: 1-800-EAT PUSSY. The stench of urine is also evident. As he changes into his swimming trunks, Ivan frowns and shakes his head. This place smells like a commode!

Walking beyond the concession stands as well as the park, which is now behind him, topless, and barefooted he heads toward the beach. "Where was you at man?" Lazarus asked. "I had to change inside of that filthy assed bathroom." Ivan answers. The thought of the smell alone still made him twitch, as he shakes his head once more.

"From confines of that facility, I don't think that time has been much of an ally."

Right now, the entire group is well relaxed, calm and at ease. Everyone with the exception of Rizzo is swimming in the water. Rizzo on the other hand, is creating a giant sand castle. Nikki, Andrea, and Denise are lying on their rafts while Laz dog paddles.

Charles, who isn't seen, is directly under them. He snorkels. Plunging into the water, Ivan himself joins them. For about a half of a mile from the dense shoreline to the center of the lake itself, to the point where he no longer feels the surface, Ivan swims back.

Returning to the sandy shore, Ivan emerges from the seaweed smelling water. As the water glistens from his well-muscled frame, his female friends began to smile.

"When I was smaller, I actually used to have a fear of water." He tells them.

"You did?" Andrea asks. Ivan nodded. "Whenever my dad would usher me to the deep end, I would literally freak out." She along with Nikki and Denise all happily nodded.

"But yet, I still enjoyed taking baths." The girls then giggled.

"How did you learn to swim then?" Denise asked. "Well eventually Denise, I did overcome my fear." Ivan begins to explain. He now rests on the sand.

Although they see Ivan as their friend, Andrea, Denise, and Nikki are still appalled by his rock hard chest, as well as his gutless stomach. He now sports a six-pack.

“Because I knew that my father would always be committed, I eventually took him up on his offer.” “That was nice of him.” Says Nikki. “Just three years ago.” He went on.

“From the very first time my parents and me went down to Orlando, before they bought the timeshare.” “We stayed in a regular hotel, the Days Inn Lakeside.”

“There was this swimming pool just outside of our room.” The girls nodded their heads as they continue to listen. “How deep was it?” Nikki asks, as she smiles and gives him the eye. “Eight feet.” Ivan says. “For some reason, I was rather curious about how to swim from the deep to the shallow end that day.” “I asked my father if he was still interested in giving me that free lesson, and he didn’t hesitate.”

“He took me over to the deep end, and I learned to kick, flap my arms, turn my head, the works. “How did you learn to hold your breath for so long?” Nikki asks.

“Everyday all year round when I couldn’t access a pool, and my parents were still skeptical about me swimming at the Y, I used to stick my head in the bathroom sink for short periods of time.” Ivan further breaks it down. “Everyday, I managed to hold my breath just a little longer.” Intrigued by his story, the girls happily nod.

“You look good Ivan.” Denise says. “Thanks, I feel good.” Ivan tells her. “Especially after that swim.” “You managed to make it back to shore, before the lifeguards stopped you.” She continued on. “Even if you are a good swimmer, they don’t know that.”

“They can’t risk it.” “Especially when they see you swim beyond the shallow area.” Nikki added. “Almost halfway to Egypt.” The others all laughed including Charles.

He emerges from the water like that of a dolphin.

Lazarus, who has dog paddled his way around the shallow areas to the edge of the deep end, now returns as well. His bird frame emerges from the water. Jokingly, Andrea, Denise and Nikki all gave him thumbs down. Lazarus grins and then nods.

“Forget y’all.” He says. Meanwhile several of the unknown girls on shore, catches a brief glimpse of Ivan. Quietly walking by, some of them are seen smiling while others wave. One young lady even takes the liberty of blowing him a kiss. Nikki laughed.

“They’re just like a pack of hungry wolves.” She says. Both Denise and Andrea nod their heads in agreement. “Even though you’re not God's gift to the female gender." Andrea began, now facing Ivan. "A lot of these girls around here, and even those back home would have no idea whatsoever." Confused by her statement, Ivan shrugs.

"And what is that Andrea?" He asks. "They wouldn't know how to approach you." Denise explains. "Because you appear more distinguished, sophisticated, and you have killer intelligence." "And you do." Denise added. "They are actually even more intimidated by you now." Once again, all three of the girls look over at Ivan. And they smile. "Take away the fact that you look fine, and of course you have a beautiful body." Nikki added. "But you also have the brains, and the talent to back it up."

"The stuff that you're up on, except for us, Atleast half of the girls where we live would have no idea of what you're talking about Ivan." Andrea continues on.

"In the coming years especially when you're in high school and beyond, these qualities that you have now, will be among your best allies." Even the boys nod their heads to the latter. "Watch." Nikki now gives Ivan a wink. "Just stay sweet and be yourself." She says. Ivan nods his head in agreement, and smiles back. "I don't have much of a choice, do I not?" He says. "For your sake mister, you'd better not." Nikki says grinning.

At this point the entire group is now focused on Rizzo's masterpiece. The latter is sand made model of the Eiffel Tower. Ivan began to smile. "Is what I think it is?" He asks.

"Yep, it is." Rizzo concurs. Ivan, like Rizzo is also artistic. Sometimes when they meet, they would often create drawings, and employ sketches of multiple subjects that could almost come to life. "So, are you coming to join the rest of us?" Ivan asks.

Lazarus meanwhile jumps back in. "In a second." Rizzo responds, as he now studies his work. Dashing his way towards the water, Ivan jumps in once more.

In the aftermath, he splashes the others. Holding his breath, he remains under the water for thirty seconds. "Hey watch it!" Denise shouts, the moment he returns to the surface. She then chuckles. "Oh, I'm sorry about that." Ivan catches his breath.

"He ain't sorry!" Says Nikki. At this point she bares a mischievous grin. "Let's get em!" Andrea suggests. The girls all attempt to double-team him. Now splashing him, Charles is already on the scene. He rushes to Ivan's aid. "Wait alright!" Andrea pleads.

She laughs and giggles as Charles picks her up. "Ok stop!" Stop!" "CHARLIE!"

Splaaash! On contact, Charles throws her thick frame into the water. Lazarus and Rizzo also joined in. And from that very moment, Denise and Nikki laughed, shared a scream and took off running. Kicking and splashing, they are both quickly caught.

"Rizzo, get away from me!" Denise smirks. "I ain't playing boy!" "No!" The moment she turns her back, Rizzo picks her up and dumps her. Splaaash! Ivan now turns to Nikki.

"As you were saying." He smiled. "You ain't crazy." She grins. "I'll be the judge of that." Ivan moves in closer. "Ok Ivan wait!" She finally pleads. "Wait!" "Wait!"

"IVAN, PUT ME DOWN!!!" Splaaash! Ivan throws her in. Emerging from the water, Nikki's long hair is almost straight. Spitting out water, she rests on the sand. Jokingly, Nikki pretends to pout. "I hate you." She smiled. Ivan, at this point began to run.

"Where ya going huh?" She asks. Getting up, she chases after him. Ivan laughs.

Early in the evening around six, two of the lifeguards finally take a break. Two others arrive shortly thereafter, to replace them. Descending from their huge white towers, the two twenty something year-olds, one male, and one female reaches the sandy surface. Assembling a net, another lifeguard (also female) donates a volleyball. Looking around, they ask several others nearby if they are interested in playing.

Emerging out of the water, Ivan and all of his friends are among the first to volunteer. They vote yes. Six other youngsters who had also been swimming, soon joins them.

Shortly before the game starts, everyone from the lifeguards to the two teams meets the others acquaintance. The name of the nicely tanned lifeguard is Steven Dunn.

About 6'-2", lean, and ripped, he wears a necklace bearing the ancient symbols of Ying and Yang. Of South Shore's 61, 517 residents 97.4 percent are black. (59,933)

The white ethnics who had dominated the area for decades has done all but diminished. They now account for only 2.1 percent. (1,295) Steve of course is among the latter.

His family, a fixture in the neighborhood since the 1930's still owns a house in the Jackson Park Highlands. Young and single, Steve is very outgoing, open minded, down to earth and enjoys reading and writing. His sexy and attractive co-worker is Ruth Spears.

With a fudge brown complexion, Ruth has long black hair, high cheekbones, and a thin shapely figure. She speaks with a mild Caribbean accent. On the opposite side of the net from where Ivan and his team stands, are the opposing players. Realizing that the latter is one player uneven, Ruth takes the liberty of filling the void. Both sides now have eight.

Closing her eyes, Ruth takes two deep breaths. Jumping up, she gives the ball a power tap. In response, Ivan jumps up and hammers it back. The visiting team scores first. "Alright Ivan!" Nikki cheers. "Go ahead with yo bad self!" Says Denise. The others all give him pounds, and high fives. The score is two to nothing. "Its your serve." A girl from the home team says. She tosses the ball back to Steve, who tosses it back to Ivan.

As Ivan sends it back, players from the opposing team all jumped up and scrambled. But yet, they still fail. Some of the players fell to the sand. The score remains the same.

Helping each other to their feet, the opposing players dust themselves off. Another player hands the ball back to Ivan's team. Hitting the ball for the third time, a heavyset youngster tries to roll with the punches by hitting it back. However, Ivan returns the favor while Riz and the others trip and stumble. The ball, once again lands on the other side.

The score is now three to nothing. By accidentally passing the ball amongst themselves in an attempt to secure it, members of the opposing team returns the ball to their guests.

Once again, Ivan comes through with an additional two points. Their total now stands at four. At this point, the players on both sides began to rotate. "Damn, you're good." Steve tells him. "Do you play for your school or something?" A player on the other team asked. "Nope." Ivan responds. "Our school doesn't even have one." He then flexes his muscles. "But it doesn't stop me from practicing." He continues on. "I often play at the park near my house." "That's good man." Says Steve. He nods his head. The next person to serve is Rizzo. Taking his place, he jumps up and smacks the ball. The other player returns the favor, but

Rizzo gives him more of the same. Upon rotation, the rest of his team falls into place. Now, it was down to Lazarus. Serving the ball to his opposition, the latter of course spikes the ball with his head, sending everybody including Ivan into a running frenzy. Nikki hits the ball, but yet it never makes it across.

The neighborhood team scores their second point. "Don't even trip man." Charles tells Lazarus. "You doing a hell of a lot better, and we've still got it." The others all gave him a pound. "Its your serve." Ivan tells the unknown heavyset youth. He sends the ball back to him. "Alright, let's do this." He says. Smacking the ball back over to the visiting team, Ivan also spikes the ball with his head. He grins. "You're not the only hard headed person." He tells his opposition. The other youth smiles, and nods his head. "I'm impressed." He tells Ivan. The score is now six to two. Both sides continue to rotate.

After the game both teams shook hands and then parted. Meanwhile, the two lifeguards are finally off the clock. Clad in their street attire, both Ruth and Steve now walk to their vehicles. Ivan and his friends on the other hand return to the picnic area. Carrying their duffel bags, and their backpacks, the seven of them rests at a nearby table.

"That was fun." Ivan began. "Yes, it was." Nikki yawned. "It was nice of those lifeguards to arrange the game." Rizzo added. The others all happily nodded.

"We had a chance to play against some of the locals." Charles slips back into his shirt.

"That was almost a landslide victory." Says Lazarus. "Man, they got creamed."

"There had been a few occasions in which they tried give us a run." Denise pointed out.

"But, it was still a good game." Says Andrea. She appears rather satisfied.

Situated to the northeast, miles beyond the shoreline is Downtown. Among several of the landmarks to be seen is the world's famous Sears Tower, the John Hancock Center, The Prudential building, Oil Standard, The Drake and so on. As the sun fades into the west, Ivan and his friends grabbed their belongings and returned to the field house.

North Lawndale

Back in this neighborhood that Ivan calls home, during mid to late evening hours; many people particularly the younger generations are still out thus enjoying the warm spring air. On his block are the usual elements, both good and bad. Directly in front of a house next door, are several girls. Some preteens, others slightly above they are spotted jumping rope. A much older group, presumably in their teens is situated in front of a brown (three story) multi-family building. With a heavy-duty extension cord hanging from the first floor window, it is linked to a large boom box. Playing what sounds like House Music, these energetic young ladies are seen dancing, and practically shaking everything that God (no blasphemy intended), their mothers, and even their fathers had given them.

Clad in body shirts, tight jeans, and mini skirts with some wearing designer jumpsuits , a smaller congregation entertains a group of passing young males. Flattered by their gestures, the entire party of five all smile and wave. From there, they move on. In the middle of what is Lexington Street, is a "slap boxing match." Along this brightly lit corridor, the two combatants consist other teenage males. Across the street in front of a three flat, five to six others look on. "Don't let em take yo money!" Says one of them.

The two squaring away is a short heavyset individual, clad in white sneakers, a T-shirt, and black overalls. His competitor, a lanky young man clad in a tank top, red sweats, and black sneakers are literally smacking each other! However, like that of traditional boxing, both fighters must at all times keep their hands up. And of course, stick and move.

"He ain't got no money!" Says the short gladiator. Hell hath no fury, as he continues to break down is opposition. At some point, he even knocks off his opponent's cap.

At the end of the block near Spaulding Avenue, others play for money by way of shooting dice.

Thompson Residence

Ivan's parents, along with his grandmother all sat on the front porch. They too are reaping the benefits , given to them by Mother

Nature as they inhale her perfect blend of freshly cut grass, pollen, as well as man-made fossil fumes. The color of the sky has now become like the sea: clear, blue, and last but not least dark. Visible to both the human followed by the naked eye, is a bright crescent moon. On this block, all is well.

The 9:00 hour is near, as Ivan enters the porch. "I'm back, everybody." He announces. "Hey son, did you have a good time today?" His father asks. "Yes, I did." Ivan says, with great satisfaction. "Did you all enjoy the beach, and the mall?" His mother asked smiling.

"Thanks for coming back on time." Mr. Thompson ruffles his son's hair.

"No problem, Dad." Ivan chuckles. He jokingly parries his father hand. "Which mall did you go to?" His grandmother asked. "North Riverside." Ivan softly responds.

The well-preserved senior nodded and smiled. "Right, its out there on Harlem and Cermak. She reminds herself. "That was nice." "Where's Nicole?" Mrs. Thompson asked. "She is checking in with her mom as we speak." Her son explains. She nods.

"Charlie, and Laz is back around the corner already." "And Mr. Davis is on his way to drop off Riz." "That's good." Says his grandmother. "Well, I guess I'll check in." Ivan Says to all of them. "Well you live here, why not?" His father says jokingly.

"Go ahead man." Mr. Thompson playfully shoves his son as he walks into the house.

Down in the recreation room after reading several pages of Sun Tzu's "Art of War," Ivan places a marker on the most recent page, and sets it down. The latter novel sits on a brand new glass table. The night is still young. He thought, as he peers out the window.

Beginning his descent from the guess room to the hallway is Mr. Thompson. "So what's up Kung Fu Joe?" He jokingly asked Ivan. "Oh, I was just reading and relaxing." He answers. "What gives dad?" "How about a game of pool?" Mr. Thompson suggests.

"Always." Ivan smiled. Sharpening a cue stick, Mr. Thompson hands it to his son. He then collects one for himself. Racking up the balls on a nearby pool table, Ivan breaks them. As he, Ivan himself claims the solid colors, his dad of course summons the stripes.

"You want to know about the basic fundamentals of winning?" Mr. Thompson began. Aligning his cue with that of the white ball, he summons the latter upon that of his stripes. "When have you ever known me to turn down good advice?" Ivan smiled.

"Damn, you've got a point." Says his father. "I have to remember, I ain't talking to your brother." "You actually listen." Snapping his cue directly into the white ball comes a chain reaction. As the white ball makes contact with most of stripes, a few of the solids are also moved. But however, the impact wasn't powerful enough to disperse the latter.

Four of the stripes meanwhile are seen landing into four pockets. The skilled pool master takes his cue and re-positions himself to the opposite side of the table.

"And its not so much about winning at sports, or about how many fights you win." Mr. Thompson continues on. "Its about winning at life, plain and simple." His son nods, as he continues to listen. Snapping his cue into the white marker once again, the ball of course does make contact. But yet, instead of directing the other stripes to other pockets, the white ball only taps them. Mr. Thompson sighs and then chuckles. "You're up, man." He tells Ivan. Dispatching his cue, Ivan himself takes to the opposite corner of the table.

"Often times, it is quite unfair, it can be hard at times, and in some cases, it can be dirty as hell." Aligning his cue with the marker ball, as he seeks to deploy his solids, Ivan is now focused. Snapping the cue into the marker, comes the chain reaction. A few of his solids make the cut. Four pockets facing the south are quickly filled. "Good job." Says his father. "You were focused, I likes that in you." "I learn from the best." Ivan replies.

"I'm not perfect son, but I do my best." "Touché." Says Ivan. He now re-positions himself. "But, anyway the point that I'm trying to make." "Is that no matter what happens, never give up." "Whether it pertains to your dreams, your goals, always be persistent." "And just like you have been in your books, your martial arts classes, and not to mention, this game you're playing as we speak." Mr. Thompson continues to break it down. "Always remain focused." As Ivan deploys his ordinance for the second time, he nods his head. Another solid ball is sent to the side pocket. "And like they say, Ivan."

"Shit happens?" "You should always try to do whatever the hell you can, to Atleast, and I mean Atleast." "Expect, the unexpected." "That helps, you can be rest assured."

"Duly noted." Says Ivan. He continues to reposition himself. "And last, but not least."

"Remain positive." Mr. Thompson concluded. "I'm quite the optimist, these days." Ivan tells him. "I can see that." His father tells him. They now continue to play.

5

THOMPSON RESIDENCE, TUESDAY 11:45AM

After a full hour of practicing his Taichi out back, Ivan now meditates. For the next thirty minutes, he remains focus. With his mind now free of worrying, free of doubt, and not to mention fear he slowly rises to his feet. Glancing up at the sky, he bows. "Hey grasshopper!" His mother yells out the window. Ivan happily nods.

"Yes, mother?" He says. His impersonation mimicked that of Psycho's Norman Bates.

Mrs. Thompson laughs and shakes her head. "You've got a phone call." She informs him. "I think its Donnie." Ivan nodded. "I'm on my way up, thanks."

Horan Park

Established in 1924 to accommodate what was then a fast growing neighborhood (East Garfield Park), this existing parcel of land included playground equipment, a small brick recreation building, and a playing field. The latter was flooded in the winter for ice-skating. The park was named for Albert J. Horan (1894-1960) who had been elected alderman of the surrounding 29th ward. Having served as an aviator in World War I, Horan was co-founder of the Cornwall Post for the American Legion.

The parkland was officially purchased by the city in 1948. Five years later, the park was slightly reduced in size when the southeast corner was taken for construction of the Eisenhower Expressway. The city transferred Horan Park to the Chicago Park District in 1959. In the mid-1970's, the park district expanded Horan by greening over South Albany Avenue at the edge of the park, and acquiring two acres between Albany and Kedzie Avenues. Ball fields were installed; new playground equipment, and basketball courts were added. The park is now roughly one mile long.

On the eastern leg, near the Eisenhower on ramp, there are slides, toddler swings, and a spray pool. The original field house has been replaced. Its successor, a large cabin-like dwelling now sits along the southern edge.

Our Lady of Sorrows of Basilica, a catholic elementary school, its National Shrine, and its landmark tower is seen to the north. (Circa west Van Buren Street)

Nicholson Residence

Located on the southern edge of the park, this is the home of Ivan's former rival turned ally. Donnie Nicholson, fourteen years old was born into a family of seven.

With four brothers, and three sisters, Donnie is the fourth child. He has an older brother who works the meat and produce departments at the Down Home Supermarket.

The latter sits on the park's westernmost edge. Angela Nicholson, forty-three years old is a single working mother who had been long separated from her husband. His whereabouts remains unknown. A full-time employee with AT&T, Mrs. Nicholson also receives public assistance and employs a fixed mortgage for the current greystone (a three flat) that she proudly owns. Our Lady Of Sorrows, the landmark tower is across the street. Ivan steps up to the porch and rings the bell. A tall bronze complexioned gentleman in a blue lab coat, turtleneck, jeans, and work boots answers.

"Hey, what's up Ivan?" He says. "Goin' on man?" They shake hands. "Not, bad Tobias." Ivan tells him. "On your way to work?" "Yep." He responds. "How's your sister?" "Jen's, doing pretty good?" Ivan says. He smiles. "That's good." Tobias nodded.

"Don's upstairs." He then directs Ivan. "Thanks." "Hey, have a good one down there." Ivan tells him. The bright, handsome twenty-one year old is just leaving for work.

"Oh, I plan on it." Tobias says with greater confidence. His job is right next-door.

Heading up the stairs of the aging structure, Ivan walks under a bright skylight and goes left. Entering a short hall, he is now in the living room. At this time, Donnie is the sole occupant in the building. Situated in the living room, he plays The Last Battle on his Sega Genesis. "What's up Don?" Ivan says, now approaching him. "Trying to kill this last boss, and shit." Donnie gives him a pound, while continuing his game.

But yet, he still lucks out. "Damn." He chuckles. "Try this again later." Shutting off the console and the TV, he wraps up the controller.

Horan Park

Like that of any other weekday, especially during "clean up week", or in the terms of the layman, Spring break; the park is bustling with activity. Scores of youths are seen, working the basketball courts, while others play tag football. Two seniors are spotted playing chess on the designated tables nearby, while the younger children (some being supervised) embrace the swings and the slides available. Two little girls are seen running through the spray pool, while their father happily looks on.

Meanwhile, Ivan and Donnie are in the field house. Playing a game of ping-pong, Ivan takes the lead. "Its yo serve man." Says Donnie. Ivan paddles the ball back into his direction. Don hits it back. Ivan does the same. Ivan, with everything that he has paddles it even harder. Donnie, at this point must work twice as hard as he relentlessly hustles from side to side. Back and forth, he paddles away. What the fuck? Donnie thought.

Facing his friend as the game continues, he only chuckled. Without breaking a sweat, Ivan smiled back. "Goddamn, Ivan its only a game." Don laughs. "But, it ain't nothing wrong with a little competition I guess." Ivan strikes the ball, but this time Donnie misses. Walking to the end of the room, he retrieves it. The park supervisor walks in on them. Taking note of them he laughed. "How did you end up becoming so competitive?" He asked Ivan. "You even became a fitness freak." "What happened?" "You are Ivan right?" Ivan nodded. "C'mon Louis, you know its me." He says. "Stop playing."

"But, I'm glad you finally developed some confidence." Says the tall and heavy park supervisor. Before returning to his office, he gives the boys a pound. Meanwhile, it is Donnie's turn to serve. "After this, we start a new game." He says. Don dispatches the ball. Ivan nodded. "Game point." Ivan pounds the ball back. Donnie follows up, and returns it, but he summons it to the northwest side of the table. The latter is considered out.

"Damn." Says Donnie. Quickly catching his breath, he laughed. He is no longer threatened by asthma. Since his near death experience when he was only eight, followed by his visit to the E.R. shortly thereafter, Donnie for some reason (a miracle perhaps) has been able to breathe freely. His need for inhalers is now obsolete. Anyway, Ivan tosses him a bottle of water. "Thanks." He says. Producing a second bottle, Ivan himself guzzles the latter. "Game two?" He says, now grinning. "Bet." Don replied. They now reposition themselves. Ivan serves first. "You suit is cold, I like it." Donnie says.

He speaks in reference, to Ivan's newly bought attire. The latter, a top of the line jumpsuit was designed by Nike. Bearing a bright red, white and blue color scheme all around, the trademark symbol (the renowned swoosh) is displayed on the back.

Written in cursive underneath, is the word "Flight." "Thanks." Ivan responds. "Where did you get it?" Donnie asks. Both remain focused on their game. "Montgomery Ward." Ivan answers. Receiving an incoming ball, he dashes to the left and pounds it back.

Donnie swings and returns it to the sender. Ivan summons his paddle to the ball and succeeds, but yet it goes northeast. "Its out." He confesses. He tosses it over to Don.

"That's cool, I wasn't trying to contradict myself by asking you." Donnie explains.

Dispatching the ball with his paddle, Donnie doubles up. Ivan meanwhile employs his backhand. In a smooth, but yet relaxing motion Ivan rotates left and then right.

Executing another backhand, Ivan whacks the ball and retreats side to side. Hitting the ball, just inches above the net, Donnie misses. "I say that because, a good name brand is a good name brand." He breaks it down further. Picking up the ball, Donnie throws it to Ivan. "No matter where you get it from, or how much it costs." Ivan nodded. He knew where his friend was going. "A lot of our peers, ain't that bright when it comes to shopping, and spending they money." "They think that you gotta, spend a arm and a leg at a joint like Brier's or Footlocker." "And they got the nerve to make fun of you, because you shop at places like Montgomery Ward or Famous Foot Wear."

"Unlike most of the other kids in our school, you know how to save your money, Ivan.

"You dress better, you've got raw taste; shit you've got it goin'on!" "And that ain't nothing new." It is now Ivan's turn to serve. He directs the ball with his paddle.

"Since second grade, I always knew you was a smart nigga." Don openly admits . He smiled. "And, I was jealous of you man." "I should have known." Ivan smiled back.

" That was why, I used to always fuck with you." "Even though I used to whoop yo ass back in the day, you still put up a crazy fight." You was strong, before you worked out."

At this point, the young men played almost relentlessly, hitting the ball, paddle-to –paddle (nonstop), left and right, side to side; whack after whack. Dashing to the left once more, and then to the right, Ivan executes another backhand causing Donnie to miss for the fourth time. It is his serve. "But, I kinda got what was due to me that day."

"After I threw you in the garbage, my asthma started actin'up lost my inhaler, my boys left me to hang, and I thought that was it." Donnie shakes his head. His chuckled.

"As it turns out, the person who saved my ass was the very same nigga I threw in the garbage." Ivan smiled. "That had to have been nobody but God, I was sure of it."

"It was." Says Ivan. Serving the ball for the seventh time, Ivan paddles it away.

Retreating to the left of the table, and then to the right, Donnie continues to hustle as he strikes back with his paddle. Ivan whacks at the ball from a side angle, while Don countered. Employing a left backhand, Ivan finally scores. Donnie laughed.

"That was nice." He says. "So, what's this beef between you and Curtis?" Donnie asks.

Ivan shrugged. "Well you know me Donnie, my beef is with no one." He began.

“Like I told Riz last month, I wish I knew.” Donnie nodded. “I remember hearin’ about him trying to get you jumped, and you made him look twice as stupid.” Says Donnie.

“And you almost sent Malik’s fat ass to the morgue, by damned near choking the shit outta him.” Ivan nodded. “This is game point by the way.” He announces.

Whacking the ball with his paddle, Donnie successfully hits it, but yet for the third time he sends it off to the side. Another out. “What’s my record now?” Ivan asked.

“Two to zero?” Donnie nodded. He chuckles at the latter. “We’ll play one more.”

“I saw some of the dudes, staggering and limping when they crossed the bridge.” Donnie recollects. “He was slapping Des around like his bitch.” “I knew you had something to do with it.” “And Malik ain’t shit.” “Jumping on the bandwagon, and ridin’ Curtis ‘s dick all of a sudden.” “I’m the one nigga, they won’t step to.”

“Malik ain’t really the bullying type.” Donnie continued on. Ivan nods his head in agreement. “He’s just hard headed, and can’t leave well enough alone.” “Neither will fuck with me, because all I have to do is make a phone call.” “You know my godfather Terrance right?” “Yeah, I know him.” “He’s a F.B.I. agent, here in the city.”

“Well, check this out Ivan, he’s also what they call a cleaner in the Fifth City Crime Family.” “If they was to even look at me wrong, both Curtis and Malik disappears.”

“ I hear that.” Says Ivan. He smiled, and shook his head. “There is a such thing, as going to far you know.” “Word.” Donnie replies. He gives Ivan a pound.

The two position themselves for the last and final game. Taking up their paddles, Ivan is the first to serve. Like I said, on the day of my birthday.” He began. “Its going to be a new day.” “And it is, man.” Donnie assures him. “Everybody’s comin around, trust me.”

“At school, and over here.” “Hell, I’m quite sure, all is well around yo house.”

“Curtis and me, was supposed to throw down the next day.” Ivan sends off the ball.

“We met in the Golden Dome up at Garfield Park, to fight in the ring.” “The ref laid out his ground rules, rang the bell, shook hands, I bowed and I was ready." "I was there." Donnie reminded him. He whacks the ball. Ivan summons a backhand, and scores.

"For some reason, Curtis who was looking all sad and guilty just turned and walked out." "Because, he knew he was wrong." Donnie pointed out. He picks up the ball.

"And more than likely, beyond all reasonable doubt Ivan, he was gonna lose."

"Curtis hasn't said a word to me ever since our initial confrontation." Ivan whacks the ball. "In fact, he's been staying out of my way, and so has Malik." He misses.

It is his serve. "That's a good thing." Says Donnie. He delivers a backhand, while Ivan follows though and employs one of his own. "But still, watch em." Donnie advises.

"No telling, what they on." "Shit, I still don't trust them." "Oh, I'm watching them." Says Ivan. Whacking the ball, it flies beyond his side of the net, and lands onto Donnie's.

Attempting to paddle the ball back, Donnie hits the ball twice without sending it over.

This is also declared an out. "For the time being, I'm going to accept that as a truce."

After taking on Donnie in a game of basketball, Ivan summons his bike, puts on his helmet, and refills his canteen. Adjusting the headphones to his Walkman, he rides out of the park. Pedaling east On Harrison Street, Ivan surpasses all of the local traffic.

Passing its namesake housing projects between Sacramento Boulevard, and Francisco Street to his left, the young cyclist passes along a corridor flanked by an auto shop, a multi-family apartment building, one story cottages (some dilapidated), a storefront church, a vacant lot, a convenience store, and three well worn two flats. All of which, are situated to his right. Crossing the intersection of south Francisco, Ivan rides past a car wash, a vacant factory, and another church. Two weed-strewn vacant lots are seen on both sides (left and right), followed by a lone bungalow situated to his left.

A short alley is spotted on the opposite side, facing a much larger structure to the right. The latter, which is also antiquated, is both residential as well as commercial.

Approaching California Avenue, a liquor store and a currency exchange rests on the corner. Once the light has turned green, Ivan proceeds to cross over. Continuing further east, he makes a right at Washtenaw Avenue.

Wallace Residence

Most of the land that makes up the 2700 block of west Flournoy Street is currently vacant. With the exception of only six homes remaining, many of the others had been long demolished, due to severe fire damage, decay, and overall neglect.

On this lifeless corner, scores of older men some alcoholics, some drug addicts are seen acting as lookouts for the local drug czars. Their base of operations is housed in a recently refurbished factory, located one block north. It is believed to run by a member of the 24th Mafia. Outside the complex, a long line of people, both men and women (young and old), even a few outsiders are awaiting their fix. In the hood, business is booming.

Located one block south of the Wallace House, lies another vacant lot covered with weeds and large bushes. The awful stench of garbage and human waste from homeless

residents plagues the air. The railroad embankment showcases a backdrop of makeshift homes (cardboard boxes) while long abandoned factories linger in their wake.

Carrying his bike up to Rizzo's front porch, Ivan puts it down and rings the bell. "Hello Ivan, how are you?" It is Rizzo's mother. "Pretty good, Mrs. Campbell thanks." Ivan responds. "You're looking beautiful as usual, I might add." He flirts.

Mrs. Campbell smiled. "If you keep giving me compliments like that, I'll wind up stealing you from Nikki." She winks. Ivan laughs. "Is Rizzo awake?" He asked. "Yes, he is sweetie." Says Mrs. Campbell. "Come on in." Leaving his bike and his helmet in the hall, Mrs. Campbell leads him upstairs. "What's up Riz?" Says Ivan, as he enters the living room. Seated on the couch is Rizzo himself. Playing Double Dragon on his NES (Nintendo), his two younger brothers look on. Ivan gives all three of them a pound.

"Just starting off the day with a little Double Dragon." Rizzo explains. Ivan takes a seat on the opposite couch. On the table in the center of the room, are several drawings.

"Hey Ivan, check em out." Says Rizzo. He points them out. "Wanna take over?" Rizzo asked his brother Marco. "Yeah, thanks." He quietly responds. "I spent most of the night, working on them." Rizzo began. For the next few minutes, Ivan closely examines his best friend's work. The first portrait displays, members of the group N.W.A. In this picture, they are seen engaging the LAPD in what appears to be a shootout. Ivan was astonished.

Shaking his head, he began to laugh. "I really like this, man." He says. "The more graphic, the better." "But what really has me rolling Riz." Ivan continues to point out.

"Is that there is even, a lone surviving cop on the radio calling for backup while everyone else in his unit, lies dead on the ground." "This would actually be good for a comic book, I think." Rizzo nodded. He agrees with his friend. "Go to the next one."

Rizzo's next drawing, displays Italy's renowned Leaning Tower of Pisa. The latter employs a unique blend of watercolors. "You're always on key." Ivan commends him.

"Now, I can plainly see why we're always on the same page." "Bra to the vo!"

Finally, Ivan browses at Rizzo's final piece. This particular drawing actually favors that of a special blueprint. (A mural possibly) Ivan nodded as he continues to observe.

The drawing consists of moving figures; most notably spray cans dressed as human beings. One display shows them partying inside of a nightclub, while another displays a group of men sitting in a sport utility truck. Smoking blunts as they pick up women, who are leaving, others are seen in the background exchanging phone numbers.

Surrounding all of these figures is Rizzo's signature handcrafted in blue and gold.

The latter reads: "THE RIZ" "Do you have plans for a mural?" Ivan asked. "I kind of thought about the movie, Beat Street when I was working on it." Rizzo smiled.

"You're like the mad scientist of art." Ivan chuckles. "Your work is just as comparable." Says Rizzo. "You can create some mean pictures yourself, stop fronting."

“Is this all of them?” Ivan asked. “Naw, you forgot one.” Rizzo reminds him.

Underneath the miniature mural, is a portrait of his female friend Christy.

Her features mirrored that of a younger Janet Jackson. Ivan sizes up the picture.

“So this is the girl?” He asks. “Yeah.” Rizzo responds. “She’s fine.” His friend nodded.

At this time, Marco and Rizzo’s youngest brother Roger has already left the room. Turning off the NES, Rizzo still clad in his pajamas now turns on the VCR. Popping in the movie “School Daze”, he hits the play button. “Get dressed fool, we’ve got things to do.” Ivan says with enthusiasm and encouragement. “You know people to see, some to kill, towns to be pillaged!” “The usual norm.” Rizzo laughed. “This movie is for you.” He tells him. “I know what time it is man.” Grabbing a fresh towel, Riz heads for bathroom.

Atgeld Park

Established in 1873 as Congress Park, the land for this existing park was donated to the city of Chicago by local real estate developers Frank W. and James L. Campbell. The city transferred the one-acre park to the West Park Commission in 1915, at which time the commission required an additional four acres. The following year the expanded park was renamed in honor of John P. Atgeld (1847-1902), the Illinois governor from 1893 to 1897, and an early proponent of neighborhood playgrounds. The controversial Atgeld, a strong supporter of labor, was best known for pardoning several of the Haymarket conspirators.

Stretching from Washtenaw Avenue to the west and an existing freight line to the east, its northern boundary covers Congress Parkway as well as the Eisenhower.

Harrison Street of course, covers the south. Its tan brick field house employs the façade of a historic town hall. Its playground equipment and swimming pools are located outside. Across the street overlooking the latter, is the so-called pharmaceutical plant.

Training rigorously in the field house, both Ivan and Rizzo acts as though they are champions. Shadowboxing in the mirror of the dance studio, both young men display different fighting styles. As Ivan viciously pounds the weight bag, Rizzo works his speed on a much lighter parcel. Taking a quick break at the fountain, the boys under Rizzo's boxing instructor Otis Patterson, oversees a light-sparing match. After the exhibition, Mr. Patterson advises both his student as well as Ivan to keep up the good work.

Hitting the weights in the fitness room, Ivan and Rizzo have now completed their workout. Shortly thereafter, the young dynamic duo enters the gymnasium.

Upon entry, they hook up with six other youths. The youngsters having played a game of basketball, greets Ivan and Rizzo with a handshake. They now head outside.

These young men are all close and personal friends of Rizzo. Among them is Alfred Miller. Twelve years old, he is five seven with a husky frame, and smooth brown skin.

With natural curly brown hair, and chubby facial features, the letter "A" is shaved into the back of his head. Clad in a black football jersey and blue sweats pants, he also employed white sneakers. Alfred, who lives directly across the street from Rizzo, is a computer genius. His father, a Naval Reservist is also a computer technician.

Alfred, a renown gamer is also a first rate hacker who could tap into any system in the world, anywhere, at anytime. And yet in the eyes of the Bureau, he remains unseen.

The three triplets would be the Powell brothers. They are Brian, Craig, and Jason.

Among the remaining three, there's twelve-year-old Ahmad Carr, William Kent, also twelve, and last but not least thirteen-year-old Thomas Moore.

At this time the eight of them combined, are now playing football in the open space opposite the bleachers. Their game is suddenly interrupted, when another group approaches them. Clad in white T-shirts, jeans, and sneakers; some even donned baseball caps. The few who did, of course wore them to the right. Carrying what appears to be Louisville sluggers, they obviously didn't play baseball. This thought made Ivan chuckle.

Meanwhile, Rizzo and the others exchange puzzling looks. "What the hell is this?" Ivan asked. "A re-enactment of the Warriors vs. the Riffs?" Rizzo and the rest of the gang are tickled pink at this point. They laughed themselves silly. "Can you dig it?"

"Or something more recent." Rizzo suggests. "Like that movie Colors?" Ivan grinned.

Once again, the others laughed. "You ain't right Ivan." Thomas chuckled.

While the others lined up to take their stances, Rizzo, Alfred, and Ivan commanded their lead by remaining calm. "Well, let's see what they want." Alfred suggests.

The leader on the opposing side wore jeans, red snickers and a baseball jersey. Unlike his followers, instead of wearing a baseball cap, this young man sports a furry Kangol.

His skin corresponds to that of a medium brown, while his eyes displays a mild green. Advancing closer, the angry leader stops and observes Ivan the others. He knew them.

"Wait, hold up." The scrawny youth began, now smiling. In his mouth, one tooth is missing. "This Rizzo, Alfred, and Ivan." He turns to face his friends. "I know these niggas, they cool." He gives Ivan and the others a pound. They are finally relieved.

"I know the others too, we don't want them." Thomas, Ahmad, along with the triplets all sighed as well. Fifth teen minutes later, the sky went from being cloudy and gloomy to bright and sunny. "Is everything cool?" Thomas asked the leader. The youngster nods.

"Straight up, Ready Rock." Rizzo Joins in. "Y'all walk up here, looking like the lynch mob." "Its been a fucked up assed day." Says the young man. Now known as Ready Rock. "Some fools, stuck up my cousin and took his chain and his rings." Ready explains. "Where?" Ivan asked. "By Fillmore near the viaduct." Says one of the others.

"First, they stick em up, take his ice and then whoop his ass." Ready Rock thunders.

"Y'all see anybody?" He asked. "Naw man, we just came out here." Alfred replies. "But you know, we got yo back." Rizzo reassures the heated youngster. "We'll keep you posted." Ivan added. Shaking hands with Ivan and the others, Ready Rock and his group takes off. Shortly thereafter, they all resume their game. Forming two teams once again, they all scramble, some ducking, others dodge while one runs for cover. The sun blazes.

Charging his way towards the embankment, Ivan takes a quick glance at his terrain. There is no one else in sight to tackle him. From the very moment he receives the ball from Rizzo, he takes off running. By passing his overwhelmingly busy teammates, Ivan continues his course. Jumping over his opposition, Ivan ducks; he dodges and even zigzags his way across the park. Sweating, coughing, and breathing heavily his friends on the other team are doomed. They didn't stand a chance.

Pumping away at his arms, Ivan breathes in and out as he sprints straight ahead. Upon reaching the embankment, he spikes the ball. Performing a victory dance, he removes the sweat from his eye. His breathing is less labored, as Ivan now walks back. He smiled.

"You lucky bastard." Ahmad chuckled. He shakes his head. "Rizzo's team would be nothing without you." "You really think so?" Ivan grins. "I know so." Ahmad Says with confidence. "Alright then." Rizzo quotes him. "We need a time out." He announced.

For the next few minutes, both teams took to their corners. "We're gonna shut his ass up." Rizzo tells his teammates. The others began to listen as he employs his strategy.

"Change of plans." "Ivan, here's what you're gonna do." Ivan listens. " Instead of you going for power, this time it'll be Alfred." Alfred himself nodded. "Ivan, you're the running man." "We have to do whatever we can, to keep Ahmad, Tom, and the others at bay." "Don't let em touch you." "Why would I let them now?" Ivan chuckled. "Duly noted." Rizzo Says. "The rest of you, do what you do." "Defense." He then claps his hands. The others follow his lead. "Let's take em to the cleaners!" Says Alfred.

Snapping the ball, Rizzo motions for Ivan to get as far as he can from Ahmad players, while Craig and the Powell brothers wrestles their opposition to the grass. As Ivan runs his course across the field, Alfred slams and tackles the resistance. Ahmad now has second thoughts as the defensive tackle closes in. So does Thomas. Focusing on Ivan who is already halfway toward the playground, Ahmad and Thomas quickly take a shot.

But however, before they can even make it beyond Washtenaw Avenue, comes the light show. "Oh shit!" Prroooofff! Craaash! Both Ahmad and Thomas were sideswiped.

Smelling the earth, Ahmad and Thomas are now helped by the very person who sacked them: Alfred. Dusting them off as a gesture of good sportsmanship, he sends them on their way. "Go Ivan!" He says, encouraging his fellow teammate. Rizzo cheers also.

Maintaining his wind, Ivan doesn't look back. Continuously jumping ducking and dodging, he succeeds. Stopping at the wrought iron fence facing the pool, Ivan spikes the ball. Doing the M.C. Hammer, he wipes away additional sweat. It was the final touchdown. Ahmad and Thomas who had been briefly hurt, lives.

The two of them along with the rest of their team, congratulates Ivan and the others. "Damn, you taking steroids?" Ahmad jokingly asked Alfred. The husky computer genius chuckled. "I was so sure we had yo ass." Says Thomas. They both turned to Ivan.

"You know to get sideswiped by Alfred, is like making friends with a Mack truck." Ahmad Testifies. He shakes his head and laughs. "Both Ivan, and Alfred got a lot of power." Rizzo added. He checks his watch. "It was still a good game." Craig replied.

"It could have been worse." Thomas began. "Atleast, we still managed to score something. "That's true." Rizzo Says with honesty. "Is anybody hungry?" Ivan asked.

"Yeah." The others reply in unison. "Let's go to Robert's down the street." He suggests. Rizzo and the rest of the group nodded. "The bill is mine." Ivan announced.

"Cool." Says Ahmad. Now leaving the park, they head toward California Avenue.

6

CALIFORNIA AVENUE

Walking out of Robert's, a local rib shack on the northeast corner at Harrison, Ivan, Rizzo, and the rest of the party all began to venture south. "Why in the hell do you call that guy Ready Rock?" Ivan asked. Crossing the street, they all walked past Pete's. One of two convenience stores on the corner, the latter unlike its competitor on the northwest corner (California Sunshine), is more of a low budget Walgreen's by comparison. The Harrison/California currency exchange is directly across the street.

"It doesn't look like he's on freebase or anything, to say otherwise." "What's the story behind his name?" The Powell's laughed. "Naw man." Rizzo smiled. "Everybody calls him that because he's usually on top of things, you know; always alert, and always

prepared." "Or to put it in simple English." Alfred began. "He's Ready to Rock." Ivan nodded. "Almost like you, so to speak." "And like Me." Rizzo continues on.

"He boxes up at Atgeld, and he's really quick on his feet." "Dude is good." "I remember one day, Otis paired me up with him during practice, and we fought to a draw." "Twice." Rizzo holds up two fingers. "In one of his matches, I've seen his ass knock one nigga out the ring!" "Yeah, well Atleast he helped old boy up." Ahmad added.

"His real name is Raymond Hudson." Craig informed him. Ivan shakes his head. "I'm quite impressed." He says. Crossing an alley on the next corner, they pass an abandoned playground. The metallic skeletons that once held the children's slides as well as the swings are still present. Only a corroded igloo and a set of rusted monkey bars remain.

Behind it on the same parcel of land, is an unused parking lot. Empty cans of motor oil, a stripped van, old tires, and the chassis of what had been a Chevy Impala are among the sole survivors. Dead batteries, and weeds also exist. An existing auto repair shop is located next door. Having strolled past the lot, Ivan, Rizzo and the others observes a crowd of mostly older teens as well as adults. What they are rooting and cheering for isn't obvious. Climbing over a small fence, Ivan and the others decide to have a look.

Upon working their way through the masses of spectators, the boys encounter the unimaginable. In the middle of the lot are two vicious dogs. Squaring away face-to-face as they attempt to maul one another, more than likely to the death, a young man somewhere in his late teens to early twenties is also seen. Clad in a red designer jumpsuit, a matching Kangol, and sneakers (the same color) he collects money from some of the spectators. Placing their bets, the unidentified male keeps it moving. Money talks.

Two other men are situated in the alley nearby. Leaning against the wall of the auto shop, as they smoke their squares, they also employ two other barking and growling hounds. Their leashes remained bound to a common pole beside the garage.

Parked in front of the lot of this depressed, but yet lively avenue is a black Chevy Malibu. The driver talks on his cell phone while the song "Dope Man" summons the alpine. Nearly everyone is rooting for Killer. Killer, of course is the huge pit bull now mauling away at his opposition. His rival, another huge canine is named "Armageddon." Armageddon appears to be part Rotweiler and Dalmatian.

The huge black spots on his huge coat are evident. Ivan thought, as he and his friends continue to look on. However, the clash of the four-legged titans takes an unexpected turn. A partially gnawed and beaten up Armageddon, somehow regains his strength.

Growling and biting back, the clean saliva that is ejecting from the recipient's mouth has now become bloody and somewhat meaty. It looks like Killer's days are numbered.

"This reminds me of that Call of The Wild Story, that my mother used to read to me when I was smaller." Ivan smiled. "The story about Buck versus Spitz." Rizzo laughs.

"I know what story you're talking about." He says. Alfred also grinned. "For a time, the story focused on two of the huskies: Buck and Spitz." He began. "Spitz thought that he was God, and he always tried to bully the other dogs." "And for a little while, Spitz

actually did lead the pack." The others nod. "Then he came across Buck." Ivan comes back. "Buck was cool, a real mothafuckin' G." "He didn't bother anybody."

"Buck didn't like how Spitz was running the pack, in fact he became heated up." Ivan continued on. "But Spitz was too much of an ass, he didn't have a clue." "The next time Spitz began attacking another dog in the pack, Buck snapped off, and they went toe to toe." "Their owners Perrault and Francois saw them and broke it up." Thomas chuckles.

"Hell they were even placing bets on who would one day win." He added. "Francois, was like one damned day Buck is gonna end up killing Spitz." "And he did." He finished.

"Perrault and Francois found out the next day, when they realized Spitz was missing.

"To this day, I still like that story." Ivan chuckled. "While my brother had Old Yeller, I had Call of The Wild." He concludes. "This fight, for some reason had me thinking about it." Rizzo, Alfred, and the others nodded as they witness the current onslaught.

Gnawing his teeth into one of Killer's legs, Armageddon now tears into another. Chewing away at the side of his opponent's neck, the powerful white hybrid takes a bite at the brown pit bulls coat. At this point, some of Killer's flesh as well as his bone tissue is now exposed. He barks frantically. "So much for the one they call Killer." Ivan shakes his head. "Damn." "The killer is about to be killed by the end of the world." Rizzo added.

"Armageddon?" "That's the name of the other dog right?" He asked. The rest of the group laughs. "Hell naw!" Thomas chuckled. "Did you hear this fool?" He says.

"But that was a good one though." He gave Rizzo a pound. "I never would have thought about that one." Alfred nods. "I thought that Armageddon was outta there." He added. A few minutes later, the fight is declared over. Only Killer's partially mauled carcass remains. One of the breeders calls for Armageddon. Putting on his leash, the weary, but still beat-up canine is now ushered off the lot. The fight results in a huge upset, as many of the spectators curse themselves. Tossing their money to the pavement, they take off. Meanwhile, a fight amongst the others breaks out. Unsatisfied customers.

Exchanging punches, followed by kicking and stumping one another, one woman hits a man who is already catching a beat down from another, with a glass bottle! Realizing, his opposition is already unconscious, the couple takes off running. At the sound of a sudden gunshot, the others began falling in line. Running to their vehicles, they start their engines. The sounds of screeching tires are heard, even five blocks away.

Fortunately, Ivan and the others are able to leave just minutes before the fights breaks out. They manage to take refuge at another establishment located one block north.

The Fun Factory

Established just six years ago by Satchel Brooks, shortly after the election of the late Harold Washington (Chicago's first black mayor), Mr. Brooks, a well-connected alderman founded this establishment to best serve the greater community as well as the youths who dwell upon it. It exterior embodies the feel of an exquisite nightclub.

Hanging above the entrance are two flags. One American, the other: the continent of Africa. On the inside, one gets a slice of pizza, an order of fries, or even a hot dog. There

is also a candy store in the back, as well as eight video games. A seating area is located near the front entrance. Beyond the cordoned off stairwell, lies a pool hall as well as a teenage dance club. Open from seven in the evening until midnight (Fridays and Saturdays) armed security is also employed. The club does not operate on Sundays.

At this time, Ivan, Riz, and Alfred are situated in the front lobby. The Powell's, Thomas, Ahmad and the others are in back performing their magic on the machines. A congregation of other locals arrives within minutes. Among them are two girls, and two boys. Three others, two more males and one female also arrive. Rizzo obviously knew the first four. They called his name. “Hey yo, what’s up Rizzo?” Says one of the boys.

“What’s going on Leon?” “Khali?” Rizzo acknowledges. Walking over, the two boys give him a pound. Once more in laymen’s terms, they shook his hand. While the girls smile and wave at Ivan, Rizzo and Alfred pretending as though they are vampires, decides to make crosses with their fingers. “Be gone evil day walkers!” Rizzo cracks.

“Whatever.” Says one of them. “Looking like Chip and Dale.” Alfred roasts. In response to his wisecrack, the other young lady blows him a kiss, turns and then pats herself on the ass. “Hi Cassandra, hello Justine.” Says Ivan. He smiles.

“Hey Ivan.” Both girls respond at once. Turning to face one another, they giggle.

“Anybody see the smack down outside?” Leon asked. Ivan, Riz, and Alfred nods. He obviously witnessed the scuffle that took place following Killer’s defeat. “They was punching, kicking, and stompin’ man.” Leon informed them. “I was like damn!”

“This had to have been right after we left.” Ivan answers. “They were cursing themselves silly when were out there.” “It was kinda funny.” Alfred added. He chuckled.

“Somebody apparently fired a gun in the air, and everybody just took off running.”

“Its quiet out there now.” Khali adds. “Cops ain’t comin.” “Sir George is still out there in his limo, his brother still collecting the paper, some of the people dropped.”

“Security is still packing heat, and on the stand by.” Obviously surprised and perhaps confused, Ivan, Rizzo, and Alfred all gave a shrug. “Whoever this Sir George is, he probably owns the police.” Ivan finally spoke. “You won’t be seeing any patrols, until it gets dark I bet.” “Word.” Says Rizzo. “Look around, this isn’t UIC or Lincoln Park.”

"This is the ghetto!" "Yeah, straight up." Says Alfred. "Everything is on CPT." The two girls now known as Justine and Cassandra have already disappeared to the back.

"Y'all coming through later?" Khali asked. "Yeah, we'll be up the block." Rizzo responds. "We're gonna conduct some business on NARC right quick." Leon began.

"Get something to snack on, and chill at Atgeld for the time being." The others nodded. "Still kinda early." "We just came from up there." Ivan says to him as he checks out Cassandra and Justine once more. "They like you." Khali tells him. "I see." Ivan responds. "They are fine." He looks back. "Well, we'll holler at y'all later." Says Leon.

As Khali and Leon make their way toward the arcade, Ivan and the rest of his group began to walk out. Cassandra and Justine now carrying trays of food take their seats.

The mastermind behind the dog fighting operations is twenty-nine-year-old George Starks. On the streets, he travels under his pimp alias "Sir George." Born May 27th, 1960, Sir George has always lived a hard life. A native of Houston, Texas, the life long hustler never knew who his father was. His mother, a prostitute who turned tricks for a living to support them both, ended up in debt with her employer who was also a pimp.

As a gesture of "goodwill" Thelma Starks, later sold her son to the man known only as "Cesar." Cesar, who also treated women as though they were his personal property, surprisingly served as a father figure to the young George. Accompanying him on his daily strolls, George learned first hand, the tricks and the trades involving his master's occupation. As Sir George came of age, he also began selling drugs.

Making money hand over fist, Cesar was greatly pleased with his protégé. As a result Prince George as he was called at the time, was later given the job of managing his mentor's books. Occasionally, whenever Cesar was away on business, Prince George was left in charge to manage his workers. And of course, the latter served him well.

They always had his money. Never a penny short and they were always…on time.

Not once did Prince George ever had to raise a hand, unlike that of Cesar. Cesar, of course was strictly hands on. However at the time, the "apprentice pimp" was also a Psychology major. He enrolled at Texas State University where he earned himself a bachelor's degree. As a great mathematician, with a minor in chemistry, Prince George was eventually able to cook drugs. But yet, one-day George's life takes an unexpected turn. One hot summer evening in June of 1979, Cesar was gunned down as worked his usual corners by a family member of one of his "employees." He was later pronounced dead. Shocked by the violent death of his mentor, as well as that of his mother, the following year Prince George decides to leave Houston; and buys himself a one way train ticket. Almost twenty hours later, he arrives at Chicago's Union Station: via Amtrak.

In 1980 at age twenty, Prince George eventually locates other family members; including an uncle and a younger brother that he never knew. Having dropped out of the drug game, George explores another avenue. At the time, William "Willie" Brown his uncle a loan shark, legendary pimp, and arms dealer had his own gambling operations based on the city's far west side. It is believed that he later educated George as well as his brother, the basic fundamentals of dog fighting. The senior hustler has long retired, and now lives in Barbados. Prince George is rendered obsolete. He later becomes Sir George.

Today, Sir George and his younger brother, nineteen-year-old Ricky Devreaux are both partners in their current operations. Just to the west, both brothers also run a strip along west Madison Street in an area called "K-Town." The smoke has now cleared.

California Avenue

Along this East Lawndale corridor, it is business as usual once again. Scores of pedestrians are now visible; auto traffic resumes heavily in both directions, businesses continue to thrive, and last but not least so does the usual elements.

With a resurgence of spectators, Ricky resumes his placing of bets, money collections and so on. The kennels are still full, dogs trained, fed and more of the like.

Ivan and the boys resume their endeavors along this avenue as well.

Returning to their initial spot in where the dogfights are usually held, Ivan suddenly has an idea. “So what are the odds?” He asked the others. Rizzo and the rest of the group shrugs. “The odds of what?” Rizzo asked. He then nods. Facing the now empty arena, Alfred and the rest of the gang turns to the spectators. “You think we got a chance?” Thomas asked. “I don’t know.” Says Ahmad. The three triplets (The Powell’s) look on with curiosity. “It ain’t like we playin games down the street.” Ahmad reminds them.

“What do you call playing NARC or Outrun?” Thomas drills him. “It doesn’t matter if you spend twenty five cents, Fifty cents, whatever.” “Straight up.” Rizzo added. “The last time I checked, that was still considered gambling.” He continued. “Hell, going to the game room is no exception.” “Its nothing more but a casino for minors, Ahmad.” Ivan further points out. “If you beat the game, would Roxie or Melvin give you back your money?” “I don’t think so.” Says Craig. His brothers chuckled. “That’s my point.” Ivan smiled. “You DON’T get your money back, if you lose.” Says Alfred. He laughs.

“You’ll be lucky to get one credit.” Rizzo cracked. “Ivan’s got a point.” “At least if you work the slots, or play blackjack, and you win.” Alfred steps in. “You’ll definitely get yo paper.” “You’ll never leave empty handed.” “But if you lose.” Ivan began. “You’ll definitely be S.O.L!” He chuckled. “Shit outta luck.” Ahmad finishes.

“The same rule applies to this as well.” William speaks for the first time. “If we spend whatever we have, and we lose given that most of us ain’t always loaded.” He now faces Ivan. “We’ll be ass out.” The others nod their heads in agreement. “But, if we win, we’ll spend the next week and a half living large.” Rizzo reminds him. “Of course, we couldn’t tell anybody.” Ivan nodded as he listens to Riz. “And its not so much about others sweating you either." "Word." Ahmad finally agrees. "Its the exact opposite."

"Aight then, its on." He says. "Let's do this." Ivan responds. For the entire group, their decision is unanimous. "How much money does everybody have?" Rizzo asked.

"Damn, I've got Atleast seven." He says. "I have five." Alfred announces. "We have fifth teen altogether." The Powell's all smiled. "That's cool." Ahmad nods. "You can put me down for my last four." He added. Thomas produces a ten, while William throws in another ten. Ivan, the rich man in comparison throws in a whopping forty.

The others stare at him, shake their heads and then laugh. "Ok, Mr. Rockefeller." Says Alfred. Collecting all of their funds, Ivan then takes them over to Ricky. At this time, Rick himself is in the alley across the street. Sporting a red designer jumpsuit, a matching Kangol (concealing a Jeri Curl), a bright gold chain and suede sneakers, the junior partner looks at Ivan and then smiles. As he takes a drag from his Cuban, the young man closes his eyes and inhales. Blowing clouds of smoke into the air, Rick is now relaxed. He opens his eyes. "This is the real shit." He says to one of his bodyguards.

Meanwhile, the sentry himself who employs his own brand couldn't agree more.

Ricky turns back to Ivan. "So what's up little nigga?" He says. Ivan smiled back. The freshman hustler extends a hand. Ivan pounds it. The armed sentry also greets the youngster. "Well first, I'd like to say that's a nice gat." Ivan began. "What is it?" "A nine?" Ricky laughs in response to his comment. The guard himself just smiled.

"Thanks Lil' Homey." He responds. "And yeah it is. Suddenly, the big man chuckled.

"Hold up!" "Wait a minute!" He says. "What would you know about guns and triggers?" Ivan smiled. "Uh, my father collects them." He began to explain. "An ex-military man, and former marksman." Ricky nodded. "I like him." He tells his bodyguard. "He looks like a smart little nigga." The unknown sentry added. He nods.

“Are you from around here?” Ricky asks. “Yeah, I am.” Ivan assures him.

“You seen to have like an accent, that’s my reason for asking.” Ricky explains. “But anyway, its cool.” “How old are you man?” He asked. “Thirteen.” Ivan answers.

“ I had a birthday two months ago.” “Aight.” Ricky nodded. “I came to see you about placing a bet.” Ivan finally explains. Both men are now appalled. “No trick.” Ivan assures them. “No wire, no hidden mikes, none of that.” “All in good fun.” “Just me and partners across the street there.” As Ivan points to the lot, Rizzo and the others (now in plain view) all wave back. Ricky smiles and shakes his head. “So how much you got?” He asked. As an honest gesture, before handing him the money, Ivan first counts it.

“Eighty huh?” Says Ricky. His bodyguard also counts it. “Nothing personal.” Says the sentry. Ivan smiled. “I believe you were just doing your job sir.” He says happily.

“You guys are good to go.” Ricky announces. “Its a bet.” The two shakes hands once more. “What’s yo name man?” Rick finally asked. “Ivan.” “Like the Russian dictator from wayback?” Says his bodyguard. “Ivan “The Terrible.” Ricky helps him out.

“I’ve always been down with world history and shit.” He points out. “Hell, I’m still in school.” Rick added. “What year?” Ivan asks. “I’m a senior at Whitney Young.” Ivan nodded. “And one more thing, stay in school.” Ricky tells him. “I don’t think I have a choice, uh… “Oh, I’m Ricky man, my fault.” Says the high school student, slash hustler.

He finally introduces himself. “Your parents ain’t gonna let you drop out, I knew that one.” “That means they care.” Ricky pointed out. “I’m graduating in two months myself.” “I spoke with one of your bookies, and they’ve got me down for Ice.” Ivan reminds him. “Cool.” Says Ricky. “You ready?” He asked. Ivan smiles. “I was born ready.”

“Well, let’s do this little homey.” Ricky replies. “And may the best dog win.” Ivan nodded. “Word.” Rick smiled. After giving the men one last pound, Ivan heads back.

Shortly after Ricky collects additional money from more incoming spectators, a half hour later, and the names of the next two combatants are announced; the fight begins.

Security is seen covering all four corners of the makeshift ring as they rotate every thirty minutes. A midnight blue, unmarked CPD vehicle slowly cruises along the avenue.

Pulling up to a bus stop on the corner near Flournoy, one of the guards briefly hands the officer on the passenger side a white envelope. Apparently pleased with the contents inside, the officer clad in plain-clothes gives a signal to his partner on the driver's side.

Nodding his head towards the guard, the senior officer urges him to return to work.

As the trainers bring two more hounds into the ring, the crowd cheers.

Between the two Dobermans, are the names Fire and Ice. Ivan and the boys, of course roots for the latter. It is on; from the very moment the trainers remove their leashes.

Retaliating immediately, Fire returns the favor. Ice's tan coat now displays a dark red patch of open flesh. Fire's coat is comparable. Both animals maul, they growl, and they slob. Pinning one another to the ground, the bout intensifies. It is no holds barred.

Ice attacks his opposition viciously. Ripping his teeth into Fire's flesh, it will be the fifth time for which he has employed such an act. The boys are almost in a state of disbelief as they look on. "Oh shit, Ice is gonna win!" Alfred babbles. The Powell's are completely hoarse. Ivan and Riz shake hands. The others meanwhile clap. A frustrated and determined Fire attempts to reach his opponent's jugular.

However, it appears as though his luck has run out. Ice quickly turns the tables. He even bites the top of his head. "Finish his ass!" Says one of the spectators. "Its over." Rizzo nodded. "It look like, we'll be paid after all." Ahmad added. "I told you so." Said Ivan. "My instincts doesn't fail me too often." He tells them. Ice goes for the jugular.

YIPE! Tearing into Fire's main artery, the fight is over. Fire is dead. Ice wins.

7

Following the onslaught between Fire and Ice, a bout that resulted in large sums of money for those who placed their bets (namely on the latter), Ivan and the boys are no exception to the rule. Ice, the breadwinner is long removed from the ring.

Meanwhile, a trainer comes to remove Fire's chewed up carcass. Wearing protective clothing, the gentleman scoops up the remains and throw them into a garbage bag. "Well, let's get our money." Ivan Says. The others nodded. Before they could meet with Ricky, one of the guards stops them. Ivan and the others are now puzzled. The gentleman smiled. "Relax, chill nobody's jacking you." He says. The young men sighed.

"The man himself wants to see you." The sentry announces. "In fact, HE wants to pay you." "We should have known." Ivan shakes his head. Rizzo and Alfred both chuckle. "And once again y'all, congratulations." The guard shakes hands with them.

"Thank you sir." Says Ivan. "Follow me please." Says the stocky gentleman.

Busy Bee Lounge

Situated just two blocks south at the corner of Polk Street, this establishment has just recently moved from it previous location on West Harrison. Also under new management, this is also the office as well as the hangout of Sir George himself.

As Ivan and the others are escorted in, they spot his limo immediately. The latter is parked along the side street, opposite the entrance. From the moment the boys entered the lobby, several of the patrons many of whom are over twenty-five briefly stares.

"So what's good Mary?" The guard asked the bartender. The petite and dark-complexioned female looks up and smiles. "Right now, it looks like you." She says.

"Let me guess Miles." She began. "Your new trainees?" The cream suited clad guard grins. "You're funny." He says. "Its kind of a long story baby, I'll tell you later."

"But for the time being, get these young bucks something that won't get us in trouble." The woman first studies Ivan, and then the others. "Cokes it is." She says.

Shortly thereafter, the guard heads to the back. As she serves the boys the boys their drinks, the bartender looks at them and smiles. "Does your parents know you're here." She teases them. Ivan and the others meanwhile laughed. They now feel more at home.

Five minutes later, the guard returns to the lobby. "He's ready to see you." He tells Ivan. "And by the way Mary, George says give the others another round." "On him."

"Well, that's what I'm paid for." Says the bartender. "This way sir." The man directs Ivan.

Located in the back near the restrooms is Sir George's office. Reading the Chicago Sun Times at his desk, Sir George himself hears a knock. "Come on in man." He says.

"Thanks a lot Miles appreciate it." Giving his boss a nod, the guard takes off.

Clad in a black suit, a cream-colored shirt and red tie, George is actually a fairly handsome gentleman. About five foot seven, he has smooth brown skin, a goatee, and a relaxed fade. (Curly) To appear more distinguished, George even wears eyeglasses.

Ivan is now seated before him. Sir George smiled. "I take it you've met my brother." He began. The two shake hands. "He's my partner in crime." Ivan nodded as he listened.

"I notice there's a slight resemblance between you two." Ivan says smiling. "He's cool, make no mistake." "Ricky learns from the best." Sir George insists. "So you guys were among my youngest patrons huh?" He asked Ivan. "Very much sir." Says the young man. George chuckled. "You don't have to call me that man." "You can call me George, shit." "I'm not old." "And I can plainly see, that you're a respectful young man anyway."

"I take it that you've already heard of me?" George asked. "Very much, I've heard your name come up from time to time." Ivan answers. "So what brought you all over?" George asked. "Actually, we were rather curious." Ivan responded. "Given that we were already passing through." He went on. "My friends and I noticed the rather large crowd, and at first we were somewhat thinking, that maybe it was like a regular street fight."

George nods as hears word from word. "It was my idea to wanna place a bet, and I talked it over with my friends out there." "So you're their leader?" George asked.

He was obviously impressed. "I guess you can say that." Ivan answers. "You know, Rick filled me in on some things." George tells him. "In reference to your character, and you appear to be quite intelligent." "Given the age that you are." "What grade are you in?" The educated hustler asked. "Sixth." Ivan answers. "Bullshit." George chuckles.

"More like sixth, going on twelfth." He roasts. "You don't seem like you're from around here." Ivan chuckles at his last statement. "What your brother told me was comparable." He says. "But there's nothing wrong with that." George reassures him. "There's actually one suggestion that I'd like to make." He began. "Given that I like you already." "Curiosity is like a double edged sword, and one can lose his or her life if they're not careful." "Just like the theory of curiosity killing the cat?" Ivan asked.

"Exactly." George snaps his fingers. "Some things are meant for you to see, others are not." "Of course, my operations are an exception to the first rule." Ivan nodded.

"Here, take some M&M's man." George hands him a glass bowl. "Thanks." Ivan responds. "No problem." Says the young lounge owner. "My favorites." Ivan crunches away. "Same here." Replied George. He laughs. "Well Ivan, here's your fraction."

Sir George hands him a thick white envelope. Ivan takes a peak. He nods. "I've got one more suggestion." George began. He now gets up to open the door. "Like I tell my brother, as you know he's a senior at Whitney, stay in school." "Mind over matter."

"I plan on it." Ivan tells him now getting up. "That's good." George shakes his hand.

"If you need anything, one of my girls whatever." "Even if you just wanna talk, you know where to find me." "Thanks George, I really appreciate it." Ivan says.

Returning to the lobby area, Ivan summons the others.

Miller Residence

Seated in the dining room, Ivan, the man of the house (Alfred) joined by Rizzo and the others now count their stacks. Playing on the stereo in his mom's entertainment room is Special Ed's (A New York rapper) "I've Got it made."

I'm your idol, the highest title
Numero Uno, I'm not a Puerto Rican
But I'm speakin, so that you know
And understand, I got the gift of speech
And its a blessin, so I preach the lesson
I talk sense; condense, into the form of a poem
Full of knowledge, from my toes
To the top of my dome.
I'm kinda young----but my tongue speaks maturity
I'm not a child, I need nothing for security
I get paid when my record is played----to put it short
I got it made.

"Is this a dream?" Alfred asked. He chuckles and shakes his head as he counts his bills. The others follow suit. Ivan and Rizzo laughed. "Nope." Ahmad responds. "Its for real G." "We're still in the real world." Ivan explains. "We've won." The Powell brothers had now regained their voices. "It was rather kind of Miles to give us a ride back here." Says Jason. His two siblings nodded. "Basically, he did it for security reasons." "I know it."

"You've got some envious assholes sticking people up for their sneakers, caps, and starter jackets and shit." Ivan adds. "What do you think they would do with plain, good old fashioned money?" "Yeah, straight up Ivan." Says Thomas. A chill runs across his spine. "Remember, what Ready Rock said about his cousin?" Rizzo asked the others.

"Word." William nodded. "You've always gotta watch your ass around here." Ivan suggests. "Sir George told me the same thing today." He tells the others. "That's right!"

Thomas snaps his fingers. "You met with him up close, and personal this afternoon."

"We've always seen him and Ricky on the strip, but we never really talked to them." Rizzo breaks it down. "Basically Hi and Bye." "My mom actually went out with him for a minute awhile back." Alfred added. "They're still good friends though." Ahmad clears his throat. "He's flesh and bone just like the rest of us." Ivan says with mild disdain. "George is cool and all, but he's not a saint." "He then smiles. "Stop riding."

"But I can still fill you in on what we've talked about." "Please, do tell." Says Riz. "Well for starters." Ivan began. "He asked me why we came over, filled me in on what Ricky told him, in reference to my character." "Shared some of his life stories, and gave me a lot of words of advice." The others nodded their heads. They were obviously impressed. "Shared some M&M's, and then gave me the money." "That's cool."

The others all respond at once. Ivan looked at them and laughed. They gave him a pat on the back. "And right before I came out, George told me if that if I ever needed anything, including one of his girls, or whatever." Ivan concludes. "Just stop by."

"Ah Shit!!!" Says the others. "That means you in with em." Says Ahmad. He shakes his head. "This is unbelievable." Says Thomas. "You've just made friends with a renowned hustler and his partner. "This can only mean one thing." Alfred began.

"And what's that?" Ivan asked. He acts as though he has no idea. The others give him the eye. "You're coming up in the world, Ivan." Rizzo gives him a pound.

"Who want some Kool Aid?" Alfred asked. Everyone in the group raised their hands.

Alfred retreats to the kitchen shortly thereafter. Five minutes later, Ms. Miller arrives. "Hello boys." She says. "Hey ma." Says Alfred. Kissing her cheek, he hands his mother a glass of Kool Aid. "Thanks." She tells him. "So how are you guys doing?"

"We're doing great, Ms. Miller thanks." Ivan happily responds. "How was work?" Alfred asked. "Tiring, but still productive." She tells her son. Rachel Miller, twenty-eight is employed as a postal carrier. She works out of the main post office located downtown.

At this point, she still dons her uniform. Single and divorced, the resemblance between the young mother and her son is comparable. Her sex appeal enhances her full-figured frame as she now retreats to the living room. At the touch of a remote, she activates the television. Releasing a loud sigh, Ms. Miller falls onto the nearest couch.

"Let me help you out a little." Says Alfred. He helps her in removing her work boots." "You guys have a good friend here." She tells his friends. "Thank you sir."

Now surfing through multiple channels, the woman of the house discovers what is known as The Movie Channel. "So are you guys having fun?" Ms. Miller asks.

"Yes, we are." Rizzo answers. "What have you done so far today?" Alfred's mother asked. "So far, we hung out at the park." Alfred himself began. "We were at first on our way to see Ernest, then an altercation broke out on the corner, in the lot." Ms. Miller nodded as she listens. "As a result, we had to take a detour." Thomas added. "So we just chilled at the Fun Factory." "Some people obviously lost some money on those fights again." She guessed. "They can't put it all on George and his brother for losing." Ms. Miller went on. "There is something called freedom of choice, you know?" She smiled.

"If you decide to gamble away your money in whatever way, shape, or form then that's on you." "Why should the actions of a few ignorant individuals, spoil things for the rest of the community?" Ivan shrugged. "Only God knows, I guess." He answers.

"You can say that again." Ms. Miller chuckled. "How are your parents?" She asked.

"They're doing pretty good." Ivan responds. "My mother is on vacation like us." Ms. Miller nodded. "That's right, you did tell me she worked for the Board of Education."

She then guzzles away at her Kool Aid. Returning to the room with other glasses, Alfred now serves his friends. "Thanks a lot Al." They tell him. Alfred nodded.

"We played football up at the park earlier." He began to tell his mother. She listens.

"For awhile, we had Ivan play as our running back, and of course nobody could catch him." "I bet, they couldn't." Says Ms. Miller. "Ivan has changed a lot." Rizzo tells her.

"He certainly has." She says, now studying him. "You've slimmed down quite dramatically." Ms. Miller began. "And yet, you've become quite buffed as well."

"You're looking good." Ivan smiles. "Thanks, Ms Miller." He says.

"Like they say, you only look as good as you feel." Alfred's mom added. "Anyway, Ahmad here got mad and started talking trash, because his team was getting served." Rizzo began. "Whatever, man." "We were killing y'all out there." Alfred points at him.

"So we made a switch on them." Rizzo added. He laughed. "You're still salty." He says to Ahmad. "For awhile, Ivan was our defensive tackle." Ms. Miller nods.

"But he later changed places with me." Alfred explains. "Ok, so after our little time out, we got ourselves repositioned." "Both Ahmad and Will deserved a chop, like it was nothing. "While everybody else had their hands full, with the other players." Thomas began. "I'm guessing at first, that all Ahmad and William could see was Ivan."

"Even though they saw their teammates were overwhelmed with players from the other side, they were actually looking good for a minute." The others laughed as they continue to listen. Ahmad and Will they go ahead, they run after him." "But before they could even pass Washtenaw, Alfred sideswipes them!" "They both got sacked." Rizzo laughs.

"Both Ahmad and Will looked as though, they've been hit by a truck." Said Ivan.

"It was so funny, Ms. Miller." He continues. "I can imagine." Says the head woman. Seconds later, the phone rings. Ms. Miller summons the receiver located next to her. She answers. "Hello?" The boys meanwhile, enjoy another round of Kool Aid.

New Prospects Food & Groceries

Located across the street from Sir George's killer canine coliseum on the corner of Flournoy and California, this store is owned and operated by Mohammed Aziz.

Aziz, a native of Riyadh, Saudi Arabia has been a fixture in the neighborhood for ten years. Just to the right of this establishment is an existing Spirit of "76" gas station.

As Ivan, Rizzo, Alfred and the others walk in, they are first greeted by the sound of the motion alarm. The sound corresponds to that of a doorbell. Its speakers are suspended between the entrances itself as well as the cashier's booth. The store consists of two narrow aisles, stretching from the main point of entry to a deli located in the rear.

A single surveillance camera is seen behind the counter. Another stands to the right of the overlooking the exit. "How are you guys doing today?" Mr. Aziz asked.

The short but heavy Arab-American takes note of them from the cashier's booth, as he tends to other customers. He waves at Ivan and rest of his group. "We're good as usual Mo." Alfred Says. He grabs a box of Lemonheads situated on a bottom shelf near the deli. Ivan picks up a box of Boston baked beans, while Rizzo and the others procure the Jawbreakers. "How's your mother?" Mr. Aziz asked Alfred. "She's fine." Alfred Says.

"She just got off of work." The storeowner nods. "Is Ernie in?" Thomas asked. "Yeah, he should be back there." Mr. Aziz answered. The young man that he employed behind the deli counter is eighteen-year-old Ernest Blackwell.

Earnest who only lives four blocks away, attends Jones Commercial High School located in the Loop. He is a senior as well as a law major. Just two days ago, Ernest received a letter in response to his application for Harvard University.

The young man who recently ranked number two out of three hundred and fifty other students has been accepted. He enrolls in August. “Hey, what’s up Ernest?” Says Ivan.

“Yo, what’s going down fellas?” Says Ernest. He gives all of the boys a pound.

Putting on a pair of plastic gloves, he opens the door to a refrigerator in the corner of the shop. Removing several packages of meat and vegetables, he opens them.

“So Harvard accepted you huh?” Jason asked. Ernest nodded. “Congrats.” Says Ivan.

“Thanks.” Ernest responds. “Like my pops always used to tell me.” He began. “You always have a choice.” “Straight up.” Alfred added. “You can always better yourself.”

“Like Public Enemy said last year.” He went on. “Don’t believe the hype.” The others finished. “Even in the hood, you still have a choice, you have still have options.”

“You don’t have to always rap your way out, or play sports.” “Or better yet, the worst case of scenario, sell drugs or join one of the gangs.” The others nod.

“Ain’t nothing fabulous about prison, and besides.” Ernest chuckled. “I value my rectum.” Tickled pink by Ernie’s latter statement, Rizzo’s laugh mimics that of a chipmunk. The others are also cracking up. “So what cases do you have in mind?” Brian asked. “Mostly civil, some class action, corporate cases and last but not least, a few criminal cases.” Ernest answered. “Especially if I believe that person is wrongly accused.

“Cool.” Says Ahmad. “Why the hell is this?” William asked. “You have a lot of poor and low income students going to the best high schools, while you have those who are rich and well off, and yet they attend schools over here like Crane, Marshall, or Manley?”

“Because they’re looking for trouble.” Ivan answered. “Yeah, he’s right.” Says Ernest.

"That's usually the case." He continued. "When I graduate, I plan on getting my law license, become a lawyer and start my first practice over here." Ivan and the others nodded. "That's not such a bad idea." Says Thomas. "Give something back."

Ernest, standing at five foot seven employs a slender, but yet ripped frame. A disciple in the arts of Muy Thai, and standard Kickboxing, he is also a registered voter and very well cultured. Alfred's parents were very young when they got married.

They were together for only five years when Mr. and then Mrs. Miller filed for a divorce. The latter was triggered by infidelity caused by Alfred's father.

However, to this day they both still have joint custody, in addition to child support. (Courtesy of Mr. Miller)

Alfred of course has no siblings. Sometime ago, following his parent's divorce he was often picked on by other youths. One day, Ernest was on his way home from school as he crossed a viaduct near Francisco Avenue. He spots six boys within his own age group. At this time, they are beating a much smaller Alfred almost senseless.

With his bike on the ground, an also younger Ernest becomes angry and agitated.

Ordering them to leave him alone, one of them gives Ernest the finger. Another urges him to "push on." Urging for the hoods to pick on someone their own size, the group's leader becomes heated. With their attention no longer focused on Alfred, they now turn to the challenger. They are no match for this rising young student.

Calling upon the numb chucks from his belt, Ernest aborts a series of bricks, bottles, and rocks thrown at him. Those who are responsible are among the first to retreat.

Those who didn't employ weapons, employed themselves head on. Cracking his knuckles, Ernest delivers pre-emptive blows, multiple kicks, takedowns, excessive blocks, and of course elbows. The brawl is over before it even begins. Now petrified, the leader attempts to flee.

But however, before he is able to cross the street at Fillmore, a car sideswipes him. Helping Alfred to his feet, Ernest summons his bike.

The two have been like brothers ever since. Although Alfred's dad is the driving force for role models, Ernest falls into the second category.

"My game plan in reference to giving back to the community." Ernest began. "Is to help those who help themselves." The others nod as they continue to listen.

"One of the key building blocks for a thriving area." "Those who are always are always dependent, and lacks the willingness to help themselves." "Stay away from people like that." "They will only slow you down, you'll be wasting your time, energy and shit like that." "People like this will even try to take advantage of you." "I bet." Says Ivan.

As Ernest spreads his words of wisdom among the boys, he yet manages to still make sandwiches for his customers. The smell of different meats, spices, and seasonings fills the air. Like an ancient warrior, Ernest takes his chopping knife and tosses a foot long loaf into the air. With the employment of his blade, the skilled swordsman slices the bread in half. Ivan and the boys followed by Mr. Aziz and a few patrons all clap.

Fifteen minutes later, the store becomes crowded. "I'll holler at y'all later, it looks like its getting packed." Ernest explains. "Alright, bet." Says Rizzo and the triplets.

Shaking hands with the lone neighborhood employee, the boys all split. "Peace."

Young Residence

Just one block west of California on the 2800 block of Flournoy, this is the home of eleven-year-old Leon Young. The building is a pink and white single-family cottage.

Leon, another close friend of Rizzo also has a series of talents. Among them is making people laugh, dancing, acrobats, as well as picking locks. His grandfather, a local locksmith and his grandmother, a longtime employee of the Chicago Transit Authority, has raised Leon since he was three years old. His mother, a heroin addict later died.

His father who sold drugs is now incarcerated. He serves a ten-year sentence.

Upstairs in Leon's bedroom, the junior host hangs out with four of his best friends. Among them is Alfred, Ivan Thompson, (of course Rizzo) and last but not least, there's Thomas Moore. The others had long split, following their meeting with Ernest.

It has been two hours since they began playing video games. On the NES, for which Leon himself owns; the group now plays "Skate or Die." As Ivan waits his turn, he discovers a small mouse in the doorway. Perhaps it is just a vivid of my imagination, or did that mouse just nod his head. He asks himself: Did that mouse just say hi to me?

Seconds later, the mere rodent disappears. Ivan nods his head. I didn't see you.

And with that, he now returns to the screen. The latter is shown in black and white.

"It's your turn, Ivan." Leon says. The host sends him a controller.

Manufactured by Konami and its affiliate Ultra Software, this game is the projected forerunner of an up and coming genre: Skateboarding. Skate or Die, which was released early last year, employs different skating styles. Among them is "The Joust, "The Downhill, "The Freestyle", and last but not least; the renowned "High Jump."

In reality, in the world of Skateboard such styles really exist! Ivan, a huge fan of this game enjoys the latter. At this point, the game has been switched to this mode.

"You know that you need a Freedom Stick for that right?" Says Rizzo. The Freedom Stick is a wireless controller used mainly for fighting games or otherwise shooting games. “Not necessarily.” Says Ivan. He now removes his jacket. “I’ll show you.”

As Leon and the others look on, they exchange concerned looks. Moving back and forth while pressing the “B” button, Ivan’s character suddenly began to pick up speed as he goes back and forth between two thirty foot ramps. Leon and the others are now appalled. “What are you?” Leon began to roast. “Some machine?” “Johnny Five?”

They all laughed. Gaining full momentum of his character, the latter begins to employ a multitude of unspeakable tricks. But yet, after performing so many stunts, Ivan’s character eventually loses his stamina. As a result, he falls off of his skateboard.

Hitting the pavement below, Ivan falls through the earth. Furthermore, jokingly to add insult to injury; a black hole is seen where his body landed. Leon and the others are tickled pink. Rizzo’s face is completely red at this point. He too can’t stop laughing.

“How do you do it?” Leon asked. “Well a guy at my school, allowed me to keep this very same game.” Ivan began to explain. “For about a week.” The others nod.

“As an insurance policy, I gave him Mike Tyson’s Punch Out.” “Fair trade.” Says Thomas. “Having mastered every different style.” Ivan continues. “Comes this one.”

“I’ve spent an entire week mastering, this particular form.” “And as a result, one day….

“I just began toying around with the controllers, namely moving them back and forth.” Ivan now demonstrates. “And the next thing I knew, I began picking up speed.”

“Finally, I decided to experiment a little, test the waters.” “And suddenly, those points began to quadruple.” “I was on a roll.” Ivan now hands Leon the controller.

Although Leon is unsuccessful in duplicating most of Ivan's tricks, he yet still manages to master a few. The results for Rizzo and Thomas are comparable.

Only Alfred comes close. He finishes out second compared to that of Ivan himself.

Leon's grandmother, a dark, slender, and slightly grayish woman looks in from the doorway. "What are you all laughing at?" She says smiling. "Up here smoking refer?"

"Naw, grandma." Says Leon himself. "We're just playing the Nintendo here." Leon explains. "Ivan was just showing us how to master one of the skateboarding games, with one of his characters, and he ended up taking a fall." The woman, Mrs. Payne nodded.

"I take it that you are all having a good time." She says.

"Well anyway, I am heading back out to pick up some groceries."

"I trust that you boys won't tear up my house."

"Well of course not." Says Leon. He smiled.

"We'll be more than ready to help, when you return Mrs. Payne." Says Rizzo.

"Until then, carry on." Mrs. Payne says to them. She happily nods.

Leaving the room, Leon's grandmother descends to the front door.

8

FLOURNOY STREET

Located at the corner near Francisco Avenue lies an existing brown bungalow. To the right of this occupied dwelling is a huge lot, as well as that of another home.

However the white-two story frame, which occupies the far right, is dilapidated, vacant, and obviously abandoned. Ivan, Rizzo, Alfred, and Leon all hang in the vacant lot. Thomas, who is still seen, reunites with the Powell's. They are all performing flips at this point. Taking turns on what appears to be a discarded mattress, the boys execute death-defying acrobats! The vacant structure, an obvious health hazard remains open.

The chipped enamel, cracked paint, and bare window frames (not even boarded up) makes it all the more evident. Even the front door is missing.

Within the confines, the stench of mildew, decaying wood, plaster, and human waste is present throughout the entire house. Ragged clothing and deteriorating furniture still remains in one bedroom. Among the first four to warm up, there's Ivan, Rizzo, Alfred, and Leon. Taking flight from the first floor window, they each began to flip forward. Landing on the mattress, supported by a box spring, they return to the surface.

Shortly before returning to the mat, the boys began to stretch. Leon is among the first. Donning a gray sweatshirt, jeans, sneakers, and a dew rag (concealing his dreads), he closes his eyes and takes one deep breath. Standing two feet shy of the first floor window (In what used to be a dining room), Leon runs and then jumps.

Rolling into mid-air, he flips and makes a smooth landing. "Tada." He says. "Tada?" Alfred began to roast. "Where's your base?"

He asks. "You sound like a straight up fruity boy man!" The others quickly laughed. "Mary Lou Retton?"

"That wasn't what Rachel said last night!" Leon fires back. He grins. "OOOOO!" Says the others. Alfred Chuckled. He grins and shakes his head.

"Aight, tell Blanche that I've got a dust buster for her." Alfred Says. The Powell's whistled. "Cause every time that I eat her out, I get a mouthful of cobwebs!"

"DAMN!!!" Says the others. Ivan's light brown face turns red. The laughter explodes. Rizzo meanwhile goes into the building. Standing in the dining room, Rizzo takes two steps back. Breathing in, he closes his eyes. Slowly jogging, Rizzo jumps over the windowsill and flips. Landing onto the mattress, he bounces once and flips backwards. The thin, but lean youngster is back in the dining room.

Flipping for third time, Rizzo lands back onto to the mattress. He steps down. "Did somebody eat their Wheaties this morning?" Says Craig. His brothers smiled.

"That was actually sweet." Says Leon. He nods. "I learn from the best." Says Rizzo.

A few minutes later, four more youngsters approach the lot. Among them are thirteen-year-old Khali Rutherford and his brother Quincy, age twelve. Behind them are two young ladies, twelve-year-old Cassandra Walker, and her best friend Justine Knowles. The Rutherford's unlike that of the latter, actually rode their bikes. Ivan and the others have met with them earlier this afternoon. They are greeted once more.

"Doing yo flip action out here?" Khali asked Leon. "Don't I always?" Leon responds. He gives Khali and his brother a pound. "Is everything still cool?" Quincy asks.

"Word." Says Leon. "Quincy and me, just ridin around." Says Khali. "We took a tour of the best side (the west side) here, covered Oak Park's downtown, and rested at that forest preserve in Maywood." "When we made our way back." Quincy began. "Like around Fifth Avenue and Homan, some boys tried to chase us."

"They was on bikes too, but we out pedaled them." Leon continues to listen as he watches Ivan. Ivan himself now enters building. "So these dudes tried to gank y'all?"

“Straight up Leo.” Says Khali. “When we lost em at Whipple and made a sharp turn, they ended up falling like dominoes.” “It was funny as hell.” Leon laughed.

“I bet it was.” He says. Cassandra and Justine looked over at the building and smiled. They watch Ivan as he briefly stretches. Looking right back at them, he waves.

In the former dining room, the junior athlete takes three steps back. Situated in the middle, Ivan begins to run. Taking flight, he flips over the windowsill and lands firmly onto the mattress. Flipping backwards into the dining room, Ivan again flips forward.

Having landed onto the mattress a second time, he employs another backwards flip.

Surprisingly, his number of spectators has already grown. After a fourth and final flip, Ivan returns to the mattress. As he steps down, he is completely fired up.

“A Ninja With An Attitude y’all.” Leon says to the spectators. “Give it up.” The onlookers, mostly block residents all gave their round of applause. But it wasn’t over.

Ivan re-enters the abandoned house. Rizzo, Alfred, and Leon now became nervous.

“Ivan man, what the hell are you doing?” Rizzo and Leon both asked. “Shit.” Alfred whispers. Running up the stairs of this former residence smelling of damp, but yet molded drywall, Ivan quickly reaches the second floor. Going left he reaches the living room. Peering through a window, he looks down on his friends as they anticipate his next move. Even the two blossomed; females Cassandra and Justine are concerned.

Standing in a narrow desecrated hallway near a bathroom, Ivan gives himself a running start. Dashing through the house, he makes his jump from a window in the center of the living room. Running and scrambling, Leon and Rizzo place more mats in front of the building. Rolling and flipping, Ivan lands unscathed. After a brief moment of silence, the remaining spectators (namely his friends) applaud. Justine fainted. Ivan walks over.

"What happened to your girl here?" Ivan asks Cassandra. She smiled and nodded.

Justine, now cradled in the arms of her best friend also wakes up to find Ivan standing over her. "People can't take you nowhere girl." Ivan teases. "But, naw you don't have to be embarrassed, Justine." He assures her. No longer embarrassed, Justine smiled.

Cassandra giggles. "How did you do that?" They both asked. Both Cassandra and Ivan help her to her feet. "Its a long story." Says the fitness buff. "You'll see me later."

"You straight now Justine?" Alfred asked. "Yeah, I just fainted that's all." Justine assures him. The others happily nodded. "The excitement almost killed you huh?" Leon asked. "Look at ya!" Uh huh!" Back to her former self, the young lady laughs.

"Courtesy of Mr. Shinobi here." He then points to Ivan. "You'd make a good ninja for real, straight up." Khali laughed. "Damn, I wanna be like you when I grow up." He says. "You're a freak man." Leon teased him. Ivan smiled. "A freak I may be." He says.

"That's right and I'm not ashamed of it." "Because he's the good freak." Rizzo finishes. "Do you Atleast have a reflection?" Leon asked. Ivan chuckles.

"You know what man?" He began grinning. "Kiss my ass!" "Do you cross dress?"

The laughter explodes.

9

FLOURNOY STREET

Inspired by their friend's grand performance, the Powell brothers re-dedicate themselves to the mat as they take flight and perform almost back to back on their flipping techniques. Leon turns to Cassandra. "Man what y'all still doin' over here?" He teases her. "Ivan doesn't want you like that." "Both you and Justine look like a fake assed Salt-N-Pepa!" "The two of y'all ain't been watching us, until he came along anyway."

"Stop frontin." Both Cassandra and Justine smiled at this point. The two them both flips him the bird. "Its a free country." "No its not." Rizzo began to remind her.

"Its a democracy." "But, still this ain't yo lot boy." Cassandra says. She punches him in the arm. "Yeah!" Justine added. Snapping her fingers, she then rolls her eyes at him.

Putting her hands around her hips, the medium shorthaired female spins in one rhythm.

Leon grabs Justine and picks her up. "Hey!" "Stop, Leon!" "Put me down!" She shouts. She is tickled pink. For a brief moment, Leon spins her around. "Stop!"

"I'm wearing a skirt!" "Lucky you." He grins. Leon finally puts her down. Justine fixes her skirt. Shortly thereafter, they both double-team him. "Hey Leo!" Rizzo calls to Leon. Leon, who is still playing with the girls answers. "Its time for us to step."

"We're gonna holler at my cousin, and see what's he's up to." "Aight, peace." Leon responds. Shaking hands, Riz, Ivan and the others heads north on Francisco.

Martin Luther King Plaza (East Garfield Park)

Following the assassination of the slain Civil Rights leader, a housing development to commemorate his honor is later built. Rising from the ashes of what was once a commercial strip, comes the latter. Located at 3220 W. Madison Street on the corner at Kedzie Avenue, the fairly recent complex was established in 1972.

Located across directly across the street is the Garfield Community Center; also known as 10 South Kedzie (also built the same year by the city), and to the left is a vintage building. The latter built around 1910, houses a cluster of local businesses from a Walgreen's-like shop, to a mental health center, a currency exchange, a barbershop, and so on. The housing complex itself, Martin Luther King Plaza covers both sides of west Madison.

From Kedzie Avenue to the east, the complex consists of three-story twin buildings.

Roughly a half-mile long, its western boundary ends at Homan Avenue. A local daycare center compliments the northeast corner. The development houses low income residents.

Montgomery Residence #3234

The very first building, which overlooks the community center, is the home of Rizzo Harrison's cousin, Jamal Montgomery and his mother Constance.

Located on the front lawn of this dwelling, lies a statue of Martin Luther King Jr. himself as an African Chieftain. He holds a Coptic cross and a Native American prayer wheel topped with a globe. A dove of peace sits on his head and he wears the Nobel Peace medal around his neck. Geraldine Hamilton-McCullough, a chairperson of the art department at Rosary College (recently retired) was the sculptor.

Crossing the street, Ivan and Rizzo joined by Alfred and Thomas approaches the latter building. Before Rizzo is able to ring the bell, the front door already opens.

A tall and lanky young man buttoning his shirt shows a thick, longhaired young lady to the door. As she procures her purse, the youth slaps her across the rump.

"Hey what's up cuz?" The young man says. He embraces Rizzo with both a handshake and a hug. "Its on like Donkey Kong as usual." "Bruce Lee Roy, what's goin on?" Jamal adds. He refers to Ivan. "Mr. War games!" (Alfred) and Tom Jones." Namely Thomas.

The seventeen-year-old shakes hands with them as well. "Shit, come on in y'all."

"So who was ol' girl?" Rizzo asked. "Straight up." Says Ivan. She looked fine."

Sitting in the dining room, they are now playing poker.

"Oh that was Georgia, a female I just met." Jamal answers. His guests all nodded. In their left hands they each employed five cards. For whatever card holds no value, is of course thrown into the pile. As for the winning player or whoever is in the lead at that moment, is likely to salvage one or more of the cards if it proves beneficial to the latter.

"Where did you hook up with her?" Ivan asks. Picking up another ace, he collects a stack of chips from Jamal. The host himself is impressed by Ivan's competitiveness.

He smiled and nodded. "Up at the library man." Jamal answers. His cousin smiled.

"The library is still a good place to meet a female." He says to Ivan and the others. "It never fails." Jamal reminds them. "That will never play out." "Anyway, what have you got Goldie?" Rizzo asked him. Looking carefully at his cards, Jamal grins.

"Let me see, I've got two deuces, a joker, a spade, and a heart." He says to his cousin.

"You're going down." Rizzo throws down a queen and five chips.

Ivan, Alfred, and Thomas all follow suit for the third time. "I met her at the library yesterday." Jamal went on. "Brushing up to take this constitution, when school starts back." Jamal, seventeen is an only child. An Honor Roll "B" student, he specialized in numbers, chemistry, history, and plays football at North Lincoln Park High School.

"Works for me." Ivan gives Jamal a pound. "Every man has his own angle." He says.

Ivan now studies his deck. "I've got one diamond, one heart, two jokers and a king." Says Rizzo. "Damn." Thomas shakes his head. "Its looks like we're fucked."

He too observes his deck. Alfred follows suit. "Man, if this was a real game and we played for money, we would all be ass out." Rizzo added. "Literally." He sighs.

They now wait for the winning player. Ivan summons another card from the pile. He now holds seven. "Your move Jamal." Ivan Says to the host. He tosses another set of chips. Jamal meanwhile, takes another card from the pile. Both players are neck and neck. "So where is she from?" Alfred asked. "Around by Chicago and Pine." Says Jamal.

"She not only has the ass and tities, but Georgia's got the brain's too." He points out.

"Hell, this girl is actually the smartest one I've hooked up with so far."

"It ain't funny." "She's a straight "A" student, head of the cheerleading team at her school, she's bad." "What school does she go to?" Alfred asked. "Austin." Jamal answers. "A smart ass huh?" Ivan asked. "I guess so." Says Jamal.

"She even gives good head." He added. "I can imagine." Says Thomas. He smiled.

"Let's take five." Jamal suggests. Rising from the table, he heads to the kitchen.

In agreement, the others nod their heads.

Searching his kitchen cabinet, Jamal summons a bag of Doritos for his guests. His cousin, who returns from the store, produces a case of Pepsi. Distributing these treats amongst themselves, the game continues.

Jamal, Rizzo and the others continue to throw out cards. They sighed. And then they smile. "Guess I'll be taking your deed to the house." Ivan grins. He tosses out all of his cards at once. Jamal chuckled. "If it wasn't for bad luck, I wouldn't have any at all." Alfred shakes his head. Jamal gives Ivan a pound.

"Good game man." He says. "Thanks, I learn from the best." Ivan tells him. Jamal nodded.

Garfield Park

Established in 1869, this 185-acre parcel of land was originally known as Central Park. Renamed to honor President James A. Garfield (1831-1881) after his assassination, plans for the entire ensemble of three other parks in the region had been completed ten years earlier, by William Le Baron Jenney, best known as today as the father of the skyscraper. As ambitious plans could not be realized all at once, Garfield Park developed in stages, beginning with the east lagoon. Jens Jensen, who had begun as a laborer for the West Park System in the 1880's worked his way up to superintendent of Humboldt Park a decade later. The system was entrenched in political graft. In 1900, the commissioners fired Jensen because of his efforts to fight the corruption. Five years later, during major political reforms, new commissioners appointed him General Superintendent and Chief Landscape Architect. Deteriorating and unfinished sections of the parks allowed Jensen to experiment with his evolving Prairie-Style.

For instance when he took over, each of the three parks (including Douglas and Humboldt) had a small poorly maintained conservatory. Rather than repairing these structures, which each displayed similar collections; Jensen decided to replace them with a single centralized facility. Designed in conjunction with an engineering firm, Hitchings and Company, Jensen conceived the Garfield Park Conservatory as a work of landscape gardening under glass. Considered revolutionary when it opened to the public in 1908, the form of the building emulated a "great midwestern haystack," while inside the rooms were wonderful compositions of water, rock, and plants. In 1928, the West Park Commission constructed the "Gold Dome Building" in Garfield Park to provide a new administrative headquarters for the West Park Commission. Architects Michaelsen and Roanstad designed the structure. In 1934, the Chicago Park District took over when the city's 22 park commissions merged into a citywide agency.

At that time, the administrative offices were no longer needed and the "Golden Dome" building becomes the field house.

A hundred and twenty years later little has changed.

Located from as far as Lake Street to the north and Jackson Boulevard to the south. Other boundaries include Hamlin Boulevard from the west and Homan Avenue to the east. The Golden Dome and its nearby lagoon (still intact) is surrounded by trees and connects to a large path. From the main entrance lies a small bridge. A decaying gazebo is seen in the distance. On the opposite side of the "L" tracks, at the corner of Lake Street and Central Park Drive in the heart of its namesake community, lies the conservatory.

Situated in a neighborhood stricken by drugs, poverty, and crime, the Conservatory is still visited by millions. Namely from around the world.

An accordion-like bus, Man series 7001 leads a tourist charter over the lagoon via Central Park. Employed by the Chicago Transit Authority, the latter, which offers tours to various landmarks across the city, is known as the "Culture Bus."

In one area of the park, scores of children occupies a playground. Embracing the swings, slides, and jungle gyms before them on this still bright afternoon, their parents and others look on. Several families are seen engaging in cookouts, while a lone solicitor roams the perimeters. Upon spotting a marked CPD cruiser, the scrawny gentleman takes off. On the basketball courts, many teens as well as young adults play viciously amongst themselves by way of catching rebounds, free throws, followed by a dunk or two.

One player tries for a dunk, but instead catches an elbow. Falling to the ground, his opposition gives him a hand. From there, the game continues.

In the northernmost region, scores of preteens joined by younger adolescents engage in horseplay, mingling, and more of the like. Along Washington Boulevard, a red Corvette is illegally parked. Rocking side to side, the windows (although tinted) remain foggy.

The screams of pleasure behind the glass, makes it evident.

No hydraulics.

Farther north, behind the "Lake Street "L", Ivan and the others play softball. Among them: The local youths. Many of them of course, are friends of Jamal. As Ivan prepares to batter up, Rizzo on the other hand prepares to steal third.

Alfred and Thomas are situated behind a ten-foot fence. Jamal now acts as the umpire.

The home team, namely those that lives in the area plays outfield. Holding the bat firmly while he cracks his neck, a young man named "Fusion" blinks his eyes before throwing the pitch. Ivan takes a swing. With his powerful forearms, he hits the ball.

Ivan's force, complimenting both the speed followed by the trajectory; sends the ball flying! Or to become more accurate, it travels nearly one mile.

Several of Fusion's teammates tried to retrieve the ball, but yet they were too late.

Ivan and Rizzo meanwhile cover all three bases. Sprinting, running and sliding, they are now home. (Behind the fence) Two and a half blocks, in the southeast corner of the park, beyond the statue of

President Garfield and the murky lagoon, a young couple is seen having a picnic. Seconds later, a ball lands on their tent.

The gentleman and his female companion laughed.

"Y'all safe." Jamal tells the boys. He fixes his mask shortly thereafter. Rizzo smiled.

"How far was that?' He asks. "Damned near three blocks?" "Shit!" Riz now chuckles.

"You've got some powerful forearms." A young lady added. She is one of the only two females on the team. Her name: Beverly Johnson. And with her, is her sister Pamela.

They now join Alfred and Thomas behind the fence. Alfred is up next. "Its on you big homey." Says Thomas. Both he and the girls give him a pat on the shoulders.

Ivan and Rizzo are among them as well. Alfred takes the bat.

Fusion, meanwhile throws him a curve. The heavyset youngster commences to swing.

"Watch him carefully." Ivan advises. And Alfred listens. Hitting the ball on impact, employing all of his force, the poor ball travels a good ninety-five yards.

Within reach, on the intersection of Warren Boulevard and Homan, lies a gas station.

Both Alfred and Thomas cover all three bases. Clearing his throat, Alfred spits phlegm. Once again, Fusion's outfielders are too late. The Johnson sisters are next.

Fusion is dumbfounded. He shakes his head and chuckles. He and his team are only two in four. "I've been waiting a long time for this!" Says Jamal.

Chewing a stick of gum, he prepares to further strike out his opposition. "Like they say, payback is a bitch." Fusion laughs at his response. "Yeah, whatever man."

The members of the opposing team are also friends of Jamal.

Among them are Frederick "Fusion" Higgins, Crystal Haggerty his cousin, Marcellus "Mouse" Dawes, Butch Masters, and Baxter Goodman.

"So far thanks to Ivan and Alfred, we have two home runs." Thomas began. He looks through the makeshift dugout and shakes his head. "These are two of our best heavy hitters." Rizzo says to some of the spectators. Beverly takes a swing.

As her bat aligns with the ball, the tall and heavy young lady takes off. She makes second base. "Safe." Says Jamal. Her fellow teammates and the others all clap.

"Looking good!" Ivan nodded. "We've got em." "You're next Pam." Says Thomas.

Pamela on all counts favors her sister to a "T." Same facial features, braided hair (shoulder length) ebony skin and so on. While one sibling wears glasses, the other employs contacts. Pam, Beverly's junior by only one year steps up to the plate.

Fusion sends her a fly ball. Swinging the bat, Pamela misses. "That's your first strike Pam." Alfred announces. "Don't let em take you under girl!" She smiles.

Throwing her a curve, Pam this time hits the ball; but however it is declared a foul. Repositioning herself, the young lady dispatches the ball directly across the lagoon.

Stealing second and then third, Pamela returns home. Beverly who is already behind the fence, gives her a high five. The rest of the team followed suit. Both girls sweat profusely.

However, their scent tells a different story. “Somebody smells good out here.” Says Ivan. Both Beverly and Pam smiled. “Its the both of us.” Beverly explains.

“Magot Etro is our brand.” Ivan, Rizzo, and Alfred all nodded. “It smells really good.” Ivan tells them. “Thanks.” Says Pam. Taking out a bottle of Gatorade, he takes a long sip and towels his hair dry. The latter is naturally slicked back.

Reaching into his bag, Ivan summons two more bottles. “These are for you.” He tells them.” “Thanks, you’re so sweet.” Says Beverly. Both siblings accept his drinks.

“I do my best.” He tells them. “Not bad.” Pamela began. “Its rare that you will find someone, who is both cute and sweet.” Agreeing with her sister, Beverly nods.

Ivan meanwhile returns to the plate.

10

Driving his 1984 Buick Park Avenue south on Homan Avenue, Jamal Montgomery makes a right on Congress Parkway. Reaching the access ramp, he is now on the Eisenhower. As he makes the appropriate lane changes, the young motorist works his way among dozens of other vehicles. Steering clear of the much larger rigs, Jamal also keeps his distance from those who are obviously indecisive. For example: the ancient beetle (Volkswagen) in front of him. While cutting off another driver, the unidentified woman without warning is changing lanes. "I value my life." He tells the others.

Riding with him shotgun is Rizzo. Ivan, Thomas and Alfred are sitting in the back.

"Let me get away from her." Jamal chuckles. Another driver gives him the right a away. "Driving is a straight up privilege." He reminds his passengers.

The boys all nodded. "You ain't just doing it for you, you're really driving for everybody else out here too." Ivan smiled. "What did you say Jamal?" He says. "Its not a racing game?" "Straight up." Jamal responded. "The insurance is no joke either."

"For a younger person, its expensive as hell." "And don't have a accident." "Because it only goes up." Rizzo finished. "Thank you." Says his cousin. "I think its cheaper for older people." Says Alfred. "It is." Thomas added. "Because a lot of them are less likely to have an accident." "Or to say the least, they're less likely to cause one."

Crossing the underpass at Cicero Avenue, the boys all continue west.

Surrounding them is a multitude of industries. The Illinois Department of Motor Vehicles complex is to the left. At this point, the expressway now becomes elevated.

Passing along a series of row houses, bungalows, and three flats parallel to what is now Flournoy Street, Jamal, Rizzo, Ivan and the others now reach Central Avenue.

To their left Loretto Hospital, the landmark (Byzantine-style) Assumption Church, and Columbus Park are seen. An existing factory is spotted to their right.

Venturing beyond the city limits at Austin Boulevard, Jamal and the others now enter the village of Oak Park. Alfred, Rizzo and Thomas turn to Ivan. "So Ivan, I see you have like a growing fan club with the girls these days." Rizzo began.

"Word?" Jamal asked. "Word." Rizzo Confirms. "On my momma cuz."

"Given your overall gesture with the Johnson's, yeah I can believe it." Jamal continues on. His eyes are still on the road. "Givin' them Gatorade and shit." He chuckles.

"Your boy is aight with me Riz." "I think Crystal, although she didn't holler was checking you out too Ivan." Jamal added. "She might appear rough on the outside a little, but Crystal still has a cute face". Rizzo breaks it down. "And a nice shape too."

"She's a tomboy." Jamal reminded his cousin. "Right." Rizzo nods. "Damn."

"But it ain't like she's on the other team, if you know what I'm saying." Jamal goes on. "Crystal is kinda private as to who she talks to." "In other words, if we was to stick around for a little bit longer after the game." "And you were like by yourself, she would definitely come after you." "Crystal doesn't take no shit either." Rizzo tells Ivan.

"I heard that some other girl in her school was stupid enough to pick a fight with her, on the account that she felt like it." Jamal comes back. "Ol' girl slaps Crystal right?"

Ivan and the others nod. "Crystal beat her ass like a piñata!" They all laughed.

"Ol' girl, the one Crystal fucked up; was shitting in diapers for atleast a month."

"Somebody else told me, like her uncle or some man tried to molest her, and Crystal took a letter opener and revoked his manhood." "Dude still got his ass whooped by her brothers, and the judge threw the book at em." "Ten years." Jamal nods. Rizzo chuckled.

"He should have no asshole by now." He says. "Sick assed perverted fuck."

"Which takes me to the Johnson sisters." Jamal continues to drive. He briefly looks at his overhead mirror. "Beverly and Pam are really nice." "They're down to Earth."

"They're cool." "And as you already know, they like to smell good." "They always do." "Considering they on the chunky side a little." "Size doesn't matter to me all that much Jamal." Says Ivan. "Because a lot of big girls, on both counts have the best personalities." "They have great sense of humor, high on self esteem, and they're more outspoken." Rizzo, Alfred, and Thomas nodded. "Yeah, he's right about that."

Says Thomas. "Its even rumored that they give good pussy." Alfred and the others nodded. "Now let's talk about the girls who are already fully developed or smaller."

Ivan began to point out. "A lot of their personalities are the exact opposite as opposed to their larger counterparts." Jamal laughed. "Man, who the hell are you?" He asks.

"The male version of Doctor Ruth?" "Hey, its true Jamal." Thomas supports Ivan's thesis. "A lot of regular healthy females or those who are just slim are vein and straight nasty as hell." "Or better yet, bitchy, stuck up, or in some cases conniving." Rizzo adds.

"And its not a laughing matter either." Alfred pointed out. "Its nothing wrong with playing hard to get at times, but some girls and some woman, they tend take it too far."

"Especially in our culture." Ivan added. "And they wonder why a lot of brothers are passing them up for women of other groups." "It is what it is y'all."

"Word." Says the others. "Boys and men, we need love just like they do." Ivan breaks it down. "Its not just one side alone." "Amen." Jamal says jokingly. But he understood.

So did the rest of the group. They nod their heads. "Some girls really believe that they are God's gift to the male gender." Thomas Sighed. "The same with guys who favors the opposite." "Straight up." Rizzo added. "The reason why I say that Ivan has a growing fan club with the girls." He began. "Is because there are these two others."

"They are actually closer to where me and Alfred lives." He explains to Jamal.

"Named Cassandra and Justine." "Then there's my aunt, she's two years ahead of him, a high school sophomore, and then there's this girl who lives two doors down from Ivan."

"The latter he very much has already Jamal." Listening to his cousin, Jamal nods.

"She has the brains, the personality, and last but not least, the body."

"Straight up?" Jamal asked. He then smiles. "Go ahead man." He tells Ivan.

Without turning his head, Jamal gives him a pound.

Crossing the Harlem Avenue underpass to the left, is the world's famous Ferrara Pan candy factory. Home of the Lemonheads, the Jawbreakers, and the Boston baked beans; one can definitely smell the latter as they enter or exit the highway.

After Oak Park, comes the next suburb. Forest Park.

With a blend of large frame, Victorian, Queen Anne, and Chicago-style bungalows seen to the right, the Ivan and the others, chauffeured by Jamal passes the arena-like Des Plaines Transit Center. Located on Des Plaines Avenue, this building is the final stop for the O'Hare Congress line. Its adjoining yard and repair shop houses three generations of railcars.

Among them, are the red, white, and blue 2600's, the silver stainless steel 2200's and surprisingly a modest number of St Louis-built 6000's still exist.

The latter, built during the 1950's , are no longer in revenue service at this point.

Bearing a yellow color scheme, as opposed to the modern-day Spirit of Chicago or better yet, its original alpine white and green, these cars today are only used as work motors. Parked along the shoulder of the left lane, they appear to have been tagged.

Or in laymen's terms, vandalized.

The Des Plaines River sits along the western edge. Two cemeteries(Forest Home and Waldenheim) now cover both sides of the highway. A Commonwealth Edison sub-station, and corporate office is to the left.

At First Avenue, the boys now enter the village of Maywood.

The further west they travel, the greener, the quieter.

Hillside, Illinois (Cook County)

Located 14 miles west of downtown Chicago, this suburb occupies a network of expressways serving the Chicago region. Interstate 290(the Eisenhower) cuts through the village from the east, with Interstate 294 and the 290 extension near Hillside's northwestern boundary. Providing access, but at the same time dividing the suburb into distinct sections, the expressways (and earlier the railroads) contributed considerably to Hillside's development. Settlement began in earnest in the 1840's as German Lutheran immigrants established farms and built the first school and church (Immanuel) at the corner of Wolf Road and 22nd Street. Even though most of Hillside's later development was north of 12th Street, Immanuel Lutheran Church and school were included within the village limits , giving Hillside its distinctive shape.

Although farming was the major occupation in the 1850's, Marion Covell discovered a large deposit of limestone just a few feet below the surface of the property.

The quarry that he began in 1854 continued to operate until as recently as the mid-1970's, crushed stone for road building throughout the Chicago region. Against wishes of most village residents, the quarry was acquired by the John Sexton Company in 1979 and used as a sanitary landfill. Beginning with Mount Carmel in 1894, followed by Oak Ridge, Glen Oak, and finally Queen of Heaven in 1947, these cemeteries also replaced active farmland just outside of town on its western and southern boundaries.

Accessible from a station on the Illinois Central Railroad and from a spur of the Chicago, Aurora, and Elgin interurban that followed 12th Street (Roosevelt Road), the cemeteries prompted the establishment of taverns, restaurants, monument companies, greenhouses, and floral shops. The village was incorporated in 1905, adopting its name from the Illinois Central Railroad stop, which was called Hillside because the westbound trains had to go uphill at this point. The 1920's saw the first concentrated residential development in the village as more farmland was sold and subdivided.

St. Domitilla Roman Catholic Church and the Mater Dolorosa Seminary bought extensive properties here in the 1920's. Surrounded by open land for a time, these institutions were engulfed in a sea of residential construction after World War II as the local population doubled (from 1, 080 to 2, 131) from 1940 to 1950, then jumped to 7,794 in 1960. By 1980, it was down by only ten percent. (7, 694)

Hillside Mall

Adjacent to the Eisenhower Expressway, this shopping center was completed in 1956.

Surrounded by a Holiday Inn, the M&R-Loews operated Hillside Cinemas, a bowling alley, the High Point Tower office complex and a network of retail shops, an industrial park is located on Fencl Lane. Jamal exits the highway here.

In its heyday before larger malls became the usual norm, the thirty-three year-old complex was once a regional center. Although a recent facelift has failed to retain its star tenants, the shopping center still soldiers on with its namesake theaters.

Originally housing four cinemas when it opened, a deal was later struck with Loews-M&R Theaters to least additional space in the mall. As a result, a newer cinema complex is built bringing the total number to eight. Among some of the titles are Cyborg, Disorganized Crime, Scandal, Say Anything, Field Of Dreams and Criminal Law.

Accepting their tickets for the movie Cyborg, Ivan, Rizzo, Jamal and the others enters the lobby.

East Lawndale

On the corner of California and Flournoy, Jamal pulls up to drop off Rizzo and his friends. "Thanks for hooking us up Jamal." Rizzo says to his cousin.

"That was a good assed movie." Ivan adds. "No problem man." Says Jamal.

"So what you plan on doing now?" Alfred asked. "Well I've gotta head back and get some sleep." Jamal explains. "Got to start work early." "Need all of the overtime I can get before next week." "That's right school starts back." Thomas remembers.

"What about y'all?" Jamal asked. "You all have the rest of the week to enjoy yourselves." "Well we're just gonna hang out at my crib for a little longer and just call it a night." Rizzo answers. " I would." Jamal yawns. All of the boys gave him a pound.

"Tell the rest of the family, I said hi." Jamal tells Rizzo. "Aight, bet." Says Riz.

Jamal is employed as assistant lab technician at a local eye center in Lincoln Park.

After school, he repairs glasses and aids the head technician in placing special orders.

Considering that its often part time on the account of his classroom schedules, as well as his football games, Jamal with the blessings of the shop's owner and as well as the head tech, is sometimes allowed to work at home. Shortly after Jamal takes off, his cousin joined by Ivan, Alfred and Thomas all began crossing the street.

Walking down a bright-lit alley, with Ivan leading the pack, two masked gunmen around the next corner surprised them. "Y'all know what time it is!" Says one of them.

"Nobody move, gives us everything or whatever you got." Almost unfazed, Ivan and the others first looks at one another. Turning to face the jacks once more, armed with their thirty-eights, Ivan pretends to surrender. "Y'all make this easy." He says.

Tickled by Ivan's comment, the other robber chuckles. At the blink of an eye, Ivan disarms the first robber! Snapping a left hook kick around the leader's left hand, Ivan collects his gun, and throws it to the ground. Yanking off his mask, Ivan becomes furious. The unidentified young man, somewhere in his late teens, suddenly wants to be their friend. He smiles. "Hey little homey look----- Ivan gives him a palm strike to the face. The leader is out cold. "Fuck you, you little pussy assed nigga!" Says his partner.

Still pointing his gun at Ivan, the second jack now employs his trigger finger.

Repeatedly cocking the barrel, the lanky figure (still wearing his mask) is obviously nervous. In a cold sweat, he shakes and trembles. The others acting as a decoy, attempts to disarm him. Rizzo, Alfred, and Thomas slowly advance. "Get, get, get, get back!"

He demands. The boys, who are actually somewhat nervous, did what they were told.

Turning back to Ivan, he catches a rude awakening.

Ivan snaps an outside crescent kick. As a result, the older teen loses his sidearm.

Situated in his fighting stance, Ivan delivers a double sidekick. As the sole of his left Nike is deployed into abs of his opponent followed by his left jaw, Ivan then spins and delivers a rear-leg crescent kick. As the blood and saliva sprays from his mouth, the assistant robber falls to the ground. He too is out. Ivan returns to his fighting stance.

Removing the mask of his second opponent, Ivan spits on him.

"So who's the pussy assed nigga now?" He says to the knocked out gunmen.
"That's what you get for playing with guns."
Alfred, Rizzo, and Thomas are now in shock.

"Are you three alright?" "You straight?" The boys slowly nodded.

Ivan bows to his enemies. Picking up their guns, he empties the barrels.

Each hollow point shell, including those in the chambers are now removed.

Throwing the guns into a nearby dumpster, Ivan and the others take off.

However, the real action has only begun.

"Where the fuck y'all going?" A tall muscular youth barks.

Sporting dreadlocks and a bald fade, the young man wore a white tank top, baggy jeans, and black work boots. In his left hand, he holds a wooden bat.

Behind him is an army of roughly fifth teen to twenty hoods, all carrying melee weapons. Turning around, Ivan discovers another group closing in.

"Apparently they have some questions for us." Rizzo chuckled.
"Well, let's answer them." Says Ivan. He gives his friends a nod.
"This is not a drill." Says Thomas.

While Ivan and Rizzo focus their attention on the group before them, Thomas and Alfred face the other. All four are now in their fighting stances.

The first five who rushes in, Ivan snaps two axe kicks (left and right) across the head to one, stops another with a left front kick (sole to abdomen), turns around and delivers a spinning hook kick to another, and executes a double left side kick into the fourth enemy.

Foot sweeping his fifth opponent, Ivan comes in with a double jab as both hands penetrates the sternum as well as the chest. Parrying away the punches of a sixth rival, Ivan now, with both hands parries his opponent's arms from the inside out.

An example of what is believed to be the Wing Chun, Ivan strikes the sternum with a second blow, followed by a right to the throat. At this point, the opposing youth spits out blood. Now executing two tiger claws to both sides of the temple, Ivan's latest enemy collapses. Rizzo, who employs his boxing skills is also on fire.

Knocking out one hood after the other, he drives his knees into the fourth enemy and gives an uppercut to a fifth. Hip tossing another, Riz remains in his fighting stance.

Rocking on the balls of his feet, he bobs and then weaves. Snapping a left jab and then a right cross, Rizzo delivers a murderous left hook. Executing a right cross and then another left hook, the talented young boxer delivers body shots. Cutting across the ribs, the kidneys and the abdomen, Rizzo delivers two knees. With a clothesline to the neck, he comes in with his right foot and knocks his prey off balance.

The unidentified youth is out!

Alfred, who is a student under his god brother Ernest, employs his Kick boxing skills.

Deploying elbow after elbow across the faces of his opposition comes the sound of dislocated bones. Snapping a combination of multiple kicks ranging from roundhouses, to crescents, hooks, axes and more of the like, Alfred initiates several throws, parries, blocks and knees. Delivering a left jab and a right cross to his eighth opponent, the husky youngster comes around with a left back fist. Employing another back fist to a ninth, Alfred crosses his left leg behind his right and snaps a powerful sidekick to the tenth.

Dispatching a broomstick, Thomas breaks it in half.

He now has a pair of makeshift Kali sticks.

Already in his stance, the resourceful fighter employs a six-count. Repelling each and every attack delivered by his opposition, namely their weapons, Thomas takes no prisoners. With the execution of each angle comes agonizing strikes. Spinning around, a much taller fighter catches one across the face.

A black van pulls up seconds later.

With both doors sliding open, comes more youths.

However unlike their predecessors, who were hell-bent on destroying Ivan as well as the others, are here for the opposite. They have come to help.

Like that of Ivan and the others, they too are trained in the martial arts. With the employment of Kali sticks, Bo Staffs, numb chucks, and stainless steel darts, they assist the visiting team. "I'll be damned." Says Alfred as he faces another young man.

The gentleman emerging from the van's driver's side is none other than Ernest Blackwell. He smiles and then waves. From moment he steps out the vehicle, two hoods rush in. Dispatching his right elbow onto the head of one, Ernest snaps a double round house into the other. Stomach to face. The opposing leader is dumfounded.

At this time, the big youth attempts to quietly walk away. Turning to face the north, Ivan now confronts him. "How about a little exhibition?" He says.

The ringleader smiled. “Let’s do this.” He says. “Right this way.” Ivan points toward the park. About a half hour later, the mobs finally disperse. Limping, hopping and running, only the badly wounded are left behind. The streets remain littered with bodies.

All of which are still alive. Surprisingly.

Atgeld Park

Pounding their fists like true warriors, both Ivan and his opponent known only as “Mack Truck” comes out fighting. In the green space where Ivan and his friends played football earlier, is now their private arena. Dancing on the balls of his feet, Mack throws jab after jab. Cross-after cross. Combining all of his punches with his guards up, Ivan first dodges to the left and then to the right. Grabbing Mack’s wrist, Ivan plants his left foot behind his calf and sweeps him off balance. The slightly taller young man falls.

Getting up, Mack shakes it off. However, his ego remains shattered.

Executing more combinations, Ivan blocks, and then parries.

As the park lights shine, Ivan discovers an opening. In one motion, he delivers three back fists. Attacking the sternum, Ivan then strikes the throat, followed by Mack’s face.

The big man now bleeds from the lower lip, as well as the inside of his mouth. Snapping a right side kick, Ivan then combines it with an immediate hook kick to the jaw, as well as the face. Spinning around, comes a rear-leg roundhouse. The latter this time connects to Mack’s left jaw.

Breathing and huffing, Mack himself is furious.

Coming back, he returns three punches across Ivan’s face. Jab-cross-hook. Ivan is unfazed as he now cracks his neck. He feels no pain.

Snapping a crescent kick, both in and out, Ivan throttles Mack with a spinning rear-leg crescent. Executing a jab-cross of his own, Ivan jumps up and delivers a flying crescent.

Rocking on the balls of his feet, the talented young artist snaps two single jabs.

Maintaining his rhythm, Ivan snaps two more across Mack's face.

Delivering two more, he combines them with two right crosses. Applying them all at once, Ivan snaps an uppercut. Delivering one knee after the other, Ivan snaps a left roundhouse. Bending his left knee backwards, Ivan snaps the heel of his foot into Mack's face. For the second time, the big man falls into the grass. The left side of Mack's face is now swollen. Getting up for the second time, Mack storms after Ivan.

Executing a hip toss, Ivan maintains his grip on Mack's left arm.

Crossing his legs around the arm of his opponent, Ivan sits back and applies leverage.

Mack's arm is dislocated. He howls.

11

EAST LAWNDALE

As the 10:00 hour nears, the area particularly east of California is still hot following the latest melee. Meanwhile several CPD units remain parked on both sides of Washtenaw as their blue lights continue to flash. On Flournoy, E.H.S vehicles flashing their red and white lights are also parked. Dispatching neck braces, stretchers, and Intravenous tubes, the paramedics are summoned to retrieve the wounded thugs.

Their friends, especially those who were still able bodied had long fled.

Meanwhile detectives on the scene are working to acquire whatever information they can from local eyewitnesses. In the alley nearby, the would-be robbers are now accounted for. Advised of their rights, the dumbfounded and beat up offenders are handcuffed and placed in one of the vehicles. A plain-clothes officer confiscates the two thirty-eights from a dumpster nearby, while another (in uniform) collects their masks.

All through traffic along Flournoy, has been (temporarily) redirected east of California via Harrison. Amongst the dozens of onlookers on the twenty-seven hundred block of Flournoy in the heat of the night (no relation to the TV drama), the parents of the youngsters who foiled their would be "jackers" are already concerned.

Wallace Residence (The front porch)

"Have any of you heard from the boys this evening?" Ms. Campbell asked Alfred's mom. "Your guess is just as good as mine Annie." Says Ms. Miller.

Jacqueline Moore, Thomas Moore's mother, joins them as well. Those who are yet to be seen although they are not would be Mr. and Mrs. Thompson.

"Rizzo's cousin called me an hour ago, saying that he dropped Riz and the boys off at the corner." Ms. Campbell went on. The other three ladies nodded.

"I called Frank and Marie, explaining what had happened down here and they haven't heard from Ivan since he and the others left the theater." Ms. Wallace adds.

She smiled. "But for some reason, they weren't as worried."

"Could you blame them?" Asked Ms. Campbell.

The Powell brothers, who are now on their porch laugh, points and whistles as the paramedics continue to place the injured into their vehicles.

Many other pedestrians, mostly young males and a few females, all follow suit.

"What the fuck happened to them?" One of the youngsters asks. "Besides the fact that they got they Asses whopped."

"This is an onslaught." Says Ms. Moore.

"Who could have done all of this?" She says chuckling.

It is almost as though Thomas's mother is impressed. "I wouldn't be surprised if Ivan had something to do with this." Says Ms. Campbell.

"I agree." Ms. Miller supports her neighbor's case.

"Rizzo told me about the situation at the "Y" back in February."

"What happened?" Asked Ms. Moore.

"Some gangbangers tried to mess with Ivan, Nikki, and some others, and he snapped off Florence." Ms. Campbell explains. "Snapped off how?"

"Ivan took em all down, every single one of them." Ms. Miller added.

"Hell, he even knocked the leader on his ass."

"Some time last year, Ivan's parents enrolled him in a martial arts school." Ms. Campbell reminds Ms. Moore. "Ivan is really good at what he does."

"Although its been only one year, Ivan has changed a lot." Ms. Wallace pointed out.

"Both mentally and physically."

"You're absolutely right." Ms. Moore remembers.

"He used to be all plump, somewhat timid and mildly soft spoken."

"Now look at em." Says Mrs. Campbell.

"Not only is Ivan still respectful and considerate, but he is now dead handsome."

Ms. Wallace laughed. "I even see Keisha checking him out now."

"And she thinks I don't know."

"I would bet my next paycheck that Ivan was involved in this, even if it wasn't him directly." Says Ms. Wallace. "All of the boys can fight." Ms. Moore pointed out.

" Ivan was the one who taught Thomas what he knows, Alfred's god brother taught him kickboxing, and Rizzo does boxing up at the park." She continues on.

"Even though they're all great fighters, neither of them can catch bullets with their teeth." "You can say that again, given that the police picked up two older boys in the alley." Ms. Miller added. "They tried to stick somebody up, and got the shit kicked out of them." The other ladies laugh. "I'm sure they're around here somewhere."

"The boys are okay, I'm sure of it." Says Ms. Campbell.

"They're probably at Ernie's." Ms. Miller added.

"Let's hope so." Says Ms. Moore.

Before the latter could even ask her neighbor, Ms. Wallace hands her the phone.

"Whoever's responsible for this vicious assault, had done the entire community a favor." Ms. Miller chuckles. Ms. Campbell, Ms. Moore, and Ms. Wallace nodded.

"This isn't some Kung Fu flick with the poorly dubbed English." Ms. Moore snaps.

"Somebody really did a number on these hoods."

"And if it wasn't the work of one, I'm sure it was more."

Completing her phone call, Ms. Miller hands Ms. Wallace the receiver.

With the riff-raff immediately disposed of thanks to Ivan and his allies, among them is Ernest Blackwell. Joined by his dojo brothers, they now tend to the man of the evening.

Atgeld Park

Entering the confines, they all spot Ivan. Snapping his opponent's arm back into place, the now merciful victor shakes his hand. Returning the wooden bat to its rightful owner, namely Mack Truck himself Ivan bows his head.

Limping in the opposite direction, Mack walks off into the night.

"Are you alright Master Splinter?" Ernest asks.

The others including Alfred, Riz, and Thomas all smiled.

"Yeah, thanks." Says Ivan. He sighs and then laughs.

"I could have very well ended his life tonight."

"Oh, we know." Thomas nods. "That was one of the two reasons, we rushed over." Ernest assured him. "Damn, I'm surprised that your parents didn't register your ass with the state." "You're a goddamned lethal weapon." "Fuck Mel Gibson's, Martin Riggs."

"There's rumors spreading about you all round the west side now."

"You're like a myth."

"People hear about you, but most of them don't know who you really are."

Ivan chuckles. "You know, I've learned something tonight." He began.

"Sometimes, it pays to have at least a little bit of mercy." The others nod.

"Because every now and then, you too will want some."

"If you always beat someone senseless, they're less likely to learn something."

"He never lied about that." Says one of Ernest's friends.

"And eventually." Ivan went on. "To have such a reputation can destroy you."

"And of course, if you're not careful, even the most fearful individual or individuals can kill you." "And as they say." Ivan concludes. "The true art of fighting, unless the circumstances are really dire, is not to." "Word, straight up." The others reply.

Now on the front steps of the field house, the boys all hop into Ernie's van.

Blackwell Residence

Located on the twenty-nine hundred block of west Lexington Street, is where Ernest Blackwell lives. Born into a family of five Ernest Nicholas Blackwell, is second to the oldest. His brother Joshua, a newly hired C.I.A. operative now lives in Virginia.

He is twenty-one years old. Harold, his slightly younger brother is sixteen. A junior at Whitney Young high school, Harold like his brother is also academically inclined, and he holds a green belt in Shotokan Karate. His two sisters Lisa and Lana are both in the fifth grade. A family portrait hangs on the wall in the living room.

Furthermore, Ernest like Ivan still has both of his parents. Mr. and Mrs. Blackwell have been married for eighteen years. His mother works an interior decorator. His father has his own tailor shop on the near west side. Having dropped his buddies off, the responsible youngster returns to his family's two flat. This block is virtually safe in comparison to the surrounding area. Thanks in part to an effective block club.

Nearly all of the homes are well kept, lawns manicured. The housing stock consists of mostly brick two flats, two story greystones, a few single frames and one ranch.

A lone burned out tenement sits on the next corner.

Charred and boarded up, the smell of burned wood indicates a more recent fire.

Among Ernie's guests are Alfred, Rizzo, Thomas, and last but not least Ivan.

The time is now 10:30 as they all sit in the living room.

Meanwhile, his sisters along with Mr. and Mrs. Blackwell remain out front. His brother on the other hand, works the NES in his room.

"You know given your various fighting styles, you all looked really good tonight." The host began. "I'm more than impressed." "I'm proud of you." "Including my protégé."

Ernest now turns to Alfred. "Alfred man, you've come a very long way since we've met." "That's one of the many reasons why you learn to fight." Ernest breaks it down to his guests. "I'm going to the kitchen for some tea." He then announces.

"Who's down?" The others all raised their hands. "Cool." "You could have served those fools by yourselves out there." Ernest hollered behind a set of wooden double doors. "That's how good you guys are today." "Lorenzo, me and the others were just your backup." "Thanks for looking out Ernest." Says Ivan. Ernest returns with a tray six minutes later. "No problem man, that's what friends are for." The boys grabbed their cups. "Damn, this is strong." Says Alfred. He slowly sips. "Its herbal." Ivan tells him.

"For something like this to taste so bitter, you'd swear its potent." Rizzo added.

"Oh, it is Rizzo." Ernest explains. "Trust me." "I think it improves your sex drive." Ivan added. "It does." Ernest backs him up." "The hell you know about that?"

The others laughed. "My girlfriend reminds me each and every time before we do the nasty to drink some." "So how did you know those hoods were going to ambush us?" Ivan asked. "Because we sure as hell didn't." "Yeah, word Ernie." Thomas steps in. He sets his cup on the table. "At first, the two dudes tried to stick us up in the alley."

"Ivan disarmed him, I mean he hooked his left foot around the guy's hand, snatched his gun, threw it down and yanked off his mask." "And this wasn't funny man." Alfred reminds his god brother. "All we had to do was make one false move." Rizzo added.

"Let alone, one false move." "We would have made the 10:00 news." Says Thomas.

"After I snatched off the guy's mask, and took his sidearm he all of a sudden wanted to be our friend. Ernest chuckles. "He knew he was goin down, and tried to butter you up." "And he really made me sick." Ivan comes back. "I knocked his ignorant ass out."

"His boy tried to act all hard." Thomas began now sipping his last drop.

"But he was still scared, forget being nervous."

"Ol' boy tried to shoot Ivan, he was shaking, already losing his aim."

"Don't get me wrong Ernest, we were a little nervous too."

The host nodded. "Yeah, dude could've canceled y'all." He shakes his head.

"We acted as decoys, tried to distract him from blowing Ivan away…

" And it worked." Ivan reminded him.

"Ol' boy turned back around, I kicked the gun out of his hand, he looked like an idiot, then I knocked him out!" "It sounds to me, like you performed some fancy footwork Ivan." Says Ernest. "Ivan yanked off his mask, spit on him, took both of their guns and we walked off." Rizzo concluded. "Mack Truck came into the picture, talking mess, asking us where we going." "The next thing we knew forty more guys showed up, like we killed Sirus." Everybody including Ernest all laughed.

"Before we knew it, we ended up tearing them apart, then you Lorenzo, Angel, and the others showed up." "As you already knew, I engaged Mack Truck at the park, and won." "I dusted him off and sent him home." "Which really was noble of you Ivan." Ernest commends him. Ivan finally finishes his tea. The host faces his guests with only mild disdain. "You know you all could have been killed out there tonight."

"That's true." Says Ivan. "But we didn't." Ernest happily nodded.

"Well because you all fought so well, I ain't gonna ride you on it."

"As to how I knew about the ambush in the first place." Ernest began sipping the remains of his tea. "I didn't." "I just had a hunch." His god brother and the others nodded. "I remember these two dudes from work, it was like they were casing the store,

like they wanted hit it." "Mo kept telling them that they had to buy something, and they just left." "They could have been casing the entire strip." Rizzo adds.

"About a quarter to nine, after me and Mo closed shop, these same two guys started hanging out by the gas station next door, this time like they were waiting for something or somebody." "Other store owners have been complaining too."

"I believe you." Says Ivan. "Except they were unmasked." Ernest added.

"Sir George wasn't playing with them either." "What?" Asked Rizzo.

He is surprised. "They had the nerve to try to hang out in front of his lounge, try to sneak in with fake I.D's. and one of his guards scared the hell out of em."

"Right after we closed shop, and Mo left, I called up Lorenzo, Angel, Dion, and the others and we all met up in Jew Town." Ernest continues to narrate.

"We all headed back this way and found you guys."

Before Ernest could finish, the phone rings.

He picks up the receiver. "Hello?" "Yeah Rachel, they're here."

"Alright, you're welcome." "Ok, bye." He hangs up.

"Your parents just wanted to know where you guys are, that's all."

"And your mother and father asked me to drop you off Ivan."

"In about five minutes, I'm taking everybody home anyway." He yawns.

He checks his watch.

Chicago Police Headquarters Area 4
Wednesday, 10:00 am

Having enjoyed their "choke" meal consisting of a dry bologna sandwich, a small bag of Fritos, Jell-O, and a carton of low fat milk, Eli Collins and his friend Rodney Hampton both seventeen now brace themselves for the trip south. Cook County Jail.

It has been a full twenty-four hours since their stay in lockup. Since then the two would-be stick up artists have been booked, fingerprinted, and placed in a holding cell.

However, they are not alone.

Among them are dozens of other prisoners. Within the confines of this "human kennel", the occupants are to use only one toilet. A metal commode sits in the opposite corner. Many benches are employed, as well as that of one public phone.

For the majority of the males who occupied this large cell, it was as though they were still on the outside. They laughed, they joked, played cards, and even smoked cigarettes.

An older gentleman sits alone in one corner, reading a novel.

A scuffle breaks out between two others, but is quickly stopped by a patrolling uniform. Without entering the cell, the senior officer issues a warning.

Both Eli and Rodney are seated in the back.

"Them Lil' niggas was already onto us." Eli began. Still disgusted and dumbfounded, Rodney nodded. "Word E." He says. "You mean to tell me that these mothafuckas actually knew other mothafuckas?" "Shit!" "They served everybody who was wit us."

"That shit ain't normal, straight up." Says Eli.

"Especially with that Chinese looking dude." He went on.

"The last thing I remember, I told em all to give us everything or whatever they got, and the little nigga snatched my piece with his left foot."

"And they know who we are now."

"He knocked us out." Rodney holds his head.

"Ol' boy went Enter The Dragon on us."

"We good as fucked."

"I wouldn't be surprised if we saw they Asses in court." "Again."

"Word, I KNOW the judge is gonna throw the book at us." Eli sighed.

"Even if it is our first offense."

"Nobody's comin for us man."

"We ain't leavin no time soon."

"Word." Says Rodney.

"We need a public defender, just to get a goddamned plea."

"Face it E."

"We goin to 26th and California."

"It ain't no more 1100 s. Hamilton."
"We goin to a real joint this time."
"Bread and water nigga."
"Soap on a rope."
"Our momma's don't give a fuck about us."

A minute later, a blue uniform approaches the cell. "Eli Collins and Rodney Hampton?" The boys are appalled. "Who wants to know?" Asked Rodney.

Unlocking the gate, the burly officer motions them to come forward. "You're out on bail." He announces. Eli chuckles nervously. "Come on man stop playin." He says.

"I'm afraid not sir." The guard assures him. He smiled. "Let's go."

A sigh of relief is upon Rodney as he also smiled.
"Guess you heard em E."
"We out, let's go."

With his right hand focused on his revolver, the officer re-locks the gate.

"Walking out the stationhouse with their personal belongings in a plastic bag, namely their shoe laces, belts, wallets and so on, both Collins and Hampton are yet still puzzled as to who bailed them out. Perhaps a mysterious gentleman clad in a black suit, can now tell them. "My boss wants to see you." He says. "He has a business proposition for you."

A black Rolls Royce is parked in front of the precinct.

Collins and Hampton briefly turn to one another. "Damn!" Eli began.

"It can't get no better than this." Says Rodney. He smiled once more.

"One minute, we damn near on a prison bus, another minute some nigga, looking like the black assed Godfather wanna give us a job."

"Let's do this." They both said in unison. Giving each other a pound (a handshake), the boys follow the gentleman. Opening the rear door of the Royce, Eli and Rodney jumped in.

Dan Ryan Forest Preserve, 9:45pm (Far southwest side)

In a wooded area around 87th Street and South Western Avenue between Chicago's North Beverly neighborhood and a suburban village known as Evergreen Park, nineteen-year-old Kevin O'Hara and his girlfriend seventeen-year-old Natalie Foster, enjoys what would have been an intimate moment. Playing a love game of hide-and-go-seek, the two obvious lovebirds pursues one another through the seemingly pitch black forest.

Canvassing through the terrain with flashlights, the two surprises one another. They began to kiss slowly. "Are you covered?" Asked Natalie. Kevin smiled. "Always." He says. Reaching into his pocket, Kevin produces four Trojan-made condoms.

Natalie smiled back. "Yes, you are." She then whispers.

Slowly sucking away at his earlobe, Kevin picks up Natalie.

As the French kissing continues, Nat's legs are now wrapped around Kevin's waist.

Hiking up her skirt, Kevin takes Natalie into the bushes.

A blanket is already in place as Kevin lowers her short, but yet healthy frame.

As Natalie unbuckles her boyfriend's belt, Kevin, on the other hand removes her panties. Under the moon, while their flashlights still burn, Kevin and Natalie are ready to make out. "Shit." Kevin whispers. "What is it sweetie?" Natalie asked.

"I've got to take a leak." "Ok, then hurry back." She smiles once more.

"We don't have all night out here."

"You think?" Says Kevin.

"Nature calls."

Retreating to another set of bushes, Kevin makes water.

However, as he does the young man makes a grizzly discovery.

"Jesus Christ." He whispered. Kevin's face is now pale.

He runs back to his girlfriend.

Lying on her back, with her skirt high above her waist, legs spread wide, Natalie looks up at her man and grins. "Are you ready Mr. Director?" She says.

"I was." He chuckles nervously.

"It's gonna have to be a rain check Nat."

Natalie is no longer smiling. "Are you ok?" She asks.

"You look like you've seen a ghost."

"Something like that, I'll explain when we get to the car."

"In the meantime, let's get the hell out of here."

Taking his girlfriend by the hand as she fixed her skirt, the two began to run.

At the sight where Kevin began to urinate, were the two bodies of both Eli Collins and Rodney Hampton. Shot in the head at close range, both youths appeared to have been tortured and maimed. With his eyes wide open even in death, Rodney now stares at nothing. Eli, on the other hand appears peaceful. His eyes are closed. Both bodies are now cold. Stiff. The rigamortis has already set in.

12

JENSEN SCHOLASTIC ACADEMY, MONDAY

After an exciting, glorious, and adventurous week of fun in the sun, for Ivan and his friend's classes are now back in session. Each year particularly around this time, many elementary schools across the nation (including this one), will give to its students what is known as the Iowa Test. For grades Kindergarten through eighth, the latter provides a comprehensive assessment of progress among students in subjects such as Reading, Math and others in between.

Room 403

Not too long after Mrs. Holmes and Mrs. Cobbs takes the attendance, the public address system, comes to life. "Good morning, please rise and join me." Says a male voice. As the morning pledge is announced, everyone begins to stand.

Following the pre-recorded national anthems of the Star Spangled Banner, and Lift Every Voice, Mr. Rothstein, the principal welcomes everyone back.

The public announcements soon follows.

Among them is a reminder for the students (namely in the upper grades) to return their immunization forms. Following the announcement of a basketball game, Mr. Rothstein acknowledges the test. Wishing the students good luck, the P.A. system fades out. Mrs. Holmes smiled. "Well like he said, good morning everybody." She says.

"Good morning Mrs. Holmes." Her students respond.

“It’s nice to have you all back here with us.” Mrs. Cobbs added.
“Nooooo!” Says Jermaine Wilkins.

As the shortest, and perhaps not by the far the youngest in the class, Jermaine: ten-years old is the second funniest. Curtis Hawkins, a semi class bully still ranks number one. Wearing a box fade hairstyle with a shag in the back, Jermaine wears baggy blue jeans, and a pair of British Knights. (Sneakers)

The yellow T-shirt he wears has often turned heads with a lot of parents as well as staff members. The latter reads: SAME SHIT EVERYDAY.

Jermaine’s father, who actually bought him the shirt, thought it was true.

The statement that is.

Meanwhile, Jermaine’s fellow classmates as well as his teachers began to laugh.

“It’s gotta be a dream man!”

“Whatcha talking about?”

“Spring break ain’t over yet.”

Removing a safety pen from his pocket, Jermaine drives it into the palm of his hand.

He howls. For the next few minutes, the classroom becomes his audience.

They continue to laugh. “This ain’t real G, I’m still at home knocked out.”

“Hey, who got a match?”

Mrs. Holmes tries to control her laughter. "Get outta here boy." She says.

"It worked for Alice in A Nightmare on Elm Street Five." Jermaine added.

"Anyway, welcome back." Mrs. Holmes says once more.

She playfully slaps the comic in the back of his head.

"Goofy ass." The head teacher nods.

"It looks like we have a full house today." Mrs. Cobbs began. "Nobody is absent, everybody was on time." "We're definitely going to have a good day."

Mrs. Holmes now moves to the center of the room. "Let me get down to the nitty gritty." She says. "So Tamala really is a girl after all." Jermaine interrupts.

The others laughed once more. "Aight, aight." Jermaine controls himself.

Mrs. Holmes at this point is not laughing. She stares at the comic with the certainty of disdain. "Thank you." She says. Shortly thereafter, Mrs. Holmes smiled once more.

"Yo, chill Jermaine." Donnie chuckles. He shakes his head.

However Tamala Spann, Jermaine's "roastee" is far from tickled.

Although Tamala was actually nice looking, the young lady employs what is believed to be a defective gene. Presumably triggered by an irregularity involving her hormones, the otherwise physically normal twelve-year-old has a light mustache as well as other facial hairs under her chin. Behind her African and Sioux exterior, Tamala has light brown eyes. "You know what?" She began now focused on the rising comic.

"Kiss my butt Jermaine." "You are all going to seventh grade this year." Mrs. Holmes announces. The students all gave themselves a round of applause. "That's right everybody, take a bow." Says Mrs. Cobbs. "You guys deserve it, you have done a wonderful job." Ivan and Donnie gave each other a pound. "Not one person has even scored below a C." Says Mrs. Holmes. "And this is from the last two marking periods alone." "Many of you have been on the Honor Roll." "Half of you made the Certificate of Merit." To make the Honor Roll, students are required to have all A's all B's or both.

Certificate of Merit candidates are required to have both A's and B's with only a limited amount of C's. Only those who score below are excluded. "Even the so-called gifted class, Room 405 is getting a run for its money." Mrs. Cobbs added. "Yeah."

Sighs Mrs. Cobbs. "What's so gifted about them?" She asks. "I never understood that." "They ain't gifted!" Tamala blasted. "Atleast most of them, if not all of them are so phony." Says Donnie. "They so full of themselves." He goes on. "They're vain."

Denise Wilson added. "And they stab you in the back." "They're fifted."

Jermaine cracks. Mrs. Cobbs laughed. "What in the world is that?" Asked Mrs. Holmes. She chuckles. "That's what you get when you put phony and gifted together."

Jermaine breaks it down. The others laugh immediately. "The girls alone spreads more gossip than all of the STD's combined." Tamala snaps. "Including Herpes!"

"Damn, they're that bad huh?" Asked Ivan. Mrs. Holmes is laughing so hard that she nearly falls out of her seat. "You know, Tamala does have a point." Says Ivan.

"The boys on the other hand are like the Detroit Pistons, they're always looking for a fight." He grins. "Hecky naw." Added Jermaine. "They even play basketball just like them!" Ivan chuckles. "Toussaint's students are a trip man." Says Donnie.

"They're some straight hacks." "I'm telling you, a lot of them have some serious issues." Andrea nodded. "Especially Milton Brown and Joy Faulkner."

"Those two especially, they fare among the worst." The entire class nods.

"Such know-it-all's!" "And this guy Cedric Holt." Serena Summers began.

"He's think that he's God's gift to every girl here, namely on our grade level."

“I agree.” Says Mrs. Holmes. “Cedric is rather ridiculous.” “He’s arrogant and he has no idea as to how to talk to people.” “Atleast he doesn’t play with the teachers like that.”

“And then there’s this other heifer Hannah Dubois, who always turning her nose at us as well as the other class.” “Hannah needs a bath, she stank, plain and simple.”

“If you ask me.” Nikki began shaking her head. That entire room should have its own sitcom.” “Like Young Gifted and Flaky?” Asked Ivan. “Ouch.” Says Jermaine.

“As I told you guys before, two months ago.” Mrs. Holmes began.

“You are actually the gifted ones.”

“I know so, because I work with you.”

“Plus you guys are very respectful, humble as could be, and you’re always willing to learn.” Mrs. Cobbs added. “You put in five-hundred percent every time.”

“Those kids in Mrs. Toussaint’s class, and to a certain degree Mrs. Bronson’s, the intermediate class envies you.” “We could give a fat rat’s rump as to what others may say or think.” “And on a more personal note, at least when you guys fight, you have enough sense to take it outside.” The kids, especially in 405 don’t give a damn.”

“They will throw down in the middle of Reading, like they have nothing to lose.” Chuckles Mrs. Holmes. “Like for example, do you remember the fight between Darius Pratt and Lance Little?” She asked her students. They nod. “These two are trading blows like it was nobody’s business, and the other students were just plain trifling.”

“They’re cheering, and acting like a bunch of inmates.” “In a co-ed prison.” Ivan further instigates. Nikki laughs. “Oh, we remember.” “Mrs. Toussaint had to take a phone call in the office, at the time of the brawl.” “We all heard the racket, you intervened, and the next thing that we knew, you came back with Lance and Darius.”

“You kept the door open between our room and theirs, so that you could further watch us as well as the other students until Mrs. Toussaint returned.” “Meanwhile, you made Darius and Lance sit under your desk.” “And I said to the both of them, gifted my ass.”

Mrs. Holmes concluded. “And they looked real salty that day too.” Says Malik Allen.

"But the bottom line is." Mrs. Homes began. "Is that I really enjoy what I do here, and so does Mrs. Cobbs." "Unlike most of the teachers in this school, we really do have your best interests at heart, we want you to succeed, to get ahead." The students nodded.

"Just like your parents, we want you to get a decent education, have a nice job, own a Lamborghini, raise a family, buy that house in Beverly or in Wilmette."

"Remember, that's why we're here."

"Considering that our parents are paying your tax dollars." Ivan adds.

His fellow classmates laughed.

"You're absolutely right." Says Mrs. Cobbs.

"As you already know." Mrs. Holmes continues.

"Nothing ever comes cheap in life."

"To really achieve your goals, you'll have to work twice as hard."

"Respect yourself, respect others, and you'll be just fine."

"You'll be blessed."

First looking at their watches and then at the clock, the two teachers began handing out booklets. Once the booklets as well as the answer sheets are distributed amongst their students, Mrs. Holmes and Mrs. Cobbs now focus their attention on the board.

Written on the latter, are the times as to when to start, as well as when to stop.

"And by the way." Mrs. Cobbs began. "Keep up the good work."

"We wish you all the best of luck today."

"Of course, we believe in you."

"And Ivan." Mrs. Holmes began.

"Yes, Ms. Holmes."

"I understand, you are one hell of a speed reader, and your comprehension is way off the charts." "You go through more books than I can count, and that's good."

"But we need you to take your time on this one, okay?"

"No problem." Ivan replies.

Five minutes later, the testing began.

13

NORTHWEST HALLWAY, FOURTH FLOOR 9:45AM

Among the four teachers situated in this corridor, is none other than Mrs. Holmes, and Mrs. Cobbs who heads the lower sixth grade class, Dorothy Toussaint who heads the advanced, and last but not least is Lorraine Bronson who of course, oversees the intermediate. Sitting in a workstation overlooking Rooms 407 and 405, these prominent longtime educators are now seen, socializing among themselves.

Within one hour, they return to their assignments.

Room 403

"Alright ladies and gentleman, all good things must come to an end." Mrs. Holmes walks in. "In other words, your time is up." Mrs. Cobbs added. They both smile.

However, their students were already finished.

With their Spelling books and paper already laid out, (across their desks), Mrs. Holmes and Mrs. Cobbs, are more than impressed. They happily nod.

With the exception of cricket-like noises (employed by Ivan), the rest of the room remains quiet. Several of his peers laughed. "Ivan, stop that!" Chuckles Mrs. Cobbs.

"You're worst than that man off of Police Academy."
"Doing all of those different sound effects."

"You know, having a lot of talent is one thing, having too much time on your hands is another." Mrs. Holmes added. "I'll tell you." She then laughs.

"Anyway what's up with you guys?" Mrs. Cobbs began.

"You're supposed to be still writing when we come in." Her co-worker teases.

"Y'all ain't right."

"For that, we want two hundred lines from all of you."

Their students all laughed.

"I will not finish my test ahead of time."

"Where's the cheat sheet?" Says Mrs. Cobbs.

"Nah, we're just playing with you."

"So how would you rate yourselves on this first half?" Asked Mrs. Holmes.

"Ivan?" "Well, let's just say that Doogie Howser ain't got nothing on me." Says her star student. The others nodded. "I'm quite sure he doesn't." Mrs. Cobbs smiles.

"What about you Nikki?" "The test seemed rather easy." Nicole herself replies.

"Especially if you like to read." Donnie added. "Yeah." Says the rest of the class.

"Well, you guys do have a point." Mrs. Holmes polished her glasses.

She now puts them back on.

"I think you fared pretty well too." Mrs. Cobbs added.

"How well did you guys enjoy yourselves last week?" Asked Mrs. Holmes.

"You can write us an essay later."

"In the meantime, please open your hardbacks to page two-twenty-four."

"If I'm not mistaken, I believe we're on lesson twenty-eight now."

"Along with your sentences, there are the usual definitions so break out your dictionaries if you have them." "If not, we have plenty of extras available." "So help yourself." Many of the students were already prepared at this point.

However, for those who didn't, are already at the nearest bookshelf.

They were very well disciplined. "Thank a lot everybody." Says Holmes.

While the rest of the class was on the twenty-eighth chapter, Ivan who had long completed the latter is now on the thirty-eighth. (Ten chapters ahead of schedule)

As she munches on an apple, the long time educator turns to the board and began writing math problems. "Does anybody have any questions?" Asked Mrs. Holmes.

"No." Her students all reply. And with that, she now returns to her desk.

Punching away at her PC, Mrs. Holmes makes one final gesture.

"Well if you do, feel free to come to my desk here." "I won't bite."

"Yes massa." Jermaine cracks. "Oh shut up." Mrs. Cobbs chuckles.

Taking off one of her heels, she attempts to throw one at him, however the class clown catches it. "Touch down!" Jermaine holds it up. Walking over to her desk, he returns it to her. In her mind, Mrs. Cobbs wants to give him the finger.

But instead she laughs. Meanwhile her fellow co-worker as well as the rest of the class follows suit.

14

WEST PLAYGROUND

Every day after lunch from the spring to the end of fall, students are allowed one hour of recess while their teachers on the other hand gets one of their own. (An additional thirty minutes) As usual, it's just another day in the yard. Scores of children are playing softball, basketball, some girls are jumping rope while some of the boys play touchy feely. Namely with the latter. Small congregations of teachers are also seen.

Situated under the flagpole opposite a set of double doors, the modest group looks on as they sip their coffee and bottled water. Their colleagues on the other hand are either in the lounge or upstairs in their classrooms. "Hey, give me back my shoe!" A girl shouts.

Chasing a tall lanky boy across the play lot, running through crowds of other children the unidentified young lady is also tickled silly. She laughs. Mr. Dunn, the lone in-house security guard sits at his desk. Seated near the Harrison entrance, the huge gentleman now takes a walk down the hall. Upon greeting some of the staff members in the main office nearby, Mr. Dunn now canvasses the western playground. No altercations.

No injuries. With that, he goes back inside.

Eventually, the young lady catches up with the young man. Holding up one of her LA. GEAR' s, he grins. "You punk!" The girl now hits him. She punches away at his back.

"Aight girl, damn!" He pleads. The boy curls up and laughs. Near the walkway, which leads to the eastern playground, Ivan, and Jermaine joined by Omar Ragsdale and Andrea are now playing a game known as Poison Box. The object of the game is to hit the ball back and forth from one person to another, until someone ultimately strikes out.

The remaining players will continue to rotate until there are two or less individuals remaining. "Name the cities where you'll find some rappers." Jermaine deploys the ball. "New York." Ivan began. He parries the ball. He sends it over to Omar.

"Houston." Omar himself responds. He parries it over to Tamala. "Compton."

She says. Tamala then sends it Andie. "Miami." Andrea Says. She parries it back to Tamala. "The Boogie Down Bronx!" Tamala returns it to Omar. She parries.

"Oakland." He says. However, Omar loses control. "Aw junk." He says. He shakes his head. Jermaine hums out Mario's death theme. The remaining players began laughing.

"Game Over." Ivan grins. "Hey check it out man." Jermaine began. "If you give me a quarter, I'll let you continue." Omar chuckles. "Man, get yo goofy ass outta here!"

He says. "That's aight though." "I'll be back when y'all start another game."

"It's cool." Omar retreats to the basketball court shortly thereafter. There are now four players left in the square. "Name your favorite singer." Jermaine says.

The game continues. Jermaine parries the ball to Tamala. "Bobby Brown." She calls

Out. She parries it to Andrea. "Al B. Sure." Andrea says. She sends it to Ivan.

"Vanessa Williams." Ivan hollers. "Janet Jackson." Jermaine parries it back to Ivan.

"So what's new Action Jackson?" Jermaine asks.

"Been checkin out some fights lately?"

"Yeah." Answers Ivan.

"In fact, not only have I seen any Jermaine, but I even won a few."

Andrea and Tamala both smiled.

"I bet, you have." Says Jermaine.

"Nothing surprises me around here anymore."

With the four of them still parrying the ball, the formation now mimics that of a human pinball. Jermaine smiled. “Last night, they had a fight on HBO.” He began.

Ivan now parries the ball to Andrea. “You mean the bout between Tyson and Spinks?”

Andrea asked. “Yeah, I’ve seen that.” Says Ivan. “Me too.” Andrea nodded.

“At first Spinks did put up a good fight.” Jermaine began to recollect.

“But by the seventh round, Spinks started to get sloppy and Tyson saw it.”

“He just went to hammering on Spinks.”

“Tyson went to sticking him left and right.”

“He showed no mercy.”

“As I recalled.” Ivan began.

“Tyson was pouncing on Spinks so badly, that the ref himself had to stop the fight.”

“I remember.” Says Andrea.

“I saw the fight at my dad’s house.”

“By the sixth round, Spinks was like fuck it.”

“He even looked high.” Says Jermaine.

“Spinks was like, which way did he go?”

“Which way did he go?”

The others all laughed.

“I’m telling you all.” Ivan began.

“That was no ordinary fight, an ordinary fight is when you either win or lose by decision.” “Especially if you’re still standing and surprisingly, Spinks was still standing.”

“But in the eyes of the ref, it was a massacre.”

“That was why he stopped the fight in the first place.”

“No comment.” Andrea smiled.

“Whatever.” Ivan chuckles.

“I know what you’re getting at.”

“Its been strictly self-defense!”

The entire game is now declared over.

Assembly Hall (Outer lobby)

Sitting on the steps directly under the flagpole, Ivan along with Jermaine and Andrea now relax. “Man, I can’t wait for summer to get here.” Ivan himself began.

He glances up at the sky. ATA flight 501 from Atlanta now begins its final decent.

Just to the northwest (forty five minutes from where the school is located) lies O’Hare International Airport. “Me neither.” Says Jermaine. Spinning his basketball with one finger, he sighs. “I know I can’t.” Andrea added. She twists and plays with her bangs.

“My sister who attends Pine Bluff, has just moved off campus, and she has her own apartment now.” “She invited me to spend the summer with her.” Ivan and Jermaine nodded. “That sounds nice.” Says Ivan.” “I’ve got family myself in New Orleans.”

Jermaine adds. “What about you Action?” “My parents own a timeshare in Orlando.” Ivan responds. “So y’all live large like that?” Jermaine asked. He smiles.

Ivan chuckles. “We’re not like the Huxtable’s man.” He breaks it down. Andrea laughed. “Its a resort located in this suburb called Lake Buena Vista.” “Its like a half hour from all of the major attractions like Disney world, Sea world, Wet’N Wild, Busch Gardens, you name it.” “That’s straight.” Jermaine nodded. “I don’t know if I told you guys before.” Ivan began. “When I first arrived in Orlando the year before last, I actually saw Shamu.” “Straight up?” Jermaine asks. He was appalled. “That little dolphin right?”

Andrea asked. Ivan nodded. “At Sea world.” He confirms. “The first year, it was just my parents and me.” “The second year, Simon came with us.” “We all went to the Magic Kingdom in Disney World.” “Of course, that was last year.” “Sounds like you all have a lot of fun down there.” Jermaine says happily. He gets up and dribbles his ball.

“It beats the hell out of being stuck up here for the summer, I’ll tell you that much.” Ivan tells him. “I hear ya homey.” Jermaine gives him a pound.

“Hey girl!” Ivan suddenly jumps up. He grins. Nikki, who had been interacting with another group, playfully smacks him as she walks by.

As she enters the building, Nikki turns to him. She waves.

Room 403

As they attempt to solve the most recent math problems assigned to them by Mrs. Holmes, the entire class at this point become has become increasingly frustrated.

Browsing through their books repeatedly, executing formula after formula, there is no success. Even the renowned geniuses Serena Summers, Tamala Spann, Donnie, and Najee Irving are unable to connect the dots.

The assignment consists of multiplication, and addition with the employment of decimals. Glancing first at their papers, the students write continuously, they scribble, it is now back to square one. Harsh sighs and four letter words echoes across the entire room. “Man, I can’t understand this shit.” Donnie breaks his pencil.

“Where the fuck are these decimals supposed to go?”

“Even though we technically have the right answers, they are still wrong because our decimals ain’t in the right place.” Najee says. “We’ve been tryin to do this stuff forever, and it just ain’t makin no sense.” Curtis Hawkins adds. Rewriting his problems repeatedly, thus balling up paper, he sweats almost profusely. Jermaine smiled.

“You’re supposed to beat your meat on your on time back there.” He roasts.

“Man, fuck you.” Curtis thunders. The others laughed. “The only thing that’s keeping me from stumpin yo ass, besides Holmes is that you can at least back it up.”

“In other words, he’s funny as hell like you.” Says Donnie. “Yeah, whatever.” Chuckles Curtis. “Shit.” He shakes his head. “We have done this, at least half a dozen times already.” Nikki moans. At this time Mrs. Holmes has briefly stepped out.

“Where do we continue to go wrong?” Najee asked his peers. He reads the directions in his book continuously. “I’ll just copy the answers out of the teachers guide.”

Curtis now gets up. Taking with him a blank sheet of paper and pencil, he approaches the teacher's desk. Mrs. Cobbs is also indisposed at this time. "You know, that sounds cool and all Curt." Omar Ragsdale began. "But Mrs. Holmes will still wanna know as to how you did the work." "And she'll want more proof." "I don't care." Curtis responds.

He ignores Omar, and began to copy.

Ivan who is busy doing his own work, at first pays no mind to the others. He is relaxed, calm, and collective. He now looks up. He smiles. "So what's the story with you Action?" Ivan at first looks into his own book, and then back at his paper. He motions for Jermaine to have a look. The rest of the class face him as well. "What is it?"

Asked Denise Wilson. "What?" "No crickets?" "We just forgot about you so suddenly." Says Najee. "You're back here, all quiet, eatin your ham sandwich, and working in your little cubicle. (A figure of speech on both counts) "In other words, you'd have to know something." Getting up from her desk, Nikki walks toward Ivan.

"Let me see." She says. Nikki now looks on with Jermaine as well as Najee. Donnie and Serena soon followed. They couldn't believe it. They now studied Ivan's paper.

For the many who has failed, the one person among them who has had the most difficulties (namely in this subject) succeeds.

As Mrs. Holmes returns to her class, she finds her students giving one of their own, namely Ivan pounds, high fives, and pats on the back as he explains the calculations for which he has just written. The teacher herself is appalled. "Am I in the right class?"

She says to her students. She smiled. A few of them laughed. "Yes, you are." Says Ivan. "Come on in." As his fellow classmates all sat before him, Mrs. Holmes is now relieved. "I take it you were all having problems." She began now sitting down.

"We were." Says Najee. "Why are you sweating like a horse?" Mrs. Holmes asks Curtis. "Were they that bad?" The tall and powerful youth nodded. "If you only knew."

He says. "All this time the one person who was able to help us, was the one who had the most difficulties." Jermaine added. "Namely in math." "While we were like chickens with our heads cut off." Serena began. "Ivan here was holding out on us." "I see."

Mrs. Holmes nodded. “Are you trying to take my job?” She asked Ivan. He grins.

“Nah, I’m just teasing, but you did good.”

“Don’t let this subject intimidate you.” Says Ivan’s teacher. She encourages him.

“You have a lot more potential than you realize.”

“Anyway, I’ll take it from here, thanks Ivan.”

The star student returns to his seat.

15

GYMNASIUM-AUDITORIUM

It is all about testing ones courage as well as their endurance followed by their might. Yes, it is survival of the fittest as Mr. Bosworth, the gym teacher and prominent basketball coach performs his daily duties. Like that of Ivan's former teachers, Mrs. Reid and Mrs. Armstrong, Bosworth is also a firm believer in what is perceived as, "old school" corporal punishment. Unlike the traditional yardstick or rulers employed by his fourth grade counterparts, Bosworth instead summons an old fishing rod.

His targets consist of children in grades ranging from first through sixth who often opposed him. (Allegedly) Furthermore, there's even speculation that Bosworth himself, has a drinking problem. The initial rumors began three years ago, when nearly every student (except for those on his team) received an F on their report cards.

Many parents were outraged.

Pending an investigation, Bosworth was suspended with pay.

Having passed a drug test, he returns to work the following week.

Early on when he was perhaps younger, Ivan too was reprimanded. (Wrongfully)

When Ivan informed his father about the caning, Mr. Thompson gave the gym teacher an ultimatum. But yet, Bosworth defies the senior Thompson. A grave mistake.

One morning before 7am, as Bosworth left his Oak Park Victorian to go to work, Mr. Thompson suddenly confronts him in his driveway. There is now a sudden change of plans. Instead of his short commute into the city, the gym teacher now calls off.

Having sustained multiple bruises (including a black eye) from Frank Thompson's meaty punches, Howard Bosworth whose head was also shoved through the glass of his own Cadillac, now ends up at West Suburban Hospital. No charges are filed.

After taking his usual attendance, Mr. Bosworth commands his students to rise.

Lining up in columns, all of Ivan's classmates (including Ivan himself) now began to warm up. After completing a series of pull ups, jumping jacks, leg lifts, torso twists and squats, nearly every student in the room with the exceptions of a few, are extremely tired.

Now running a series of laps, many of the students continue to breathe heavily while others cough and wheeze. Ivan, of course is not among them. He now leads the pack.

"Come on man, you ain't the Road Runner." Omar tries to keep up. He huffs. He sweats, he breathes heavily. "Damn Superboy." Terrell Goodson began.

"Yo big test tube, outta this world, genetically engineered, Jessie Owens, Popeye, spinach eatin ass!" "Slow the hell down." "You makin us look really bad."

Jermaine chuckles. "Did you have some kind of accident?" "Did you get hit by lightning?" "That's alright though." Serena slightly picks up the pace.

Breathing in and out through her diaphragm, following each stride, her chest bounces.

"I'll have what he's having." Najee gasps. As Tamala trails Ivan, she takes note of his triceps, back, and buttocks. Good God! She thought. The eye candy in front of her is clad in a white V-neck T-shirt, gray sweats and sneakers. One pants leg is rolled up slightly above Ivan's knee. A towel is wrapped around his neck. Curtis and Malik who initially kept up are suddenly out of breath. “This is it Elizabeth!” Curt mimics. The others laugh.

“I’m coming to join you honey!” “I don’t know if I can keep goin, with my arthritis, and hemorrhoids.” “I’m getting too old for this shit!” Malik is now jogging at this point.

Beads of sweat rolls off of his forehead consistently. He coughs. “Jesus.” He says.

Mr. Bosworth steps out of his office and smiles. Shortly thereafter, he blows his whistle. “Halt!” “Take five, and get yourselves some water.”

While the other students retreated to the nearest fountain, Ivan retrieves a bottle of water from his backpack.

16

GYMNASIUM-AUDITORIUM

Five minutes later, the students re-enter the room. Situated on the easternmost stage opposite the Congress Parkway feeder (via Interstate 290) the class of room 403 now began their monthly fitness exam.

In front of them are four giant ropes.

Suspended high above the ceiling supported by steel brackets, the object of this drill is for each student to climb as high as they possibly can. (At their own pace)

On the account of the height, the students are urged not to look down.

And furthermore, their hands are to remain on the ropes at all times.

As Mr. Bosworth picks his Afro, he summons the first four. "Allen, Hawkins, Ragsdale, and Fox." "You gentlemen will go first." Jumping onto the ropes, the boys began to climb. Curtis, with all of his might slowly pulls himself up.

Breathing in with each tug and then out, the seemingly strong young man although he lacks the stealth begins to struggle. As for Malik, even though he manages to pull himself up halfway, moving slowly he suddenly decides to look down.

"Naw man, keep looking up!" Najee urges. "If you look down, you'll lose your concentration." Taking heed to the words of his friend, Malik takes a deep breath.

Upon tightening his grip, the semi husky youth continues to climb. He finally reaches the top. "I'm the pimp of the year son!" Malik boasts. He now slides down.

"You mean jackass of the year?" Says Cicely Parker. "Jack this ass."

"Get away from me Malik." The tall and skinny girl smiles.

He pulls down his pants and moons her.

Once Kenny Fox and Omar made it to the top of their ropes, the two nearly lost their balance when they saw Malik moon Cicely. They both laughed.

Curtis has already made it back to the surface at this point. He now rests.

Before Malik could even pull his pants back up, Mr. Bosworth summons his fishing rod. Quietly sneaking up behind him, Malik is too late. Whackit!

The sound of the rod striking his ass echoes throughout the entire gym. Malik screams at the top of his lungs. "AAAAHHH!!!! The entire class is now tickled pink.

Although the short and husky youth is no longer able to scream, his mouth yet still remains open. At this point, all that Ivan can think about is the film Salem's Lot.

As his lungs calls for more oxygen, the warm tears began to trickle.

His fudge brown complexion has now turned red. Bosworth shakes his head.

"Nobody told you to put yo ass out there in the first place." He says.

Cicely giggles and points. "That's just what you get." She tells the "cainee"

"Okay, the shows over go back to your drills." Bosworth tells the class.

He summons the next four. "Thompson, Nicholson, Cox, and Wilkins."

The boys quickly take their places.

However before Jermaine is able to carry out his assignment, he immediate begins to roast Malik. “Could I prescribe some Ben Gay?” “Some Icy Hot?” “Or perhaps some Preparation H?” “Fuck you bitch!” Malik snaps. He now attempts to chase after him.

But yet, Malik is still unable to move at this point. He moans. Jermaine pats him on the head. “I didn’t think so.” He says. “You ain’t right brother Wilkins.” Bosworth nods. “I’ll bet you four dollars, or better yet five that Ivan climbs all the way up.”

Omar dares Najee. “Aight bet.” Najee himself responds. “But I still think you’re wrong.” “Even though he might be strong, he ain’t that strong.” However, the two still shake on it. “Go.” Bosworth commands the next four. Employing all of their strength and weight as they climb, Donnie and Jermaine are moving at a seemingly slow pace.

Ivan, who is not only strong but also agile, climbs with unspeakable ease. Using only his hands, he focuses only on his breathing. Having already made it to the top, he now does three pull-ups on the adjoining bars. Donnie and Jermaine are still halfway at this point. The rest of the class is both shocked as well as stunned. Their mouths began to

drop. Even the gym teacher himself is appalled. Shaking his head, he then retreats to his office. Upon entry, Bosworth summons his coffee mug. Serving himself a freshly brewed pot from his personal maker, he then reaches into the drawer of his desk.

Inside is a bottle of Jack Daniels. Calling upon its contents, he applies two drops.

Mixing up the latter, he returns to the gym. The room is suddenly quiet as Ivan returns to his spot. Donnie and Jermaine are seen climbing back down a few seconds later.

As the rest of his peers continue to stare, Ivan smiles. He then shrugs. “What?”

17

THOMPSON RESIDENCE

Walking in from off the street, Ivan checks into his grandmother's apartment. Sarah LeMay-Cartier, was born March 10, 1921 in Clarksdale, Mississippi.

The daughter of a domestic servant (a maid) and a sharecropper, Mrs. Cartier studied to become a teacher at Tuskegee University. She graduated in 1945.

Two years later, Ms. Cartier arrives in Chicago. Almost a month later, she meets her husband, (also from the south) Little Rock-born Joseph Cartier in June of 1947.

At the time of his acquaintance with his then-girlfriend, Mr. Cartier was an established businessman. He owned and operated his own photography studio.

They tie the knot almost six months later. In September the following year, the newlyweds move into Lincoln Park. (On the near north side)

As the neighborhood underwent what was then urban renewal, the Cartier's were eventually displaced. In 1969, Mr. and Mrs. Cartier along with their five children moved into this very building. At the time, the neighborhood surrounding it had already been a casualty of job losses (not to mention the riots a year earlier) housing disinvestments, demolitions, as well as the loss of commerce.

However during this dark transition the very block, for which the Cartier's dwelled upon, remained intact. As first time neighborhood homeowners, for Mr. and Mr. Cartier, it was a "win-win." In May of 1973, their daughter Marie (then twenty-four) and her husband Frank, twenty-six along with their two children (then four-year-old Jennifer and little Simon age two) all move upstairs. Ivan is not yet born.

In August of 1978, Mr. Cartier dies. His wife becomes the sole surviving owner.

After being employed for nearly forty years as an elementary school teacher, Mrs. Cartier retires in June of 1986. Nowadays, the sixty-eight year-old enjoy visiting the museums, watching screenplays, and reading books. Furthermore, Ivan's grandmother also enjoys cooking, and studies Yoga at Loop College. Although two years shy of seventy, Mrs. Cartier is still in remarkably good shape.

Her bronze complexion is yet still radiant. Her hair (although now gray) is still long and silky. On the account that her vision has only slightly diminished, Mrs. Cartier now wears glasses. Her Creole-like exterior employs not a single wrinkle.

Mr. Thompson, in the form of a compliment once likened his mother-in-law to that of a fine wine. She was indeed blessed.

As Ivan enters through the living room, it appears as though he's in an art gallery.

Many paintings of people (both famous and local) buildings, as well as monuments cover the walls. Dozens of masks representing mostly African, Native American and some Asian cultures are also seen. Supported by both of the latter, are exotic plants.

Track lights shine in all four corners of the room.

Suspended above the center overlooking the polished hardwood, is a bright shiny chandelier. Walking into the dining room, there is no sign of her.

In the study room of his late grandfather, Ivan takes note of several books lying on the table. A King James edition of the bible is among them. Looking at an aquarium occupied with tropical fish, he moves to the next room. At this time, the entire apartment smells like fried chicken. Man, that really smells good. He thought. Continuing down a narrow hall, Ivan now heads for the kitchen. Upon entry into the latter, he finds his grandmother.

"Hi Grandma."

"Hello Ivan." Says Mrs. Cartier. She kisses her grandson's forehead.

Ivan now takes a seat behind the eat-in counter.

Besides the smell of the fried chicken that Mrs. Cartier was obviously cooking, is the smell of an apple pie baking in the oven below. "It really smells good in here." Ivan tells her. "Especially that pie." His grandmother smiled. "I bet, it does." She replies. "So what's going on grandson?" "How was school today?" Asked Mrs. Cartier as she now throws lard into the frying pan. At the very same time, the veteran cook tends to a steaming pot of collard greens on one eye and a pot of carrots on another.

"It actually went well." Says Ivan.

"Thanks."

"The first day of testing was comparable as well."

His grandmother nodded.

"That's good." She says.

Removing a now freshly baked apple pie from the oven (a pie that she made from scratch), Mrs. Cartier places it on the counter. "Go ahead and grab a slice."

She tells her youngest grandson. "You know where to find the milk." "Thanks a lot, Grandma." Says Ivan. While she summons him a plate, Ivan reaches into the refrigerator.

While getting the milk, he collects a glass along with a fork from the dishwasher nearby. Followed by a knife. "You know, even though I took Mrs. Holmes' advice and took my time." Ivan began. "I was still among the first to finish." "No speed reading."

"Good, just keep it up." Advises his grandmother. "I know you read around the clock."

Ivan smiled. At this point, he has already devoured his slice. “How do you know that?” He asks. “Your folks tell me.” Mrs. Cartier responds. She smiled back.

“Almost every morning when they wake you up for school, you’re always up to your covers in books.” His grandmother explains. “I like that.” “Psychological warfare at its best.” Ivan added. He slowly drinks his milk. “A nuclear deterrent for the mind, which proceeds to look out for the body, even while its resting.” “Eighty percent of the time, at least.” Ivan goes on. “As I understand Grandma, that even the mind itself needs rest.”

“That’s right.” Says Mrs. Cartier. Beyond all reasonable doubt, she is greatly impressed. She smiled and then nodded. Tossing flour-covered chicken wings from a brown paper bag, Mrs. Cartier now submerges them into a frying pan. The custom made see through skillet, employs lard. Turning on the ceiling fan, Ivan’s grandmother now opens the window. “You have so many God-given talents, Ivan.” She faces him once more. “Always full of surprises.” “Your grandfather would be so proud of you, had he still been alive.” “You were only two years old when he passed away.”

Ivan smiled and nodded. “I’m quite sure he’s looking down on us as speak.” He says.

The young man has long finished his snack.

“Yes he is baby.” Mrs. Cartier assures him.

“During gym class, we had like this obstacle course where we had to climb this rope.” Ivan resumes the conversation. He belches. “Oh, excuse me.” “That’s fine.”

Says his grandmother. “It was nearly thirty feet high.” Ivan went on. “Were you afraid?” Asked Mrs. Cartier. “For the first time Grandma, I didn’t think so.” Ivan answers. “Or let me rephrase that.” “I wasn’t.” “Another breakthrough huh?” Says his grandmother. “Praise the Lord.” “You SHOULD be used to flying by next August.”

“That was the very first thing that crossed my mind when I initially climbed.” Ivan tells her. “And I had done it with both speed and agility Grandma.” Mrs. Cartier nodded.

“Two of my friends, you might know them.”

“Donnie and Jermaine, they fared pretty well too.”

“It was an uphill struggle for them, but they finished.”

“But man, I surely felt the burn when I slid down though.”

Mrs. Cartier laughed.

"It was almost as though my hands were on fire." Ivan chuckles.

"You need some gloves." His grandmother tells him.

"Oh I know now." Ivan smiled.

"You know at some point grandma." Ivan begins to confess.

"I really believe it, and I'm sure that you can too."

"That you were a bit of a show off?" Mrs. Cartier guesses.

Ivan nodded. "After I climbed to the top, I started doing pull-ups on the bars."

"And of course, I didn't find it to be a laughing matter." Ivan assured her.

"Because anything could have gone wrong, like for example."

"I could have missed or somehow lost my balance."

"Or you could have been crippled or killed." Mrs. Cartier finished.

"Absolutely." Ivan responds.

"You guys would have been seeing me at the House of Branch up on Roosevelt."

" I was just hyped up Grandma."

"I'll take your word for it." Says Mrs. Cartier.

She now takes a lid off of the skillet.

"You know that you have to be very careful." The youthful elder reminds him.

"Young, agile and strong you maybe Ivan."

"But invincible, you're not." She now fixes him a plate.

"I love you just like everyone else around here."

"Likewise." Says Ivan.

"I love you too."

"Of course I didn't age this many years for nothing." Mrs. Cartier continues on.

"And you already know, that I'm far from being stupid."

"But I knew about your cousin's growing reputation, and why he, Leo, and his mother left in the first place." "Atleast Leo had enough sense not to steal from me."

She chuckled. "I would chop off that boy's arm, and throw it to the lions!"

"I knew all about Doug trying to look bigger than what he was, hanging out with the local hoodlums, thinking that they were his family, trying to look cool and junk like that."

Ivan nodded. "His mother has no backbone whatsoever." "I was at least, a little bit surprised when Doug came back to visit recently." "Especially on the account of what he put you through." "And that was very rotten thing that he did." "And whatever you did or said, that caused him to leave, I don't blame you." "But I want you to promise me this."

Mrs. Cartier looks into her grandson's eyes. "You, I don't have to worry about." "But still promise me, that you never stop being yourself Ivan." "No matter what."

"Like I told Nikki one day." Ivan began smiling. "I don't have a choice. "And you know what?" Mrs. Cartier asked. "She's right." "You don't." As Ivan eats his dinner, his grandmother playfully smacks him on the back of his head.

18

THOMPSON RESIDENCE (IVAN'S ROOM)

Having done all of his homework, Ivan rises from his desk. Placing each of the assignments in their respective folders, he turns off his desk light and falls onto the bed.

Reaching for a remote on the headboard, Ivan clicks on the latter and brings the TV to life. Surfing through what appears to be an endless network of channels, Ivan turns to BET. (Black Entertainment Television) At this time, the award Hip Hop show Rap City now airs. Among the first four videos to be seen is LL Cool J's "I'm That Type of Guy", "I've Got it Made" by Special Ed, "Buddy" by De La Soul, and "Express Yourself" by NWA. Immediately thereafter, comes another video. Unlike its predecessors, this particular video talks about stopping the violence, as well as promoting peace and last but not least unity. The group's composition employs some of the biggest names.

All of whom are from the East Coast.

Among them there's KRS-One, the lead rapper of the group B.D.P. (Boogie Down Productions). Kool Moe Dee, Brooklyn's own M.C. Lyte, and Ms. Melody just to name a few. Many others follow. Shortly after the video ends, the phone rings.

Walking toward the kitchen, Ivan summons the receiver.
"Hello?"
"What's going down Ivan?"
"Hey, what's up Riz?"
"Nothing man, I'm just working on a few sketches."
"How about you?"
"Watching Rap City."

“Straight up?”

“Yeah, In fact I was just checking out this new video from a group called The Stop The Movement.” “The song is called Self Destruction.” “That’s cool.”

“You have everybody from KRS-One to Ms. Melody, M.C. Lyte, Public Enemy, Kool Moe Dee, and a bunch of others.” “Mainly from the East Coast.” “The video sounded kinda fly.” “It was.” “So, are you still coming through?” “Yeah, just give about twenty to thirty minutes.” “Aight, cool.” Ivan hangs up.

Downstairs in the recreation room, Ivan and Rizzo are now playing pool.

Rotating almost repetitiously with their cue sticks in hand; both young men appear to be sharp and very well focused. Aligning his cue along with the marker (the white ball), Ivan zeroes in on a cluster of solid balls. Without out breaking a single sweat, the young shark unleashes his cue. As the sharp point strikes away at the marker, comes a chain reaction. Making contact with the southernmost ball, three others (including the latter) have now been dispersed. Rolling off quietly to their respective pockets, the balls now began to fall. Still holding his cue, Rizzo smiles and then claps. “I take it, that you’ve had a good day.” He says. “Don’t get me wrong, you’ve always been good at this.”

“But what you just did just now, was really smooth.” “Thanks.” Ivan tells him.

Making room for his partner in crime, Rizzo rotates to the opposite side.

Now positioning himself in the southern corner, Ivan re-pairs his cue with that of the marker once more. Snapping his cue directly into the marker for the second time, two more balls are summoned. Rolling swiftly into the opposite corner pockets, Ivan this time positions himself from the northeast corner. Aligning his cue with the marker for the third time, he smacks it dead into the center. Although the junior host succeeds by way of striking his remaining balls, they rolled slowly, continuously and quietly only to stop.

They did it so suddenly.

However, to add insult to injury, two of the pockets (located in the far left and right corners) are within reach. Ivan sighed. Rizzo grins. "What's goes up must come down." He says. Helping himself off the couch with the support of his cue, Riz walks up to the table. Positioning himself from the southwest corner pocket, the Ivan's only guest now aligns his cue with the marker. With the employment of a steady hand, Rizzo dispatches two of his own balls. Rolling rapidly on a forty-five degree angle, one immediately falls into the left corner pocket. Another: The right. Ivan nodded.

"So what went down at your school today?" He asks.

"Well as far as I was able to tell, it was nothing out of the ordinary." Riz tells him.

"It appeared to have been just another Monday."

"Well for me." Ivan began, as he walks slowly around the table.

Still holding his cue, Ivan moves to the opposite side of where Rizzo had been.

"It was actually entertaining Riz."

"And not to mention hilarious."

"On the account that I've spent most of the day laughing, it might as well have been like the Def Jam Comedy Hour." Nodding his head as he listens, Rizzo now re-positions himself. From the northeast corner of the table, he summons his cue and aligns it with the marker. With the employment of one stroke, two more balls are dispatched.

Rolling quickly across the table, one lands into the left hand side pocket.

The other: The far left corner pocket.

As he takes another position from the southwest corner, Rizzo pairs his cue with that of the marker. This time upon delivery, three balls are deployed. Parting along three separate paths, the balls began to roll quite rapidly. With two corner pockets within reach and one in the middle (another side pocket) facing the west, these three stripes suddenly comes to a halt. Rizzo sighed, shook his head and then smiled. Ivan chuckles.

"Déjà vu." He says.

"I have to give it to you Riz, you are not by far, a very formidable challenger."

"Well, I learn from the best." Rizzo himself replies.

"I'll take your word for it." Ivan tells him as he now emerges from the couch.

"Anyway, what happened today?" Asked Rizzo.

Moving toward the opposite side from where Ivan began to position himself, the humbled guest step back and watches his friend. "Wait a second." Says Ivan.

Having briefly sharpened his cue stick, Ivan positions himself for the second time.

"Well this morning following the usual public announcements, my teacher Ms. Holmes gave the entire class some good news." Ivan began.

"What was it?" Asked Rizzo.

"She announced that we were all being promoted to the next grade."

"Everybody."

"Straight up?" Says Rizzo.

"Just like when we were in Mrs. Bingham's class." He reminisces.

"Everybody entered the fifth grade."

"Bingham was a complete jerk." Ivan reminded him.

"Straight up." Rizzo agrees.

"She had no faith whatsoever in her students, and she was an old witch." Ivan added as he aligns his cue with the marker. "Bingham was always bringing up the past of other students, talking about this was why they failed and how they ended up D's and F's, practically belittling them." "Word." Says Rizzo. "The only students that Bingham really believed in." Ivan continues on. "Were those whose grades were already exceptional, long before these students were even transferred."

"And she spoiled the heck out of you Ivan." Rizzo smiled. "The only reason why she did it was because I don't know if I told you." "But my brother Simon, was also one of her students." "He was literally, the teacher's pet Rizzo." Rizzo chuckles. "And I'm assuming that the only reason why Bingham spoiled me the way that she did, was apparently because I reminded her so much of him." "But yet, Bingham contradicted herself." Rizzo points out.

"While she practically treated you like the house servant, and us, the rest of the boys the field servants, Bingham still had the nerve to tell you that you couldn't succeed."

Ivan smiled. "Well I guess I proved her wrong didn't I?" He says. "You bet your ass, you did." Rizzo reminds him. Snapping his cue dead into the marker, three more balls are dispatched. Rolling to the northernmost end, all three solids have finally reached their respective pockets. Two in the corner. One in the side. (To the right) Rizzo nodded.

"Bingham passed everybody, just to recommend that they still go to summer school." Ivan says as he now takes his next position. "Namely the majority."

"But Ms. Holmes is the exact opposite." Ivan assures him.

"With her, a deal is a deal." "There are no strings attached."

"The reason why she's passing everybody including myself, because we truly earned it."

"I believe you." Rizzo says with satisfaction. He nods his head.

"But anyway, back to the story." Ivan continues on. "Right." Says Rizzo.

"Before Ms. Holmes made the announcement, one of the most recent students in the class, I'm not sure if you're familiar with him, Jermaine Wilkins." "He's like another comic, funny like Curtis." Positioning himself from the south facing the laundry room, Ivan snaps his cue into the marker. As a result three more balls are sent out.

Traveling quickly, but yet quietly across the table all three of the solids landed almost simultaneously. "His name sounds familiar." Rizzo says shaking his head.

"Not only is he the shortest, but he's also the youngest." Ivan continues to explain.

"He's ten."

"Not bad." Says Rizzo.

"That means he's smart."

"Oh, he definitely makes the grade." Ivan tells him.

"That is exactly why Ms. Holmes tolerates him."

"Shortly before she made her announcement, Jermaine without warning just roasted Tamala." "You remember her right?" Ivan then asks. "Tamala Spann?"

"You mean Deviline?" Says Rizzo. Ivan nods. "Yeah, I remember her."

"She was really pretty."

"The only problem was that she was too hairy."

"Tammy had beautiful features and all, don't get me wrong."

"But didn't she have like a moustache and some other facial hairs under her chin?" Rizzo asked. "Yeah, that's her." Ivan confirms. "I think that it has something to do with her hormones." "Because Tamala once told me, that she had to shave like every other day." Rizzo smiled. "And she appeared twice as fine when she did too." He says.

"I used to like her." "Mrs. Holmes was like, I have some very good news." Ivan comes back. "And Jermaine said, so Tamala really is a girl after all." Rizzo's face quickly reddens. Dropping his cue, he holds his stomach and began to laugh. His laughter alone mimics that of a hyena. "He was bogus for that one." "I know." Says Ivan.

"Jermaine had the entire class rolling." "And Ms. Holmes on the other hand.

"Almost fell out of her seat." "And of course Tamala herself, didn't think that it was a laughing matter." Ivan further narrates. "I bet she didn't." Says Rizzo.

"She was the only stone face in the class." Rizzo chuckles. "But it didn't stop there."

"Before that, Jermaine had been making jokes, insisting that he was still at home."

"And him being back in the classroom was all a bad dream." Rizzo nods his head and chuckles once more as he listens. "Then he actually sticks himself with a safety pen!"

"Ol' boy is a fool alright." Says Rizzo. "Then he asked Ms. Holmes for a match." Ivan continued on. "I guess he was planning to burn himself next." "He's crazy." Says Rizzo.

"Tell me about it." Ivan chuckles. "Gym class alone was a virtual free for all."

"What happened during gym?" Rizzo asked. "Well, after the usual warm-ups, Bosworth decides to have us all climb the ropes." Ivan began to explain. "You know, like they do in the military, to enhance your upper body." "And of course, only a few of us made it to the top." "Some faster than others, namely myself." "And then there was Malik."

"In the beginning, he was doing quite well." "Malik is already halfway, until suddenly he decides to look down." Rizzo shakes his head. "He's nervous, he freezes up."

"Eventually, another guy in my class talks him through it." "He tells him not to look down, but instead to look up." "So finally, Malik pulls through, although he struggles."

"And he finally makes it to the top." "Malik climbs back down, he becomes cocky and all big headed, saying he's pimp of the year." "This tall and skinny girl named Cicely Parker called him the jackass of the year." Rizzo chuckles. "And she was right on both counts." "Malik tells her to jack this ass, walks up to Cicely pulls down his pants, and moons her!" Rizzo began to laugh. "But what he did was nothing in comparison, to what Bosworth had done." Ivan assures him. "Bosworth had Malik feeling salty."

"What exactly did Bosworth do?" Rizzo asked. "While Malik was busy mooning Cicely, Bosworth decides to capture the moment." Ivan further breaks it down.

"Like a ninja, Bosworth got his fishing rod, and quietly walked up behind Malik."

Rizzo laughs. "Poor Malik didn't see it coming." Ivan chuckled. "You could actually hear echo of Bosworth's fishing rod striking Malik's ass Rizzo." "It was like one of those earlier Kung Fu films." Rizzo, at this point is literally tickled pink. Falling to the floor, Ivan's lone guests clutches away at his abdomen. His complexion, once again turns red.

"Malik was in so much pain, that he couldn't even cry out."

"Although, you could see the tears, and even though his mouth was open."

"Nothing was coming out."

"You would have thought that he was on fire."

"Because Malik actually stopped, dropped, and rolled."

"Screaming and running."

"And of course everyone laughed."

"Even Jermaine gave him a good roast."

"When Malik found a chair, and decided to sit down."

"Jermaine was like, I could prescribe you some Icy Hot or some Preparation H?"

"Malik was pissed!"

"He tried to go after Jermaine, but he quickly found himself sitting back down."

"I bet he did." Rizzo chuckled.

Positioning himself to the west, Ivan summons his cue.

As he aligns his ordinance with the marker, he sends another ball directly into the adjoining side pocket. It is another clean break.

Now turning to face the hall, Ivan dispatches his cue toward the southeast corner.

Aligning his cue with the marker, two more solids are within reach.

Situated near the southeast corner pocket, Ivan deploys his cue.

As the latter strikes away at the marker, the marker itself collides into a blue ball nearby. As the blue ball rolls away quietly, it immediately makes contact with a "connecting" red ball. With the red being the first to fall, the blue is second.

The game is over.

"Good game." Ivan tells Riz.

Hanging up their cue sticks, both young men takes a seat on opposite couches.

"You guys have anything to drink?" Rizzo asks.

"Yeah, check the fridge in the back, I think there's a case of Coke's and a few Sunkist's on the bottom shelf." Ivan responds. "Cool." Says Rizzo. He now gets up.

"And while you're back there, don't forget to fetch me a can." Ivan reminds him.

"Thanks." "No problem at all man." Riz tells him.

For the next few minutes, Ivan begins to practice his fighting skills.

Our Lady of Sorrows of Basilica

Established in 1874 by three servants of Mary (Servites): Fathers Austin Morini, Andrew Venturi and brother Camara. The Bishop of Chicago, the Reverend Thomas Foley, enthusiastically approved their dream of a sanctuary where the Blessed Virgin

could comfort her people and honor her Divine Son. Within that first year, a plot of farmland was acquired on what was then the city's far west side. (Now East Garfield Park) It was 102 feet long, 38 feet wide, and two stories high. Midnight Mass was held on Christmas Eve, 1874. In the following year, the little church, on the site of today's Servite Monastery was beautifully frescoed.

Soon a much larger church was needed and on June 17, 1890, ground was broken for the Italian Renaissance-style church now currently seen. The building was opened for Masses within months, under a temporary roof, while the walls had reached only half of their eventual height. It was not until January 5, of 1902 that the great church could be dedicated. When improvements were made to the lower church, Father James M. Keane compiled a booklet of prayers to be used in a new service that would take advantage of this basement shrine. On January 8, 1937, the Sorrowful Mother Novena began an era that would establish Chicago's Our Lady of Sorrows as a Marian Shrine of national as well as international fame. Through the 1940's and into the 1950's the Great Novena filled the church weekly in up to 38 separate services. The Novena spread to over 2300 additional parishes at the peak of its popularity. In 1956, Pope Pius XII granted to Our Lady of Sorrows the National Shrine of Basilica, and the Basilica is increasingly being recognized for the splendor of its architecture, and the history it had witnessed.

Tragically, the upper stages of the western tower were lost to fire in 1984.

But the interior and the exterior brickwork have benefited from periodic and ongoing restorations since, resulting in a shrine that is breathtaking for the first time.

Just over a year ago, millions of viewers of the Academy Awards telecast saw the mural of St. Anthony Pucci, which fills the rear arch of the sanctuary.

A short but crucial scene in the recent film "The Untouchables" Starring Sean Connery and Kevin Costner, was also filmed here. The ceiling and the mural that was mentioned, was also employed as a backdrop. On the outside along Jackson Boulevard, a leafy and floral park lies adjacent to a large statue east of the Basilica. Located behind the property overlooking Van Buren Street lies a mile long acre of green space.

Running parallel to that of Horan Park (located across the street), this parcel of land is also owned by the parish, and remains fenced off.

Each year particularly around this time, Our Lady of Sorrows holds its annual Carnival.

The event, which is enjoyed by many whether they are local residents, regional, or other, is obviously a simple fundraiser. In the eyes of the parish such necessities like infrastructure, operating expenses, and even special projects (whether they are current or forthcoming) are to be considered. At this time, the land situated behind the property now acts as a makeshift amusement park. Many rides both great and small filters the overall landscape. Multiple vendors, as well as that of the standard booths, which houses the prizes as well as the games, are dispatched amongst the crowds.

Surprisingly, there is also a video arcade.

Security is provided by plainclothes off duty police officers, who are now seen patrolling the perimeters. Entering beyond the makeshift entrance near the corner of Kedzie Avenue, Ivan and Rizzo pays the cashiers. With their tickets in hand, they now enter the fairgrounds. Working their way through the masses of their fellow patrons, Ivan and Riz approaches the first ride to their left. The colossal structure standing before them consist of many giant loops. The tracks are suspended as high as twenty-five feet above the surface. With free speeds ranging from seventy up to one hundred and twenty miles an hour, the structure actually surrounds the entire property. A waiting slash boarding area sits directly at grade level. The screams of many passengers are heard as a thirty-foot long roller coaster, works the rails. Moving at top speed, the steel titanium cars travels on what appears to be a series of inclines. Next, having surpassed the latter comes a multitude of steep hills. Plunging almost simultaneously, the roller coaster twists and then turns. Traveling upside down, the cars plunges once more. Advancing around a series of giant loops, the roller coaster returns to the surface. The name of this ride is called the "Super Loop." Moments after the vehicle comes to a complete stop and the restraints are removed (manually), comes the passengers. While many are seen leaving in an orderly fashion to make room for others, some who are obviously ill quickly makes a run for it.

This ride becomes Ivan and Rizzo's first choice.

As they patiently wait in line, Ivan and Riz see Donnie Nicholson.

Donnie, who is already in line himself, calls them over.

"Hey, what's up y'all?" He says.

The three shake hands.

"You know you've got best seat in the house." Rizzo tells Donnie.

"Straight up." Ivan added.

"Literally."

"So, how long have you been in line man?" Ivan asks.

"About a half hour." Says Don.

"At least."

"It's a popular ride." He explains.

"Been on it at least three times today."

"It's the shit."

"I'm telling y'all."

"It certainly looks like it." Says Ivan, as he closely studies it.

"Our Lady of Sorrows is obviously well financed."

"Word." Says Riz.

"Because it's like a miniature Six Flags out here."

"You have all of these state of the art assed rides." Donnie adds.

"And a game room?"

"Might as well enjoy all of this, cause its leavin in two weeks."

Ivan and Rizzo both nodded.

"I've seen almost everybody out here today." Donnie continues on.

"From school and beyond."

"I bet you have." Says Ivan.

"Which reminds me, that I've just thought of something." He began.

"Yeah, what's up?" Asked Donnie.

"More than likely, you are already up on the recent thefts that's been plaguing the school." Ivan began. "Are you not?" "Yeah." Answers Donnie. Riz also nods.

"It's becoming a serious problem for the entire student body." Ivan began to break it down. "Namely for the sixth grade classes." "The rest of the building is fine."

"Somebody from either our class, or possibly one of the other two is involved."

"I know it."

"Fuck the no snitching policy, because there are others who are always watching."

"And these very same individuals, know exactly who's responsible, but yet they're two-faced, chicken shit, and to some extent hypocritical." "Straight up." Says Donnie and Riz. They both reply in unison. "But if somebody were to steal from them, they would be among the first to cry wolf." "I may not be Sherlock Holmes." Ivan continues.

"But if no course of action is taken, eventually Rothstein will more than likely intervene." "Understand that neither side, whether it be good or bad, likes a thief."

"Especially when it comes to internal, or in-house affairs."

"Just like those two know nothings, who were found in the Dan Ryan Woods last week." Ivan began to point out." "I knew it!" Donnie cracks.

"You had something to do with it, didn't you?"

Rizzo chuckles. "They tried to ambush you, you fought em hand to feet, you took their guns, fucked them up, and then snapped both of they necks."

"Some Kung Fu-Gangsta Shit."

"A Black Shaolin Triad."

Ivan smiled and nodded his head.

"Whatever man." He says.

"Naw, let me stop playin." Donnie clears his throat.

"But, Ivan and me were actually among the last few people to see them alive." Rizzo added. "Word?" Says Donnie. "Word." Rizzo confirms.

"Just before these dudes came up missing, they tried to stick us up." Ivan reclaims the floor. "Rizzo, his friends Alfred and Thomas, and myself had just come back from hanging out with his cousin." "We had all gone to the movies out in Hillside."

"Rizzo's cousin dropped us off near Flournoy and California, just one block east of where he lives." "Next, we all take a short cut down the alley and before we knew it."

"We meet the fake assed Frank and Jessie James."

Both Donnie and Rizzo began to laugh. "They're like, y'all know what time it is."

"Give us everything and whatever you've got."

"It was actually more of a shock at first."

"I'm like being both funny, nervous, and sarcastic."

"Let me remind you, they also wore ski masks." Ivan faces Donnie.

"And I tell them, y'all make this easy."

"The lead gunman laughed, both of them carried thirty-eight's."

"And at the blink of an eye, Ivan wrestles the gun away from the leader." Rizzo tells Donnie. "Completely disarming him!" "Neither of us, the jacks nor my friends, not even myself saw that coming." "And so it was so smooth the way he did it Don."

Donnie himself laughs and then claps.

"So I WASN'T too far off." He says.

"Well, you ain't kill em."

" I just gave them an old school neighborhood ass whoopin, and sent them home." Ivan says. "Knocked them out, yanked their masks and told them--------.

"That's what you get for playing with guns." Rizzo finished.

"Hell naw." Donnie chuckles. "You getting to be a bad mothafucka."

"Ain't ya?" "The Real life Bruce Lee Roy."

"But that was just only the tip of the iceberg Don." Ivan comes back.

"The second one after, he tried to blow my head off and after I disarmed him and knocked his ass out." "I spit on em, took their guns, unloaded them, and threw the barrels in a dumpster." "And I asked them, who's the pussy assed nigga now?"

"After I've done away with them, twenty to as many as forty more niggas emerged from the bushes." Rizzo and Donnie began to laugh themselves silly as they listened.

"Well not exactly from the bushes, but you all know what I'm talking about!" Ivan

Chuckles. "Shit." "Sounds like a scene from the Snake and Crane Secret, I know right?" "It was just Rizzo, and his two homies who also have backgrounds in the martial arts, and of course last but not least, myself." Donnie smiled and nodded.

"Talk about a helluva of a fight."

"But the Calvary arrived, not too long thereafter." Rizzo added.

"Some of our allies and mutual friends came through for us."

"In the end, those who were able to run, they ran."

"A lot of em didn't, because they were already laid out."

"The street was littered with bodies, and talk about some pain."

"I fought with the ringleader privately." Ivan added.

"Yeah, they fought one on one up at Atgeld." Rizzo points out.

"It was actually a clean fight."

"I beat him, dislocated his arm, snapped it back into place, dusted him off and sent him on his way." "You not only got balls Ivan." Donnie began shaking his hand.

"But, you also got a lotta heart."

"Thanks." Says Ivan.

At this time, the boys have now reached the center of the line.

"It was rumored that the two who tried to rob us, were later picked up by the police." Rizzo began. "They spent a night in lock up on Kedzie, and the next day somebody bailed them out." "By ten thirty the following night, they were both dead."

"Who do you think did it?" Asked Donnie.

"Some believe that it was Sir George, others believe that it was Hannibal." Rizzo answers. "Well for starters, I know Sir George personally." Ivan began.

"Besides him being a close and personal friend, he wouldn't do it because he had already made his point that night when Eli and Rodney tried to sneak into his club."

"One of his body guards saw that the ID's had the faces of older women, he threatened to call the police and they just took off." "Not to mention that the guy himself was huge, but they weren't trying to argue." "I bet they asses was mega salty." Donnie chuckled.

"They were." Ivan concludes.

"The other rumor circulating is that Hannibal swore Eli and Rodney into the gang."

"As part of their initiation, they jacked somebody's car and they passed with flying colors." "But something went wrong, from what someone else told me."

"Eli and Rodney became entirely too cocky and overconfident."

"Sticking up people at random, without Hannibal's permission, picking fights and causing friction among the rest of the gang, their allies, and especially their rivals."

"Just drawing all kinds of unwanted attention."

"Eventually a lot of higher ranking 24's made the executive decision long before they went to jail." "The next day, either Hannibal himself or one of the other chiefs of staff posted their bail." "More than likely, they were promised a promotion, but we all know the rest of that story." Donnie chuckled. "The only promotion that Eli and Rodney got was to dance with the devil." "Word." Says Rizzo. "Anyway as for my plan." Ivan began.

“I could easily just place a hidden camera or cameras, in or around the rooms.”

“That actually sounds cool.” Donnie shakes his head.
“Yeah, straight up Ivan.” Rizzo backs him up.
“Just to get the ball rolling.” Ivan explains.
“But other plans will soon follow.”
“I’ll keep you all posted.”
“Aight.” Says both Riz and Donnie.

Once again they both respond in unison.

After almost forty-five minutes of waiting in line, Ivan and his three sidekicks are now situated at the gate. “Here, take these just in case.” He says. Ivan hands each of them a stick of gum. Once they’ve strapped themselves in, a safety operator briefly inspects each car. Motioning for the control operators to proceed, the ride is immediately dispatched. Quickly gaining traction, the cars’ speeds also follows suit.

At the blink of an eye starting from zero, the roller coaster already reaches its top speed. For all of the passengers as their hearts pound rapidly, many began to scream.

As the ride quickly climbs hills only to plunge, twist and then turn, a strong wind is also felt. Chewing away at their gum as their ears began to pop, Ivan and his friends maintain their grip on the bars. After circling multiple giant loops, the ride finally returns to the surface. Stepping off, it is almost as though the ride is still going. (Namely for Ivan and his friends) As they advance toward the bumper cars, it appears as though they are traveling at warp speed. A real natural high.

19

LINCOLN PARK (MID NORTH SIDE)

Situated just three miles north of downtown, during the nineteenth century, the inhabitants of the future community area ranged from affluent residents focused on the park and the Loop, to German farmers and shop keepers oriented to North Avenue, to industrial workers living near the factories along the north branch of the Chicago River.

Most early European residents were German truck farmers, whose products earned them the nickname "Cabbage Patch." By 1852 the German community was well enough established to began work on St. Michael's Roman Catholic Church, which was named for the patron saint of local brewer and land donor Michael Diversey. The city of Chicago made the southeastern portion of the area its cemetery in 1837, but the graves proved such a health hazard that the cemetery was moved and the land re-designated Lake Park in 1864. It was renamed Lincoln Park the next year for the assassinated president.

This recreational center attracted such cultural institutions as the Chicago Academy of Sciences, the Lincoln Park Zoo, and the Chicago Historical Society. 1863, Cyrus McCormick sponsored the opening of the Presbyterian Theological Seminary in the northwest section of the area: The school was later renamed for its benefactor.

In 1871, the Great Fire swept through the entire north side, including most of this neighborhood, and destroyed many of the structures here. However, the area was quickly rebuilt. Many found housing in temporary wooden shacks before the city extended fire limits to the city boundaries in 1874. During the next two decades, industrial plants such as furniture factories and the Deering Harvester Works concentrated along the North Branch of the Chicago River. Italians, Poles, Romanians, and Slovaks worked in these factories and established the working class character of the western section.

The eastern section remained an enclave of families of middle class commuters and expensive mansions fronting the park. Among the new institutions of the late nineteenth century was Crilly Court, an apartment complex designed by Daniel F. Crilly, who selected artists for tenants. In 1898, St Vincent's College, renamed De Paul University in 1907, opened near the McCormick Seminary. By the turn of the century, Lincoln Park was established as a residential neighborhood that hosted some of Chicago's major cultural institutions. During the Great Depression, the neighborhood's housing stock deteriorated as owners subdivided and neglected their properties. After World War II, the residents of Old Town, in the southeastern section were worried that their community hovered on the verge of becoming a slum. (Or a ghetto) They formed the Old Town Triangle Association in 1948. The latter inspired residents of the mid-north neighborhood to create a similar organization in 1950. In 1954 the Lincoln Park Conservation Association was organized to cover the entire community area. LPCA pursued neighborhood renewal by encouraging private rehabilitation of property and the use of government tools such as federal urban-renewal funds and enforcement of the housing codes. In 1956, the neighborhood was designed as a conservation area, and in the 1960's the city began implementing its "General Neighborhood Renewal Plan."

Although the LPCA had consciously tried to avoid the wholesale clearance that took place in Hyde Park, it incurred the wrath of poor people who lived in the southwestern quarter of the area. The Concerned Citizens of Lincoln Park argued that African-Americans (including Ivan's grandparents) and Puerto Ricans were being displaced from their homes and priced out of the renewing neighborhood. Developers bought land near the park and high-rise apartment buildings, to the consternation of LPCA, which had hope to keep the district congenial to families. In recent years, the land values have increased dramatically, making it difficult for people and institutions in financial straits to remain here. The exodus of the poor continues even today. In 1973, the struggling McCormick Seminary sold its land to DePaul and moved south to Hyde Park.

Single professionals and childless couples are growing continuously.

The newly built high rises and rehabilitated old homes left by their predecessors, are now in their possession. It is projected that by the end of this century, Lincoln Park will be among the higher status of neighborhoods. (Namely in the city)

Along the tree-lined Armitage Avenue, bustling with traffic, both vehicular as well as pedestrian; lies a combination of upscale, exotic, exquisite, and last but not least authentic eateries. From the corner of north Sheffield to Racine Avenue lies a diverse spectrum of taverns, pubs, a lone catholic parish, a bicycle shop and a Seven Eleven.

A newly opened Starbucks coffee house, a few independently owned boutique shops, clothing stores, a hair salon, and a cleaners sits on the south side along Armitage.

Situated near the Ravenswood "L", lies a shoe repair shop and the long established Cartier Photography Studio. Directly across the street from the latter is a Laundromat.

Ravenswood trains serve the Armitage Station located on its namesake avenue, running between the Loop (downtown) it ends at a modern terminal at Kimball Avenue, in the city's Albany Park neighborhood. The station, which has been in use since the turn of the century, employs a brick terra cotta stationhouse at grade level. Its dual side platforms located twenty feet above street level still bears its classic revival design, which was inspired by the work of a sixteenth century Italian Renaissance architect.

The original peaked roofed canopies remain in place as well as the tubular railings and posts with panels of decorative, and vaguely diamond shaped metal work. Perhaps the only alterations, which had been made since its birth were none other than its paint scheme (now chocolate brown) and the current signage. The original lighting and crooked shaped fixtures also remain in place. The immediate structure employs four tracks. The Rave, which utilizes the outer tracks, summons passengers on the affected platforms mentioned. The

Evanston Express, that runs only during rush periods, bypasses this station as well as Howard trains. The latter, which emerges from a portal at Willow Street, employs the inner tracks. At this time, countless passengers are now seen entering and exiting. It is obviously rush hour.

Cartier Photography

Born May 1, 1911 in Little Rock Arkansas, Joseph Cartier Sr. had a dream.

He wanted to become a photographer, and run his own studio.

The son of bootleggers, at an early age Mr. Cartier not only learned the "family business", but he also developed an interest in boxing.

With the employment of his bare knuckles and raw power, the teenage Cartier ultimately becomes a force to be reckoned with.

Most notably amongst his peers, their parents, even the local Klan.

The oldest of seventeen children, nine brothers and eight sisters, to earn extra money, Mr. Cartier fought. As a self-educated man who taught himself to read and write, the young Joseph was never without an angle. His key hobbies at the time besides hunting, was also taking pictures. At the age of nineteen, Mr. Cartier arrives in Chicago.

With only his tripod and four hundred dollars to his name, Ivan's grandfather continued his hustle. Working at the Stockyards by day and taking pictures at night, Mr. Cartier saves just enough money to open his studio.

May 1, 1932, one day after his twenty-first birthday, marked the grand opening.

Despite the Great Depression, and more surprisingly during Urban Renewal, Mr. Cartier's business still prospered. At the time of his demise with no one else suited to run the business, his youngest son

Joseph Jr. is elected. Perhaps it was more than a coincidence. About a month before his father's death, Junior better known by his middle name as Clayton was already a college graduate. As of the present day, Clayton not only runs the shop, but he also owns it. Following the current recession, the quote that his father once made almost six decades earlier, suddenly comes to mind.

"Last hired, first fired my ass!"

For quite sometime, Ivan his favorite nephew has developed an interest in terms of holding a job, as well earning a little money. On the account of his newfound attitude on life, as well as his ability to do what is expected of him, Clayton of course says yes.

Especially after seeing his most recent report card, Ivan of course hears these words:

"How soon can you start?"

He was hired the following week.

Working four hours a day, five days a week (minus Friday and Sunday) Ivan's uncle pays him roughly fifty dollars each week. Tax-free.

While his uncle is busy catering to his clientele, Ivan at this time works not only to keep the store clean and orderly, but he is also responsible for the layouts, followed by the removals, the installations and in some cases, the re-arranging of certain backdrops.

At 6:00, His Aunt Mardi urges him to take a break.

Thanking her nephew, Mardi who is not only Clayton's wife, but also his business partner returns to the front lobby.

Retreating to his place of solitude, namely in the lower level, there are five rooms.

The first, which is located near the stairs, appears to be a storage area.

To his left on the opposite side is obviously a darkroom, on the account of the hanging exposures, a dual sink and last but not least multiple red lights.

A black curtain hangs in the doorway.

Further down the hall towards the rear, lies a recently renovated laundry room.

Also situated near the latter, is a utility room, as well as that of an office.

A much larger recreational area is located directly under the lobby.

For Ivan, this was his own personal hollideck.

Like Captain Piccard to Star Trek: The Next Generation.

From the front all the way to the rear, the flooring consist of a creamy masonry/ ceramic marble trim. The interior brick walls that was once red, was recently stripped and later sandblasted. Priceless paintings also cover the latter.

Modern candescent lamp fixtures hang firmly above the ceiling, as well as the bearing walls. Supplemented by the track lights overlooking the pictures are several plants.

Leather furniture and a huge entertainment center occupies the front, while a small bar and a refrigerator corresponds to the center.

A modest restroom is situated behind the latter.

Turning on the TV, the privileged young employee fires up the Sega Genesis.

Popping in a game, he turns it on and began to play.

Two minutes later, his aunt Mardi comes down.

“You have some company sweetie.” She says.

“Thanks Aunt Mardi.” Ivan responds.

Alfred and Rizzo descend before him.

Closely observing the room, the two gave Ivan a nod.

“It is really sweet down here.” Alfred began.

“Word em up, Al.” Rizzo added.

“It ain’t all that different than yo grandmother’s apartment, Ivan.”

“So this is what yo uncle and aunt pays you for?” Alfred roasts.

Ivan grins and then nods.

“Oh, I hustle.” Ivan assures him.

“We know.” Says Riz.

“I take it you two, were just in the neighborhood.” Ivan guessed.

“Something like that.” Rizzo began.

The two guests began to take a seat.

“My aunt had some errands to run, and she dropped me and Alfred off in front of Dennis’s.” “We hung out there, and played games.”

“The El was right next door on Belmont, so we took the first train that pulled in.”

Alfred added.

“We thought about you and got off here at Armitage.”

“That’s cool, I appreciated it y’all.”

“By the way, you’re both just in time.”

Ivan then hands one of them a control pad.

“I’ve got forty-five minutes.” He explains

“You can play too, Alfred.”

Getting up, Ivan surrenders his controller.

"Thanks." Says Al.

"What time do you get off again?" He asked.

"Nine." Says Ivan.

Alfred shakes his head.

"I can't tell everybody that I have a job either." Ivan began, as he sits on the opposite side of the room. "And, you shouldn't." Rizzo advises.

"Because, you'll have more people sweatin' you than ever."

"Or kissin' your ass in other words." Alfred added.

They are now playing Tommy Lasorda's Baseball.

"Yeah, especially the girls, both in school and around the house." Says Ivan.

"They're so ridiculous."

"They're Goldiggers." Rizzo chuckles.

"What did you say Ivan?" Alfred began to ask.

"If they didn't stand by, behind or even with you in the beginning, they can step huh?"

"That's right." Ivan says with authority.

"Bad enough, that they weren't in my corner when I being treated like a so-called nerd." "I just don't have time for their pathetic games anymore, Alfred."

"I don't blame you G." Rizzo nods.

"The only girls who stood by me from the beginning, was Andrea, Denise, and Nikki."

"And I love all three of them." Ivan concludes.

"Especially the latter."

"And some of these guys are just as comparable."

"Even though a lot of them are beginning to respect me more, there are still some brownnosers out there."

"Straight up." Says both Alfred and Rizzo.

"Like that old saying about the elephant, that never forgets." Ivan chuckles.

"We've got you Ivan." Rizzo laughed.

"Are there any new developments on your plan we've talked about?" He then asks.

"Yes, there is Riz."

"I'm going to arrange a meeting with either one or, possibly all three of the teachers whose rooms have been affected." Ivan breaks it down.

Alfred and Riz nod their heads as they continue to listen.

"It'll be the first priority upon my arrival tomorrow."

"More than likely they will say yes, and either myself or someone else will install the cameras." "The person or persons responsible will be caught red-handed."

"They'll either be suspended, arrested, expelled, or all of the above."

"For what its worth, I know for certain that Rothstein, nor Jamison will take this lightly." Ivan concludes. "Yeah. I bet they won't." Says Rizzo.

Getting up briefly, Ivan grabs his backpack off the floor.

Turning on the sound system, he places a tape into the first deck.

The latter is the most recent by their very own DJ. Killer watt.

Upon pressing the play button, is the sound of Killer Watt's voice:

You're listening another House Mix from DJ. Killer Watt
Volume Four

The opening song is Turn Up the Base by Kool Rock Steady and Tyree Cooper.

"Are you gonna get one in with us?" Asks Rizzo.

He offers Ivan his control pad.

"Yeah." He responds.

The title screen now says Golden Axe.

"You want to know what really pisses me off?" Ivan asked his guests.

"What's that?" Says Alfred, as Ivan accepts Rizzo's controller.

"I might have mentioned it before, but whenever something belongs to a student in the classroom and he or she reports it missing."

"Usually its stolen."

"That person of course, would try to find out who did it."

Alfred and Riz nods.

"Beginning with his or her fellow classmates."

"The person affected is usually upset or disgusted, and yet the other students think that it's a laughing matter."

"They will swear up and down that they don't know."

"But they never want the teachers to find out." Rizzo cuts in.

"And when they do find out, the teacher's guess is just as good as the one who was ripped off."

"Straight up." Says Alfred.

"And when the teacher demands that whoever is responsible to come forward, nobody still says nothing." "Unless the other students like you, they're gonna plead to the fifth."

"Let me give you a prime example."

"When I was in Mr. Schwartz's class, I one day brought my radio to listen to during recess." Ivan breaks it down further.

Alfred and Rizzo continued to nod.

"Along with the radio, I had a tape."

"Kenneth, our very own D.J Killer Watt, of course made it for me."

"What was so interesting about this case was that it wasn't my radio that got stolen."

"Ok, its lunchtime, and Schwartz has us all line up at the door."

"I bring my backpack with me."

"Of course, once again it wasn't my radio that was stolen."

"Instead, it was my prized mix tape."

"Now the funny part about the situation was that I still had my lunch."

"Even thieves have to eat." Ivan then chuckles.

Rizzo laughed.

"So here it is and lunch is over."

"It's time for recess."

"Schwartz retreats to the teacher's lounge, and we all go outside."

"I'm carrying my backpack so it won't seem as obvious, and I retreat towards the dugout on the west end of the playground."

"Before my parents bought me my current boom box which is twice as big, I had my little ghetto blaster that my sister Jennifer left me."

"And sure enough as if my name was Sherlock Holmes, I noticed that my tape was missing the minute I opened my bag."

"One minute I'm happy as hell like the Kool Aid man, another minute I crying like Oliver Hardy." Both Alfred and Rizzo exploded in laughter.

"Of course I didn't really cry." Ivan laughs.

"But I was pissed."

"Some of the other boys from my class who were out there with me, pretended to look dumbfounded."

"But yet, they all knew who did it."

"Especially Lenny's ass."

"Lenny was actually the one sitting closest to the thief."

"In fact, Lenny was the first person that I asked."

"He insisted that at first that, he didn't know."

"I never really liked him." Says Rizzo as Ivan continues on.

"Lenny had no backbonc as I remembered."

"He was phony, always smiling in your face, whiny and chicken shit." Ivan added.

"Curtis told me that he did it himself, but I didn't believe him."

"Because you was always used to him joking around." Rizzo reminds him.

"The next day for some reason unknown, Curtis is absent."

"He was out for like two days."

"It was said that he had a death in his family, or something."

"But anyway, back to Lenny."

"Two days later, he comes forth and he asked me if I wanted to know who did it."

"So I tell him yeah."

"He now tells me that Curtis did it."

"Curtis stole my tape."

"Faggot." Snaps Alfred.

"And because I wasn't supposed to bring my radio or anything that was proven to be entertaining to the school, without the consent of my parents or Schwartz himself I just couldn't simply tell neither."

"In other words like Ice Cube, you were ganked." Says Rizzo.

"Word." Ivan responds.

"I couldn't engage Curtis, because I wasn't strong enough back then like I am today."

"You've become his equal, like the Soviet Union to the United States." Says Riz.

"And forget about sticking Lenny in his face, I just wanted to smack him just like the little bitch that he was."

"And not to mention the rest of the class."

"Yeah, I remember." Rizzo replies.

"Even then, Nikki was in my corner." Ivan reminds his guests.

Alfred laughed.

"It's really a doggy dog world." He sighs.

"I'd have to be the most outspoken sixth grader, let alone the most outspoken grade-schooler." Ivan shakes his head.

"Sometimes it pays to stand alone Ivan." Rizzo tells him.

At this point, Ivan nears the end of the game.

It is now the final battle."

"Yeah, straight up." Ivan gives Rizzo a pound.

Looking up at the clock, Ivan shuts off the console and then the TV.

The music in the tape player ceases.

Side A is complete.

"It's time for me to head back gentlemen." Ivan says with a mild distinguished accent.

"Cool." Alfred and Rizzo replies.

"Thanks for stopping by, and give my regards to your aunt Riz." Ivan then smiled.

The boys began their ascension to the main floor.

Having met with all three of the sixth grade teachers at school the next day, Ivan also consults with the assistant principal, who in turn summons Detective Jenkins of the Chicago Police Department. Mr. Dunn, the in house security guard (also employed by the city's school board) was also in attendance. Immediately one day after the meeting, all three classrooms on the fourth floor are retrofitted with hidden cameras.

Jensen Scholastic Academy, Thursday 12:35pm
Fourth Floor

Right now all three classrooms 403, 404, and 405 are empty.

Its teachers are currently on their breaks while its students play and socialize outside.

With the lights turned off, the only lighting that is now available shines from that of the exterior. (Namely from the sun.) At this time most of the other rooms although unoccupied, remains clean. The floors are spotless, the bookshelves well organized, desks are cleared, and the computers are shut off.

Outside on the west playground near the assembling area right under the flagpole, Ivan mingles with several of his peers. Among them there's Donnie Nicholson, Kendrick Watts, Ronald Cox, Tyree Clark and last but not least Nikki.

Instead of playing their usual game of basketball around this time, the six of them decides to just simply enjoy the afternoon breeze and chill.

"Check it out." Ivan began.

"I just finished a couple of new pieces last night."

"Is anybody up for a peak?"

"We always up." Answers Tyree.

"Considering you're that good."

Ivan is obviously referring to his latest artwork.

"A lot of times his drawings and sketches are so life like, that they practically creep me out." Nikki tells the others.

"In fact, I actually have a few of them hanging up in my room."

"I even have one of Ivan's self portraits on the back of my door."

"Yeah, he's good." Ronald nodded.

"Shit, what else is new?" Says Donnie.

"Anyway, I'm gonna head up and get them." Ivan now heads through the double doors.

"I'll be right back."

"Aight." The others all reply in unison.

Fourth Floor hall

Jogging up the stairs from the north side of the complex, Ivan walks beyond the double doors leading into this partially desolate corridor. Quietly roaming the hallway, he witnesses the unimaginable. (Accidentally so to speak)

Several of his fellow students are ripping off a classroom.

His classroom.

Desperately gathering as many of their peer's personal belongings as possible while another acts as a lookout, Ivan on the other hand remains unseen.

He watches them from around the corner.

Shaking his head, he silently chuckles.

Oh, hell no! He thought.

Perhaps the one thing that he finds appalling minus the fact that they were actually bold enough to break in and steal the items of other students, was that they had chosen his room once more. To say the least, Ivan commends them on their discretion by way of not tearing up the room, as well as their time frame. The tall and bulky youth who stood guard was also smart enough to keep the door closed.

However, little that they knew was not only were they being watched by Ivan, but also by none other than big brother. The hunters have become the hunted.

Now smiling, Ivan decides to lend them a hand.

"What the fuck you want man?" Asked the tall and overweight youth.

Turning around to face his friends who at this point are ready to leave, the large boy suddenly looks as though he's seen a ghost.

Dropping to his knees, the young man struggles to breathe.

He passes out shortly thereafter.

Emerging from his shadow as though he's a warrior sent back from hell, is Ivan.

Already in his fighting stance, he quietly steps over the former look out.

The others, who are obviously startled, dropped their duffel bags.

Another attempts to succeed where his predecessor failed.

"Mothafucka, you ain't that tou---!"
Ivan quickly snaps a left jab.
The second youth is already unconscious.
A third dashes in and tries to throw a punch, but Ivan surgically cuts him off.
Folding his arm back, a grotesque popping sound is heard.
With complete control of his wrist, Ivan dislocates the boy's arm.
As the youth grips his shoulder (which is also severed), he moans.
To finish him off, Ivan slams his head into a desk.
With another following suit, Ivan parries his hand and delivers a back fist.
Dislocating the arm and shoulder of enemy number five, Ivan tosses him to the floor.
Engaging his sixth opponent between two desks, the young man attempts to throw an axe kick. Missing Ivan who now dodges him, the boy instead strikes an empty chair.
Coming back with a sharp kick of his own, Ivan prevails.

The heel of his left foot descends upon the boy's knee causing his entire leg to fold back. From what appears to be the sound of cracking bones, his leg is obviously broken.

As he now screams, Ivan shuts him up with a palm strike.

Before the seventh fighter could even advance, Ivan kicks the desk causing him to topple and collide. Falling face down, the young man hits another.

"Don't forget to clean up before you leave." Ivan says to his now vanquished opposition. Shaking his head, he bows. Crawling and moaning, the seven hoods all of whom Ivan had known are dumbfounded.

Walking out of his classroom, he embarks upon another encounter.

Jumping back into his stance, Ivan gives two incoming hoods storming in from the southern stairs a front kick to the abdomen. Left and right.

Another attempts to attack him from behind, but instead catches a right foot. The latter smashes directly across his face as Ivan crosses his left Nike behind his right.

Sliding across the floor (namely on his ass) the shorter youth knocks over several of his friends who also try to rush in. Catching the left fist of his eleventh rival, Ivan twists both forward and then back (along with his left arm) and ultimately flings his wrist.

The young man goes down hard.

Clutching at his lower back, the husky hood moans, and grits his teeth.

Snapping the left side of his right foot across the shin of number thirteen, Ivan turns his body bends his left knee and kicks up. Executing a double jab (left and right) into the abdomens of two others at once, Ivan then smashes both their heads together.

In conjunction with his most recent strikes, Ivan roars.

The base in his voice corresponds to that of pure rage and ferocity that goes unmeasured. Forcing his last opponent into a limbo-like position, Ivan chops him in the throat. Literally.

Hiding around the corner of a nearby workstation along the north hall, thirteen-year-old Cedric Holt, and his female friend twelve-year-old Hannah Dubois are scared.

Perhaps they messed with the wrong student.

Without being seen by Ivan who now walks toward the southern stairs and their friends who are still laid out, Cedric and Hannah makes a break for it.

They retreat to the northern stairway.

20

DR. JAMISON'S OFFICE (THE ASSISTANT PRINCIPAL)
FIRST FLOOR, FRIDAY MORNING

Glancing at the video footage retrieved from the hidden cameras upstairs, Karen Jamison and Mrs. Holmes who are also joined by Mrs. Cobbs, Mrs. Toussaint, and Mrs. Bronson are all but surprised.

Exchanging looks that employs the uttermost of disdain, they suddenly began to chuckle. Rolling the footage repeatedly, the five women shook their heads, smiled and then pointed at the monitor. As the assistant principal struggles to keep a straight face (as though trying not to laugh), Mrs. Holmes chuckles. Mrs. Cobbs, who is obviously impressed, nods her head. While Mrs. Toussaint appears nauseated and frail (apparently she's disgusted), Mrs. Bronson on the other hand is somewhat embarrassed.

Dr. Jamison stops the tape.

"I've known Ivan for a long time." She began.

The four teachers all nodded as they continue to listen. "His sister Jennifer and his brother Simon were also students here." "And their grades were equally exceptional."

"For most of his life, namely from when I first met his acquaintance, Ivan has been through a lot." Holmes, Cobbs, Toussaint, and Bronson all sat before their head boss.

Situated on a common couch, which overlooks Dr. Jamison's desk, they all sipped on Espresso. "Why is it that I'm not surprised?" Asked Mrs. Holmes.

"Your guess is just as good as mine." Mrs. Cobbs replies

"Ivan was always a good kid." Dr. Jamison continues.

"I could tell Karen." Mrs. Holmes tells her boss.

"I remember taking over for Pauline Rubin, the old Assistant Principal." Dr. Jamison comes back. "Because she was retiring." "I remember her." Says Mrs. Toussaint.

"Ruby was always down to Earth."

"Just before she was tapped as being Adam's assistant, she was formerly the Guidance Counselor." "Back then, I was just a mere substitute teacher." Dr. Jamison continues on. "And she told me some things about Ivan, as well as some of the other teachers who worked here at the time."

"How long ago was this?" Asked Mrs. Holmes.

"Just seven years ago." Dr. Jamison tells her.

"Ruby said that Ivan was just a first grader when she met him."

"Even she told me that Ivan was a good kid."

"Everybody, from his teachers to his peers and even his family gave him a hard time."

"The two teachers that Ivan had back then, a Mrs. Haas who Adam eventually fired, and her no-backbone having maid Joyce Conway really treated him, pardon my language ladies, like a piece of shit." "I'm surprised that Adam didn't fire her." The assistant principal now faces Mrs. Holmes. "If you asked me, Rothstein should have fired her ass too." Says Mrs. Cobbs. "Good for nothing Aunt Jermina-----. "Yes massa!" "No massa!"

"We sick boss! "I don't blame you Vearline." Dr. Jamison commends her.

"You know that it was rumored that Haas who was both German and Dutch although American-born was racist, and she didn't like children." "Particularly, those of color."

"Others said that she was sexist, because she was more favorable toward the girls as opposed to the boys." "I can believe both." Says Mrs. Toussaint. "Haas was really nasty with her students." Jamison resumes. "She practically yelled at them, and abused them."

"Both verbally and physically." "And guess who was number one on her hate list?" Asked the assistant principal. "Ivan, who else?" Says Mrs. Holmes.

"Ms. Rubin told me that Haas really did a number on Ivan."

"She harassed him, terrorized him, and humiliated him almost every day."

The other four women are shocked as Dr. Jamison continues the story.

"Conway sometimes watched her but did absolutely nothing."

"Once again, I have no idea as to why she's still working here."

"And off the record ladies, there are others just like Conway and Haas who still works here." "So why in the hell are they still here Karen?" Mrs. Holmes asked with authority.

"Politics." Dr. Jamison says with mild disgust.

"They should have been out the door a long time ago." Mrs. Bronson added.

"The only reason why Adam eliminated Haas was mainly because of political pressure." "That was exactly how much heat she brought to Rothstein."

"A lot of parents, the alderman, and other major players were really outraged." Says Dr. Jamison who now offers her employees a mint. They all accept.

"I can imagine that." Says Bronson.

"These others will eventually have their day, I can assure you."

"What did Ivan's parents do about the situation?" Asked Mrs. Holmes.

"They actually played him left field Sharon." Jamison reluctantly responds.

"As you guys know, you too Vearline."

"Ivan is from a strong working-middle class family." Jamison began.

"His mom, who you'll see from time to time, as you know is a teacher at Walt Disney."

"His father, works as a site manager for Garfield Equipment Company on Carroll."

"You know, where they build heavy machinery."

"Rocky, the man you replaced Vearline the Howard-turned professor is his brother."

Both teachers nodded. "And Mrs. Thompson is also a member of the local school council." Mrs. Cobbs reminds her. "Right, thanks." Her boss acknowledges.

"I understand that Mr. and Mrs. Thompson, has nothing more but the best of intentions toward their son." Dr. Jamison now refills her cup.

Offering her four upstanding employees another, they all decline.

"Suit yourself." She smiled.

"Mo, for me."

Mrs. Holmes laughed.

"But sometimes, they can be a bit egotistical, ignorant and power hungry over Ivan."

"I also found this out back when Ms. Rubin was the Guidance Counselor."

"You're serious?" Says Mr. Holmes.

"I'm afraid not Sharon."

"Ruby was actually the one true friend that Ivan really had."

"He used to talk to her all the time."

"I bet he did." Says Mrs. Holmes.

"Could you blame him?"

"Of course not." Says Dr. Jamison.

"Now what I meant about Mr. and Mrs. Thompson playing Ivan left field was that they knew about Haas and Conway all along."

"Maybe in their own sick way, they especially Mr. Thompson, was probably trying to give a Ivan a crash course on racism."

"As a former child psychiatrist, forget Dr. Spock, what Ivan's parents did was still wrong." The four other women continue to nod.

"Just a few years before Rock was assigned to work with you Sharon." Dr. Jamison began. She now turns to face Mrs. Holmes. "He used to be a sub."

"On a few occasions whenever Haas and Conway couldn't make it in, Rock would sometimes fill in for them." "And he told me some things about Ivan's dad."

"Rocky told me about how his brother would punish Ivan whenever Haas gave him bad reports, knowing good and well they weren't true."

"I never pictured Mr. and Mrs. Thompson like that." Says Mrs. Cobbs.

Mrs. Toussaint and Mrs. Bronson nods.

"Neither, did I." Mrs. Holmes herself answers.

"So basically you're telling me Karen, that Mr. Thompson was trying to boost his ego in an attempt to look like he was taking care of business."

"Exactly." Dr. Jamison points a finger in her direction.

"One prime example was that Haas accused Ivan vandalizing a textbook."

"But as it later turned out, the book wasn't vandalized."

"And that in fact, what Haas and Conway discovered was that the alleged graffiti was actually part of the book." "And furthermore, all of the books carried it."

"It was actually art." Mrs. Holmes nods her head with disgust.

"This Haas was really one stupid bitch, wasn't she?" She quietly thunders.

"Apparently she was." Says Mrs. Bronson.

"Ruby said that Ivan told her that his father didn't believe him, about not writing in the book, and he whooped him." "So in other words, Mr. Thompson whooped Ivan until he got a false confession?" Mrs. Cobbs tries to guess. "Yes, he did Vearline." Dr. Jamison replies.

"Ivan's father literally pushed him so hard, that Ivan was actually the only child to have multiple migraines." "Again, Ivan was just six-years old. "And Rock told me, that even though he and his brother got along, it was still like north vs. south when it came to raising their children." "I bet it was." Mrs. Cobbs chuckles. "He even told me that all that Ivan's father ever did, well at least most of the time was play politics."

"When word had finally gotten out about a boycott, a lawsuit and an internal investigation, all of a sudden Mr. and Mrs. Thompson wanted in." Dr. Jamison comes back. "They were wrong big time." Mrs. Toussaint added. The assistant principal along with the three other teachers all nodded. "Mr. Thompson, an obvious, self appointed opportunist was so puffed with pride that he couldn't even admit to his son that he made a mistake." "He instead, tries to buy his way out by giving Ivan some lavished present."

"But moreover ladies, that was only the tip of the iceberg." "Another reason why Ivan had such an uphill battle especially with his teachers, was because his parents were so over conservative, self righteous, and not to mention overcompensating."

"That they believed that old school myth that the teachers were always right, and the students weren't." "They must have been frozen in time or something." Mrs. Holmes cracked. "Hello?" The others gave her a high five. "Its 1989 goddammit!"

"You said it yourself Karen, just because a lot of these teachers have multiple degrees doesn't mean that they belong here." Mrs. Holmes recants.

"Yes, I did Sharon." Dr. Jamison reminds her.

"And to add insult to injury, Ivan's parents would often tell him that if any teacher was to strike him, whether it be with a ruler or whatever, tell them."

"And when he did, Mr. and Mrs. Thompson would suddenly pull a three eighty."

"He used to tell me himself."

"That was really a bogus thing to do." Says Mrs. Bronson. She shakes her head.

"In other words they did nothing."

"Unless, they so-called felt like it."

"And they kept doing it for years, up until now."

"His two siblings didn't fare any different."

"Even though Jennifer and Simon had the best grades, the perfect test scores and so on." "Neither, was anywhere close to bright when it came to minding their little brother."

"They practically beat Ivan as though he was Kunta Kinte."

"Atleast, they didn't chop off his other foot." Mrs. Holmes said with mild disgust.

"From the first grade up until now, Ivan was the most hated student in this school." Dr. Jamison reclaims the floor. "Not only did his peers despise him, but what was more disturbing, was that a lot of the teachers too." "Why did they hate him so much?" Asked Mrs. Toussaint. "Because he was more intelligent." Mrs. Holmes answers.

"Even though Ivan himself didn't see it, the other kids and the teachers obviously did."

"They tried to kill that poor boy." Dr. Jamison says as she finishes her second and final cup. "I'm really proud of Ivan today." The assistant principal happily admits .

"I hear that he has a job." Says Mrs. Cobbs.

"He works at his uncle's photography studio up north." Her colleague reminds her.

"That's good." Dr. Jamison nods.

"He learns his first trade, discovers the fundamentals of hard work, and last but not least, Ivan makes him a little money."

"For the simple fact that Ivan didn't give up, he hung in there, and didn't become anything like the very people who picked on him, my hat goes off to him."

The others nodded.

"Instead of him getting mad, or even Ivan became smarter, more creative, and more productive." "Even against his enemies."

"You know, for what it's worth." Mrs. Cobbs began.

"As many times as I reprimanded students for fighting, I've finally come to several conclusions." "If you can't always turn the other cheek in real life, what makes you think that you can always do it here." "Face it, you can't always walk away from a situation."

"Especially if your immediate safety is threatened."

"I think that some of these traditional school rules are nothing more but just plain bullshit." Mrs. Holmes adds. "For example, two students are fighting."

"There's one who is who is honest, hardworking, and upright."

"The other is a renowned troublemaker."

"For the sake of argument ladies, let's say that Student "A" has tried everything in either his or her power, to get along with Student "B.""

"However, Student "B" still doesn't want to act right."

"He or she becomes more ignorant, more provocative, and Student "B" punches "A" first." Everyone including Dr. Jamison herself agrees. They nod their heads.

"Student "A" hits back."

"The last time I checked, that was self defense."

"And yet, we the teachers tell the students that they shouldn't take matters into their own hands." "It's almost as though, we're sounding like hypocrites."

"And yet, we have the nerve to punish both sides, because of something for which only one started." "That's really stupid." "I agree with you Sharon." Says Dr. Jamison.

"Seriously, but you still have to think in legal terms."

"Like if an altercation breaks out between two students, and if one or both gets hurts given that the incident happened on school property, both the school board and the city could be held liable." "That's why Adam's not playing around."

"But what if there are sometimes circumstances even beyond the control of those who are usually good?" "Take Ivan on this tape for example."

For the seventh time, the young assistant principal rolls the footage.

"Jesus, this boy is really good!" Mrs. Holmes whispers loudly.

"I figured Ivan was working out and all, he started shedding weight and then buffing up." "But I didn't know he could fight like that." She now chuckles.

"His parents enrolled him in the martial arts a year ago." Dr. Jamison explains.

"He really did a number on them too."

"Ouch, he's gonna need a chiropractor!" Mrs. Bronson points at the screen.

"These other boys especially, and even some of these girls had better watch out."

"I'd like to ask, where in the hell did this boy come from?" Asked Mrs. Cobbs.

Sometime ago while on their very first date, Nikki asked Ivan a similar question.

"It was like he came from out of nowhere."

"Not too long ago, Ivan was like this timid fat kid who otherwise kept a low profile."

"One minute, he's an honor's student, another minute he's a super jock!"

Mrs. Holmes chuckles. "Someone tells me that he speaks three languages too."

"I can believe that also." Says Mrs. Toussaint.

"He does." Dr. Jamison confirms.

"It takes just one of him to make all of my kids look like modern-day cotton pickers." Mrs. Toussaint roasts. "And I've got the so-called gifted class."

"Ain't that a ------."

"You ain't right Shirley." Mrs. Holmes shakes her head.

"Well at least, we know who our thieves are." Jamison finally points out.

"Some of these boys doesn't even attend this school anymore."

"Once we get them, we find the mastermind.

The others nod.

"Before we call Michael to pick them up, I'd say we give them a little time to recover."

"They're damned well gonna need it." Mrs. Cobbs snaps.

The bell sounds.

"Its time for you ladies to clock in, and head up." Dr. Jamison advises.

Punching in, the teachers go to work.

Monday Morning (The Following Week)

Waking up, all is well for twelve-year-old Harvey Holloway.

Having breakfast with his single mother and his younger sister, all is well.

Stepping out of his family's apartment on west Franklin Boulevard without being jumped on or shot at, all was well. Catching the daily school bus, all is well.

Arriving at Washington Irving Elementary where he is enrolled, all is well.

Upon entry into the crowded lobby, his grim-faced, mildly shocked, and seemingly concerned principal summons the tall and overweight youth.

Thinking nothing of it as he shrugs, nods, and then smiles, Harvey joins the man in his office. Even as he walks in, all is well.

About thirty minutes later, two uniformed CPD officers flank Harvey.

With his hands cuffed tightly behind his back, the dumbfounded youngster is no longer smiling. He shakes his head in disbelief.

"C'mon, watch your head buddy." Says one of the officers.

Taking the fresh-faced cop's advise, Harvey ducks his head as he now takes the back seat. As the white and blue marked Impala takes off along Oakley Boulevard, a senior gaunt-faced official radios in. All is not so well.

Jacob Beider Public School (East Garfield Park)

Located along a crumbling and blighted commercial strip along Kedzie Avenue near Walnut Street is where twelve-year-old Willie Garrison is enrolled.

Having received a left jab where his mouth is for not only talking shit to his nemesis this past Thursday (namely at his former school), but also Lil' Willie had the nerve to try to engage his opposition, head on. Perhaps, Willie failed to remember that the "good ol' days were of course like Milli Vanilli's career: Dead.

A former student of Jensen, Willie was once enrolled in the gifted program where he used to maintain straight A's. The oldest of three children, Willie like most of his friends and fellow peers never knew who is father was. Is it his mother who struggles to wear both the apron as well as the pants. By day, Estelle Garrison, age twenty-seven is a package handler employed by UPS. However at night, Ms. Garrison moonlights as a part time exotic dancer. Working at Club Babylon in the expanding South Loop area (Downtown), her stage name is simply known as "Heart Attack."

Given to her by the club's owner slash her boss, Guy "Lucky" Peters, Peters himself deemed her name appropriate on the account of her overwhelmingly gorgeous body.

Willie, who is once again the oldest of three, his brother Marcel, age ten, and his youngest sister Marisol, age nine, was recently elected as the man of the house by his mother. Besides taking care of his younger siblings, it was also required for Willie to not only maintain his studies, but to also generate additional income.

About a year ago, the young man suddenly embarks upon the wrong path by selling drugs. As a result, Willie was both arrested and expelled.

In addition to one night in jail, a judge sentenced him to two weeks of home confinement.

Prior to his first run-in, Willie sold marijuana to pay for not only his apparel, but also to cover his mother's phone and from time to time, the cooking gas.

Surprisingly, although Ms. Garrison cursed her son for the fact that he had been caught, she yet, still commended him for his illegal contributions.

About two days later after a CCS officer (Cook County Sheriff's) deactivated his electronic bracelet, he was advised by his Uncle Harry who was once in the game himself, if he's to remain in the business, never again sell his products out in the open.

Furthermore, he should always know his customers, his competitors, and always remain discrete. Harry also advised him to keep his eyes open for stick up artists, as well as that of police officials. In an effort to avoid taxation, never sell on occupied gang turf.

Especially if he's working alone, and with that Willie takes Harry's advice to heart.

Willie's connection to Ivan goes back to as far as the fourth grade.

Back then he too played a part in making his enemies' life a living hell.

To add insult to injury, although Willie was believed to have stolen countless items from Ivan, the rest of the class remained silent.

As in the case of what Willie attempted to do last Thursday.

Once again attempted.

Payback was truly a bitch.

When Willie sustained Ivan's killer jab, the dope man/thief was instantly knocked out.

He awoke with a bloodied nose minutes later.

Four days later, Will remains dumbfounded.

Determined to move forward and forget about his defeat, he planned to collect his cut for the items he had stolen and hang it up.

Well, at least he thought it was that simple....

Early in the morning at his usual time, Willie arrives on the playground, he shoots hoops with some of his peers, and he attends his classes. At noon, he has his lunch; he flirts with the girls and chills with his homies. At twelve-thirty, while most of his class enjoys recess, Willie along with several of his friends remains in the cafeteria.

Producing a pack of cards, Will and his friends distributes them amongst themselves and began to play. Within his circles, are Mustafa Henson, Kris Mathews, Quentin Leaks, and Bernard Shaw. Perhaps what is interesting about these four young men was just that last Thursday they all had their limbs either dislocated or broken.

Almost one week later, they are now completely healed!

"So the rumors are true." Mustafa began. He studies his hand. "About what?" Asked Kris. He acts as though he has no idea. "Ivan fool!" Mustafa punches him in the back.

"Ivan's got some balls for a change." Quentin chuckles. Mustafa tosses out two of his cards. Willie retrieves them and throws out two of his own. "Buddhist fist and Dragon claw himself." "The Last Dragon in the hood!" He shakes his head.

"And Harvey's big ass was the first mothafucka to feel his wrath."

Kris throws out three of his cards. Willie claims them. "That nigga at first looked like he'd seen a ghost or some shit." Mustafa continues.

He summons two cards tossed out by Bernard. "Then he looked like he was havin' a heart attack and passed out." "Next thing we know, we see Ivan's mothafuckin ass behind him." "All lean and buffed, something he wasn't before." "Damn y'all, wasn't Ivan like fat and slow?" Asked Bernard. Still glancing at his deck, he appears to be baffled.

"Hell yeah!" Exclaims Kris. For Kris, Bernard and Quentin, it seems as if their game is at a standstill. Glancing at their hands, they have yet to find their matches.

Willie at this time has nearly a full deck while Mustafa trails him. "We all practically used to bum rush his ass." Quentin reminds them. "And every time when either his brother Simon or his cousin Doug showed up, we'd break." "And if both of em came with they homies, we'd definitely run." "Word, anybody else other than those two wasn't helping em." "Ivan was a loner, the enemy." Willie added scooping up three more cards.

"Nobody liked him." "Hell, not even the teachers."

"Shoulda listened to Donnie a long time ago." Kris sighs.

"You know, he said we'd go too far."

"And did we listen to em?" Asked Bernard. "Hell naw."

"Then we tried to take his shit along with everybody else's, and got schooled big time."

"It's a good thing that yo uncle is a chiropractor Q." Says Willie.

"Because we weren't supposed to be here in school this afternoon."

"Straight up, word Will." Bernard praises.

"We should have been wearin' leg braces, casts, and arm slings for at least six months."

"Going to physical therapy and shit."

"At least Ivan gave us enough time to straighten up the room, and get ourselves together." Says Mustafa. "At first, I thought he was gone trick off."

"But he didn't." "In fact, when did Ivan ever trick?" Asked Kris. "Never."

"Hold up, Kris." Willie began chuckling.

"You was gonna take Ivan's sketch pad, wasn't you?"

"I kinda liked them." Kris vaguely explains himself.

"Greedy ass bastard." Willie calls him.

Kris shrugs. "What?" He says.

The other boys grin and shake their heads.

"Aight, check this out." Willie began.

"From this day forward, we don't fuck with Ivan no more."

"He never did nothing to us."

The others nod their heads in agreement.

"After Cedric pays us for this job, we hang it up."

"On my momma, something tells me things is gonna get hot at our old school."

"Fuck the dumb shit."

"Word." Says the others.

"And I win." Willie announces.

Tossing all of his cards in front of his boys, they all sighed.

"No you don't." Says an older male voice.

Standing before them so suddenly is Detective Michael Jenkins of the CPD.

Clad in plain clothes, the twenty-nine year old wears a shoulder holster. With two side arms supporting the latter, the silver of his badge deflects incoming sunlight from the outside. With the concealment of body armor inside his shirt, Jenkins wore another side arm (a nine millimeter) onto his left hip. On his right is a standard radio along with cuffs and last but not least, pepper spray. Four uniforms join the fresh-faced veteran.

"Ah, damn." Says a now disgusted Willie.

The rest of the group suddenly looks ill.

Kris soils his jeans.

And the winner loses.

The New "Skool" Café, 4:30pm

Located on the corner of west Harrison and south Sacramento, this establishment is often well patronized by both elementary as well as high school students in the immediate area. During both peak hours (the early morning and late afternoon), youngsters would hang out, eat, socialize and go to their respective institutions. The end of the each day was of course vice versa. Open from six in the morning until nine in the evening, this fairly new establishment actually does correspond to that of a café.

In addition to the traditional fast food it serves, there is also a special menu for broiled as well as baked dishes. Freshly made pastries supplement the candy bar, followed by sodas to warm beverages. Originally a local greasy spoon known as "Lil' Milt's since this decade's beginning, the initial eatery closed last year. Some say it was because of code violations, others, higher property taxes. The existing residential units that occupied the second floor were eventually vacated. For three months, the entire building remained empty. By late spring, the property is acquired by former neighborhood resident Eugene Jernigan and his wife Bertha. Mr. Jernigan, a southern native, WWII veteran, Civil Rights activist, and former city employee has long moved to the suburbs.

It is rumored that he and his wife still owns their graystone on west Lexington.

The latter is located two blocks south.

Upon making their purchase, the Jernigan's came up with the name to reflect those who are more than likely to come in: The young people.

However, during non-peak periods, the establishment is actually visited by both the old as well as the young. The staff, which consists of one manager, an assisting manager, and four cooks, all dwell among the populace. There are also two waitresses who live in the immediate area. On the first floor, the layout employs a small dining lobby as well as an extended sit-in counter. A universal grill, oven and deep freezer overlooks the latter.

Four coin-up games are situated along the northern wall.
To the right is the sole main entrance.

On the second floor of what had been a four bedroom apartment was later gutted.

A year later, it employs additional seating for the overall establishment. A spiral staircase summons additional customers from the main level.

On one wall, there are images of historical figures (heroes, heroines, leaders and etc.)

Another bears images of those more recent from athletes to singers.

Situated among the masses is the late Harold Washington, as well as the recently released Nelson Mandela. Mandela, the highest-ranking member of the ANC (African National Congress) and a prominent citizen of South Africa was persecuted for his opposition against Apartheid. He spent twenty-seven years in prison as a result.

Just last year, Mr. Mandela was released.

There have been rumors spreading here and there about him running for president.

F.W. De Klerk, a white Afrikaner is the current head of state.

The next major election is to be held in 1994.

Portraits , artifacts, and other memorabilia are also scattered about throughout this room.

For rare and special events, a modest soundstage and microphone sits between two restrooms. At this time of the day as usual, the restaurant is quite is quite busy.

In the background, a remake of Stephanie Mills' "Whatcha Gonna Do with my Loving?" by Inner City is heard. The waitresses, two area high school seniors are seen working tirelessly as they tend to their customers' every need. They are cheerful, energetic and surprisingly happy. The janitor, a high school junior clad in his street clothes keeps the floors shining. And the manager does what he does best: Manage.

Sitting at a table overlooking a strip mall housing only a liquor store and a beauty supply shop, Maxwell Hopkins is nervous. So are the five other youths sitting with him.

They appear as though someone has died.

Among the five others, there's Scotty Winfield, Lance Crews, Lawrence Penn, Dean Kensington, and Martin Frye. The food for which they had ordered, still sits before them.

Cold and literally untouched.

The boys instead, sip away at their drinks.

"Okay, I need to be re-enlightened as to what happened last Thursday." Max began.

"Uh, we got served." Scotty drags.

"Ivan morphed into his new alter ego Kaos, and punished all of us."

At this moment, his tone corresponds to someone who suffers from partial brain damage. Scotty himself is obviously still distraught, over his flawless defeat.

"We straightened up his room just before the others came back." Lawrence adds.

"Everybody left, we limped to the bus stop and boarded that number seven."

"We saw Q's uncle on Taylor and he fixed us up."

"You know, the man's dope like that."

Max nodded. "At least Ivan didn't drop a dime on us." Martin crunches his ice.

"To hell with trickin', he could have killed us." Dean yawns.

The light complexioned and otherwise radiant youngster appears rather groggy.

"What made Ivan become like this man?" Asked Lance.

"They said that he was having personal problems at home too."

"Damn." Scotty sighs. "Rumor has it, he drove his cousin Doug out of town."

"Why is that?" Dean asked. "Because Doug sold him out." Max answers.

"Doug wanted to be a gangster with the Two-Four Nation, and he practically served Ivan up to em on a silver platter." "I heard that Ivan beat him, until he was unconscious."

"I bet he did." Dean chuckles meekly.

"His entire family dogged him out." Max reclaims the floor.

"It was like we lost World War III up there last week."

"We misjudged Ivan from the get go." He finally admits .

"He was always smart, and intelligent y'all."

"Straight up Max, Ivan should've been in our class." Martin shakes his head.

"Yeah, he's definitely different." Dean added.

"I say its time to just leave em alone." Max suggests.

"Straight up." Says the others.

"I don't know if y'all heard, but the police picked up Harvey early this morning at his school." The rest of the group is now stunned by Maxwell's news.

"It gets worse." He continues.

"Willie, Mustafa, and the others got picked up at theirs."

"Does Cedric know?" Asked Dean.

"Where is he anyway?"

The rest of the group shrugged.

"He's probably kickin' it with Hannah or something." Says Scotty.

"I tried to call em at first, then I paged em."

"In fact, they're still locked up down the street." Max added.

"This thing is getting hot G."

"I'm gonna cash in what I've already got and leave it at that."

"Word, straight up." The others reply in unison.

"From here on out, Cedric's on his own."

"Hey, yo Scott leave Eva a tip."

Tipping the waitress three dollars, Scotty catches up with the others downstairs.

Jensen Academy (The next day)

At 9am, Max and his friends joins the long assembly line leading upstairs.

They are obviously on their way to class.

Just as Max himself begins his first flight up the northern stairs, someone suddenly taps his shoulder. The results are comparable for that of his friends.

A group of plain-clothes officers (male and female) leads them out the building. “I’ll be damned.” Max began.

“Not necessarily man.” The lead detective himself, Mike Jenkins says.
“In fact Max, today’s your lucky day.”

While his boys are cuffed and placed in the back seat of separate unmarked Impala’s, Max himself is not only spared of being in restraints, but Jenkins also allows him to sit in the front. The sincere detective in fact, opens the door. “No trick Max.”

Perhaps it is his lucky day.

21

AND SO THE GAME OF "LET'S MAKE A DEAL" BEGINS

The band of young thieves that Detective Jenkins himself calls "The Son's of Ocean's eleven (although there were actually thirteen) are eventually bailed out by their legal guardians and have already began making deals with the D.A., their public defenders, and last but not least, a juvenile court judge. Perhaps now the only missing piece to the puzzle is none other than their leader (who is still unaccounted for), and his accomplice.

Having been tipped off two days prior by an unknown source, Cedric Holt fakes a sudden case of the stomach flu. The very next day, all of his teachers including Mrs. Toussaint marked him absent. Meanwhile, Hannah Dubois, his lovely accomplice continues her daily classes, maintains her grades, socializes and of course goes home.

With her beau to consider, Hannah also takes the liberty of bringing Cedric his homework. For Cedric, his feelings are comparable.

It has been one full week and Cedric has yet to return.

Monday

In her sixteen years of teaching, Dorothy Shirley Toussaint has worked with all types of children. She has seen it all. She has heard it all.

Well at least she thought she did.

Two weeks later, her world is all but turned upside down when Mrs. Toussaint viewed the footage of her prized winning students (seven of them), her academic thinking tank stealing from their own classmates, their friends, their fellow peers and so on.

The married mother of four couldn't believe it, and yet she still couldn't.

Although she managed to keep a straight face and somewhat laugh at Ivan who made virtual mincemeat of her students who tried to break in his classroom, Mrs. Toussaint was still hurt. She was still shocked, and perhaps somewhat distraught on the inside.

On the very same evening as she had dinner with her family, Toussaint become somewhat ill.

In room 405 where she is now teaching her students Geography, Mrs. Toussaint still notices the seven empty seats.

Seven would be brilliant minds.

Or to be more accurate, brilliant slash young slash promising.

In the exact same order.

It is almost eleven thirty as Mrs. Toussaint continues the completion of her Geography lesson.

"How long do you think the Earth has been around?" She asks her students.

A pocket of hands began to rise.

"Alright Justine, what have you got?"

"One point five billion." Justine herself replies.

"That's good." Mrs. Toussaint nods.

"It's been around a lot longer than every current living thing combined."

"The Dinosaurs, other non-human animals, humans themselves and surprisingly even plants." "So it was basically like the current Mars?" Another student tries to guess.

The young man is twelve-year-old Arnold Coulter.

"Yeah, something like that Arnold."

"Except that the Earth even then still had water, there was also rain." Mrs. Toussaint further breaks it down. "It was rumored that Mars was exactly like Earth once, and that its inhabitants were human." "But we'll save that theory for another day."

"Are you guys familiar with the phrase "Its a Small World?"

"Yeah, uh-huh." Answers the entire class.

"Well over a billion years ago, the world was even smaller." Toussaint further elaborates. "All seven continents as you currently know them made up one huge mass of land." "And its oceans, one big assed-----!" Her students laughed.

"I mean one large body of water, my fault."

"One single ocean on the planet!"

"Imagine if such a continent still existed, let alone in the present."

"Could you?" Mrs. Toussaint now asks her students.

Some nod. Others smile.

When Toussaint's star student Justine Thomas answered her question as to how old the Earth was, the former Job Core educator has already enlist several other facts on the board. Among them is the name of what used to be a super continent, Earth's true age, as well as the teacher's short hand drawing of the planet, its ancestor continent (namely Rodinia), and what is supposedly a large body of water.

"Just try." Toussaint further pushes her students.

"First imagine what the world have been like today, had all seven continents remained in place." "Now imagine if there had people, live stock, buildings, cities, you name it."

"Imagine a family trip by more than likely a high speed train, going from Chicago to Timbuktu." "Chicago to London." "Traveling from here to Paris."

"Washington to Shanghai."

"Munich to Tokyo."

"Or better yet, Belize City to Buenos Aires."

"You know, that would actually be cool." Says eleven-year-old Laila Page.

"Straight up." Adds another female student.

"I think that the wildlife in rural areas would be even more plentiful. A male student began. "More fruitful as far as hunting, fishing, and recreation."

" I believe that people would have gotten along a little bit better." A second young man replies. Others nodded in response to the answers being given.

"Maybe a little less pollution." Says a third female student.

"I think had there been any wars or border conflicts involving one or more countries." Another male student began to speak. "They would have been twice as likely limited."

"Very good." Mrs. Toussaint commends her students.

"The beef would have somewhat ended before it even started."

"I've got ya."

"So we're talking about a semi-utopia?"

"That's fair enough."

As the entire class began closing their books, Toussaint checks her watch.

"Well, its time for our breaks, we'll do some more of this tomorrow."

"Hannah, see me after class."

"Five minutes."

"No problem Mrs. T."

As the rest of her peers line up, Hannah waits to speak with her teacher.

While the rest of Toussaint's class continue down the remaining flights of stairs (along the north corridor) Toussaint herself shares a few words of wisdom with Lil' Miss Thang.

Both student and teacher are rather far from idiotic.

"So how's Cedric?" Toussaint began.

"Actually, he's getting better." Answers Hannah.

The seemingly privileged young lady who is deemed the fourth most "sexiest" amongst her male peers continues to act normal.

"Cedric is just getting back into solid foods." Hannah continues.

"He's more than likely to be back within three days."

Toussaint shakes her head and smiles.

"That's good."

"You know you guys make a great couple."

Hannah blushes.

"You are every bit as a good friend to Cedric as he is to you."

"You guys have been friends since the Kindergarten."

"You're every bit as intelligent, compassionate, and most of all quite beautiful."

"Both of you."

"You have just as many gifts, and talents like the rest of the students."

"You obviously know what this is about don't you?"

Without patronizing her teacher, Hannah instead gives a nod.

"Hannah, I know all about Cedric's little crime ring he ran here at the school."

"I know that he bailed out on Max, Lance and the others by not showing up for school last week." "He obviously knew about Officer Jenkins' visit, because somebody tipped him off." Hannah tries to speak shortly thereafter. "I know it wasn't you."

Toussaint announces. "As I understand it, Max and the others are in a heap of trouble."

"They're facing at least six months to a year in the Audy Home, a another year of probation, and its even possible that they might kicked out of here."

"They're already making deals with a DA, their lawyers, and a judge as we speak."

With the rest of the class already on the main floor, the two now walk alone.

"It's gonna be trick fest eighty-nine, because Max and the others are gonna roll over."

"Your boyfriend is finished, kaput, terminado."

"They're really upset Hannah."

"It was bad enough that they got their butts kicked by Ivan, but for Cedric to suddenly abandon them is like an act of treason."

"They really feel betrayed."

"Cedric, Max, you guys were all best friends."

"What makes you think that he won't do the same thing to you?"

"He'll have you in the girl's wing of the Audy Home."

"Come out in six months with a flat chest, a fade better than his, and you'll sound like El Debarge." Hannah's white chocolate complexion turns pale.

"You might want to consider spending less time with him."

"Hannah, you're not a bad student."

"A little conceited, but you're no Catwoman."

"You know you can talk to me, right?"

Hannah responds with a slow nod.

"Think about it."

As they continue down the first floor hall, the two go left toward the custodian's office.

On opposite sides of the latter is the teachers' lounge as well as that of the cafeteria's main kitchen. It is at these particular points where the two began to part.

"And by the way, tell Cedric that I said thanks for the homework"

Nodding her head once more as Hannah looks back, the young lady summons a tray.

West Playground

On the basketball court, Ivan and his friends as usual are going at it.

Parrying, bumping, and falling (followed by an occasional elbow), the group is playing what appears to be known as "alley ball." Tackling his way through the crowds of both his fellow teammates as well as his inter-opposing rivals (who are also his friends), Ivan smashes through the latter like that of a human bulldozer.

"Mercy is for the weak." He taunts.

Dribbling and spinning around his opposition, Ivan takes flight.

Shooting the ball from the rims right side, he makes his shot.

The Wilson quietly goes in.

“Hey damn man!” Says some of the other players, who at this point are seen holding their heads. One young man (obviously in pain) clutches away at his lower back.

Now running with the ball is Yusef James.

He gives it to Sergio Valentine who charges down the court and began dribbling circles around his opposition. With the execution of sudden sharp turns, faking and dodging, the lanky giraffe-like youth forges ahead. As he now positions himself in the center of the court, Sergio makes his shot. The score is tied. (Twelve and up)

“Deeze nuts!” He boasts.

“Grow some first!” Nikki fires back.

Donnie grins. “You heard the lady.” He began.

“Stick defense and dunk more.”

“No nuts no glory, c’mon.”

“Stop bullshittin, two up.”

“Check.” The junior captain calls out.

He bounces the ball to Kendrick who then sends it back.

Furthermore in response to Nikki’s comment about Sergio growing some nuts, others just laughed, pointed, and whistled.

Bouncing the ball twice, Donnie takes flight on the balls of his feet.

From where he stands, the tall and thin (but yet well-ripped) youngster jumps up and dispatches the Wilson. As the ball makes a thunder-like sound against the backboard, the latter object still makes it through. The score stands at fourteen to twelve.

With players on both sides hustling, blocking, and jumping up relentlessly for an opening, Donnie who is already preoccupied with Kendrick, Sergio and Morris Parker calls for Ivan. Ivan, who is already nearby, receives the ball from his captain.

When Kendrick’s other teammates attempt to stick defense against a now sweaty Ivan, Ivan himself who accidentally flings his perspiration throws the Wilson over to Nikki.

Nikki in turn gives it to Terrell Hall, who at this point is also surrounded.

Sending the ball to Christian Vance, Christian summons it to Tyree Clark.

Taking it to the hole on opposing player Ferris Ferrer, Tyree executes a layup.

Sixteen to twelve.

As the wind blows west and the pigeons fly about, all of the players began to scramble and hustle. Ivan briefly towels himself dry before resuming his game.

With an increased heart rate, his brute strength, and impeccable reach, Ivan takes flight high above his defense-sticking opposition.

Dribbling and thus bouncing the ball between his legs like an actual pro and of course far from tired, Ivan executes his footwork.

With all of Kendrick's players now hunting him down for the ball, Ivan blinks his eyes and begins to fake, to duck, and then dodge.

Spinning and turning at multiple angles, the young athlete takes off down the court.

"Somebody stop him!" Kendrick hollers.
Most of his players are out of breath at this point.
Ivan is already out of reach.

Ken's team tries to keep up with the charged up Ivan, but they're too late.
As his fellow teammates ran with him, Donnie grins at his mock rival.

"You small wonder assed mothafucka!" Yusef James chuckles.

He covers his mouth and coughs briefly.

With no one to stop him (which isn't the first time), Ivan takes flight, grabs the rim and slams the ball. Eighteen to twelve.

"Now that's how the fuck you supposed to play." Don gives Ivan a pound.

The rest of the group also commends him.

"Nice one." Kendrick gives Ivan a high five.
"Thanks." Ivan responds. He smiled.
"A worthy mock opponent."
"Why don't you call him a frienemy?" Nikki suggests.
"Word says Ferris."

Dashing across the court with his fellow teammates, Donnie bounces the Wilson.

Attempting to keep Kendrick as well as his two star players at bay, Donnie searches for one of his own. Desperately looking over to his left followed by his right Donnie spots a now open Nikki. Ignoring her bouncing breasts, he throws her the ball.

Before Morris, Chris, and Sergio could even touch her, Nikki herself has already taken flight. Situated in the middle of the court, the young lady successfully makes her shot.

Three points.

As the ball quietly flops through the net, the bell rings.
Twenty-one to twelve.

Recess, on the other hand is now over as the teachers return to claim their students.

Old Town School of Folk Music (Lincoln Park)

Just one block east of the Ravenswood "L" and the Cartier Photography Studio along west Armitage, Ivan walks into this building.

Established in 1957, the Old Town School of Folk Music covers a wide range of music, dance, theater and visual arts courses to every social demographic and age group.

There are roughly seven hundred accredited class offerings; private workshops and lessons that cover a growing range of genres.

The thirty-two year old establishment is housed in a large three-story storefront on the corner of north Fremont.

Since she was younger, music has always been among Nicole's many talents.

From the time that she was five years old, Nikki has been a master at playing the piano. At seven, she learns to play the clarinet.

At ten, a fast blossoming Nikki masters the art of playing the saxophone.

Today, Nikki now learns to play the violin.

Shortly after her arrival in Chicago last year, Nikki's mom immediately enrolls her here. She began her Violin classes around the same time Ivan's parents, enrolls him in the fighting arts in a school on the other side of town.

Room 318

Situated on the west end of the building opposite the roaring "L" trains, longtime symphony conductor Matthew Vogel instructs his students.

At thirty-five, Vogel is among a handful of young teachers.
The youngest, Rebecca Cox is twenty-four.

Born in Providence Rhode Island but raised in Europe where he also received his education, Vogel has done several of his own performances here in the U.S. and abroad.

Although he no longer performs on the account of his current profession (his second love), the recently married instructor yet still produces songs for current as well as up and coming musicians.

Smooth, distinguished, and well spoken, Mr. Vogel is also fairly observant, he never misses a beat and at often times, can be quite humorous with his students.

After an hour of warming up their instruments, studying their notes, and thus making the necessary adjustments, all of Mr. Vogel's students began to play.

Immediately, simultaneously performing more as a live group as opposed to a class.

As the young, slender and blond haired conductor directs his students with his wand, he began to smile.

Among his top five students, of course, there's Nikki (who is now seen playing in the front row), Jessica Flanagan joins her along with Emmanuel Singh, Vincent Kim, and Ruben Martin De Porres.

It is now 7:50 in the evening.

With the incredible energy, the enthusiasm, and last but not least, the will to go all the way, all of Mr. Vogel's advance students (considering its only a small class) takes it to the max. Without breaking a single sweat (literally!), the entire class of nearly twenty is playing as if they're in the White House.

Or perhaps Carnegie Hall.

Relaxed but extremely focused, the students are one with the instruments.

As the thin metal summons the appropriate notes, they proceed to follow their instructor's lead. George Lloyd originally composed the sounds that are now heard above the roaring "L" trains. Mr. Vogel's students successfully picks them up.

Also in attendance along with the students and the lone conductor are presumed to be friends and possibly family members of the performing parties.

From time to time, Nikki's mother at least once a month will watch her perform, while her closest friends (namely Denise Wilson, Andrea DuPont, and Charles Davis, not to mention her number one fan Ivan himself) will visit her classes on a weekly basis.

Having really outdone themselves at this point, and with the consent of their teacher, the students stopped playing.

As the seemingly noble pupils stand and bow, the small audience before them began to clap. "Great job everybody, have a safe and pleasant evening." Says Mr. Vogel.

"Until next time, good night."

Although Andrea, Denise and Charles had been there the entire time to watch Nikki perform, Ivan for some reason was unable to make it.

He was obviously working in his uncle's photography shop just two doors down.

But however, as Nikki and the others began to leave, Ivan himself arrives.

The young workingman takes the liberty of carrying her case.

"Thank you." Nikki smiled.
"Well, it's the least that I could do." Ivan began.
"I'm sorry that I was unable to be here."
"My uncle's shop was rather busy."
"And he really needed my help."
"Oh, we understand." Andrea says happily.
"Gotta make your money."
"Hey, at least he's paying you overtime." Denise grins.
"We can imagine." Says Charles.

"Anyway, it's almost nine, we have to get out of here." Ivan checks his watch.

"You took the words right out of my mouth Ivan." Andrea chuckles.

The group now makes their way towards the exit.

As sunset gives way to nightfall, a light wind blows in from the east.

The dual platforms of the yet still busy Armitage station can't appear to be anymore livelier than they already are. Besides the visible presence of passengers, the station's incandescent lighting employed by humming transformers acknowledges the rails with a soft glow. The aisle of high wattage bulbs along the edge of the wooden platforms (namely above track level) makes the prewar stop resemble a marquee.

At this time, it is obvious that the stationhouse below is unmanned.

An overhead sign now illuminated in red urges the passengers to pay on the train.

Turning the curve at Willow Street, a single pair of dual white headlights appears. The wayside markers located above the latter are red and green.

Approaching the northbound platform, a married pair of Budd 2600's is now in plain view. Its destination markers indicate a Ravenswood "all stops".

The two-car train while calling for passengers summons a bright blue spark.

"Fullerton is the next stop." The conductor announces on her P.A.

As the doors began to slide shut and the conductor closes her window, the train departs.

Just getting off of a pay phone with his parents on the southbound platform, Ivan turns and faces his friends. "My dad is gonna pick us up at Homan." He announces.

The others nod.

"What happened to Rizzo tonight?" Denise asks Ivan.

"He's hanging out with his father." Ivan explains.

"Yeah, that's right." Nikki shakes her head.

"He did mention that to us yesterday."

"You are really good at what you do." Andrea began to tell Nikki.

The entire group is now seated on wooden benches.

An old interlocking tower, which is all but dormant, sits only a few inches to their left.

This tower was added in the early 40's to initially observe and control the crossovers to the nearby State Street Subway occupying the center tracks.

Today, interlocking is no longer controlled from this station.

The existing tower now serves as a field office for the signal department.

"Word, Nikki was definitely throwing down tonight." Charles adds.

"But she always does Charlie." Ivan reminds him.

The star musician smiles as she listens to her friends.

"That violin that she's playing, is only a mere appetizer as opposed to what she can really do." "You guys have been to her house." Ivan continues on.

"Nikki also plays the piano." "She plays the clarinet." "Even the sax."

"Of course, there are too many instruments to name."

"Are you a descendant of the fiddler?" Charles began to roast Nikki.

Nikki simply smiles and gives him the finger. "Whatever." She tells him.

"You ain't right." The others reply at once.

"But I do come from a long line of musicians though." Nikki answers to Charles.

"My grandfather back home was a blues singer."

"I had a great grandmother who did opera."

"Then I have aunts and uncles also back down south, who specializes in almost every instrument known to man."

"Well at least some of us were already aware of that." Ivan responds with a wink.

"I used to actually watch you play your violin in your backyard from time to time."

"Whenever I strolled through the alley."

"Regardless of what some of the others in the neighborhood thought, I thought that you sounded great." "So what if it is the hood."

"He was stalking me." Nikki says to the rest of the group.

She playfully punches her neighbor.

"We weren't yet fully acquainted then." Ivan explains to the others.

He looks at Nikki and smiles back.

Emerging from the illuminated portal (the State Street Subway) near Willow, another set of dual headlights emerge. Situated above them are two green wayside markers.

Rolling unto the elevated from the incline below, an eight car Jackson Park-Howard "all stops" train employed by Budd 2600's and Pullman 2000's bypasses the station.

The impact of the wind as well as that of the passing cabs nearly blows off Charlie's Kangol. "That was exactly how I lost my hat at Six Flags once." Ivan says to him.

"And what was so ironic, was that I technically didn't lose it."

"I was on the Iron Z, when it just flew off."

"The park officials insisted that it was nothing that they could do."

"And they knew where it was, because I told them."

"My uncle Nate was really pissed with one of the supervisors."

"But he still bought me another one."

"There was no need to trip any further about it."

"Things can be replaced, people can't."

"Amen brother." Denise says. Her tone mocks that of an evangelist.

"You're quite talented too Andrea." Says Charles.

He adjusts his Kangol before putting it back on.

"I'm sure that you have many other talents, don't get me wrong."

"I'm not trying to impose any self racial stereotyping."

"But you can sing pretty well and really dance too."

"I'll do." Andrea shrugs with both modesty and humility.

About fifth teen minutes later, a single overhead light with a wayside marker of red and green comes in to view. The destination markers for this particular train are situated below the windows of both the passenger as well as the motorman's cab.

A married pair of vintage PCC rail cars employs the incoming Loop-bound Ravenswood train. Built by the St. Louis Car Company between 1950 through 1959, the 6000 series unlike that of its modern-day off springs consist of die cast metal, blinker-type doors (folding doors) and bullet shaped lights. By way of compensation for its lack of central air units , this aging series allows its passengers to open windows with the use of overhead cranks. However, in an effort to make sure that a rider doesn't lose his or her limbs, each window is retrofitted with a special guardrail as well as a written warning.

The latter is posted in English and Spanish.

In addition to their recently adopted (Spirit of Chicago) color scheme, their slightly tinted windows and modernized destination signs, these particular relics are among the sole survivors. While many of their cousins are either being utilized as manual laborers (work motors), retired or just simply scrapped, these cabs are yet still making it.

Screeching twice as loud with every turn.

Screeching with authority.

And with that same authority, the less crowded train roars into the station.

Its traction as opposed to the higher performing cars causes the antiquated unit to jerk to a complete stop. The doors open shortly thereafter. A middle-aged conductor in the second and last car peers briefly out of his window.

Ivan and the others board the second car.

Immediately after the conductor closes the doors, the train jerks back into motion.

The P.A. system whines as the conductor makes his announcements.

"Sedgwick and North Avenue will be next."

"Please have your fares ready."

"This is a southbound Ravenswood train making all stops around the Loop."

"For your own safety, please do not lean against the doors.

Traveling through the nightly, urban, north side landscape in what is still Lincoln Park; the group's train lead by car 6150 passes through a neighborhood emerging from decades of disinvestments, poverty, and partial job losses. Namely along the eastern section.

Along west North Avenue to the to the north, there are recently built market-rate townhouses. To the south along north Larrabee situated over Terry's Red Hots and a nearby track and field for Cooley Career Magnet High (sometimes known as Lincoln Park South), lies the debris of what used to be row houses.

The ruthless housing projects of Cabrini-Green lingers high above Cooley, but the downtown skyline however outshines them both.

Cutting through a short network of trees, existing frame homes, side streets and newly constructed but still empty strip malls (along North Avenue but over an alley), Ivan and his friends reach the Sedgwick Station. Screeching along a curve just beyond the latter, their trip continues. Other points of interest includes the never closed Oscar Meyer meat facility, Schiller Elementary, a garage housing recreational horse carriages (including the horses themselves) and more homes.

Mixed used buildings from converted lofts to thinning industries also exist.

Making a transfer connection at the Clark and Lake stop downtown, Ivan and company now boards a westbound Lake and Dan Ryan train immediately following the Ravenswood they had just alighted.

Turning a curve at Wells Street and heading back to Kimball, their six-car unit of 1976 Boeing-Vertol 2400's and the most recent 2600's are now clear to leave.

Having crossed Tower 18(At the Wells intersection), the florescent-lit cabs cross Wacker Drive and then the Chicago River.

Now crossing the corridor for Metra's (suburban) Union Pacific and Northwestern branches to Harvard and Waukegan, the group's first stop is the Clinton-Northwest Passage Station. With the exception of the recently added fluorescents, orange sodium vapor lights, and modern signage, the 1906 built station remains in remarkably sound condition.

There are escalators, and stairways connecting to the adjoining Northwestern Terminal next door. The latter was added in 1970.

"We heard about what happened at the school last week." Andrea began.

Situated onboard the first car, everyone is now focused on Ivan.

"We all know that it was you Mr. Ivan the Terrible." Denise adds.

"That was really a brave thing that you did." Nikki also says.

"Oh, we have our sources mister."

"Oh, I have no doubt." Ivan responds smoothly, calmly and of course happily.

Without warning, Nikki kisses Ivan across the cheek.

"Thank you." His closest neighbor then says. Ivan himself blushes.

"You ended up getting back everything Cedric's wannabe thieves and gangsters took."

"How did all of this jump off?" Charles asks.

"It was actually more of a surprise." Ivan began to explain.

"I was just going upstairs to get my sketch pad, and there they were."

“Harvey, Willie, Mustafa, and Kris, these guys don’t even attend the school anymore.”

“Just helping themselves, like they were shopping at Marshall Fields or Sears.”

“Acting as though our classroom room was their corner, so I did the unimaginable.”

“Those three attempted to summon many others, but they failed.”

“As to you doing unimaginable Ivan, yes you did.” Charles chuckles.

“You guys know that although I really don’t like to brag.” Ivan began.

“I actually hurt them pretty bad.”

“So what’s the difference between hurting someone pretty good vs. pretty bad?” Nikki asks. She glances at him for a moment.

“Well, when you fight a person.” Ivan began to elaborate.

“And he, she or they become visibly bruised, scarred or whatever other external lacerations that they may sustain.”

“And yet, they are still able to stand, limp or walk away, then it was a clean fight.”

Nikki, Charles, Denise and Andrea all happily nodded.

“BUT, when you attack them striking internal vital areas, dislocate or even break one or more of their limbs, then that’s what you call a brutal assault.”

“Let alone, if you knock them unconscious based on the impact of your blows.”

“Damn!” Charles shakes his head.

“You’ve got that right.” Chuckles Denise.

Getting off at the historical Homan Avenue station directly above Lake Street, Ivan and his friends goes through the westbound stationhouse, immediately before reaching the surface. Pulling up in his SUV directly along nearby Garfield Park, Mr. Thompson summons for Ivan and his friends to hop in.

Montclare

Sharing borders with the nearby suburbs of both Oak Park as well as Elmwood Park, this neighborhood was annexed by the city of Chicago in 1889.

However, the first spurt of growth didn't occur until 1912.

Presumably in conjunction with the extension of streetcar service along Grand Avenue.

William Sayre, and his family contributed acreage for community use in 1916, which along with another piece of donated property, later formed Rutherford-Sayre Park.

The park was divided down the middle by railroad tracks that marked the town's southern boundary. Settlement concentrated in the southeast section near the community's namesake depot, but was hampered until utilities and paved streets were added in the 1920's. Single-family structures, mainly standard bungalows, predominated the area. Some residents found employment at light industrial plants along the CM&SP railroad lines that bounded the northwest side neighborhood on its eastern and southern edges. Most of the workers crossed into neighboring communities where factories were plentiful. Housing extended north of Diversey Avenue in the 1930's, a combination of bungalows, ranches, and Tudor houses.

Hugging the city's western edge, Montclare retains an identity more suburban as opposed to urban. Pre-World War II commercial development was minimal.

The only shopping had been a retail strip on the corner of Grand and Harlem Avenues.

In the 1960's this strip experienced decline and deterioration as stores left and newer shopping centers were built in other surrounding areas.

Most notably the Brickyard shopping center, and the newly built Bricktown Square plaza located on Fullerton Avenue. The latter also houses a Cinema complex.

However, the residential areas remain intact.

Population figures for 1970 were at 11,675.

Although Poles, Italians, and Germans account for the majority, the neighborhood has now seen a rise in Greek, Ukrainian, and Lithuanian residents.

Another visible influx is also seen among Lebanese-Americans followed by Hispanics. Despite a recent rash of racially motivated incidents, the African-American population is unfazed. As the newest addition to the area, they too continue to grow.

Cedric Holt and his mom are among the latter.
Originally from the North Lawndale neighborhood, Margot Judith Holt, thirty-eight, a marketing executive along with Cedric, her only child moved here just three years ago.

Although the Holt's didn't endure any racial slurs or perhaps vandalism to their newly bought Victorian in the 2300 block of Oak Park Avenue, many of their white ethnic neighbors instead shared nervous looks.

Their attitudes toward their lone black neighbors remained somewhat negative during the Holt's first year.

Also during this time, the late Mayor Harold Washington wins a second term in office.

About two months later after the Holt's move in, he suddenly dies.

It was as though the long time residents had practically worked in shifts as the Holt's went on about their daily lives. At least several residents had already begun consulting with a realtor. The Holt and their fellow constituents only chuckled.

Three years later (The Present Day)

The very person who occupies City Hall, is none other than the very same man that Harold Washington defeated six years earlier: Richard M. Daley.

Although it was stated that Washington had a massive heart attack, others suspect that he had been poisoned.

Meanwhile, in the Montclare area, the social tensions escalate.

However, thirteen-year-old Cedric Holt remains on high alert.

Holt Residence

Having played sick for almost two weeks in the wake of his mental defeat by Ivan, and a narrow escape from the police at school, the handsome but yet vain Lex Luther –like youth improvises. At 2:30 in the afternoon, Cedric is home alone.

Ms. Holt will not be home for at least another two hours.

Still clad in his pajamas, he cleans up his room. Cedric changes into his workout clothes shortly thereafter. Descending into the basement, which also houses a recreation room and two additional bedrooms, he turns on the stereo and began to exercise.

Jumping rope, Cedric does several sit-ups; pushups, and curls several weights.

At about five foot four, the coming of age youngster is relatively quite ripped; his medium brown complexion is without blemishes, let alone not even a pimple.

His closely cropped hair employs shiny thick waves.

Now putting on some gloves, as well as ankle wraps, Cedric then goes to work on both a punching as well as a kicking bag. Now shadowboxing, the lean youth concentrates on his fighting form. Kicking, blocking, and spinning around throughout the entire basement, Cedric attacks his phantom opposition.

Unleashing a kiai upon every strike, the freshman disciple returns to his stance and bows. Currently, Cedric holds a gold belt in Tae Kwan Do and he also studies kickboxing at Keller's Dojo. He was recently promoted.

Having completed his exercises, Cedric towels away his sweat and heads for the shower. Putting on some more clothes, he then enters his mom's study.

Browsing though her collection of novels, he finds a book entitled "To Catch a Thief."

He flicks through the first ten pages when he suddenly hears the doorbell.

Walking hand in hand, Cedric along with his girlfriend and fellow classmate Hannah Dubois passes the Shriners Hospitals for Children before cutting across Rutherford, Sayre, and Rutherford Sayre Parks. The unmanned Mars Station sits in the middle.

Servicing both community residents as well as employees from its adjoining factory (the company that makes M&M's, Mars, Snickers, and so on), the station calls for trains on what is known as Metra's Milwaukee District/West.

As usual at this time, the sun shines to the west.

Now strolling along the tracks, Cedric and Hannah continues west to Harlem Avenue.

Approaching what is also a dividing line in terms of different municipalities, Harlem (Route 43) borders both Chicago's Montclare neighborhood as well as the Village of Elmwood Park. The latter whose housing stock mirrors that of its eastern neighbor, sits directly across the street.

Just beyond the railroad crossing to their right, Cedric and the biracial Hannah continue one block along north Harlem.

Many businesses from independent retail, local service shops, two auto dealerships, and a few eateries cover both sides of this further congested avenue.

A passing commuter train is responsible.

Directly on the next corner at Grand Avenue is Salvatore's Pizza.

Salvatore's Pizza

Established nearly two decades ago around June of 1970, this pizzeria is among a few hangouts for many local teens in the area. The menu corresponds to both Italian as well as American made dishes. It opens from eleven in the morning, until twelve midnight Monday through Thursday. Friday and Saturday, the hours are extended until at least two A.M. On Sunday's, the shop closes at eleven. Forty-two-year-old Salvatore D' Angelo and his wife Judy, forty-one are both the founders as well as the co-owners.

Both Cedric and Hannah decide to walk in.

But however, before they do a flock of youngsters (all of whom are white) attempts to hassle them. One of them the presumed leader, a tall chunky and spike-haired boy tries to block their way in.

"And who the hell are you man?" Cedric asks with disdain.
He shakes his head and chuckles.
"The Fuhrer of the hood?"
The wannabe minuteman youth smirks while his friends laugh.
"You're funny." Says the leader.
"Pay your cover charge and we'll let you in."
"You're cool." The leader then tells Hannah.
"A black tax?" Cedric playfully laughs it off.
"Ain't this a bitch?" He turns to Hannah.
"They think you're Caucasian." He whispers to her.

As he pretends to reach for his wallet, Cedric surprises the bigger kid.

Grabbing the back of his neck, the recently arrived resident pulls down his opposition and snaps his right knee across his face. Turning his huge body counterclockwise, Cedric rolls him to the ground. The leader tosses, he turns and then he moans.

"You black motherfucker!" Another youth roars. Already in his stance, Cedric gives him an inside roundhouse knocking him clean out. Another rushes in and catches a spinning hook kick. Snapping a left front kick into another (stomach to face), Cedric employs a combined (right) hook kick-sidekick into the head of another.

He is too is out. Taking it to a medium weight, Cedric administers a spinning roundhouse in mid fight. Landing his left Adidas across the face of the olive-complexioned youth, sweat and saliva quickly surfaces. Dancing on the balls of his feet, the no holds barred resident summons a left jab-right cross to another. Two others attempt to attack Cedric from behind, but are suddenly stopped by Hannah.

Spraying one boy with mace, she also kicks him in the groin. Dead center. Punching another in the stomach, Hannah then gouges out his eyes. He is temporarily blind.

He howls. Delivering a solid left hook across the face of another racist hood, a sixth catches a spinning backfist from Cedric. The left side of his face is swollen and purple.

Snapping a right front kick to the seventh, Cedric, stops the eighth fighter with an uppercut. The disposition of his blow is first summoned to the stomach followed by the chin. Falling back in a seemingly slow motion, this would be tough is out.

"YOU FUCKING KUNG FU NIGGER!!!" A ninth hood tries to tackle Cedric to the ground, but is stopped with two elbows to the spine.

The seemingly possessed youth slowly collapses.

Snapping two knees into the stomach of his last opponent, Cedric turns him counterclockwise and rolls him to the ground.

At this point, they are all laid out.

"Look where your hatred has taken you." Cedric began. He now brushes his hair.

"So this is how you all get down over here huh?"

"You might want to consider coming out of your social bunkers."

"It's almost a new century."

"Enjoy the rest of your day."

Giving his estranged neighbors something to think about as they toss and turn on the ground, Cedric once more takes Hannah by the hand.

They now enter Salvatore's.

22

RAINBOW BAPTIST CHURCH, SUNDAY

Reverend Combs is just getting warmed up for his regularly scheduled sermon.

He makes a grand entrance just as his wife raps up her Sunday lesson. The first lady herself currently teaches the adults as well as the teens, while the first family's oldest daughter Audra works with the children. At this time, the special offerings are paid, prayers are said, and all three groups have reunited. Following a brief moment of fellowship, a devotional service begins. Standing at the pulpit before God, with his microphone, the actual well to do Pastor prays for everyone.

Whether it is for a special blessing, a summary of deliverance, the Lord's general wisdom, mercy or perhaps his general understanding, this is the place to be.

Although many leaders are made, very few are born.

And Thaddeus Elmer Combs II are among them.

Born to Thaddeus Jr. and Dinah Combs in October of 1949, here in what was then a socially changing and diverse neighborhood, the third generation Mr. Combs is next to the oldest of four children. His father, a well-connected minister and butcher shop owner from the rural south, and his mother, a beautician who had her own shop and choir director opens this church on September 26, of 1959.

Prior to its current tenant three decades earlier, the brick storefront building was once the home of a kosher deli. Enlisting himself in the Navy after high school, Mr. Combs completes a brief tour of duty in Cambodia before returning home to attend Roosevelt University in 1969. While majoring there in Law, a then twenty-year-old Combs meets Marilyn Thornton. Just two years younger, Ms. Thornton was then a Psychology major.

They were married within one year prior to each other's acquaintance.

The recently wedded Mr. and Mrs. Combs graduated around June of 1974.

Two years later in addition to their first child Audra, who was then six at the time, the Comb's then had another daughter named Cecilia.

Furthermore at the time of Cecilia's birth, the young father is immediately blessed with his first job at Bookman brothers, a local law firm.

Under his father, a friend who was also a bishop in Christ, as well as a few other dignitaries from elsewhere, ordains the then twenty-eight-year-old Thaddeus as a regular full-fledged minister. Knowing that this was among his many callings, the second Thaddeus humbly accepts. Many rejoice.

The latter immediately came to past following his first job.

For some time prior to his founding which was then unknown to most of his congregation, the eldest Combs even as he ran his meat shop at the same time fought a battle with Multiple Sclerosis. For many years, the preceding Pastor who is now pushing seventy very much had it well under control.

However, in recent years following the birth of his then most recent granddaughter, the disease suddenly began to reject the senior Combs treatments.

Experiencing an increase in relapses, exacerbations, and acute flare-ups for at least three straight years, the longtime entrepreneur and founding pastor is ultimately forced to retire. A week before Thanksgiving in November of 1979, his son Thaddeus II barely thirty succeeds him. God himself swears him in literally through his own father, his predecessor, other body members as well as other spiritual leaders from elsewhere.

Although the eldest Combs is no longer the pastor, his positions as the overseer and founder however remains intact. His wife of fifty years now known as "Mother Combs" remains at his side. Their children now run the businesses for which they owned.

The first family itself now lives in the suburbs.

In conclusion if it is not mentioned, the longtime church is situated here on the corner of St. Louis Avenue near Flournoy Street, a seemingly quiet residential area.

The Thompson house is around the next corner.

The good Pastor and his wife Marilyn also known as Sister Combs still have many friends in the community, and among them are the Thompson's.

As newborn infants, Ivan and his siblings were all baptized here.

Those within his circles (namely Charles, Nikki, and Lazarus) those live the closest are also members here. Charles and all of his siblings when they were infants were too baptized here. The Davis household sits only three doors down.

Nikki and her mom are among the most recent members.

Just two weeks following their arrival from Atlanta, Ms. Sanders and her daughter followed suit. The single but still attractive young mother acts as the treasurer as well as an usher. Of the many houses of worship that occupies this struggling community, Rainbow is classified as one of the most active beacons in terms of finding jobs, voter registration and food drives, youth programs, and other key necessities that upscale communities would otherwise take for granted.

Currently in this somewhat stuffy sanctuary, which mimics that of a live theater, there are many members as well as some visitors. Twenty-three total.

Among the masses who occupy mostly the rear, and center (with special VIP's situated in the front), there are just as many young adults as there are seniors.

For the first time since its opening thirty years earlier, the congregation is now seeing new life as its number of both preteens and adolescents began to rise.

Ushers accommodate the latter by dispatching additional folding chairs.

The overall sermon itself is truly not by far a long shot, God's ultimate house party.

Within the confines of the sanctuary, many people are shouting, dancing, screaming and thus jumping for joy.

They jump for joy for their Lord and Savior, The Lord and Savior.

Christ Jesus himself.

The thirty-nine-year-old pastor who will turn forty this fall is still in robust condition.

About five foot nine, Combs stays fit by employing cardio related exercises along with some weightlifting. His relatively lean and muscular frame makes it evident.

Mr. Combs attire beneath his black and gold robe consist of a red and black suit, which corresponds to a tie (also black) as well as a pair spotless gators.

Seated behind him there's his wife and first lady (Marilyn), of nineteen years, his daughters Audra who is eighteen, Cecilia now thirteen, and Thaddeus III twelve.

To all of his friends, the third human sequel is simply known as "T3."

Also in attendance are the original founders, none other than his parents.

The eldest Combs, sixty-nine now appears to be frail and gray. Seated alongside his wife, a gold cane rests to his left. Happily facing his family before him as well as the entire congregation, Mr. Combs first looks up at the ceiling by giving honor to his true maker, his Lord, as well as his friend of all friends.

Facing his son as he preaches the word, a very pleased Elder Combs shakes his head.

As beads of sweat rolls down his face and neck, the current pastor paces back and forth with his microphone almost as though he is rapping.

While delivering his message, his daughter Cecilia pours him a glass of water.

An usher hands him a fresh handkerchief.

Although he fails to show up for the early Sunday school lesson, Ivan yet still makes it in for the regular service.

As he proceeds through the tinted double doors, the suave young teen with his shinier than usual slicked back hair, designer tux, and matching dress shoes (well-buffed) makes a grand entrance before the entire congregation.

Receiving the shockingly handsome youth warmly (namely with smiles, nods and a few waves), they briefly resume their course.

"Hey there 007." Says Ms. Sanders.

"You look really nice."

Handing Ivan a program, Nikki's mother then kisses the top of his head.

"Thanks." He almost blushes.

"You made it just in time baby."

Directing him toward an aisle located in the center, Ivan takes a seat.

His peers are already seated before him.

Nikki who is joined by both Charles and Lazarus greets him.

"Hey you." She says.

"Didn't think you'd make it."

"I called you not too long ago, and your dad said you weren't up yet."

"Straight up." Says Lazarus.

"Yeah, he told me." Ivan yawns.

"Last night, I stayed up watching Friday The 13th: The Series."

"Freddy's Nightmares too."

Nikki, Charles, and Laz all nodded as they listened to the word at the same time.

"They were both pretty good." Nikki now opens her purse.

She produces a small bottle of lotion.

Unscrewing the top, Nikki extracts a wad of it rubs both of her hands together.

"Yeah, I've seen Friday the 13th, but I didn't watch Freddy's Nightmares." Says Charles.

"I was out by the time the latter came on."

"I know I've seen them both, and Showtime at the Apollo." Lazarus adds.

"The episode that aired last night was actually a follow up." Charles began.

"It was about that cursed coin that was used to bring the dead back life."

"But to do that, the person who owned it had to take at least one life in advance, in order for it to work." Ivan finishes. "Just like that crooked cop for example, who used it to resurrect his dead partner." Nikki joins in.

"Jack and Ryan ended up having to used the coin for themselves to bring Mickey back."

"At the end, they failed to retrieve it because that old taxiderming building collapsed.

"And those demonic worshippers went right down with it."

"They killed Mickey with it at first when she ended up too close."

"But at least Johnny and Jack succeeded this time, in terms getting it back." Ivan concludes. Nikki puts the Jergen's back into her purse.

"Johnny and Jack had a huge argument over the coin, because Johnny had also used it."

"There was another earlier episode when Johnny's dad, who was a security guard ended up being killed at his job." Charles reminds them. "About three years earlier."

"You mean that episode about the jacket right?" Nikki asks.

"He was killed in an apparent break in at the museum where he worked."

"It had old World War II memorabilia, and among the artifacts, there was this cursed jacket." Ivan quickly recalls. "Some guy had broken in, surprised Johnny's father, took the jacket, and tried to pin the murder on Johnny himself."

"Depressed because he and his dad had a tradition where they would usually go fishing at least once a year, Johnny ended up taking the coin, went to cemetery where his father was buried, exhumed his body which was still in remarkably good shape, and brought him back." "Mickey on the other hand was still traumatized because of what had happened to her." Lazarus cuts in. "When Johnny asked her how did it feel to be dead for that moment, Mickey told him that she just felt cold."

"Because Johnny was trying to determine what he would expect from his dad once he revived him." Ivan finishes. "Jack threatened to fire Johnny because, what he felt John was doing was wrong." Nikki reclaims the floor. "Although he did, use the coin to bring back Mickey." "Eventually Johnny had no other choice, but to return his dad back to his resting place." "Considering that he was experiencing a mild case of memory loss, and at Jack's request to so, Johnny used that very same coin to kill him." Nikki concludes.

"He lost his father twice if you think about it." Says Lazarus. He shakes his head.

"Kinda bogus." "Straight up." The others whisper in unison.

"Just before I crashed, I recorded some mixes off the radio." Ivan begins.

He now browses through his bible.

"Speaking of House music, my brother has some new tapes for you all." Charles announces. Ivan, Nikki, and Lazarus all nod their heads.

As he brings the devotional part of the service to a close, Pastor Combs now urges every member to stand. At this point, the praise team as well as the choir assembled by Rev. Constance "Connie" Delaney also rises. Elder Ezekiel Majors works the Yamaha while T3 gets down on the drums. Another young man does his thing playing the bass guitar. The youthful and energetic choir orchestrated by Rev. Delaney takes the lead.

The star singer, a tall blond haired dark complexioned woman named Melissa Hendrix hits unspeakable high notes while at the same time, managing her vocals to a point that the rest of the choir is able to keep up. Verse after verse, melody after melody, this group literally brings down the house. The rest of the congregation continues to rejoice.

Some dance. Others cry. Many wave their hands. Two members actually perform flips this time, while the rest (including the visitors) clap.

The younger current Pastor who is now seated looks on and nods his head with great satisfaction. Among the various songs being performed, there's "An On Time God", Ones Secret Place, and I'm Still Alive. Briefly Sister Combs (the first lady) takes the mike for a moment and sings "Getting Your House In Order."

Suddenly a few women jump out of their seats and began to shake and convulse.

This has nothing to do with neither medical-related complications nor does it pertains to any mental ailments. They are actually in the best of spirits . They continue calling upon the Lord's name. The two middle-aged females now dance. They are experiencing what is known as the "Holy Ghost." Shortly thereafter, two nurses are motioned by Ms. Sanders to accommodate them. A third member is heard speaking in tongues.

"Amen!" Everyone says.

After a full hour of praying and meditating, Pastor Combs is ready to speak.

Now getting up with his bible in his right hand, the tall dark and handsome gentleman approaches the podium. "Amen, glory to God everybody." "Why don't we give the Lord one great big round of applause." The entire congregation claps.

The Pastor briefly speaks in tongues.

"I don't know what you all come to do." He begins.

"But I've come to serve Jesus, the Living God, God Almighty."

"Alpha, Omega!"

"The beginning and the ending!"

"Amen." The entire congregation responds.

"Today's sermon is about never giving up."

" Make it plain now." Other members respond.

"We'll be reading from the books of Job, Corinthians, and Romans."

Many members in the congregation are now turning pages in their bibles, while others of course commence to take notes. "If you have found it, just say that you're on your way." He smiles. "I'm on my way." Several others reply in unison. "If you didn't, just say that I'm working on it Lord." "I'm working on it Lord." Replies the rest of the congregation. They all smile and began to chuckle.

"You see, when it comes down to the word of God." The Pastor began.

His words are clear, concise, but yet still relaxing.

He slowly paces back and forth. Once again, he smiles before the congregation as the latter begins to nod. Their showers of praises are continuous. "Glory, Hallelujah."

Says Ms. Sanders. She briefly speaks in tongues. "When it comes to keeping the faith." "You have to exercise." "EXERCISE I SAY!" The Pastor's voice is now thunderous. He preaches with the true authority. The conviction. The substance.

The truth. The Father himself gives all of which onto him. The Heavenly Father, Christ Jesus, Jehovah, The Messiah. "EXERCISE!" "Walk by faith and not by sight."

"Amen!" Says the rest of the congregation. "You have to exercise your faith whether you're a novice Christian, or in the simplest of terms, a baby or beginner."

"You can be a junior or senior, or one with more experience." The voice of Pastor Combs falls to several notches at this point. His tone is smooth, sharp, but well controlled. "You always have to exercise." He preaches to his flock.

"Come on now, say it with me saints." "To exercise." "To exercise!!!" The congregation quickly replies. "That's right, to exercise."

"You can always be physically fit."

"You can be mentally fit."

"But are you spiritually fit?"

"Well?" Says the rest of the congregation.

For a brief moment, Pastor Combs takes the mike and steps down from the pulpit.

He closely observes all of those before him, thus going from aisle to aisle.

"In the word, you have to train yourself." "Condition yourself."

"Life itself is like a race."

"And it doesn't matter how you start, but it's how you finish."

"Although Philippians 4:13 says that I can do all things through Christ who strengthens me, namely you all saints." "At the very same time, in Christ we are more than just conquers." "Life is a race that everybody wants to win, to prosper, to succeed and more of the like." "Make it plain." Says one listener. "Preach on it." Another replies.

"Some clap. Others nod with equal satisfaction.
"The Kingdom of Heaven is the finish line."
"Well?" One member stands.
"And it doesn't matter what place that you fall in."
"Or how you finish out."
"As long as you just finish the race." Several claps continue.
"But if we truly want to prevail in this race that we call life, we need Jesus."
"He will tend to your every need."

"Jesus is the coach of all coaches, the King of all captains."
"His word alone is even the breakfast of all champions."
"He'll train you if you let him."
"The things that we all go through are just routine exercises."
"Routine exercises on a minor scale as opposed, to what we can really go through."
"Things that we could ultimately face."
"Things that we will sometimes face."
"What you say?" "Preach black man?"
Several of the members laugh.
"Amen." Says Melissa. The model-like young woman throws up her hands.
"You have your brothers and sisters in Christ here on earth."
"You have your Angels in Heaven cheering for you."
"Of all living beings in the this world and possibly beyond, God is the one true person."
"The one true person who really wants you to make it."
"He will never forsake you, nor will he sell you out."
"Amen." Says the rest of the congregation.
"Jesus doesn't allow you to endure things as a means of belittling you."
"Nor does he allow you to withstand things that will tear you down."

As the Pastor continues on with his sermon, his voice employs a mild southern flavor.

"But to elevate you, to build you up for bigger and better things."

"Just as the Lord had done for Job."

"Even though Job himself, didn't see it."

"For all he knew at the time, God was picking on him."

"And Job, was also a man of God."

"There were many times that he wanted to give up."

"Not to mention that God eventually had a pep talk with him."

"But even as modern-day Christians ourselves."

"We become doubtful, all of which are tricks of the enemy by the way."

"We want to throw in the towel, to give up."

The bass in the Pastor's voice resurfaces with unspeakable energy.

"We're down, but not out!"

"At times, we retreat!" "But NEVER, in defeat!"

"Visibly open, and NEVER discreet.

"Although Satan's principal goals are to Kill, Steal, and destroy."

"His central goal is to throw you off of your game, to distract you."

"Make you lose focus."

"Whatever it takes to deter you from reaching the finish line."

"Just like you're racing cross country for example."

Wiping away sweat from his face and forehead, the Pastor pours himself another glass of water and takes a few sips. He motions for Cecilia, his second daughter to come forward shortly thereafter. Both Cecilia and Audra who are quite beautiful closely

resembles their mom. With a smooth double chocolate skin tone, the two girls have relatively long shoulder length hair and light brown eyes.

T3, who is of the youngest (Cecilia's junior by only one year), closely favors his dad.

"So you're in a race." Pastor Combs continues on. Smiling and waving at the others, Cecilia assists her father in what is obviously a mock race. "You're running through the designated paths that they would say like in a forest preserve." The rest of the congregation smiles as it look on. For a moment, Pastor Combs allows Cecilia to jog alone. Up, down and around the aisles of this medium sized sanctuary.

For a brief moment, the Pastor sits in the front row among his V.I.P. guests.

He still holds the mike. "You're up against many other runners."

Pastor Combs now motions for five other members to come forward from the center row. They now join the second first daughter. "At some point, you end up having the other runners eat your dust." The rest of the congregation responds with laughter.

The other mock runners become weary and they each step to the side one by one.

"And usually, they'll have spotters out there watching you, making sure that you don't cut any corners." "Because that's considered cheating and that would get you disqualified." "And just when you think that you're home free at the Promised Land, it turns out that there is still one other runner out there." At this point in the demonstration, Ivan represents the opposing runner. Both he and Cecilia chuckles.

"And he will of course do anything to win." The pastor returns to the podium.

"Even if it means to cheat." "Just like the Devil if you look at it." "His actions are comparable when he realizes that he doesn't stand a chance."

"Especially against the Lord who also created him."

"I actually knew this guy when I was running in school, literally get himself clocked."

"For trying to force another runner off the track."

"And of course he was disqualified."

Within one inch of the finish line (Namely the middle exit) Ivan playfully attempts to throw Cecilia off, but she finally prevails. Laughing once more at the two young people, the congregation including the guests all applaud.

"Before we all head out, once again the message behind this brief demonstration and the service at large, is never give up."

"Stay encouraged, and most importantly just hang in there."
"The Lord hasn't forgot about you."
"He loves you."
"God won't give you anymore than you can handle."
"He always has your back 24-7, 365, thick and thin."
"In other words, help is on the way."

"Everyone have a bless week, you are now dismissed."

23

As Ivan's friends mingle and fellowship with the overall congregation (Situated in the central lobby) not too long after, he himself breaks the ice. Ivan now greets the Pastor and his first lady.

Around this time the head clergyman and his very attractive wife are now seated amongst key members from the ushers (including) Nikki's mother, also known as the treasurer, Nurse Laura Chandler, Rev. Delaney, and Elder Majors just to name a few.

However, before the lone youngster is able to speak, the conference is already adjourned. Upstairs in what used to a residential unit is now a recently converted dining area. A large kitchen occupies the rear while a medium conference room which doubles as a classroom for younger Sunday school students, is situated along the left of a narrow hallway. In the dining area where a growing number of members are now eating, the latter mimics that of a more upscale environment.

Plants, a small makeshift fountain and last but not least several paintings and a few sketches corresponds to the visible brick walls throughout this entire floor.

There's also some track lighting, which highlights a picture of the church's founding first family in what was formerly a living room.

Another portrait of Martin Luther King hangs on the left wall.

The slightly tinted windows offer a view of a vacant lot supported by a backdrop of brick flats and gray stones on a following street.

Finally the buildings that once housed the former Sears-Roebuck headquarters are also seen. Its historic landmark tower stands out.

"And how are you Brother Ivan?" Pastor embraces.
"I thought that I was the only man on a mission."
Ivan and the head clergyman share a laugh.
Mrs. Combs smiles as she herself greets the junior member.
"Blessed as usual." "Is it obvious?"
"Minus the bragging rights." Ivan playfully clears his throat.

"Are you developing a sense of humor?" Asks Elder Majors.
He pats Ivan on the shoulder and grins.
"That's a good thing though son."
"We're all glad that to see that you're still emerging from your shell."
"We hear a lot more about you these days." Rev. Delaney begins.
"Enjoy the sermon today?" "As always." Ivan humbly replies.
"For as long as I've been listening to your sermons."

"I knew for certain that each and everyone is actually based on someone's day to day issues and circumstances right here in the church." Ivan points out to them.

"And of course, my grandmother has also informed me.

The older clergy members nod their heads with the greatest of satisfaction as they continue to listen. "As in the case of today's sermon, the topic of never giving up was about me." Ivan deciphers. "I knew that." Grins Pastor Combs.

"You never gave up." Adds Sister Marilyn.
"A true fighter you are." She then smiles.
"We are all proud of you Ivan, and may the Lord continue to bless you."
"As we understand, you've really been through a lot." Says Rev. Delaney
"We've been aware of this for years." Adds Nurse Chandler.

“You’ve been dragged through the fire, the ice, and even the mud.”

“At school, at home, and even within the community.”

“Man, the devil really tried to do you in.” Says Elder Majors.

The heavy bald man (with a shaven head and goatee) first nods as he reminisces.

“And we heard about your fallen out with your cousin.” Says the Pastor.

He along with the other members tries to be less judgmental as they continue.

“What he and your brother did to you was really wrong.”

“And to a certain degree, you were technically within your rights to lash back.”

“When you do wrong onto others, you still reap what you sow.” Adds Sister Combs.

“His punishment was warranted in other words.”

“And I hear that he hasn’t returned since.” Nurse Chandler chuckles.

“We hear that you have been cleaning house also.”

“Your enemies are really becoming your footstools.” Pastor Combs almost laughs.

“Although violence is never the answer, you still have a right to defend yourself.”

“Rumor has it, you’re really good Ivan.”

“Your fighting skills are also a gift.”

“God has really been good to you.”

“Blessed you with more talents than you already know.” Says Sister Combs.

“The Spirit tells me that this is just the beginning with you.” Her husband prophesizes.

“With the permission of my Sifu, I’d be more than happy to show you guys a demo whenever the next Men’s Day, Women’s Day or even the next Youth Day comes around.” “There could even be a nice exhibition without the swords.”

“That would really be nice.” Says Ms. Sanders.

"On a more personal note." Ivan begins.

"I'm quite sure you all recall my hot tub incident."

The pastor and his counsel all nod their heads.

"That was my closest attempt to actually throwing in the towel by the way."

"When I woke up in the hospital, there was actually this young nun standing over me."

"Fairly nice looking, early to mid twenties and given her accent."

"I would have gone along with Italy."

"Obviously God-sent, Madonna I think that her name was."

"She wasn't the singer, nor was she the Virgin Mary."

The others continue to nod as the young man speaks.

"But she actually gave me my friendly pep talk."

"Madonna advised me not to give up, hang in there, and whatever was troubling me."

"She said would eventually pass, and prayed over me."

"My parents and my grandmother entered the room shortly thereafter."

"We've been praying for you and your family too, since day one." Adds Elder Majors.

"Well, I wasn't yet called into the Ministry." Pastor Combs begins.

"But my father, my mother, Elder Majors here, Nurse Chandler, and some others."

"Actually baptized you." The Pastor tells Ivan.

"You were just a baby." The other members smile as the Pastor continues on.

"It was his Christening as I remembered."

"Rev. Delaney and Sister Sanders, this was long before you two came to the city."

"Your parents and your grandparents, your grandfather when he was alive."

"Were in attendance, they brought you here."

"Ivan really was the biggest thing out there." Adds Sister Combs.

"You've grown from being a little butterball to being quite handsome."

"Without sounding vain guys." Ivan begins to blush.

"But I've been hearing that a lot lately."

"So how's your job at your uncle's photography shop going?" Asks Rev. Delaney.

"It's been going pretty well." Ivan responds happily.

"I feel like more of a business person."

"That's good, you're staying busy." Elder Majors shakes Ivan's hand.

"Learning fundamentals of hard work, making an honest pay, learning to budget."

"And still enjoy your youth."

"You've got it made." Adds Ms. Sanders.

"And as far as your grades are concerned, keep up the good work."

"I plan on it." Ivan now faces the remaining masses within the church's lobby.

Cascade Bowl

As Ivan and his friend's walks in, they find that the establishment is literally jammed packed. Nearly every lane is occupied at this time with the exception of two.

These particular lanes, which remain off limits to the general public, are reserved only for V. I. P. use. At this time, Ivan who is still joined by Nikki, Charles, and Lazarus now represents this group. By Sam's standards (Namely Ivan's uncle), such a party also includes family. The Combs' children, mostly notably Cecilia and T3 have also come along. Its just another Sunday of hanging out after church.

Now clad in their regular street clothes, Ivan and his friends immediately put on their bowling shoes before returning to the lane.

"Hey, why don't we play in teams?" Suggest Cecilia.

"I vote yes." Says Nikki.

"Likewise." Adds Ivan.

"How about a game that involves a battle of the sexes?" Asks Charles.

"I think he's really onto something." T3 smiles.

"Cool." Replies Lazarus.

"You ain't say nothing but a word." Cecilia claps.

"You know, I'm down with the idea and all." Nikki shrugs.

"But aren't we short of like two people?"

"We don't think so." Says two unknown voices.

Two tall twins who are dressed alike (literally) emerge from the crowd.

Clad in tight jeans, sneakers, and spandex body shirts displaying their modest figures, they even have long shoulder length French braids.

At times whether they are spoken to or not, these girls will almost speak and answer as though they are one. "Veronica?" "Valencia?" Cecilia calls out.

It is the Day twins Veronica and Valencia.

Born just two minutes apart, and both thirteen these girls are both into making their own designer clothing, and likes to collect dolls.

Their favorite sports consist of tennis, basketball, and to a lesser extent softball.

Veronica and Valencia both live with their parents in a neighborhood further west known as "The Island." Their father works as a cab driver for Checker while their mother on the other hand, is employed by the city. She works as a cashier on the Chicago Skyway. Eight hours a day, five days a week.

Ivan, and Charles in particular along with both the Comb siblings and the Day's sisters are all lifelong friends. "Either I've been hit on the head, smoked a lotta weed, or I'm straight up seein' double in here." Lazarus shakes his head.

He smiles at both of the girls. Veronica and Valencia now laugh.

"Hey what's up?" Says Veronica.

"Hi Ivan." Both girls respond in unison.

"Hey double mint, I mean hi." Ivan accidentally cracks.

Cecilia laughs. "Now we have a game." Nikki says with optimism.

As a noble gesture of goodwill on their part, Ivan and his fellow male teammates allow their female counterparts to play first. At this time, Cecilia is up.

Dispatching a medium sized ball from the rack, the preacher's daughter who already has the figure of a woman in her early twenties sizes up the pins before her.

Taking fourteen small steps to her left, Cecilia positions her self just two inches shy of the gutter (also to her left) and slowly lowers her ordinance.

Quietly stepping back, Cecilia an obviously skilled bowler rolls back her ball and sends it off. Rolling and thundering alongside the left gutter, the ball suddenly shifts.

Traveling slightly to the right at least by one inch, the maroon ball strikes the southernmost pin as it continues to shift north.

However, an immediate chain reaction results in the toppling of all remaining pins.

Cecilia scores the first strike.

Her fellow teammates cheer her on.

Nikki, and the Day sisters all give Cecilia a high five.

The boys all smile and look on as though they are impressed.

And sure enough they are.

Ivan himself applauds Cecilia on her well-calculated strike.

For the time being, he sits. He observes. He studies.

Calling upon another ball from the rack as the lane itself summons other pins, Cecilia repositions herself. With her mind only focused on the game at hand, the bowling goddess opens her eyes and casts away. As her second ball rumbles consistently this time to the left, Cecilia achieves a double strike.

As her teammates began to whistle and clap they once again give their girl a second high five. Ivan on the other hand claps twice and then smiles at the competition.

"Why don't you just hit a gutter already." Lazarus playfully scoffs.

The score is already forty to nothing.

Cecilia, Nikki, and the Day twins all laugh.

As Cecilia positions herself a third time (this time in the center), she this time takes one small step immediately to her left. Casting off her third ball she steps back and releases her payload onto the lane before her, Cecilia dispatches the ball down toward the newly summoned pins. The young lady hits a third strike.

"If there's anything that you all can do, we can do it better." Nikki teases Ivan and the boys. She sticks out her tongue. "Boo!" Says T3, Laz, and also Charles.

They playfully give the girls a thumbs down.

The score is fifty to nothing.

Calling for a fourth ball, the buck seemingly stops here for Cecilia who is apparently on the roll. She positions herself within the center of the lane as mechanical hands slowly lays down more pins. Upon sending off her fourth ball with the employment of the same motion and momentum, only five pins out of the ten are knocked down.

Cecilia sometimes known as Lady "C" by her dad is at this point somewhat frustrated.

"Ah man, come on." She shakes her head.

"You still did good Cecilia." Veronica assures her.

"Ah ha!" Charles snickers. "What?" "No forth strike?"

"Where's your magic mushroom?" Teases Lazarus.
"Like off of Super Mario Bros."
"Word, she shrunk." Roasts her brother.
"Forget y'all." She says with a mild suburban accent.

Cecilia collects another ball and takes her position once more.
Upon impact, the five remaining pins all collapse.
She closes out with a spare. Fifty-five to nothing.
Ivan smiles once more. "Hmm, very good." He says.
"But brick didn't hit back." His tone mimics that of Bolo Yeung's.

Yeung, a long time Hong Kong born actor, just a year ago portrayed Chong Li.
He was the opposite of Van Damme in the martial arts film entitled "Bloodsport."
"Whatever, Ivan." Cecilia chuckles. "I'm so not liking you right now."
The rest of the group is tickled pink, as Ivan's mock tone coincides with the latter.

Eventually Ivan and the boys finally get their shot, and they ultimately catch up to Cecilia as well as the rest of her team. The game is literally a dead heat.

Even if its all in good fun, Ivan and his friends yet still play.
They play to win. Right now it is Charlie's turn to play.
Rising to his feet, he procures a ball from the rack.

"Make me proud son." Ivan says jokingly.
Charles laughs. "We're onto em now." Replies Lazarus.
"You boys are gonna have to work a lot harder to get your meal tonight." Teases Nikki.
"Pay to play." Cecilia adds. "Yeah, play hard or go home." Veronica and Valencia says at once. "Ok, Double mint twins." Cracks Lazarus. An unidentified passerby responds with a laugh. Staring at the Day sisters as he continues on about his way, the young man almost bumps into several other patrons nearby.

Positioning himself to the right near the north gutter, Charles summons his ball.

Taking a step back, he unleashes his payload.

Rolling along the side of the hardwood lane, Charles' strong heavy hand knocks down all ten of his pins. It is now his fifth consecutive strike.

Ivan and the rest of his team cheer him on.

Repositioning himself within the same spot, Charles dispatches another ball.

Eight of the ten pins are executed.

It is now an ugly split.

The husky almond complexioned youth is twice as focused as he determines how to alleviate what appears to be a gap within the remaining two pins.

"So what!" Says Nikki.

"You ain't gonna get it." Insist Cecilia.

"I've got five dollars saying that he won't."

"Have my money ready church girl." Cracks Charles.

Moving to his left, Charles takes his position and rolls his ball.

As the ball travels at light speed down the left side of the lane, a nearby pin (the last of two) falls. However, mysteriously whether it was the wind from his ball or an unknown glitch, the second pin also collapses. The players from both teams are now appalled.

"What the hell?" The Day twins blurt out.

Ivan and the rest of Charles' team laughs.

"Dude, you cheated!" Says both Veronica and Valencia.

"I've heard stories about loaded dice." Cecilia begins.

"But a loaded bowling ball?"

Nikki tries to hold back tears as she laughs continuously.

Her caramel complexion turns red.

"Come on now, y'all know that I wouldn't cheat." Charles grins.

"We're just playing with you." Says Nikki.

The blood from her facial features has now cleared.

"It was a lucky shot." Says Ivan. This is Charles' tenth spare.

Both T3 and his sister who learned the game under their dad both have six strikes each.

Nikki and the Day's all have four while Lazarus, has a solid three.

Despite a gutter ball at the beginning of the game, he still holds seven loose spares.

Meanwhile, Ivan who's really been on a roll has a total of eight.

Putting on his special gloves, he summons a ball from the rack.

Immediately after the next row of pins is dispatched, Ivan now puts on his game face.

With his mind being free of whatever outside interference, Ivan takes his position.

Situated within the center of the lane, Ivan slowly steps back.

As he prepares to make his delivery, the not so obvious bowling counterweight briefly closes his eyes. As he opens them once more, Ivan is now ready.

He quietly sounds off.

As his ball roars down the center of the lane, his ordinance knocks down every visible pin. Shortly thereafter, Ivan executes a backwards victory flip.

Charles and the others cheer him on once more.

"Boo, you're a showoff." Nikki and the other girls all reply.

The best for last is indeed saved.

24

LOOP (DOWNTOWN)

In what is known as the city's central business district located south of the main stem of the Chicago River, Chicago's downtown better known as the Loop initially adopted its name from an earlier cable car system. The latter was believed to have run directly within the heart of the city.

This concept later included the ring of elevated rail tracks for rapid transit lines (still in use), which aligns this area with the other neighborhoods.

Completed in 1897, this particular loop created an intracity transportation system that helped insured the dominance of Chicago's historic core in the development of this second largest metropolis. All of the city's nineteenth century rail depots were located on the edges of this central district, creating a circle of stations around the hub of this city that never sleeps. Jean Baptiste DuSable, a black Haitian (also Chicago's founding father), established a trading post on the northern branch of the river in the late 1870's.

Fort Dearborn followed on the opposite side in 1803-4. South Water Street, along the southern bank, became a hub of activity in the 1830's, with Lake Street; a block to the south, soon began picking up the character of a retail street.

During the walking city era, the Loop area accommodated all of the functions of the city near the main stem of the river.

The diverse nature of the population in the center of the city meant that most of Chicago's older ethnic groups can point to origins in the city's historic core.

As early as the 1850's the area south and west from State and Madison Streets had a German character, although people of every background lived here, including African-Americans, Chinese, and last but not least, the Irish.

As the commercial district expanded toward the railroad stations, it pushed areas of blight, vice and transient housing just ahead of it, often creating pockets of inexpensive housing just beyond the depots.

The Civil War brought rapid growth down here thanks to the use of streetcars, which initially appeared along State Street in 1859.

At the very end of the war Potter Palmer engineered the shift of retail commerce from Lake Street to State Street by erecting a splendid hotel (Now the Palmer House), a larger commercial emporium, and other mercantile buildings along State Street.

The reorientation of this business district was already underway by the time the Great Fire struck. As a result, the entire central area was completely obliterated.

The fires destroyed many residential dwellings, historical churches, as well as school buildings within the heart of the city.

However, the rise of the skyscraper shortly thereafter reinforced Chicago's trend toward commercial growth. As a result a new distinct character for its downtown district was born. With an established skyline, the latter abruptly becomes a symbol for the entire city. Improvements in transportation enabled residents of a then expanding city to maintain contact with this central area.

Buses eventually replace the electric trolleys as well as the inauguration of two subway lines. Up until nearly four decades ago (sometime during the early 1950's), the people of Chicago actually had just two neighborhoods: their particular residential area and last but not least, this very community right here.

Back in the day, this area was once an ideal place in terms of work, recreation, government services, and what else? Shopping.

However, after 1950 in response to the outward pull of suburban development in a much newer automobile metropolis, the importance of this area grew less.

Today it no longer functions as a second neighborhood for countless citizens, and retail sales here (Downtown) accounts for a much smaller portion of the metropolitan total.

Although an extended and more luxurious business district exists along the northernmost Michigan Avenue, and although residential high-rises overlook east Randolph Street and Grant Park, its landmark theater district (namely its movie palaces) is not as fortunate.

Along Randolph between both State as well as Dearborn Streets, where a combination of independent designer clothing stores exist such as "The Randolph", Sports City, a video arcade known as the Treasure Chest, a lone Burger King franchise, as well as that of a Mr. Submarine, lies a darkened United Artist Theatre.

Formerly owned by the ABC Great States chain, and later Plitt Theaters, this palace that faces a more modern office complex (Daley Plaza) has been closed since last year.

Prior to its closing, it was independently operated and it still aired first run films.

Now the building has become a "cinema tomb". Its future remains uncertain.

Its marquees and overhead billboards are still displaying what is believed to be the palace's last and final showings.

Among them are "The Hidden" and "Stranded."

Situated across the street overlooking McDonald's, is the Woods Theater.

Located in the fifty-four West Randolph building which also houses existing offices and a Manny's Restaurant, the movie palace that employs a Venetian Renaissance-type exterior is another to lower its curtain. Previously owned by Plitt's successor Cineplex Odeon, this palace, which also aired first run films till the very end, closed its doors back in January. Unlike that of its brother across the street, the marquees are both bare.

Its main entrance is boarded up.

From its grand opening seventy-two years ago (circa 1917) up until this year, this theater was also the last surviving single screen palace ever known in the Loop.

Just one door down on the very same block of north Dearborn Street facing a newly built parking garage near Lake Street, is the short-lived Dearborn Cinemas.

Previously known as the Michael Todd Theater, which was initially run down, the M&R theater chain purchased it and converted this building into a four screen multiplex just four years ago. For some undisclosed reason although the Dearborn was a more highly patronized complex as opposed to its next-door neighbor, the promising younger theater closed its doors sometime last year. It is believed that live acts will later take over.

On the north side along Randolph where a currency exchange, a Garrett's popcorn shop, a Shopper's Corner, and a Ronny's Steak House exists, lies Oriental Electronics.

Perhaps what is so significant about this particular store was that there had been a theater on this very same sight, which had also carried that name: The Oriental.

Prior to its closing just eight years ago, the theater was already reduced to showing only films that young teenage males found appealing.

The only piece of evidence that points to its former existence is a rusted bare canopy that once supported the marquee. Underneath, a white makeshift banner displaying its namesake electronics store is seen.

It is believed that this downward trend began sometime during the late 1970's.

In a newly expanding "South Loop" (The Near South Side), where many former industrial buildings are being converted into lofts, there is a recently opened cinema complex (built from the ground up) known as Burnham Plaza.

Situated near the Columbia College Campus on the corner of East 9th Street and South Wabash Avenue, this six-screen small stadium-like building is the very first theater operated by Cineplex Odeon, to ever open its doors to the city.

On Michigan Avenue overlooking Grant Park, a theater specializing in both foreign films as well as those, which pertains to the performing arts, is also seen.

The latter, a longtime veteran of the M&R franchise is commonly known as the Fine Arts. Roosevelt University sits directly to the left, while the live performing Auditorium Theater sits to the right.

Treasure Chest

Situated on the south side of Randolph Street, this establishment from the outside bears a bright, red and white façade. Mimicking what appears to be a casino from its bright neon sign, perhaps in its own right the Treasure Chest isn't too far off in terms of legalized gambling. Its only distinction as opposed to slot machines is that this entertainment venue instead, houses video games. In the front lobby, this shop has many gag gifts as well as a sizable amount of novelties.

In the center of this now one story building (there was formerly an upstairs that once housed a “magic shop”), patrons, can enter various raffles, contests, and play special games. In return, various prizes are won.

The establishment, which was founded by a Ralph Baer (whether or not if this gentleman is still the owner), once again had a second floor.

As the result of a fire (sometime during the 1970’s), this floor was destroyed.

In the rear, numerous video games as well as pinball machines exist.

Among the many patrons who now occupy the floors of this seemingly cluttered and more so crowded thoroughfare, the vast majority appear to represent every demographic.

Even some rival gangs are seen as they congregate here and there.

However, unlike their predecessors of the previous decade whose reputations once made the Loop an unsafe place to visit, these present day factions choose to remain neutral. Thanks in part to their leaders, the mayor’s own gang: The Police, and to a lesser extent the hardworking and taxpaying citizens.

Having played almost seemingly endless rounds on games such as Super Mario Bros, NARC, Sega’s Altered Beast and Outrun, Capcom’s Final Fight and Konami’s Teenage Mutant Ninja Turtles, Ivan and the rest of his group try their luck at Double dragon II (the latest installment of the Technos Japan most recent franchise), as well as Contra and Punch Out. It has been over an hour since Ivan and his friends arrived.

It is about four in the afternoon.

After beating his entire group single handedly, in some cases barely in what is now Air Hockey, two unidentified youths, a tall heavyset Hispanic male and a leaner but shorter Filipino, obviously American-born on the account of his unaccented English accepts Ivan's challenge. They introduce themselves as Gerald and Martin.

Playing more intensively than ever, the games at first are literally tied.

Toweling himself dry, Ivan accepts a Coke given to him by Gerald.

"Thanks man." Ivan tells him. He shakes his hand shortly thereafter.

"Man bro, you look like you're playing at the Chicago Stadium." Chuckles Martin.

Nikki and the others began smiling. "I have overactive sweat glands." Says Ivan.

Charles and Lazarus shake their heads.

"He's been sweating like this ever since he became more active." Explains T3.

"It doesn't even matter how much water or Gatorade that our friend drinks."

"Dude just sweats, like it ain't nobody's business." Lazarus adds with a shrug.

"Damn, I don't get it." Both Gerald and Martin nod as they listen.

"Well, at least Ivan doesn't have to worry about pimples like the rest of us." Cecilia says.

"Yeah, his skin is quite oily and less likely to dry up." Nikki finally speaks.

Having finished his drink, Ivan now sends two more tokens into the machine.

Back in the front lobby lies a lone red machine known as the "Skill Crane."

Operating what appears to be a mechanical or robotic-like hand, Ivan manages to grab at least three stuffed animals. Among them is a fluffy white rabbit, a panda, and what appears to be a giant tweedy bird. Reaching for what appears to be a medium sized Snoopy, Ivan summons for the latter.

"This is for you." Ivan turns to Nikki.

He hands his best female friend the giant tweedy.

Adoring her fluffy and feathery stuffed animal, Nicole blushes.

"You're so sweet Ivan, and I meant what I said before."

"Thanks." She then hugs him.

"And this one is for my second best friend, who's of course like a sister."

Ivan surrenders the panda to Cecilia.

"Thanks Ivan." Cecilia smiles. "You are sweet."

"I guess that my two cousins can have the other two.

"Anyway, let's get something to eat."

Stuffing the remaining animals into his duffel bag, Ivan and his friends finally began to leave.

Ronny's Steakhouse

Established over twenty-six years ago with another restaurant on Van Buren Street and Wabash Avenue although it specializes in charbroiled steaks, there are many other dishes to choose from on the menu. Not to mention desserts.

With three levels of seating and a buffet section on the ground floor, there is a large screen TV showing movies like Dangerous Liaisons and Tequila Sunrise in the central dining area. Masonry checkerboard tiles covers the often-spotless floors, while colorful neon signs remain visible throughout the entire lower level.

Bonsai plants are also situated at each table as countless masses from all walks unwind, kick back, and enjoy their meals.

As the smell of seasoned and well-cooked entrees ascends to the air, the sounds of r&b classics (widely known as Dusties) are heard. Most notably Marvin Gaye's "Let's Get it on." A limited number of video games are also situated downstairs.

Its exterior façade pays homage to what appears to be a green and white fifteenth century English castle. A large clock displaying Roman numerals and two dark hands rests in the center. Both of the latter now declares it to be officially, 5pm.

Ivan, Charles, Lazarus and Nikki along with the Combs' siblings are all seated upstairs.

Laughing, mingling amongst themselves, and dining on a family-sized thin crust pizza, the young group is still having a good time.

Now playing is Eddie Kendrick's "Going Up in Smoke."

"You know, Nikki here is right." Ivan begins.

"I really have to remember as to why I began training in the martial arts."

"We know how you think Ivan." Charles adds.

"Truthfully I really wanted to beat that guy silly as we walked out."

"He was ignorant anyway." Says Cecilia.

"First he bumps into me, second he doesn't say excuse me, and third this guy had the balls to appear all nonchalant." "Like what you gonna do about it?"

"Look on the bright side man, ol' boy still got what he deserved." Lazarus reminds him.

"Word, straight up Laz." Ivan responds.

While Nikki serves herself three additional slices of pizza, she also takes the liberty of serving her friends. They all thank her.

"Just when he thought he got off easy, he acts all cocky, nonchalant, and he has the nerve to pound his chest." Nikki begins.

She struggles with a string of cheese that now binds her pizza as well as her lower lip.

Ivan stares at her for one moment and then smiles. "What?" She says.

“Oh nothing.” Replies Ivan. “Why don’t you two get a room already.” Cecilia chuckles.

“Yeah.” Adds her brother. “But homeboy behind him, made him look real salty.”

Charles adds. “Just who in the world did this guy think that he was?” Cecilia asks.

“Tarzan?” T3 laughs. “He really did look retarded.” T3 himself replies.

“Dude just appeared like a total jackass, just sitting in the middle of the floor.”

Adds Ivan. “People were just laughing at him.”

“Like a lost Garbage Pail Kid on crack!” Charles snaps.

The others laugh. “That’s what you get for being ignorant.”

“You reap what you sow.” Says Nikki. “Touché.” Reply the others.

“So who’s watching the game this evening?” Asks Ivan.

The entire group raise their hands.

“ The Bulls are playing Detroit right?” Asks T3. Ivan nods.

“I ain’t missing this game for the world.” Says Lazarus.

“They’ve come a long way since last year.”

“If you’ve seen them throughout the regular season, the Bulls have been on a roll.”

Adds Charles. “I’ve been keeping tabs on them myself.” Says Nikki.

Cecilia pours herself another glass of Pepsi.

“This could really be the year for Chicago.” Nicole continues.

“I’m keeping my fingers crossed.”

“Yeah, you have to.” Cecilia tells her.

“For the simple fact that the Pistons are really tough.”

“And they like to hack a lot.” Says Lazarus.

“They’re always playing off script.”

“If I didn’t know any better, I’d swear that the Pistons have some issues even on the court.” Adds Charles. “Playing against them won’t be easy.”

“Now as far as the Bulls making the playoffs.” Ivan begins.

“The chances are all but slim.” The others nod to his comment.

“It looks like the only key roadblocks is Salley, and Lambeer.” T3 adds.

"When Lambeer fouls, he acts as though he's always looking for a fight." Ivan replies.

"Its like he bumps against you deliberately when he's playing against you." Adds Nikki.

"Forget about him sticking defense, and I think that Lambeer is mental."

"Now their most recent player, I think is Dennis Rodman-------." She briefly pauses.

"Yeah, Dennis Rodman." Ivan confirms.

"He gets like five to maybe ten rebounds per game, and his defenses is just as good."

"Rodman, he prolongs his game play for almost a good twenty minutes at least."

"Now Green, Dantley, and Johnson is no joke either."

Ivan, who is so impressed by Nikki's knowledge of both teams, begins to smile.

Cecilia, T3, as well as both Charles and Lazarus who are also listening to Nikki are somewhat clueless as to what Ivan „s thinking about.

Despite the fact that they all know that both he and Nikki has some feelings for one another, they have yet to determine the extent.

Or to put it in plain English: The magnitude.

She's definitely my kind of girl. He thinks quietly to himself.

"Thomas and Dumars is like the Piston's equivalency to Jordan and Pippen here."

"But on a clear and rainy day if you take away the fouls, Detroit can really back it up." Says Cecilia. "You can do all but write them off." T3 says.

Briefly covering his mouth, he belches.

"Is the Bulls playing at the Stadium or are they playing in Detroit?" Asks Lazarus.

"They're playing here tonight man." Says Charles.

"The game starts at eight." Ivan reminds the rest of the group.

"We'll get back home just in time to watch."

A waiter takes the liberty of bringing the group "doggy bags" as Ivan and his friends split their bill. Cecilia and T3 summons a respective four-dollar-tip.

Gold Coast (Near North side)

Alighting a northbound "All Stops" Englewood- Howard train at the Chicago Avenue subway station underneath State Street, Ivan and his friends make their ascension from the dual platforms by escalator, up to the mezzanine level.

Built in 1938 and opened in 1943, with the exception of the current signage, maps and modern-fare controls (save for the agents booths), most of its features dating back to the height of the Second War remains well intact.

Previously bearing a dingy brown color scheme, also reeking of urine, this station now bears a color scheme which consist of both a bright fire engine red as well as a peach-like yellow. The globes, which protects its age-old fluorescents, are now clean.

The graffiti, a common pest throughout most the stations along this corridor is almost non-existant. Plain-clothes officers hide among the countless passengers who are now seen coming and going. On the southbound platform, as a middle aged but well-groomed musician does wonders with his sax, a seemingly endless number of coins (and the occasional dollar) falls almost simultaneously.

Even on a bright Sunday evening, forty-five-year-old Riad "Raymond" Khan still gets his hustle as a delegation of obvious tourists pays for snacks at his concession stand.

The roaring trains below continue to run every five to seven minutes.

With its northernmost terminal at Howard Street located in the Rogers Park neighborhood, that in part shares a common border with the City of Evanston (which is actually a north suburb), the State Street

Subway (namely the North-South route), employs two separate terminals for two separate branches as it continues south.

The Englewood Branch, which leaves its partner, the Jackson Park Branch continues west along 63rd Street (directly above an alley), where it ends in its namesake neighborhood.

The Jackson Park Branch that eventually separates from its Englewood cousin, turns to the far left and continues east directly over 63rd.

The latter ends at a former through station in the Woodlawn neighborhood, at University Avenue. This particular branch (which makes up all three lines) is not by far the most heavily traveled route. Service to its namesake park was suspended in 1982.

Now on the surface, Ivan and his friends now stands on what is now Chicago Avenue and State Street. More people are outside than ever at this time as they begin the rest of their journey on foot. Ignoring a lone panhandler who is seen near the station entrance, the young explorers continue east.

Along this stretch, an assortment of fast food restaurants such as: Burger King McDonalds, a Taco Bell, and an independent greasy spoon known as the Coast covers the northern section of Chicago Avenue. Between the latter and the corner of Wabash, lies an existing parking lot. A twenty-four hour Dunkin Donuts also exist between both the Taco Bell as well as the occupied lot.

To the groups right between the ongoing traffic that covers both directions, is a lone Catholic Parish. With a high school campus corresponding to the latter, a sizable church exists on the State Street side. It is best known as Holy Name Cathedral.

Just one block east beyond Wabash Avenue across the street lies a cluster of other shops and stores. Among them is a recently opened Blockbuster Video, a White Hen Pantry, and an independent florist. On the opposite side lies a cluster of vintage historic storefronts mixed in with brownstones.

Recently planted trees compliments the latter as does a set of vintage-like streetlamps.

Among the tenants is a Beck's bookstore, a vision center known as Out of Sight, a Seattle Café, a Margie's Tavern, Seoul Soul, an authentic Korean restaurant, and a boutique shop known as "Head over Heels." A lone currency exchange (also opens 24 hours) sits right next to it. Just to the east at Rush Street lies a five-star hotel known only as "La Tour." Crossing the intersection of Pearson Street facing a Banana Republic, which overlooks a Walgreen's across the street, Ivan and the others are now at what appears to be Michigan Avenue.

In the small park that surrounds the historic Water Tower, many spectators look on as three lone skate boarders performs seemingly countless tricks on their own makeshift ramps. An older gentleman seated on a bench who is obviously blind (although he still wears sunglasses), somehow does multiple sketches of those around him.

Literally. Even without the knowledge of those closest to him, he yet still creates their images; everything from apparel, to facial features, everything.

Although the unidentified gentleman expects very little, he yet still rings several dollars per sketch. Ivan and friends crosses Pearson and cuts through this park.

"Hey check this out." Ivan says to the others.

He along with Nikki, Charles, Lazarus and the Combs' all head over to the coin fountain where the visually impaired artist is sitting.

Closely observing the man's sketches Ivan and his friends, are literally blown out of this world. They are fascinated. "Unbelievable." Nikki began.

Although the gentleman is unable to see the young group, his evolved sense of hearing already summons their footsteps. The man smiles.

"Not to me it isn't." He says. "I've been doing this for a long time."

"Without me being rude sir." Ivan begins.

"Was I born this way?" The man finishes.

"Not really, in fact I lost my sight when I was very young."

"And no you're not being rude young man." The man answers him with a mild southern accent. "I sense something about you." "You're quite observant, intelligent, diplomatic, and you have a kind heart." "And the Spirit tells me for a young man, you don't appear to take any nonsense." "How old are you?" "About twelve or thirteen?"

"I'm actually thirteen." Ivan tells him. The rest of the group are equally appalled.

"This man doesn't even know you Ivan, and he's got you down to a "T." Lazarus chuckles. "That means he truly has a gift." Ivan informs him.

"Actually, we all have gifts." The man says.

"Courtesy of the Lord, and you just have to dig deep within into yourself to find them."

"Just like your friend here."

As soon as Ivan and his group had walked over, the man had already began his composite sketches. Not to mention that he was actually done within a matter of minutes.

Apparently shocked and overwhelmingly surprised, Cecilia covers her mouth.

Her smooth and relatively gorgeous complexion (dark chocolate) turns red.

"Please don't pass out on me young lady."

"Breathe Cecilia, c'mon." Ivan rubs her hand.

Cecilia accepts Ivan's advice and takes three deep breaths.

"The people in this picture looks exactly like us, ah man." Charles laughs.

"Thank you sir." Says Lazarus.

"You're welcome youngster."

Having already shaken the gentlemen's hand, Ivan and his friends humbly accepts the picture. Bowing his head to the elder, Ivan and the others continue their journey.

John Hancock Center

Upon their entry into the main lobby, Ivan and the rest of the group boards an express elevator for the top floor.

Situated across the street from the Water Tower Place complex in what is eight-seventy five north Michigan Avenue (less than two blocks where the Magnificent Mile merges with Lake Shore Drive), this 100 story, and 1,127 foot skyscraper was constructed under the supervision of Skidmore, Owings, and Merrill, with chief designer and structural engineer Faziur Khan. When the building topped out on May 6, 1968, it then rivaled New York's Empire State as the world's tallest building.

Six years later, this building was rivaled by a then newly completed Sears Tower as the world's tallest building. This twenty-one-year-old building is named for the John Hancock Mutual Life Insurance Company, as well as one of the first original tenants.

The skyscraper that is also 1, 506 feet (if one includes the antenna masts), it houses many offices and restaurants, followed by seven hundred condominiums and contains the third highest residence in the world.

As the elevator doors open, Ivan and his group somewhat staggers.

They are now on the top floor.

Observatory

"Man, I think my equilibrium is off." Lazarus begins.
"You know, it does feel like we've boldly gone where no one else has gone before."

Adds Charles. “I feel like a dwarf with a hangover myself.” Says Cecilia.

“I actually felt my ears somewhat pop.” Nikki puts two fingers to her nose.

“We were on an express elevator.” Ivan reminds them.

“The effects are almost similar when you’re on a plane.”

“It was a straight shot up from one all the way up here to a hundred.”

“Now imagine being on a 737 or a DC 10 at thirty thousand feet.” Ivan continues on.

Blowing his nose from the inside out, he blots out the excess air that has temporarily obstructed some of his hearing. “We’ve never flown.” Says both Charles and Lazarus.

“Neither have I.” Nikki shakes her head.

However although Nikki herself has never been on an airplane, she is still impressed by her friend’s knowledge of anything that pertains to the laws of physics.

Or better yet, on the account of her gorgeous smile and glowing red dimples, it is Ivan himself who impresses her. “But we have.” Says Cecilia.

“We know exactly what it feels like.”

“Going on vacation with our parents to Jerusalem and Ghana.”

“Fifteen hours in the air.” Adds T3.

“You know we’re so high up, that it almost feels like Heaven.” Says Charles.

Ivan and the others laugh.

Like that of the Sears Tower which stands in the heart of the financial district, this complex which is mainly in more of a residential slash commercial setting, on a bright sunny day such as this; one can see at least four states.

Four states alone from this very floor.

Among them, there's Illinois (the main base), Iowa, Indiana, and last but not least Wisconsin. At this time, the blazing sun is now situated to the west.

The birds began to follow.

In what dubbed as the "Windy City", a city of roughly four million people at this point, now resembles a giant model.

At least for Ivan and his friends who are currently, looking down.

From what is more than just a simple view of an entire region, or a metropolis to be more formal; the group is actually getting more bang for their buck.

From Ivan's west, he catches a glimpse of the entire west side of Chicago.

Not to mention its inner ring suburbs.

Among his points of interests, he discovers its renowned Medical District, a line of moving vehicles (presumably the Eisenhower Expressway), miniature trains in the median, pieces of a dwindling industrial hub, and the Chicago Stadium to the north.

A network of housing projects to the right such as Rockwell Gardens and the Henry Horner Homes are seen.

Further to his west, there's the main post office, the University of Illinois Campus, as well as a cluster of other neighborhoods in between.

Now peering beyond the city limits , Ivan now sees what appears to be Brookfield Zoo, the Village of Westchester and more of the like.

There was also a body of water that resembles the Des Plaines River.

From Nikki's south, she catches a glimpse of Comiskey Park (home of the White Sox), as well as everything: both east and west of the Dan Ryan Expressway.

Among these points of interest namely to east, there's the semi-suburban Hyde Park neighborhood, the University of Chicago, and even the entire boulevard system.

Railroad yards(both passenger and freight), blighted buildings(including the housing developments of Stateway and Robert Taylor), Harold Ickes and others.

As Nikki employs her telescope further east, she discovers a spectrum of multiple well-kept homes, tree-lined streets, an existing industrial belt, a network of rivers, connecting highways and a shipyard.

Both Cecilia and T3 respectively look on to the north.

With their telescopes zeroed in along the blue shoreline, they discover moving vehicles, complimented by high rises, beaches, residential subdivisions, (Cecilia sees Wrigley Field: home of the Cubs), as well as two passenger rail lines.

At some point, T3 insist that he's seen some people despite his location.

Charles and Lazarus who looks to the east catches a clear evening view of Chicago's far southeast side. The latter that appears to be blanketed by existing mills, and other industrial buildings, also gives way to beaches, forest preserves, cars on what appears to be the Chicago Skyway, and last but not least a smorgasbord of residential gems.

Connecting dots all the way to the doorsteps of outlying villages such as Burnham, they now adjust their telescopes. Having discovered what is obviously a landfill, the boys are now zeroing in what is now Northwest Indiana.

Lazarus himself takes note on what appears to be a blighted and somewhat desolate town. In his eyes the latter (presumably Gary), appears to be more like a scene from Cyborg or better yet Mad Max.

"Jesus, we're actually looking down at the entire metropolitan area." Charles begins.

"Like some type of larger scale model."

"On my both my mother and father, this is straight up amazing."

"And to a lesser extent Charlie, the people really do look like ants." Adds Lazarus.

"You've got all of the roads looking like something out of a Tyco catalog, and the rail lines mimicking one gigantic train set."

"The view really is wonderful." Says Nikki.

"It really is." Cecilia backs her up.

"When the temperature is really beautiful, you can actually see four states." Ivan informs them. "You've got Iowa, Indiana, and Wisconsin."

"It's literally like the Sears Tower, only three stories shorter."

"That's really good to know Ivan." Nikki softly responds.

"Yo, word." Says Lazarus.

"Did you know that there are talks of another skyscraper being built?"

"Yeah?" "Where?" Asks T3. "Right here in Chicago." Ivan replies.

"So in other words, Chicago would still retain its status as having the world's tallest building?" Asks Cecilia. "Yes, it would." Ivan says to her.

"It is supposed to be over a hundred and twenty-five stories."

"Damn." Says Nikki. Ivan grins.

"That was what I said." He responds.

"Have any of you guys seen Poltergeist III?"

"Yeah." Says the others.

"If you remember, that movie was actually filmed in this very building."

"It sure was." Cecilia snaps her fingers.

"I think there was a scene on like the forty-fourth floor, or somewhere."

"That's where the pool is." T3 reminds his sister.

"It didn't matter where little Carol Anne went." Says Nikki.

"Because those spirits would always find her." Ivan shakes his head.

"If you remembered from the first two films, it wasn't the entire family they wanted."

"They only wanted the girl."

"And by the way, did you know that in real life she was actually a teenager?"

"Heather O' Rourke I think her name was."

"You mean the girl who played Carol Anne?" Asks Cecilia.

Ivan nods his head. "She actually passed away not too long after the project was done."

"She only seemed younger on the account of her height." Ivan continues on.

"But she was actually a little older than we are."

"The doctors though that she had Crohn's Disease." Adds Nikki.

"They actually gave her a medication, that was supposed to treat it."

"But the drug instead, made O' Rourke feel worse." Ivan finishes.

"It caused her to develop cardiac arrest, putting her out for good."

"But as it turned out, she was actually having intestinal problems, and she needed surgery." "It was later revealed that Heather went into septic shock."

"She never pulled through." "And that was messed up too." Lazarus shakes his head.

"Ol' girl was really good playing her."

"Her parents sued the hell out of that hospital too." Nikki adds.

"I can remember the very first Poltergeist that came out." Ivan begins.

"And it actually scared the shit out of me."

Both Cecilia and Nikki began giggling.

Ivan chuckles. "What?" "I ain't playing."

Charles attempts not to laugh while Lazarus snickers.

"Man, get outta here." He points and then whistles.

"You mean to tell me that Down Lo Ho here was scared of Poltergeist?"

"I was only five man." Ivan grins.

"And you had Simon's immature ass, my own brother telling all of our friends on the playground." "But at least, the other kids didn't give a damn Ivan."

"It was a good chance that some of them watched it, and they were scared too."

Charles reminds him. "When one of the paranormal guys started peeling off his face."

"That really WAS gross." Says Cecilia. "I peed in the bed myself Ivan, don't feel bad."

"Simon was actually more of an asshole back then, than he is now." Ivan nods.

"Both he and Jennifer." He now chuckles.

Continuing their tour of the complex, the group returns to the elevators.

25

SOUTH LOOP (NEAR SOUTH SIDE), WHITE PALACE GRILL

Located on the corner of east Roosevelt Road and south Canal Street, Herbert Schwartz is seen here.

Sitting at a table overlooking the southern backdrop of existing rail yards and warehouses some still occupied, although many are vacant with the Chicago River flowing three blocks to the left; Schwartz is having dinner with a younger woman.

Mingling, laughing and even holding hands briefly under the table, this couple appears to be having an intimate moment.

The unidentified petite female who is presumed to be somewhere between the ages of eighteen to twenty-four, has long dark curly hair, bangs, and a long ponytail.

With red hoop earrings, a matching sweater, and skin just as smooth as porcelain this young lady dons a pair of tight gray jeans as well as pointy black heels.

As clear-framed glasses covers her dark brown eyes, the woman is obviously a looker to one of the cooks behind the counter who is quickly joined by a waiter as well as a dishwasher. For at least one moment, it appeared as though these men were in somewhat of a trance. They eventually snap out of it. The woman grins.

Adjusting the pearls around her neck, she finishes her coffee and eats the remnants of her dessert. For a brief moment, even Schwartz himself finds this entertaining.

He is already done with his own meal at this point.

Slowing licking her lips in a not-so-obvious seductive manner, the young lady smiles.

"I have an oral presentation for my Speech class this evening." She explains.

Schwartz smiles. "I'd be more than happy to assist you Ms. Holly." He says.
"And I'd like to give you one of my own."

The woman now simply known as Holly laughs.
"You are such a dirty old man!" She whispers loudly.
"Check please." Says Schwartz.

Stepping outside in the pouring rain that now showers this suddenly warm city with temperatures in the mid sixties, Schwartz and Holly now retreats along a busy but not congested east Roosevelt Road.

Clad in a maroon turtleneck concealed by a tan sport coat, and matching trousers, this would-be gentleman (on the account that he's actually married), and would be great teacher allows the condensation to descend upon his curly toupee as he surrender his umbrella to Holly. Splashing water as Schwartz and Holly continue to sprint, the now carefree couple runs at least two blocks left before stopping at the corner of south Jefferson Street. Stopping to catch their breath, they began walking down the latter.

What is actually a two-way thoroughfare to their right is now a one-way side street.

Along this tree-lined stretch, which literally bears no outlet, is surrounded by several industrial buildings. Namely manufacturing plants as well as the central operations for United Parcel Services (also known as UPS). Countless namesake trucks are seen departing and arriving beyond their designated checkpoints.

The shadow of the Dan Ryan Expressway dwells high above the twenty-five-year-old facility. Right now, Schwartz and Holly are situated at the corner of east14th Street.

Producing his keys, Schwartz pushes a button on his chain.

A red vintage 1963 Porsche, which still shines from an earlier wax (despite the now dwindling rain), suddenly comes to life in front of a fenced off lot.

Parked at very end of the block along 14th (namely along the south side of the street), there appears to be a black stretch limo. An unknown occupant and his driver looks on at the all but odd couple. About three or possibly four spaces to where Schwartz parked his car, another vehicle, a silver Mercedes blinks it headlights.

The motorist in the nearby limo responds by briefly flashing, his own lights.

After Schwartz opens the door for his female passenger who is more than honored by his gesture, he walks over to the opposite to let himself in.

But however, before he is able to situate himself behind the wheel, eight professionally dressed gentleman all within their mid twenties, to late thirties; four exiting the Benz the others the limo (all of whom are black), confronts him.

Holly gasps. Schwartz, for at least one moment appears startled and mildly nervous.

Little miss Holly tries to hand over her purse.

“Sir, would you please step out of the car?” Says one of them.

The leader of the group, a rather tall and somewhat muscled fellow (well groomed) with a long braided ponytail and bangs motions him to step out.

"Let me guess." Schwartz begins.
"You want the car?"
"Actually, we're not here to rob you." The man says.
"In fact, you can keep all of your personal belongings."
Holly meanwhile is staying put.
Schwartz at this point is leaning on the hood.
"We don't want your money lady." Says another member in the group.
"In fact we don't even want you."

Perhaps what is funny that although Holly herself is relieved that the men didn't come to cause Schwartz or herself any harm, she still feels insulted that none of the men finds her attractive. This gentleman who is obviously young as she is, chuckles.

At this point, even Schwartz himself is relieved.

"But however." Another male in the group begins.
"We're still going to need you to come with us."
"There's someone who wishes to speak with you."
"I can't do that." Schwartz replies with mild disdain.

Another man attempts to escort him to the Benz, but Schwartz quickly snaps him a left jab. Snapping a right cross at another, and thus mixing it up with a third man.

Bobbing and weaving on a fourth, the physically flabby schoolteacher snaps a jab-cross and an uppercut to a fifth before being struck from behind.

The cold steel barrel of a handgun from another member in this unknown group takes the credit. "This guy is really an asshole." Says the party's head person.

At some point during his short struggle, Schwartz dropped his keys.

Another man summons them.

Holly who is now frozen with fear still remains put.

"Take care of the man's car, there's not to be one scratch on it." Says the groups' leader.

The much younger man who sports a modest fade and goatee replies with a nod.

"And you Cory, take this young lady where she needs to go."

"Alright Josh." He slowly opens the door for a now horrified Holly.

"Your sugar daddy has a public relations meeting to attend right now." The young man only known as Cory extends a hand. "He'll call you later."

"Besides, you won't be disappointed." Cory winks at Holly.

Holly's at first deathly pale skin becomes radiant once more.

She smiles for the first time since her rendezvous with Schwartz back at the Palace.

Taking the hot young college student by the hand, Cory escorts her to his car.

Herbert Saul Schwartz, thirty-nine is employed by the city school board. As a veteran (with over twenty years experience), Schwartz now teaches fifth grade at Jens Jensen Scholastic. He lives in the West Ridge neighborhood on Chicago's far northwest side with his wife Marilu of eighteen years(who also happens to be a teacher), and his two children. There is even a family dog, a golden retriever named Dawn. Dawn, obviously a female given the name recently had several puppies.

Seemingly well-respected figures in their community, Schwartz along with his wife are both the children of German-Jewish immigrants.

At the height of World War II, their parents managed to escape Hitler and his killer, sadistic Nazis and arrived in the city around August of 1941.

Frederich Horowitz, who came with his wife Gretchen (before Schwartz their oldest of four children were born) later changed his surname to the current.

In his youth, Schwartz took up boxing not only as a fun sport, but he also employed the art as a means of self-defense.

Namely as a deterrent against both racial and religious taunts.

Mentally as well as physically.

Attending Theodore Roosevelt high school in his former Albany Park neighborhood, Schwartz majored in Art, Physics, and Carpentry.

The young overachiever excelled at all three classes.

Schwartz was elected valedictorian at his graduation in June of 1967.

Enrolling at Princeton University where Schwartz studied to become a teacher, the lean and robust youngster meets an equally young Marilu Weiss, a fellow major.

One hour later

Waking up feeling sore, appearing both bruised and battered, Schwartz finds himself seated in what is presumably an undisclosed location.

The latter appears to be an office.

Upon the observation of his persons, the captured and roughed up educator discovers that he is suddenly without his clothes.

All that remains to be seen is a pair of boxers and a white T-shirt.

Searching high and low for his designer bifocals (which also remains unaccounted for), Schwartz finally discovers them directly under his seat.

With his vision no longer blurred, Schwartz studies his terrain.

His presumed captor, who now enters the room clad in a two-piece business suit, takes a seat at the desk in front of him.

Reaching into his top drawer, the man who is somewhere within his late thirties to early forties summons a bottle of Scotch.

Dispatching two glasses from a nearby cabinet as well as ice from the refrigerator, the seemingly suave, well fit and handsome gentleman whose complexion favors the color of an almond, his hair naturally curly pours one serving for himself and another for his guest slash captive. Schwartz's eyes now widens with fear.

"Good evening Mr. Schwartz." The man says.
"I take it you didn't see this coming at all."
Schwartz's drops his mouth.
"Please don't piss on my Persian." The man now grins.
"The bathroom is right behind me."
Schwartz quickly heads to the bathroom.
"This means that I finally have your attention."
Schwartz moves his seat closer to the desk.

His hairy hands continue to tremble as he accepts his drink.
"If you had only been willing to hear me out during our initial conference at the school." The man begins. "You'd be still out enjoying your date right now."
Schwartz slowly nods as he sips his drink. "As I recalled the other day, you told me that if I didn't like how you ran things in your classroom, I could transfer Forrest to another school." Schwartz continues to plead to the fifth as he listens to his captor.
Schwartz raises his hand. "Oh, your little lady friend is okay."

"One of my youngest brothers took her home earlier."
"And your car is being dropped off at your house by the way."

"Your taste for vintage sports cars is impressive."

"I own a sixty-three Ferrari myself, Mr. Schwartz."

"My friend, you have absolutely no idea as to how lucky you are tonight."

Schwartz continues to nod.

"As you already know, Forrest is my son."

"And at some point, he hasn't been quite the same on the account of his mother's demise." "As well as that of my wife's."

"And for a time he was a bit of a goofball, but he has long since gotten it together."

The man slowly sips his drink. "And we both know that Forrest is a good student."

As Schwartz maintains his silence, he pours himself a second helping.

"Very good." The man commends him on his silence.

"Enjoy your second glass, on me."

"As I remembered, you weren't the professional that I expected that day."

"In fact, you got very short with me Mr. Schwartz."

A lump now forms within his throat at this point. He coughs.

"I summoned you here this evening on the account that Forrest told me, that he had to go to the restroom." "He tells me that you tried to deny him of that right."

"Forrest openly admitted to me, that he defied you."

"And I certainly, can't penalize him for that given the circumstances."

"He walked out of your class anyway." Schwartz clears his throat once more.

The wannabe tough guy of the evening now bears the look of one who is guilty.

"I would have questioned your authority, and walked out on you too."

The man chuckles. Schwartz is now feeling sick.

"So what if he needed a pass." "But that is only the tip of the iceberg."

"Forrest tells me that, that you treat him as well as the rest of the class like criminals."

"And that you watch over them as they're going to the bathroom."

"I find it relatively preposterous, and to the extreme."

Schwartz now receives a cold stare from his captor.

"I guess this is the part when you're allowed to speak." The man smiles once more.

"Yes, it is Mr. Smiley." Schwartz meekly replies.

His voice corresponds to a man who has been kicked in the groin.

The man now known as Mr. Smiley shakes his head.

Mr. Smiley pours himself a second drink. "Even if it is just a safety concern."

"The school is small, you have a guard, and there is a police station right next door."

"I understand although that the neighborhood can be a bit rough, you still have more hardworking people, and yet everyone still knows each other."

"And as for your treatment of the girls, as I understand is comparable."

"I'm surprised you don't walk into their bathroom."

"Are you a pedophile Mr. Schwartz?" "Of course not."

Without emitting a single odor, the scruffy looking teacher farts.

"Let me remind you sir, that you are a teacher."

"You are not juvenile corrections officer."

"Furthermore, Forrest told me that after he went to the bathroom, you asked him to leave." "And at the end of the day, you gave him this note for me to sign."

Mr. Smiley produces a written note from the inside of his jacket.

"Of course you know how this works Mr. Schwartz, if you ever worked at some industrial plant, and some site foreman or some supervisor attempts to write you up on a charge that you knew was bogus." "What would you do?"

"Especially if the latter job that you had was unionized?"

"I'd put down refuse to sign?" Answers the distraught educator.

"That is correct." Says Mr. Smiley.
"And right now, I simply refuse to sign this."
Mr. Smiley immediately rips up his letter. Schwartz is dumbfounded.
"You really should be a shame of yourself sir."
"You look down on those students as though you're so superior."
"As though they are under you like animals in a zoo."
"Half of the time, you choose not to assist them, and you expect for them to excel."
"You blow them off, always telling them to put their hands down."
"And you will help them only when its good for you."
"But yet, you appear to have no problem issuing failure notices."
"Is this how you treat your own children?"
"No it isn't sir." Schwartz sadly nods.
"I hear similar stories from a few other parents."

"If I honestly didn't know any better Mr. Schwartz, I'd say you are a bigot."
"You know, we're far from different."
"So what, I'm African-American and you're a Jewish-American."
"Historically, we had to jump the same hurdles, we've supported one another, and of course our list of positives rivals that of our negatives."
"But most importantly Mr. Schwartz, we're all human beings here."
"God created us all to be equal."

Mr. Smiley now checks his watch.
"As you may know, I'm not a gangbanger, I'm not a gangster, nor do I have any ties to organized crime." "Despite my clout, of course." Mr. Smiley grins.
"I am a legitimate businessman." "I own and operate one of the finest restaurants in the city, I pay taxes just like yourself, I am a

homeowner, have a timeshare in Jamaica, I have a family just like you, and last but not least Mr. Schwartz: "I own three dogs."

"The point that I'm making here is that I will kill to protect my children."

"And I take it that you will kill to protect your son and daughter, am I right?"

"Yes, I would Mr. Smiley." Schwartz humbly replies.

"And by the way, I didn't mean to interrupt your date." Mr. Smiley apologizes.

"But I had to let you know where I stand when it comes to the safety of my children."

"I have a date myself tonight, and would you believe." Mr. Smiley begins.

"This will be the first time that I have ever been out with another woman since my wife died." He shares with his son's teacher. "I understand." Says Schwartz.

"You know, I'm quite sure that your family has to be worried sick about you."

"Consider this meeting my friend an intervention, a warning, and a suggestion all rolled into one." "And please listen to me carefully sir."

"First, you might want to take it easy on your students."

"I've known half of them since they were toddlers, and they're all good kids."

"Second, treat them as though they are yours."

"And third, if I ever hear that you've been either mistreating my son or let alone any other child in your class, in the school, or wherever."

"You can be rest assured that the word termination will not only apply to your job."

"Do we have an agreement?" Asks Mr. Smiley.

"I believe we do." Schwartz quickly replies. Yes, we do." They shake hands.

"Have a good evening, I'll give you a ride home."

Mr. Smiley shows Schwartz to the door.

West Ridge (Chicago's far northwest side)

Also known as West Rogers Park and sometimes North town is nestled between Ridge Avenue and the North Shore Channel. Potawatomi established villages in this area in the seventeenth century but were forced to abandon their claims in a series of treaties between 1816 and 1829. Indian Boundary Park, which is situated on Western Avenue and west Lunt, was actually part of the native succession.

Especially along the northern section.

During the 1830's and 1840's German and Luxembourger farmers settled out here and a small community known as Ridgeville grew up around the current intersection of Ridge and Devon Avenues. During most of the nineteenth century, this quiet neighborhood remained relatively rural. St Henry's Roman Catholic Church served both the religious and social center of the community. The area was home to two cemeteries (Rosehill still in use), and St Henry's, and the Angel Garden Orphanage. Truck farms, greenhouses, and the open prairie characterized much of the area. Disagreements with its neighbor (Rogers Park to the east) about taxes for local improvements led to the incorporation of West Ridge as a village in 1890. Despite local controversy over annexation to the city in 1893.

Proponents prevailed and this area was voted in.
Unlike Rogers Park over to the east, annexation was no quick fix in terms of growth.

The number of those who lived over here at the time remained roughly under five hundred. At least until 1900. No prominent businesses really existed.

Community residents for a time had to either travel to Rogers Park or Evanston to acquire their goods and services.

However, after 1900 this was when the fun began as the pace of growth accelerates.

Brickyards that formerly dwelled along the North branch of the Chicago River moved into the area (now Kedzie Avenue) to take advantage of the natural clay deposits .

The construction of the North Shore Channel of the Sanitary District of Chicago here in 1909 increased the amount of clay available.

Scandinavian and German workers moved from other parts of the city to find jobs in the expanding brickyard operations and workers cottages appear in the western part.

Real-estate interests began to market this then new neighborhood both locally and nationally. The end of World War I triggered a real estate boom.

Brick bungalows and two flats became the dominant residential structures here.

Apartment buildings also appeared, but yet the quality of transportation was poor.

At least in reference to its facilities.

Before the 1930's, a limit was once imposed upon for larger multi-unit buildings.

But however, by the end of the 1920's Park Gables and a number of Tudor revival apartment buildings clustered around Indian Boundary Park.

A tennis club built in the Tudor revival style opened at 1925 W. Thome. A business district along Devon Avenue also came to came to life during this period as the area's population swelled from about 7, 500 in 1920 to almost 40,000 by 1930.

By this time, the locals sought the needed goods and services right here.

Unlike many other Chicago neighborhoods, West Ridge actually grew steadily during the 1930's. Population growth and economic development however did not alter the overwhelming residential character of the community.

This area has no industrial base of any kind, and its key economic base is primarily commercial. Population growth necessitated more housing units and of course, larger multi-units grew visible. One of the largest residential construction projects in the city during the 30's, the Grandville Gardens (still occupied) in the 6200 of north Hoyne, was built in 1938 to meet further accommodations.

The end of World War II sparked a final surge that began to level off as recently as the late 1960's. A large number of Jews moved out here from other parts of Chicago and were joined by a steady stream of Russian and Polish Jews.

Although the pace of growth has slowed in the last two decades, this neighborhood is still becoming a popular destination for many other ethnic groups.

Its commercial centers not only serve the Jewish population, but Middle Easterners, Pakistanis, Indians, and Koreans are also included.

Such a colorful mixture is seen here on Devon Avenue.

The bustling business strip still retains it suburban-like feel.

Schwartz Residence

In the 6000 block of north Talman Avenue, a quiet tree-line corridor aligned mostly prize-winning bungalows and Tudors; this is where Herbert Schwartz and his family live.

The latter was more of an inheritance on the behalf of Mrs. Schwartz's parents who have long retired. Her parents now live in Miami.

In the past eighteen years of their marriage, the Schwartz's have called what is a trendy English Tudor, their home. Just last year, the couple dispatched a second mortgage for its timely renovation. The latter was completed over a month ago.

Stepping out of the shower after her aerobic training, Marilu Schwartz slips into her robe and blow-dries her hair. Getting dressed, the married mother of two puts on a body shirt and jeans. Her selected attire not only reveals a gutless stomach, but also this hot momma has what appears to be a very firm, upper body.

Slipping into her sandals (toes open), Mrs. Schwartz now tends to dinner in the kitchen.

Diana, her eleven-year-old daughter who was hanging with some friends, suddenly returns home. The young brunette girl who appears rather curvy enters the house, still jamming to her Walkman. David, her twelve-year-old son walks in with Dawn.

The loyal canine quickly rushes to her bowl.

Also in his possession, are several movies followed by multiple snacks.

Leaving the flicks on the living room table, David who favors that of his dad briefly runs a vacuum over the carpet.

Diana returns to the dining room to help her mom set the table.

Not to long after the Schwartz children check in, the doorbell rings.

"I'll get it mom." Shouts David
"Thanks Dave." His mother commends him.

In front of their Tudor, a black stretch limo with tinted windows is briefly parked along the curve. David as well as the few visible residents at first, think nothing of it.

And surprisingly, they even flash a common smile as they wait for the occupant's response. However, when one of them discovers a brown plastic bag being ejected from the rear, the onlookers are no longer smiling. They now exchange concerned looks.

Among the residents, there is a young female jogger, a middle-aged gentleman watering his lawn, and another who appears to be a Rabbi.

He dons the traditional attire of one who apparently, runs a synagogue.

An off duty postal carrier (still in uniform), is also present.

Not too long thereafter, a man clad only in his T-shirt and boxers also come flying out.

His body falls to the pavement and rolls several inches toward the Schwartz house.

Moaning tossing and turning, the man struggles to his feet.

Several others emerge from their homes to assist David.

"Dad, what happened?" Asks David.

Mrs. Schwartz and Diana quickly rush to their provider's aid.
"Dad, Herbie honey, what happened?" Reply both the wife and daughter.
"Are you okay?" Asks the wife.
"I fell." Her husband lies.
Fixing his toupee, which now hangs halfway, Mrs. Schwartz, kisses it.

Before anyone on the block is able to make out the plates of the mysterious black limo, the latter along with its occupants are now long gone.

This very same vehicle begins its descent on what is now the Edens Expressway.

Indeed, Herbert Schwartz is a lucky man.

The New Skool Café, North Lawndale
Tuesday, 3pm

Cedric Holt faces a dilemma, along with his not so obvious girlfriend and his tag team partner Hannah Dubois.

The very friends that they left to hang following their surprised defeat by an unusually fast and much stronger Ivan Thompson, as well as their unexpected run in with the police are now sitting before them.

Cedric and Hannah had taken the initiative by meeting them here just fifteen minutes earlier. With no complications on behalf of his peers or even his teachers, with written statements disclosed by both his mom as well as his doctor, Cedric finally returns to class. Upon entering the restaurant, Maxwell Hopkins leads his group upstairs.

With him, there's Scotty Winfield, Lance Crews, Lawrence Penn, Dean Kensington and last but not least Martin Frye.

Taking their usual seats near the window (which in part faces the strip mall), the boys each summons a white envelope.

Their facial expressions remains unchanged as opposed to their last meeting.

However, upon this encounter with their would-be former friend, Max and the others are actually hoping to shed some light as to why were they were almost left high and dry at the hands of the very person who sits before them.

The very person, a friend they've known many years.

Shaking their heads and then sighing as they slowly rip open their envelopes, Max and the others began to smile.

They each have a card expressing the apologies of none other than Cedric and Hannah themselves. Facing their friends, they too began to smile. Also inside the cards, Max and others each receives twenty dollars.

"Had you all chosen not to show up, we wouldn't have blamed you." Cedric breaks the silence. "What we did really was bogus."

"On the account that Ced and me really did you guys wrong, we deserve more than just the book thrown at us." Hannah adds a comment. Max and the others agree.

They all nod their heads. "Apparently, you all know why you're here." Cedric gives them a warm smile. "As a gesture of goodwill slash no heart feelings, you are all welcomed to order whatever it is that you want on the menu." The junior host announces.

"It's all on me, straight up." He produces a credit card from his wallet.

For one moment, Max and the others all exchange satisfying looks.

Now rising from their seats, both Cedric and Hannah commence to embrace their friends. Just as Cedric walks around shaking their hands, and thus giving pounds; Hannah kisses them. To Cedric, they are all like family.

Shell Gas Station, Near West Side

Pulling up to this service station situated on the corner of west Van Buren and Racine overlooking the Eisenhower Expressway, thirty-five year-old Eugene King shuts off his Suzuki Sidekick at pump six. Reaching into his pocket, the personal banker who was otherwise on his way home can't seem to find his wallet.

Thinking back a few hours earlier as he stopped at a restaurant for lunch five minutes away, King suddenly remembers a young man bumping into him as he left.

The unknown youngster apologizes.

"Slick little son-of-a-bitch clipped me." He says to himself.

Sitting in his jeep for a moment, he reaches for his phone.

"So the police detained you all for damned near four hours just to say that they had nothing on you?" Asks Cedric. He is obviously appalled.

"Word Ced." Max reluctantly answers.

But Max and the others know the real deal.

They follow the script. Hannah also has a part.

Cedric remains clueless as he hears more about their previous ordeals.

At this time, they are all walking along what is now Sacramento Boulevard.

Mostly vacant lots surround the latter, as well as a lone abandoned graystone, which is boarded up. Two crumbling row houses: one maroon and one gray is also spotted.

At some point many others along this stretch joined them.

The remnants of an inside wall (presumably the hallway), still clings to the maroon building to the left. As of today, both buildings remain occupied.

Another lot occupied by two lone vehicles, a tow truck and a Coupe Deville is parked along the latter.

Crossing an alley, Cedric and his friends walks past the Lighthouse Baptist Church before crossing what is now Lexington Street. From this point the scenery somewhat improves.

Venturing further south, the recently shuttered St. Francis Xavier Cabrini Church, its former rectory, and adjacent private school (also closed) sits at the corner of Polk Street.

A joint greasy spoon restaurant and game room is situated directly across the street.

Perhaps what is rather intriguing about this particular establishment given its size is that the building itself, actually used to be a garage.

A small wooden garage that once corresponded to a now fenced off yard, as well as an occupied dwelling. As for the makeshift establishment, fewer youngsters are seen coming and going. The sound of coin up machines such as Alex Kidd in the Enchanted Castle, Arch Rivals, and Budokan: The Martial Spirit are heard as Cedric and the others walk by.

Passing by Monique's, a local tavern, which often opens an hour before dusk, and closes an hour before dawn, the group continues past Manley High School to their left.

One hour earlier when hordes of students stormed out of this complex to go home and elsewhere, only a few remain to be seen. Most notably a congregation of male students who are still clad in their basketball uniforms.

Directly across the street, lies a row of existing residential two flats while a tan brick structure, A.R. Leak Funeral Home looks on from the right.

The one-story building employs the façade of what appears to be an elegant ballroom.

"You'd have to be of low class to get in there." Says Dean.

He points to the building and laughs.

"Yeah, very low." Hannah grins.

"Very, very, low." Adds Lance.

"They provide either the suit or the dress for you, they'll call in some outside beautician to take care of your hair and makeup, fix you up real good and get you ready for your

last and final party." Cedric responds. "Because a funeral is nothing more than an eternal Bon Voyage party." "The only difference is, is that you're gone for good."

"At least, until Christ himself comes back here."

"No blasphemy, straight up." Hannah and the others nod their heads.

"I've heard that they snatched up Harvey, Will and the others at their schools." Cedric continues on. "You know something told me not to show for school that day, I didn't know why, couldn't place a finger on it, but something just told me not to come in."

"And what was funny y'all, I wasn't even expecting for the police to show up and round up everybody." "Not even Hannah here had a clue."

"She told me what happened with you later."

"We tried to tell you Cedric." Max begins.

"Yeah, the day before." Adds Lawrence.

"We all met back at the New Skool the day Will and the others got picked up, to address everything and we tried to page you two."

"We were out by Hannah's house, and the battery to my pager gave out."

"Damn, aight I guess we can let that one go." Martin smiles.

"But why did you bail out on us when we was getting our asses whooped by Ivan?"

"Word, if it wasn't for Quentin's uncle, we would have all been permanent cripples." Scotty over exaggerates. "But naw, straight up Cedric we would have been messed up for damned near the entire year." "Ivan has turned into a mothafucka!" Lance suddenly shakes. "Damn, I was NOT banking on that." Adds Lawrence.

"Buffed, slim, strong and quite fast."

"And he's actually cute now." Says Hannah.

Her eyes are almost glassy at this point.

Shaking his head, Cedric points at her and then smirks.

"Ivan practically took us all down in one motion." Dean breaks it down."

"He was like a ferocious assed lion and shit." Scotty chuckles.

"He's really been working out." Hannah says to the rest of the group.

"I know for certain Nikki's probably happy."

"Perhaps, I've misjudged him all this time." Cedric begins.
"May, he's not the punk ass I thought he was."

"And Ivan's become super smart too." Says Max.
"He's doesn't go looking for immediate, outright revenge like a normal nigga would."
"Ivan is all about the mind, and he reads and studies just as much as you do Ced."
"Maybe more than you, I hate to say."
"Ivan has this thing for allowing his enemies to come to him…how does he do it?"

"Only God knows." "His enemies actually comes to him, and he just throws down."

"And so far Ced, Ivan's been winning."

"I understand that you've had a lot of trash to take out around your recent crib." Max continues on. "But this situation is different man."

"I know you're training too, and without a doubt we know you're good."

"But if you ever have to fight Ivan, you'd best to be careful as well as focused."

"He ain't bullshittin, he's strictly business."

"You've heard the rumors about what Ivan did to his cousin."

"I remember everything." Cedric reminds him.

"You know, it wasn't that I was so much afraid of Ivan." He interrupts Max.

"I retreated mainly because I wasn't quite ready for him."

"But the next time you will be." Hannah finishes. She takes his hand.

"But we'll worry about that when we cross that bridge." Cedric comes back.

They now began crossing under a viaduct.

Roosevelt-Sacramento Flea Market

Facing the scenic Douglas Park where Sacramento merges and becomes one with two other boulevards; Sacramento Drive curving to the far right which ultimately turns into California Boulevard, and Farrar Drive which runs east, Cedric and his friends arrive here. Also on the corner of west Roosevelt Road, this store is actually housed in what was formerly an auto repair shop. Joined by many other independent but yet struggling businesses (many housed in well worn and dilapidated buildings), this fairly new shop; a little over a year old employs all types of bargains.

Open from ten in the morning until seven in the evening during the week and ten until six on weekends, many of the patrons who are seen here shopping are none other than local residents. With the internal façade of a market-like setting, vintage fluorescent shop fixtures, and an overhead skylight that welcomes the sun, everything from electronics, to jewelry, clothing, music, and even snacks are sold.

Also in the center lies a lone booth that specializes in airbrushing custom made T-shirts, jeans, and other street attire followed by a booth that specializes in all African or

Afro centric based products. Directly next to the latter is a booth for women who wishes to get their nails polished. The music that is being played on the speakers consists of mostly present day R&B songs such as Soul II Soul's "Keep on Moving", Guy's A Piece of My Love, Smokey Robinson's Save the Best For Last, and Vanessa William's: "I'm Dreaming."

There's also a blend of House, some Rap, but most notably: Hip House.

Upon his arrival, Cedric embraces Willie Garrison, Harvey Holloway, Mustafa Henson, Kris Mathews, Quentin Leaks and last but not least: Bernard Shaw.

Despite how happy he is to see the others, Max is yet still appalled.

"I thought you said Will and the others wanted nothing else to do with you." Max turns to Cedric. Both Cedric and Hannah began smiling. "I lied." Willie laughs.

"No shit." Scotty chuckles. He shakes his head.

"But we'll talk in a little bit." Says Cedric.

"Right now, we gotta clock in."

"We're here at the right place, at the right time y'all."

"Hannah and me has spent at least a month checking this joint out."

“As you all know, it’s the Flea Market.”

The others all nod their heads as they continue to listen.

“And we’re here at the busiest time of the day.”

“The perfect time.” Hannah adds.

“Security here is quite limited on the account that the guy who owns this shop, is a not so obvious cheap ass.” “There’s only one guard who can only see so much, but still watch out for him.” “The owner has yet to employ any metal detectors, but still be careful.” “Just act natural, don’t draw any unnecessary attention, and just blend in.”

“This time, no one is to be left behind.”
“You ready?” “Alright, let’s go.”

Slowly working the crowds that consist of many patrons coming and going, Cedric and the others all began splitting up. Before initiating their own spree, Cedric and Hannah briefly steps into a booth where they began taking pictures.

Having discovered their own niches, Max and the rest of the group began their “assignments.” As each of these skilled shoplifters began placing items into a basket, they also at the same time dispatch others.

Upon placing the items slowly into their pockets, they all move on.

To make the latter seem less obvious, the group actually pays for their items at the nearest checkout counter. Now situated near the main front entrance along with Hannah and their own items, Cedric checks his watch.

In as little as thirty minutes, this young but yet efficient group has already stolen more items than they actually paid for. Mission Possible.

Lincoln Park

Having worked just four hours at his Uncle Clayton's photography studio, Ivan embraces both he and his Aunt Mardi before heading out.

Entering the stationhouse to the Armitage Avenue stop near the corner of north Sheffield Avenue, Ivan pays the ticket agent who then activates the Visifare turnstile.

A turnstile that is situated near the agent's window, this more modernized version (which is a mainstay in all 143 stations), not only keeps a record of how much money the agent collects, but it also allows the customer access to the platform or platforms once he or she has paid their fare. Among the other commuters are many teenagers who attends the neighborhood's namesake high school just several blocks east.

Given that its rush hour besides the seemingly never ending foot traffic to and from, an interesting assortment of railcars are also seen at this time as Ivan ascends to the northbound platform. As a six car train of Budd 2600's leads a southbound Ravenswood "B" train into the station, a mixed train of both Budd 2600's and Pullman 2000's (all sharing the Spirit of Chicago color scheme), dispatches an Englewood-Howard "A": also heading south down into the subway.

Manufactured in the now defunct Pullman Plant on the city's far south side, its namesake series; the 2000's was first introduced to the system in 1964.

These cars were among the first of its kind to be air-conditioned, equipped with fluorescent lighting, blinker type doors, and picture-like windows along its sides.

Its more recent siblings are not by far comparable.

They ushered in a newer generation currently known as the high performance series.

Turning the curve at Willow Street above the latter as they screech two times as loud are the St. Louis-built 1-50/61-65 series.

With a single overhead light and two white wayside markers, these particular vintage cars are also the brethren of the slightly older 6000 series.

Built in 1959 and 60, this pool of double-ended cabs were originally suitable for a one-person single unit operation. Built with parts salvaged from dismantled PCC streetcars, they were later modified to act as operating cabs creating longer trains.

Prior to certain branches at some point lacking a third rail, these cars once utilized overhead trolleys or pantographs as a means of collecting power.

Bearing the same present day scheme as its siblings and offspring's, the slightly wide six-car unit now roars in Ivan's direction. Roaring past the station on what is the inside track, its roller curtains identifies the latter as the Evanston Express.

Boarding a Ravenswood "A" train led by a pair of 6000's, Ivan boards the latter for a short ride to the Fullerton station. Dashing across the overhead walkway for a Jackson Park-Howard "B" train on the opposite side, he makes it.

Exiting the "Art Modorne" designed subway stationhouse for the North-Clybourn stop underneath North and Clybourn Avenues, Ivan heads east along North Avenue alone.

Walking alongside an existing co-op housing complex, he crosses the street at North Larrabee and stops at Terry's for an order of Thai noodles.

Chinatown (Armour Square)

At this time complements of daylight savings, the sun yet still shines along west Cermak Road. People from everywhere still continue to pour in.

Whether its to take pictures, score some souvenirs, dine out or perhaps a simple tour, the neighborhood remains a must see.

Even as the seven o clock hour approaches.

Jing Wu Institute, Studio 212

Already clad in his training attire, Ivan enters this rather large room. Placing a tape in the stereo, the obviously dedicated young student begins to stretch.

Executing a series of twists, bends, and splits , Ivan now commences to do push-ups not only on his palms but he also manages to do another fifty on his knuckles, as well as another fifty on his fingertips.

Now alternating by doing only twenty-five on each arm individually, Ivan returns to his feet and began doing jumping jacks.

Now jumping rope, as be breaths in and out, the already sweaty warrior athlete, towels himself dry before putting on his hand wraps and then his gloves.

Playing on the stereo at this time is a more recent song by rappers Eric B. and Rakim entitled: "Follow the Leader."

Rakim'll say
Rakim'll say
Rakim'll say, Follow the leader
Rakim'll say, Follow the leader
Rakim'll say, Follow the leader
Rakim'll say, Follow the leader

Follow me into a solo
Get in the flow you can picture like a photo
Music mixed mellow maintains too make
Melodies for MC's motivates the breaks
I'm everlastin', I can go for days and days
With the rhyme displays that engrave X-rays

I can take a phrase that's rarely heard, flip it
Now its a daily word
I can get iller than „Nam a killin' bomb
But no alarm Rakim will remain calm

Now dancing on the balls of his feet while in his fighting stance, Ivan first dances two steps forward. Rocking on the balls of his feet, he quickly goes to work on a bag nearby.

Snapping a left jab, a right cross and then a left hook with both the speed and unmeasured power; Ivan quickly steps back while still rocking.

With his breathing well under control, Ivan quickly repeats this drill.

Going at it almost nonstop with his kiai's mimicking that of a snake as he delivers his strong, quick and yet powerful combinations, his momentum within minutes gradually increases. Now executing quick left jabs followed by matching right crosses soon thereafter, Ivan snaps a ferocious left back fist and then a right.

Delivering a Tiger claw to what would otherwise be the temple, Ivan quickly snaps a left She Xing (snake hand) and then a right to what would otherwise be the throat.

Now turning to a big blue dummy to his left, the relentless pupil swiftly parries its arms (both left and right), and quickly snaps his right fist directly into a would-be

sternum. Changing stances, Ivan then snaps a left double sidekick (stomach and face), and comes around with a double hook kick.

The latter first lands his heel directly into the dummy's face, while the balls (namely supporting Ivan's left foot) makes contacts with the back of the head.

Let alone while actually engaging his real opposition on the streets, Ivan has actually left many of his enemies unconscious. However as of right now, this is only a drill.

Fortunately enough, each of them only escaped with what they considered a bad headache. But yet, they live.

Snapping a right spinning hook kick to a speed bag directly behind him, Ivan delivers a left double sidekick to another imaginary opponent before planting the sole of his left foot into another.

Turning to the north, the fierce young man who was born in the Year of the Dragon who yet employs the strength and the heart of a lion, now snaps the sole of his right foot.

Executing the ridge of his right foot into an imaginary shin to the east, Ivan executes a left backfist to the face.

Now delivering a left dropkick, he returns to his stance and begins to snap a continuous combination of front kicks, roundhouses, and axe kicks.

As Ivan remains in his stance (with his hands up), he now spins all across the room delivering multiple crescent kicks.

Now jumping up in mid air, Ivan finally delivers a spinning flying crescent to an otherwise taller person.

Returning to his stance, Ivan switches twice before going after a lone Wing Chun dummy to his far left. Executing multiple blocks at an alarming speed, the fired up student now throws in multiple punches and kicks at the dummy's wooden knees.

In such a smooth and more rhythm-like motion, Ivan now combines all three movements (including parrying) before returning to his stance.

Bowing his head to the wooden dummy, Ivan leaves the room.

26

STUDIO 114

After a half hour of training his students with the medicine ball, Mark Choi now commands them to rise.

Prior to this exercise where each student focused on his or her breathing, which also coincides with the strengthening of his, or her abs, Master Choi's disciples has so far completed several other warm up drills.

So far they have done a sizable number of push-ups, jumping jacks, crunches, sit-ups, and last but not least, torso twists.

Having already spent one half hour stretching, the students now meditate.

The room has suddenly grown completely silent.

For the next fifteen minutes, these obviously well disciplined, well trained and equally dedicated teens all have one thing on their mind; learning to fight.

"The true art of fighting isn't always about physically crushing your opponent." Mark begins. At this time he now studies his pupils.

He now silently moves about. Pacing back and forth with his hands folded behind his back, this fresh face young master employs great patience.

Mark literally treats his pupils as though they are his own siblings. His blood.

While at the same token, Mark not only expects the best out of his students but he also brings out the best. “Nor is it about seeing how much pain that you can inflict upon your opposition.” “In reality, forget about what you see in the movies or on TV.”

“That is just strictly for entertainment purposes.”

Mark’s entire class remains seated before him.

The students continue to meditate.

“I’m quite sure that many of you, or better yet all of you are fully aware of this.”

“To be a real martial artist regardless of what system that you learn, your form, or let alone your skill level.” Mark continues on. “You have to have peace.”

“And if you ain’t got it, get it.” “You may rise.”

Rising to their feet almost at once, many of Mark’s students are tickled by his first expression. They laugh. “It doesn’t matter how many others you have defeated, regardless of your reputation.” For one brief moment, Mark studies Ivan.

“The worse fighter that you could ever be is one who always bears a grudge.”

“One who is often angry, and in some cases; “One who is just looking for a fight.”

“In other words, you’re looking for trouble.”

“You could also be a bully, and misuse what you’ve been taught as a means of superiority, power, or as they say; “Bragging rights.”

“Great power comes with even greater responsibilities.”

“There have been many great students before you who has come and gone, on the account that they’ve been misusing what we are teaching you today.”

Mark’s students all acknowledge his wishes with a simple nod.

“If I myself or whoever is training you suspects or even get a hint that you are using your techniques to cause deliberate harm, you will be banished.”

“Some or perhaps many of you might want to pass on what you are now learning.”

“If you remain committed.”

“To attain true excellence in any style, one must be at peace.”

“He or she must be also humble.”

“And I just didn’t get this off of some old school fighting flick.”

“This is real.” The Sifu/ Law major assures his flock.

He then chuckles. “That’s how you win.”

“In most dire situations, you can either talk your way out, or simply just walk away.”
“Sometimes depending on where you are.”

“It wouldn’t make you a wimp, or a coward or a punk ass because you decide to take a much higher road.” Mark’s students began laughing much more.

“Straight up, seriously.” “You know as they say; “Live today fight tomorrow.”

"Did any of you know that you can often defeat your opponent without even lifting a single finger?" Mark now asks his pupils. They all respond with mixed emotions.

"Yeah, in fact by just using this." He points to his left temple.

"This is not by far not only your biggest, but this is also your muscle of all muscles."

"Your brain." "Which should be your key arsenal in terms of outthinking your opponent." "Just like a chest game if you look at it."

"And if you know for certain that you can't either walk away or better yet talk your way out of a situation, then you go to Def COM One."

"Also keep in mind, that you can sometimes come across those who are stronger and faster." Mark now returns to the front of the room.

"And also, that's why you're here."

For the next hour, the students now began practicing their fighting stances, their common forms as well as their kicking and their punching.

As the entire class reviews each of the latter all at once (even though they're only shadowboxing), the sounds of their strikes can still be heard.

As Mark roams about studying each of his disciples, he happily gives them a nod.

Having learned to break their falls for another fifteen minutes, the students now began jumping back off the floor and back into their stances.

Their motions appear visibly rhythm-like, relatively smooth and most of all on point. The Sifu claps.

"Time everybody." Mark applauds.

"Well done, take five."

As the students return before their teacher, they each began to take up their Jian.

Invented some 2, 500 years ago in China, the Jian is a double-edged straight sword that was believed to have existed as far back as the seventh century.

Most notably during the spring and Autumn Period.

One of the initial specimens was the sword of "Goujian."

Historical one-handed versions varying namely from 45 to 80 centimeters (17.7 to 31.5 inches) inches in length. The weight of the average sword of 70-centimeter (28 inch) blade length would be in range of approximately 700 to 900 grams (1.5 to 2 pounds).

There are currently two-handed versions used for training by many styles in the Chinese Martial Arts. In Chinese folklore, it is known as the "Gentleman of Weapons", along with the Gun (staff) Qiang (spear) and the Dao (sabre).

By way of employing such a weapon or to be more accurate a tool, one can employ many fighting styles.

"Last week as you guys remembered." Mark begins.

"Namely on how to grip your ordinance as well as using the basic stances."

"This evening, we will focus on a series of deflations." The twenty-year-old Sifu now takes his stance. All eyes are now on him.

"This side of my body where I'm holding my sword is known as my tight side."

One student, a Ukrainian-born teen raises her hand.

"Yes Jessica?" Mark responds.

"Why is it called your tight side?"

"Because when you swivel and spiral down into position to deflect a thrust coming down to that side of the body, it is a tighter twist to really reach the opposing sword than it would be compared to the side of your body."

Apparently satisfied by her teacher's answer, the tall blonde girl responds with a more satisfying nod. She faces Ivan for a brief moment, smiles and then waves.

Ivan follows up with a smile of his own as he waves back.

Now dispatching his blade at a rather sharp angle, Mark summons the tip (going down) by way of utilizing the flat. Without blinking an eye, he deflects his mock opposition in one rapid motion.

While at the same time he pivots so smoothly, he remains silent.

"Another example, you could parry with your blade tip going up." Marcus turns, he pivots and he parries his sword as he goes up.

"However, I wouldn't advise it on the account that you could damage your sword in the process." "And that is why you may want to consider striking down."

"I know it seems quite difficult and all, but hey at least your sword will remain in one peace." "That's when you also live to fight another day."

"Remember, your ultimate goal is to stay alive."

“Otherwise, you’ll die one bogus death.”

Ivan chuckles. “I’d certainly hate to lose my head in a situation.” He says.

Several of his classmates are tickled. They laugh.

“Yeah, I bet you wouldn’t.” Mark playfully ruffles his hair.

“Yeah, word man.” Says Diego Salazar.

“Same here.” Adds Thomas Wang.

“And that’s why you have to continue practicing.” Mark reminds them.

“Now on the easy side.” He resumes

“Is the opposite side of your body here, what is known as your sword arm.”

Tipping his blade up, as well as his palm, Mark spirals a clean deflection to this particular side. “Music please.” He says to one of his students.

Samantha Triplett who is just within reach of the stereo system flicks on the power.

Now playing is the song “No One Can do It Better” by a Texas-born rapper known only as The Doc. Born Tracy Curry, the twenty-one year-old is now a member of the L.A-based rap group N.W.A. O’Shea Jackson, better known as Ice Cube has recently left the group. Out of the original five members (minus Cube), there are now four.

Among them there is Dr. Dre, Eazy-E (the founder), M.C. Ren and last but not least D.J. Yella. Jerry Heller, the founder and owner of Ruthless Records, manages the group.

This is the listen to, so ask not a question
Not to be taken as a simple suggestion
But a warning, to whom it may concern
If knowledge is the key, then I think its time you learn
For there is not the problem
So leaders are acknowledged, I don't follow them
I turn to another degree and find the D-O TO THE C and
Growing like a tree and
Cause much destruction cause I'm crushing
Complimenting much, yeah but never blushing
Hard like a criminal, and cause I'm subliminal
In my own right I'm dope, cause its the original
Funky, unmistakably so when the vocals are done, then you know
Its all a matter of setting a date
For America's most complete artist, but wait
Make sure that you keep the facts in mind
Don't mess with the great, cause the Doc is like a nine
With a voice, telling you the bullet's direction
I'm talking murder, but that's another section
I need to explain by keeping my composure
There's no joking a sucker but villain, and you'll kill him
So he's in fear, but there ain't no need in spilling your guts to a nut,
No I'm not your equal
Meaning you're equivalent, I'm all like heaven sent
I got it together so clever
Remember this forever
No one can do it better

Coincidentally, on the account of Mark's superb demonstration this song (right now) suits him quite well. Despite his advance level of expertise, he only sees himself as "A Master" as opposed to "The Master."

"Here, I use a tie up, a palm up, spiraling up a deflection to this side."

Mark then swings his sword up on an angle and deflects another phantom attack.

He basically goes up and around.

"This is called the easy way because it takes less effort than the tight arm."

Now in their stances with one hand protecting their faces and their legs rooted, the students all at once, simultaneously turns and then pivots.

They immediately abort their enemy's attacks.

Turning, twisting, and spiraling with unspeakable rhythm (with minor struggles on the parts of some), each student repels what would have been open cuts or possibly life threatening stab wounds. They continue to repeat these drills for the next fifteen minutes.

Follow another brief intermission, the students now return to the front of the room.

"Kudos to all of you on your last performance." Mark begins.

"Please give yourselves a round of applause."

His students all began clapping.

"Before we all go home tonight given that we've covered the basic fundamentals in reference to stopping would-be attacks, or simple deflections."

"We will now learn what is known as the Four Corners."

"But, before I get to that."

"Keep in mind that our movements comes from the entire body, not the arms."

"You must turn your waist because it gives you the power that you need to either deflect or otherwise deliver a strike to your opponent.

"Also this enables you to easily get out of the way of a thrust or even a straight downward strike with the least amount of effort."

"Plus, if you can direct a strike off script or off line without even moving your feet then you'll have the home court advantage."

"Or in plain English, the fight will be yours."

"So what is the Four Corners?"

Mark who is now armed with his Jian once more takes his stance.

"The high easy side, otherwise known as the shoulder opposite your swords arm."

"The high tight side, otherwise it's the shoulder of your sword arm."

"The low tight side, or you can just simply call it the thigh on the sword arm."

"The low easy side, or just call it the thigh opposite the sword arm side."

As he explains the motions to his students, the junior master displays every detailed move as he dances, spins, turns, and spirals.

However, the latter remains well controlled as he summons a combination of both strikes and multiple deflections.

Without really breaking a sweat, Mark returns to his fighting stance.

His students exchange looks that coincides with their confidence.

"This going to be a two-person drill, so please grab a partner."

And just as the students began to partner up, Mark motions for four others to come forward. "Ivan, Diego, Linda, and Tommy." They quickly join their Sifu as the rest of the class looks on. "Here's the fun part ladies and gentleman." Mark begins.

Many of the others laugh.

Smiling and waving at their fellow peers in front of them, Mark's not so obvious prized students now take their stances.

Surrounding their teacher with the employment of their own swords, they obediently await his instructions.

"Here are your deflections that makes up the four corners." Mark now demonstrates.

"A mo deflection to the high easy side."

Ivan, who attempts to attack Mark from the front (namely to the left), thrusts to the high easy side. However, Mark quickly dispatches his sword initiating a deflection to the high tight side. Having deflected the blade that would have possibly severed his throat, Mark turns his waist to the left and summons his blade to what would have been Ivan's heart. Ivan's deflection toward Mark is comparable.

Now focused on an advancing Diego Salazar to his right, Mark abruptly deflects his strike, and thrusts back at his left shoulder. Diego follows suit.

Thomas "Tommy" Wang makes a thrust at Mark's high tight side, while Mark deflects by spiraling down. Turning his waist right in with an elbow going up, Mark then tips his blade going down. In an actual fight, Tommy would have been deemed less handy. Meanwhile Tommy deflects and strikes back.

The beautiful and pretty Linda Lau thrusts her sword at what would have been Mark's shoulder, while under her blade he responds by actually turning his blade under hers, deflecting and then reversing.

Returning to their stances just as Mark returns to his, they all bow.

With Ivan, Diego, Tommy and Linda rejoining the rest of the class, the room is now energized. As the students now practice amongst themselves, another song entitled "The Formula" (also by the Doc) is now heard.

Daytime in the Windy City officially becomes night.

Streetlights illuminate.

Buildings young and old, great and small began to glow.

Its world's famous central skyline is definitely, no exception.

Most notably is the Sears Tower.

Its blinking antennas greet the now dark and purple skies.

Countless front and rear headlights (automobiles) cover all of Lake Shore Drive in both directions. As a new moon shines down upon the waters of what is now Lake Michigan, a few small boats are also seen. They hover about namely along the northern shores. The well lit, but almost deserted Oak Street beach, lies within distance.

Chinatown (Armour Square)

A six-car train of Budd 2600's and Boeing 2400's leads a southbound Lake-Dan Ryan "all stops" into the Skidmore-designed Cermak Station.

Manufactured by Boeing-Vertol in Philadelphia around 1976 with the last car being delivered in 1978, the 2400 series appears quite similar to its Budd brethren.

Despite the differences between the front and rear ends, both series of rail cars employ sliding doors, fluorescent lighting, air conditioning, and designated seating.

Having discharged a sizable number of passengers, the train departs.

Situated to the right of the station, is the mile long "Franklin Feeder" ramp.

This particular ramp provides access to motorists who wish to reach the Dan Ryan Expressway. Directly across from the school, lies a nearby parking lot and neighborhood mural. Standing at a pay phone, Ivan contacts his parents.

Diego, Tommy, and Linda are still with him.

"Yeah, they're all here with me Dad."
"Diego too."
"Right, I understand."
"No problem, thanks."
"I'll tell him."
"We'll see you in a little bit."
"Alright, love you too bye."
Ivan hangs up the receiver.
"So what's up?" Asks Diego.
"My father says that he has spoken to your parents." Ivan explains.
"And he's taking you back to your crib too."
"Aight, cool." Diego responds.
Tommy and Linda are rather pleased.
They happily shake their heads.

Crossing the street, Ivan and his friends now venture along Wentworth Avenue. Although now brightly lit and still dense, the pedestrian traffic slowly dwindles.

Just beyond the community gate south of Cermak flanked by replicated traditional lanterns (hanging on wires), which are reinforced by the city's own streetlamps lies more shops. This section perhaps the central core is roughly six blocks long.

Just beyond this point at 26th Street and the Stevenson Expressway (I-55), the area becomes residential. Ivan and the others now head down 23rd Street.

Wang Residence

Located along a relatively quiet tree lined street surrounded by brick flats, bungalows, vintage, (courtyard) apartment structures, and a few cottage frames is the home of the Wang Family. They live in a family owned newly refurbished two flat near the corner of Princeton Avenue. With the second floor used as guest quarters, Tommy, who also has a sister named Lilly (just two years younger), and his parents all live on the first floor.

His father Tim Wang, a prominent doctor and his mother Cindy, a realtor are both fourth generation U.S. born citizens. Tommy who is thirteen and his sister, eleven represents of course the fifth. Although the Wang's embrace their Chinese heritage and they speak the language of their grandparents, the primary language in this house is still English. Despite the occasional trips to the mainland every other year as well as the occasional Dim Sum and other dishes from the east, many of the Wang's views, their tastes, and let alone their attitudes leans toward the west.

While Tommy and his sister enjoy listening to modern-day American cuts (R&B, House, Rap, Rock and so on), their parents on the other hand favor mostly the Dusties. A bright American flag situated onto the brick canopy blows freely.

Courtesy of a mild wind from the Lakefront.

After playing a game of pool down in the family's recreation room followed by a half hour of browsing through multiple comic books, Tommy and his guests play a few games on his Turbo Graphic 16 before eventually returning upstairs.

Having played tennis out back for another thirty with his friend and lifelong neighbor Linda taking on the winner, Tommy and his two other buddies Ivan and Diego are now situated in the dining room.

"Who's down for some Scrabble?" Ask Tommy.

"We're always down." Says Ivan.

Not too long thereafter, Tom's sister Lilly enters the room.

She is initially passing through to grab a snack from the kitchen.

"Hey guys."
"Hi Lilly." Everyone replies.
"Hey Lill, why don't you join us?" Her brother happily suggests.
"Thanks." She tells him.
"This game would be no fun without you." Linda and Diego add.

Ivan, who is smiling pulls up a chair.

"How was class tonight?" Lilly asks.
"Fine as usual." Says the others.
"We practiced under Mark, using the blades." Linda tells her.

Tommy, who now summons the board game from his room, places the latter on the table. "That's nice Lilly replies. At this point everyone gets a stand as well as their choice of letters from the box. Linda who is also a player acts as the scorekeeper.

Almost immediately, Lilly has already pieced together one long word.

Brandishing her discovery before her brother and his peers, she flashes a smile.

"Man, what a show off!" Tommy teases her.

Playfully, Lill sticks out her tongue.

Ivan, Linda and Diego all began smiling at both of them.

Linda takes down her score.

"You are really good Lilly." Says Ivan. He smiles.

"She comes into the game already outscoring us."

"And what is her first word?" Diego asks.

"Outstanding." Tommy shakes his head.

It has only been two minutes, and yet the young lady who closely resembles her brother creates at least three more words. Sighing and grinning, Linda once again takes down her score. Lilly manages to create two more before eventually painting herself into a corner. As she summons more letters from the box, the obviously competitive player is suddenly puzzled. Tommy chuckles. "What's the matter?" He says.

"Brain baffled?"

"Dude, whatever." Lilly snaps.

Obviously tickled by Tommy's remark, as she laughs Lilly's face is suddenly red.

The others also began laughing.

"I'm next." Tommy announces.

In response to his sister coming up with words off of the top of her head, Tommy fires back with five of his own. Linda takes down his score.

Coming up with at least three of her own, Linda now maintains her record.

The game really begins to pick up as Ivan and Diego weighs in with their choices.

It appears as though they are all playing word tag with one another.

However, the game remains in all and good fun.

27

THOMPSON RESIDENCE, NORTH LAWNDALE

Despite the poverty, the disinvestments, and the crime that surrounds them, this well kept two flat which mimics that of a mini mansion is very much like the Thompson's own personal oasis.

With two medium-sized lawns (accounting for their front yard), surrounding the sidewalk directly in front of the vintage structure, a hissing sprinkler summons water onto the freshly laid sod below. Both of the latter is protected by wrought iron fences which in part corresponds to solar powered tier lights and two recently planted trees on the inside.

However, despite this rather scenic property the Thompson's greatest showpiece is none other than their backyard.

Previously owned and occupied by an elderly Italian couple, Mr. and Mrs. Cartier bought this building from the latter around September of 1969.

In the last twenty years since their acquisition of this decades old relic, little has changed on the very block that surrounds it.

Despite social change (the exodus of white ethnics), all of the homes that are visibly seen remain intact.

In the shadow of what had been the headquarters for Sears-Roebuck two blocks to the south, lies an unused parking lot.

The latter site, which is across the street from the Thompson house, had also previously shared what was formerly an auto repair shop. (Also owned and operated by Sears) The former department store and landmark tower is directly across the street.

Arriving from the Lincoln Park community, the Cartier's soon bought what was formerly the Campanili House.

After selling their home, Mario Campanili and his wife Gina eventually moved to California. To Ivan's grandmother, it seems as if it was still yesterday when she and her now late husband moved in.

Today, even though the Thompson's adore every square inch of their award winning home, their pride and joy is once again their backyard.

The overall landscape employs what the Thompson's call their own private park.

A sizable patch of grass (just as green as the pastures mentioned in the Lord's Prayer) overlooks an enclosed porch followed by a combination of mulch, rocks, and beautiful red roses. Additional tier lighting is dispatched all across the spacious yard, immediately at sunset. At sunrise, the latter cease to exist.

A makeshift stream flows across the middle, supported by a scenic fountain and a recently planted tree. Two smaller trees supported by alpine green shrubs conceals the foundation of a very sound two-car garage.

There are even two motion sensors: One attached to the garage, the other: The building. An alarm system provides additional security for the entire building at large.

Attached to the porch lies a recently built patio.

It appears to be a very bright and rather pleasant Thursday afternoon.

School is apparently out, as the bird's chirp and yell.

Children are both seen and heard as they too enjoy the semi warm weather.

The typical hangouts (namely the corner stores, restaurants, game rooms and parks), also the local "Y"(YMCA) is already bursting with preteens and adolescents as they emerge from their respective schools.

Meanwhile, here at the Thompson Residence Ivan who is situated out back, listens to another mix tape and reviews many dance moves.

Rizzo, who is his lone houseguest, joins him.

Surprisingly on the account that both young men are talented athletes, lyrically inclined, and humble fighters their dancing skills on the other hand, are comparable.

Ivan, who is really a true natural, tried his shot at Break dancing just a few years earlier. Of course then, he was only eight.

At that time, he along with his cousin Doug literally took the block by storm.

Both were literally good at it.

Presumably, when nearly everything in his much earlier life began to go sour Ivan just simply stopped dancing. However with everything moving full speed into the right direction, the young man for whom Ivan's mom called "Gene "The Killer" Kelly has now returned. It has been a little over an hour since Ivan and Rizzo owned it up.

Now maintaining their rhythm as the two face one another, they begin moving their arms and shoulders. Shuffling their feet, the skilled youths began turning and spinning before kicking up their feet. Tapping soles, Ivan turns and does a split.

Giving each other some dap (a handshake), Ivan and Riz takes a break.

The two suddenly hears what appears to be clapping and cheering.

Now looking towards the alley, Ivan and Rizzo find several girls who are obviously impressed. "When I can learn?" One of them, the presumed leader asks.

Smiling and waving, Ivan motions for them to enter.

"Actually, we'd be more than happy if you would join us." Says Rizzo.

"The gate is open, please." Ivan waves his hand.

His tone is quite distinguished as he now speaks.

The girls began giggling.

The leader who appears to be husky, but yet still beautiful is actually turned on by Ivan's gesture. The freckly-faced, light brown complexioned female (who also appears to have natural red hair) smiles before eventually moving on.

Meanwhile, the others follow suit.

"Feel free at anytime." Ivan hollers out to them.

"The big girl knows that she's wearing that skirt." Rizzo begins.

"Well, hey man she does look good in it." Ivan points out.

"Would you go out with a big girl?" Asks Rizzo.

"Of course I would." Ivan abruptly answers.

"In fact, I'd go out with any girl whose self esteem is off the charts."

"Anything else in between Riz is a bonus."

"Hey, I hear you on that." Rizzo gives Ivan a pound.

"As long as they're not vein and talking down on others, they're okay."

"It's really nice out here today." Rizzo begins.

"Word, it really does feel like summer." Ivan adds.

"We've has quite a few gorgeous days, but they were nothing like this."

"But I wouldn't put that Starter coat in storage just yet." Ivan shakes his head.

"Yeah, straight up." Rizzo replies.

"The other day, we were just talking about your crib."

"You know, Thomas, the Powell's, and Alfred."

"It ain't like we're on skid row or nothing." He continues on.

Ivan nods his head as he continues to listen.

Riz catches a brief glimpse of the entire yard, and then the area that surrounds it.

"We were basically just saying how nice it was."

"And straight up, on just my momma it really is."

"Both in and out."

"And we're sitting in the best part of it right now."

"And even though all of the other homes on your block are cold, your crib is more like the White House." "You all have good taste."

"Thanks." Says Ivan.

"Like I told some people at school recently, we're not the Huxtables but we do alright."

"Socially, this actually used to be a nice neighborhood."

They are now seated.

"Including your block Riz."

"My grandparents ended up having to move out of Lincoln Park, because of Urban Renewal." "Basically, they got priced out." Rizzo abruptly replies.

"It costs nearly an arm and a leg to live there now, and yet the prices are still rising."

"My grandparents, namely my mom's parents used to own a house on Seminary."

"Just off of Armitage Rizzo."

"So they used to live just around the corner from the shop." Rizzo implies.

"It was relatively convenient." Ivan confirms.

"My grandfather founded the studio back in the 1930's."

"Straight up?" Rizzo responds.

"Lincoln Park almost, since its founding has always been home to at least a tiny number of black residents." "I never knew that." Rizzo replies.

He is obviously appalled by this little known fact.

"A lot of the white ethnics especially, tried to buy my grandfather out."

"Especially during the depression."

"But he said damned that."

"And my grandfather was no punk at all."

"He truly held his own Riz."

"When he lived in the south, he always used to have the Klan by the balls."

"Those rural crackers had no choice but to respect him."

"Growing up in Little Rock, my grandfather was a skillful boxer, he hunted, and took pictures." He literally made his money hand over fist."

"With four hundred dollars in his pocket, he rode the train to Chicago, did the Stockyards and opened the studio." "My grandfather never gave up."

"No matter what despite the depression, despite urban renewal, and having to lose his home, he was not selling his business." Rizzo continues to nod his head.

"My grandfather taught himself to read and write."

"From what my grandmother told me, he was a natural born mathematician."

"He was good with numbers."

"Lincoln Park used to be a regular working class neighborhood."

"A social melting pot."

"Some parts were actually poor, not just Cabrini Green alone."

"And many of those who were displaced on the account of what was really gentrification, were of course black and Puerto Rican."

"Damn." Sighs Rizzo. "I can believe that."

"My grandparents bought this house from an aging Italian couple." Ivan continues on.

"About twenty years ago."

"My grandmother said that this neighborhood was heavily mixed when she and my grandfather arrived." "By the mid 70's, it was mostly black.

"For a time, so were the businesses."

"By the early eighties at least, most of the stores became Arab-owned."

"My grandmother told me a similar story." Rizzo cuts in.

"She moved over here just one year before the riots."

"She told me that everything had really gone downhill, after King's demise."

"And to this day, this neighborhood is still trying to recover."

"If there's another thing that I find disturbing, and please don't get me wrong."

"I'm not being socially biased."

"But when you tour other ethnic enclaves here in Chicago, what do you see Riz?"

"I notice that most of the businesses in the latter reflects of course, its key demographic." Rizzo smoothly replies.

"Yeah, that's right." Ivan says abruptly.

"But when you're here on the south and west sides in neighborhoods that are largely black, its businesses are often run by those who are not."

Nodding his head, Rizzo continues to listen.

"Would you like to know what's really disturbing Ivan?" Rizzo begins to ask.

"Yeah, what is it?" Says Ivan.

"Every time that our people become well-established in terms of running a business, there is always some non-black person, either an Arab or a Korean who is always so quick to want to buy us out." "And most of the money spent to support these businesses, doesn't even stay here." Indicating that he totally agrees, Ivan nods his head.

"Not to mention that we're often being overcharged for food that is sometimes spoiled, but most of the time, its outdated."

"Why is that by the way?" Rizzo asks.

"We seem so stagnant."

"It all goes back to slavery I believe." Ivan replies.

"For a time in here the U.S., it grew to a point that countless slave owners were actually losing control over their captives."

"The slaves were becoming more educated, and sometimes actually overpowering their so-called masters." "They started revolts, and began escaping."

"Good for the slaves." Says Rizzo. Ivan chuckles.

"Just like the slaves who had taken control of that Spanish vessel in the Atlantic."

"I think it was the Armistad." "Right?" "Yes, it was." Ivan abruptly answers.

"They killed the entire crew, namely their owners."

"But the ship was eventually intercepted by the Americans."

"Anyway, slaveholders especially in the south were literally petrified."

"Then one day, a man." Ivan begins.

"A West Indian born Anglo, named William Lynch soon gave birth to what was dubbed as "the art of war" for slave holders."

"His sick, twisted philosophy to ensure that the slaves remain passive and obedient, although sometimes resulted in death, humiliation, and vicious assaults was otherwise strictly psychological." "That the latter was actually carried out by pitting the slaves against one another." Ivan continues on. "Male against female."

"Young against old." "And perhaps to a lesser extent, dark against light."

"This is still evident even as the twentieth century comes to a close."

"How we were taught believe that we're a poor people, or that we can't keep a job or run a business, or better yet we simply can't stick together on the account of too much bickering, swindling, flaring egos or just overall self-hatred."

"Despite of everything that our people have fought for and accomplished since we were forcefully brought here, and we have come a long way Riz."

"We still remain quite hesitant when it comes to other issues."

"Namely, crime, drugs and poverty."

"But hey, we still have ways to go and another century is just eleven years away."

"That's true." Ivan says happily.

"Hey yo, check this out man." Rizzo begins chuckling.

"Leon's a fool, he's sick G."

Ivan is already beginning to laugh.

"What the hell did he do this time?" Asks Ivan.

He sighs and leans back in his chair.

"He was showing us this girl in a house next door to him right?"
"It was me along with Alfred, the Powell's, and Khali."
Ivan nods his head as he continues to listen.
"She was sitting on the toilet in the bathroom."
"Was that the best that you people could do?" Ivan begins to roast his friend.
"She was rather nice looking." Rizzo tries to make his case.
"Alright, carry on." Ivan says, as he appears to be somewhat impressed.
"I could understand if you peaked into the bedroom, or at least catch the girl as she takes a bubble bath, or maybe even a shower."

"But naw, you had to catch her on the toilet." Ivan and Rizzo are now both laughing.
"Man, y'all goofier than I thought."
"But the story gets better Ivan." Rizzo tries to control his laughter.
"Just to show you how retarded Leon really is."
"When the girl realized that she was being watched, she cursed us out."
"There was this fan sitting right in the window directly above her head."
"Leon's crazy ass kept jerking it until it fell on her back."
"And we all just broke, took off running."

At this point, both Ivan and Rizzo are laughing insanely.

"Hey what's going on out here?" Asks Mr. Thompson.
The head of the house smiles at both of them.
"Y'all high or something?"
"Naw Dad." Ivan says to his father.
"Rizzo was just telling me this rather goofy story, that's all."
"Yeah, alright." Mr. Thompson replies.

He then hands them each a bowl of Jell-O.

"Your mother just made this, I'm sure the two of you will like it."

"Thanks, Dad, thanks Mr. Thompson." Says both Ivan and Riz.

"By the way, it's your turn to take out the garbage."

"No problem, I'll grab that for you right away."

"Thanks son." Mr. Thompson happily responds.

Having finished their deserts as Rizzo now browses through what appears to be the latest edition of Playboy magazine, Ivan returns onto the wooden deck.

With his electronic dartboard in his left hand, he then places the latter onto a hook.

Setting up the scoreboard, the junior host summons his darts.

"So what do you think of my latest issue?" Ivan asks in reference to his magazine.

"This is nice man." Rizzo responds.

Licking his thumb, he slowly turns the pages.

Like a young man who truly enjoys what he sees.

Ivan smiles at the thought.

"And the piece with Latoya, is real nice."

"Oh, I know." Says Ivan.

"Why don't you hold onto it for a couple of days, that way you can enjoy it better."

"Straight up?" Replies Rizzo. He is appalled.

"Yeah, man go ahead." Ivan reassures him.

"Thanks." Shaking his head, Rizzo gives his friend a pound.

Now collecting some darts of his own, Rizzo joins in.

Casting his first dart like trained ninja, Ivan makes a clean hit.

"Twenty!!!!" Shouts the computerized ref.

"Nice shot." Says Rizzo.

"You think that was dope Riz?" Ivan asks his guest.

"Check this out."

Removing a bandanna from his pocket, Ivan then covers his eyes.

For the moment, everything is completely pitch black.

Upon reaching for another dart, he makes another shot.

"Twenty!!!!" The machine says once more.

"What the--------." Rizzo begins laughing.

At the very same time, he is shocked. Overwhelmed, and perhaps somewhat appalled.

"How did you learn to do that?" Rizzo asks.

"Well actually, it's something that I've been working on for quite some time."

"Something pertaining to my martial arts training." Ivan begins to break it down.

"Although my instructors hasn't yet trained me, I thought I'd just take the initiative."

"You know experiment a little." Rizzo nods while hearing his friend.

"So I spent at least one full week, namely around the house here wearing a blindfold."

"Just to get a feel of what it's like to actually be among the visually impaired, I've been wearing this." "And surprisingly, my mind somehow takes over."

"It's almost as though I can still see Riz."

"You know, I can't even seem to explain it." Ivan shrugs.

"Like my brain employs some type of backup system."

"My hearing is beyond heightened also."

"Man, that's tripped out." Rizzo responds.

"You think?" Ivan chuckles.

"Another gift maybe?" Rizzo asks.

"It doesn't sound too far off from that saying, walk by faith and not by sight."

"It doesn't seem too obvious." Says Rizzo. He smiles.

Ivan summons another dart.

"Nineteen!!!!" "REMOVE YOUR DARTS!!!"
"You're just blessed man." Says Rizzo.
"Its your turn man." Ivan announces.
As he now rises from his seat, Rizzo takes up his darts.
"PLAYER TWO!!!!" The machine responds.
Rizzo sends off his first dart.
"SIXTEEN!!!" The machine says.
"The human body is just full of mysteries." Says Ivan.
"Word." Rizzo replies.
"You know, another possible factor." He begins.
"Is that you could also be responding on instinct as well."
"I couldn't agree more." Ivan happily replies.
Rizzo now attempts to summon a bull's-eye.
He misses, but yet he tries again.

North Lawndale

Despite decades of disinvestments, the lack of commerce, and the job losses in most parts this neighborhood (most notably the last twenty years), at least half of its housing stock particularly along the area's southern edge appears to be well preserved.

Situated just five miles west of the Loop (downtown), and thus circumscribed by railroad lines on three sides and extends north within blocks of the Eisenhower Expressway, this west side community is home to some of Chicago's poorest black residents. Once a haven for evacuees from the Great Fire, this area was also home of the city's Jewish ghetto. The neighborhoods landscape was divided among two-flat homes (most notably single bricks, greystones, and later bungalows), Douglas Park, and massive industrial buildings. Early on, the area successfully met the needs of both its industrial as well as its residential populations.

After Chicago annexed part of what had been the Cicero Township in 1869, a real estate firm known as Millard& Decker built a residential suburb.

They called it “Lawndale” in reference to a harmonious union of its inhabitants.

This new western development’s fireproof brick buildings welcomed the people and the businesses that were burned out by the catastrophic blaze.

Near the end of the nineteenth century, many industrial workers settled here.

The McCormick Reaper Works opened a plant in the Lower West Side neighborhood directly to the east in 1873. The opening of the now recently closed Western Electric plant in nearby Cicero in 1903 and the headquarters of Sears Roebuck & Co (also shuttered) in 1906 brought North Lawndale’s population to 46,225 by 1910.

During the second decade of this century, Russian Jews became the dominant group here. Eastern European Jews still living along the Maxwell Street ghetto on the Near West Side, actually mocked those for having pretensions of upward mobility.

In fact, they even called this area “Deutschland.”

Although not reaching the economic height of the city’s German Jews at the time, the neighborhood’s fast growing population established their own small city of community institutions, including Mt. Sinai Hospital (still in use), Herzl Junior College (today Malcolm X), several bathhouses and a commercial strip on Roosevelt Road.

A study conducted in 1946, revealed this neighborhood (North Lawndale) housed roughly 65,000 Jews, approximately one quarter of Chicago’s Jewish Population.

Fourteen years later, 91 percent of the neighborhood’s 124, 937 residents were black.

African Americans began moving in by the early 1950’s, some directly from rural southern states, others displaced from their Lincoln Park and south side homes by urban renewal projects. In response, white residents moved out to northern neighborhoods such as Rogers Park, West Ridge, and various suburbs. No new housing was built here.

Well at least, during that period.

As a result overcrowding became imminent, ultimately giving way to physical decline. By 1957, the city declared the latter as a conservation area.

Perhaps another black eye for many of the new residents who now called this neighborhood home, no work was available.

To be more accurate, the local factories only hired and employed those who no longer lived here. Consequently, the local consumer base became much poorer.

As a result, tensions grew between the whites who worked here during the day and the blacks that lived here. In 1966, the poverty that altered this area prompted Martin Luther King Jr. to literally set up shop for the northern Civil Rights Movement.

Although his visit was highly symbolic, attracting much attention, there was still very little change. However after King's assassination, the area did change.

West Side residents here and in Garfield Park across the bridge rioted.

Although commercial centers run by whites were the key targets of physical attack, some residential areas burned as well.

Most of the small businesses and larger plants packed up and left not only because they lost their insurance, but it was also because they feared more riots.

International Harvester, which was actually in South Lawndale, closed its factory in 1969, and Sears (as it was mentioned earlier) moved it global headquarters downtown in the fall of 1974. The community-based organizations that King inspired-the Lawndale's

People Planning and the Action Council and the Pyramid West Development Corporation-had tried, but failed to attract new industries to employ the residents and newer housing to revitalize the neighborhood.

The area's population has dwindled from its peak back in 1960 to 47, 888 in 1980.

Almost ten years later, this trend slowly continues.

Just south of the Eisenhower Expressway which runs parallel to Harrison Street at this point between the New Look Lounge west of Kedzie Avenue which is covered by a row of existing brick two flats (all twin structures), and a school bus garage at the corner of Spaulding Avenue, lies the Roscoe Factory.

Since 1921, this particular factory specializes in making uniforms, floor mats, mops, and towels. Customers who chooses to do business with this company, also has the option to rent the very same products mentioned above.

This establishment along with a few others (which are scattered about throughout the neighborhood) is among the sole surviving industries that decided not to leave, and have long opened their doors to area residents.

Most notably in the wake of the riots.

And once again surprisingly, the historical tower of the former Sears Headquarters remains to be visibly seen. What is to become of this building, only time will tell.

DuPont Residence

Located here in the twelve hundred block of south Central Park Avenue, is the home of Andrea April DuPont. Many residential dwellings mainly brick flats, greystones, and multi-family buildings, as well as a few local businesses are seen.

The brown two flat that Andrea and her mom calls home, is located just off west Roosevelt Road. In its heyday before the riots, and even during white flight the latter employed many vibrant businesses as well as a sizable number of movie theaters.

Today, all that remains to be seen along this particular corridor (most notably between Pulaski Road and Kedzie further east) are a few liquor stores, some fast food "greasy spoon restaurants", three nationals (most notably Churches Chicken, KFC, AND Popeye's), a few barber shops, a beauty salon here and there, second rate corner stores, and a lone Marathon gas station. In between lies more parcels of vacant land.

What was formerly the Lawndale Theater near the corner of Pulaski and what used to be the Central Park near its namesake avenue are now churches.

The exterior façade for both structures (minus the marquees) remains well intact.

Besides a small clinic near the corner of Homan Avenue lies the existing Buddy Bear Grocery Store. A recently built housing development (private) Plaza Courts sits directly across the street. Another piece of vacant land bearing a "for sale" sign is on the opposite side. The neighborhood's only financial center, the Community Bank of Lawndale is seen in the distance while a recently built McDonalds rests near Kedzie.

Along the westernmost corridor where Andrea resides namely along Roosevelt here, many groups of young people (and some old) are seen hanging out in front of what remains of this once "golden corridor." Despite of the anti loitering signs that are posted on some of the establishments, the panhandling, the gambling and other illegal activities continues. Its survival of the fittest.

A young juvenile snatches a woman's chain as she waits for a bus near the Wild West Submarine restaurant near the corner of Avers Avenue.

He desperately tries to flee, but instead catches a rude awakening.

In response, before he is able to cut across the nearest alley ten other youths quickly catches him. They beat him viciously.

Meanwhile, in front of a boarded up storefront, drugs are being sold by another teen who is clad in a very bright designer sweat suit.

Four motorists pulls up one at a time just as the young dealer reveals himself from an adjoining gangway. The young man is extremely mindful of his surroundings.

Having covered all four directions, he quickly produces his bags.

Upon this rather smooth and yet very brief transaction, the gentleman collects three unmarked twenty-dollar bills. Placing the bills into his already swollen bankroll, he studies his surroundings once more. He vanishes shortly thereafter.

Michelle DuPont, thirty-three is of course Andrea's mother.

The single mother despite her "high maintenance" appearance is actually quite down to earth, considerate, outspoken, and humble.

A college graduate with a degree in business, the knockout woman who could easily act as a double for Vanessa Williams owns and operates a prominent boutique shop right here in the neighborhood. The mortgage for this very house where she and Andrea dwells upon is also in her name. At this time, Ms. DuPont is currently at work.

Her daughter meanwhile, who is out of school for the day, is here at home entertaining her friends. The weather that was once bright and sunny outside now turns gloomy. Within one hour, the sound of thunder is heard.

"Yo momma is so short, she tripped and fell over some chopsticks and broke both legs." Ivan roasts Charles. Uncontrollable laughter and a few whistle echoes throughout the entire house. "Hey y'all, check this out." Charles gets the attention of the others.

“Yo momma got two feet growing out of her tities, she fell down and kept running!”

Everyone, including the hostess is practically in tears.

Among her guests are none other than her friends Ivan, Nikki, Charles, and last but not least Lazarus. Also in attendance is her friend and neighbor Tiara Henderson.

“Yo momma ain’t got no teeth saying betcha bite a chip!” Rizzo snaps on Ivan.

“Good one!” Ivan acknowledges.

He claps his hands and points.

The faces of both Nikki and Tiara are both red.

Their eyes are literally watery from the continuous laughter that has plagued them.

The same can almost be said for Andrea whose complexion complements the flavor of double chocolate. Her cheeks are somehow fire engine red.

“Man Riz, y’all so poor that you’ve got mice actually in shackles singing let my people go!” “Pharaoh!” “Pharaoh!” “Let my people go!!!”

“And that concludes today’s battle of the yo momma wars.” Says Charles.

The sound of the thunder outside roars louder.

“How about you and me have a freestyle battle?” Ivan suggest to Lazarus.

“Yeah, aight word.” Lazarus abruptly responds.

“Let’s do this.” “Maestro.” Ivan says to Andrea. “Please.”

Switching her stereo in her mom’s entertainment room from 1390 AM which plays mostly House songs, a blend of rap, and some R&B from eight in the morning till eleven at night, Andrea now puts in an instrumental tape of “The bridge is over” by KRS One from the group B.D.P. Andrea now imitates the sound of a bell as Ivan and Lazarus prepares to rap. The others happily listen.

I'm Lucky Lazarus, You can't step to me cause I'm hazardous
I'm the man of the hour
Is that yo hygiene I smell, goddamn!
I think you need a shower
So tell me, aren't you glad you used Sure?
Its still funky in here
And you smell like horse manure
You call yourself Ivan "The Terrible"
Of course you never lied
Like a thief in the church
Stealin' from the collection plate
And never paid a tied
I'm like the hitchhiker on yo momma
Saying thanks for the ride

For the next two minutes, everyone including Ivan (who just lyrically got his ass handed back to him) is speechless. Appalled, impressed, but far from embarrassed.

Ivan already has on his game face.

Andrea brings him a glass of water.
Taking one single gulp, he smiles.

Giving Lazarus a pound, he bows his head.

I'm Ivan "The Terrible" homey
Your times up
I hope you've got my cash
I'm the real Bruce Lee Roy
Breaking my foot off in yo ass
I'll blitz you, snap yo neck
And even rupture yo spleen
Like Megatron goin off
I'll have you on the run like Star screen

For you to try roast me
You must be insane
Now you're feeling like the Scarecrow
If I only had a brain
What's the matter?
Are you constipated?
It looks like you're doing that dance
If I didn't know any better
You took a shit in your pants

Andrea and the others are already laughing and cheering as Ivan continues his lyrical assault. Lazarus smiles. It appears as though he is almost blushing at this point.

You call yourself Lucky Lazarus
You claim to be hazardous
Hell no, I ain't havin this
I'll eat you alive like six wings on the menu
This is real life
Your time is up
And you ain't go no continues!

Appearing as though he wants to go another around, Lazarus surrenders.

He walks over to Ivan and embraces him.

"This was his best battle this evening." Rizzo says to the others.
"By comparison to the way Ivan roasted me Laz, you were like the big one."
"The both of you were really good." Says Andrea.
She and the others agree. They all nod their heads.

"How about we try Truth or Dare?" Andrea suggests.
"That's cool." The others reply.
A heavy shower now becomes visible on the outside.
Heavy precipitation covers the windows.

As the sky grows somewhat darker, there is even a brief display of lightning.

"You're up first handsome." Andrea points to Ivan.
"Truth or Dare?"
"Dare." Ivan abruptly responds.

Walking towards the refrigerator in the kitchen, Andrea who is clad in a blue body shirt revealing her well blossoming figure and a long knee length skirt which still displays her curves, she removes two eggs. Dispatching another glass from the dishwasher, Andrea cracks the shells and pours the yokes into the glass.

She looks at Ivan for a moment and then smiles.

" I dare you to drink these eggs." Andrea hands him the glass.
"You ain't no punk, tell them what yo name is." Rizzo says to Ivan.
Nikki is feeling somewhat sick at this point as she now looks on.
"Kunta!" Ivan pounds his chest.

With no hesitation whatsoever, Ivan takes the glass from Andrea and quickly drinks the liquefied yolks. Andrea, Nikki, and Tiara are all appalled.

They cover their mouths.

"Son of a---------!" Charles chuckles.
"He actually did that, damn!" Andrea tries not to laugh.
"You've got to be nuttier than a Snickers." Nikki shakes her head.
"I think that you have entirely too much time on your hands." Says Tiara.
She pats on Ivan's hard stomach.
"Oh, I was just playing when I dared you." Andrea jokingly replies.
"You know you deserve a chop, Andrea." Rizzo playfully chops her on the shoulder.

"Whatever." She replies. "Nikki, you're next."

"I don't know why you're so appalled as to what he just did."

"You're almost just as daring."

"Anyway, Truth or Dare?" Andrea then asks.

"I dare you to run outside wearing nothing but your sports bra and boxers."

"Just once." "Ooooooh!" Says the others.

Nikki's face turns red.

Ivan, Rizzo, and the other two boys all point and whistle.

"You all make me sick." She says now smiling once more.

"But they can't watch me undress."

"There's the bathroom." Andrea points toward the back.

Now stepping out clad only in her gray sports bra (plus boxers) and showing what is surprisingly a well-toned stomach, Nikki darts out into the pouring rain.

Running around the block once along Lawndale Avenue (which is now rather deserted on the account of the weather), she is already back inside.

"Does anybody have a camcorder?" Ivan says to the others.

"Yep, its right here." Andrea produces what appears to be a PXL 2000.

Turning on the camera, Ivan records the footage.

Nikki quickly flips him the bird and runs off to the bathroom.

"And cut!" Ivan now turns off the camera.

A fun and bright rainy day.

28

JENSEN SCHOLASTIC ACADEMY, FRIDAY

Immediately following recess, Mrs. Holmes and her co-worker Mrs. Cobbs along with their students now return to their classroom.

About fifteen minutes later, Mary Wentworth the Music teacher arrives.

Upon greeting her fellow colleagues, who are now seen walking out for their last and final break the London-born teacher then greets her students.

Now cutting to the chase, Mrs. Wentworth begins her lessons.

The daughter of Ghanaian immigrants who originally settled in the United Kingdom, Mrs. Wentworth has been a naturalized United States citizen for over ten years. She graduated at the top of her class at the University of Oxford in 1978.

A married mother of three, Wentworth's external appearance is more pleasing as opposed to the opposite. Mainly her personality.

At about five foot four, although lean she yet still has quite a shape.

Clad in a tan business suit, a medium skirt and matching heels, her light mocha complexion is smooth, radiant.

Her hair, which is at shoulder length, is straight, and rather shiny.

Underneath her long bangs is a pair of clear thin-framed eyeglasses.

Unlike half of the faculty (most notably the other teachers), and like that of her two colleagues who had just left, Mrs. Wentworth's intentions toward her students are surprisingly good. However many of her students and some of her fellow co-workers still view her as an arrogant, narcissistic, queen bee bitch.

And they stand correct.

However, her time has come.

Having spent the first half hour learning and thus studying classical songs most of which coincides with Jazz, R&B, some hints of Gospel as well as a few traces of Ragtime, Mrs. Wentworth then introduces them to another song.

Collecting one set of notes from her still respectful students, she then hands each and every one of them another booklet.

Inside are notes for the song entitled "LaBamba."

The latter is a Mexican folk song originally out of Vera Cruz, which was ultimately adopted by the late Ritchie Valens over thirty-one years ago.

And it was actually a top forty hit in the American charts.

It was covered by many other artists, most recently Los Lobos, whose version reached number one here in the U.S. and the U.K. just three years ago.

A movie was just released around the same time bearing the same title.

To break the ice, Mrs. Wentworth who of course knows the song like the back of her hand, takes her place on the piano.

Without even breaking a sweat, she allows herself to get warmed up as she operates the keys. She is focused, but relaxed.

In less than five minutes, she is ready.

Now briefly getting in tuned; note after note (even word for word) despite her already pleasant singing voice, Wentworth clears her throat and begins her introduction.

Para bailar La Bamba
Para bailar La Bamba
Se necessita una poca de gracia
Una poca de gracia
Para mi, para ti, ay arriba, ay arriba
Ay, arriba arriba
Por ti sere, por ti sere, por ti sere

Yo no soy marinero
Yo no soy marinero, soy capitan
Soy capitan, soy capitan
Bamba, bamba
Bamba, bamba
Bamba, bamba, bam

As the minutes continue to pass, slowly but surely most of the class catches on.

Ivan, who is actually fluent in Spanish, was of course no stranger to this song.

When Mrs. Wentworth began testing the vocals of her students individually (following a group test), she is literally caught off guard. Appalled. Dumbfounded.

So is the rest of the class.

Only Nikki, Andrea, Denise, and Donnie Nicholson knew what to expect.

Now smiling, Wentworth urges Ivan to repeat his notes.

For one moment, Ivan nearly sounds like the late singer.

The class, who is obviously impressed, applauds him.

"Where are you really from man?" Curtis Hawkins cracks.

But yet he walks over and gives Ivan a pound.

" You ain't as dumb as I thought you were." Malik Allen adds.

The two boys clap once more.

For the next fifteen minutes, the entire class continues to practice.

Having concluded another lesson with her regularly scheduled class, Mrs. Wentworth now attempts to have a little fun.

Trying for the first time to appear somewhat hip, she puts together a rap.

Wentworth entitles it "Tell me Too."
In between the namesake chorus, the students identify themselves.

Now clapping their hands, the song begins.

Tell me
Tell me too
Tell me
Tell me too
"Serena Summers."
Tell me too
Tell me
Tell me too
"I'm Donnie Nicholson."
Tell me too
Tell me
Tell me too
"Kenny Fox."
Tell me too
Tell me
Tell me too

At this point, Ivan takes over

My name is Ivan Thompson
Like Nat, I'm Unforgettable
Being Strong, Intelligent and Dangerous
They call me "Ivan the Terrible."
And if you cross paths with me
You'll wind up feeling regrettable
Making you feel black and blue
You know that the answer is true
Any last words?
Or maybe a confession?
Or you can tell me too

Exchanging more appalled looks, the entire class cheers him on.

"What the----------." Jermaine Wilkins begins.

He chuckles. "What is this?" "The Ivan/Kid Capri/Prince Paul Remix?"

"Forget the shell." Says Serena Summers.

"Ivan's out of his cave!" In response, the rest of the class laughs.

Ivan himself smiles at the thought.

"You actually have a lot more heart than I thought too." Says Malik.

Eventually he too shakes Ivan's hand.

"Its been rumored that you can actually rap." Says Tamala Spann.

"And yet we've never heard you, except for the talent show."

"Why don't bust another little rhyme for us." Another student insist.

"Ok, let me see all of the hands for those who want to hear Ivan rap." Says Wentworth.

The vote is already unanimous.

"Let Nikki take over the piano for a moment." Denise Wilson suggests.

Nodding her head thus indicating that she agrees, the music teacher gives the ok.

Pinning her long curly hair back, Nikki positions herself on the piano. Putting on her glasses she begins to work the keys. It is like night and day as the gifted and much younger musician gets down. "Go on with yo bad self." Says both Andrea and Denise.

For one moment, it appears as though Mrs. Wentworth is jealous.

In the absence of a tape player or even that of an instrumental cut, both Ivan and his friend improvises. Nikki now plays what is obviously KRS One's "I'm Still Number One." "Go ahead Nikki!" Donnie claps. Ivan takes his place in front of the room.

"I want to dedicated this to you Mrs. Wentworth and many others." He announces. "This is for you." Ivan now points to the smiling music teacher.

Madame Wentworth I admire your dedication
Your sophistication, for what its worth
You're on the west side of the Atlantic now
So welcome to my turf

A true educator, a scholar who put in many years
All the modeling, the picture taking
The blood, sweat and the tears
You claim that you wanna make a difference
We can see that
We have no doubt
But for you to talk down and belittle us
You gotta cut that out
You're turning red
Are you angry?
Like Milli Vanilli
Of course you know it's true
We're human beings, poor maybe
Not some animals in a zoo

At this point Mrs. Wentworth is actually turning red.

Although angry, she also becomes dumbfounded.

Meanwhile, the rest of the class is speechless.

As Ivan's peers continue to hear him out despite being shocked, they are still impressed. To assist Nikki who is still playing the piano, the rest of the class began to clap. Ivan, on the other hand is just warming up.

You think you're so beautiful
So tough and so cool
You're nothing but the epitome
Of an educated fool
So what you went to Oxford
You live in Forest Glen
You say you're born again, but yet you still sin
You're paid to educate, unify and regulate
But instead you divide and conquer
Brainwash and miss educate.
My main goal as well my peers here
Is to reach for the stars
Careers that we enjoy

The money, homes and the cars
Heaven and Hell
With or without you we'll still prevail
Don't you have a oven to put your head in?
Or why don't you fry on the third rail

The entire class cheers loudly and applauds Ivan once more.

I Promise you
You won't be the first or the last
You're like a wet dream on steroids
Take the stick out yo ass
It's not about black or white
Upper or Lower class
You tell us to say no to drugs
But you're the main one smoking grass
You keep it up
Trust and believe
Your career will be deceased
Broke and no pension
To redeem yourself , You'll have to see the priest

"Enjoy you're the rest of your day Mrs. Wentworth, see you next week." Says Ivan.

By the time he began to speak, the suddenly embittered music teacher storms out.

She slams the door.

The entire class gives Ivan another round of applause.

Maureen Headley who is walking down the hall passes a now pissed off and ashamed Mary Wentworth who is now calling for the elevator.

Before she is able to find out what is wrong with her friend and colleague, the obviously defeated music teacher is already out of sight.

While other groups of children who are accompanied by their teachers resume their sessions in the workstations nearby, the twenty-five year old Spelling and Language Arts teacher then shrugs. Walking into room 403, she greets both Mrs. Holmes and Mrs. Cobbs who has now returned as well as their students.

"What's with her?" Headley asks her two co-workers.

"Your friend just got her ass handed back to her by a sixth grader." Holmes explains.

"Lyrically." Says Cobbs.

"You know, her intentions toward the children here are actually good and all, but yet Mary still acts as though she doesn't know how to talk to them." Headley begins telling Mrs. Holmes and Mrs. Cobbs. "We know that." Mrs. Cobbs answers.

"I thought that at least that It would be a parent who was upset." Says Headley.

"I've warned her plenty of times myself."

"And supposed if a child does step out of line, instead of just simply reprimanding him or her, Mary always likes to put on a minstrel show, putting on all types of these b.s. Theatrics, further belittling a child and has the audacity to feel proud afterwards."

"So she really went too far this time huh?"

Both Holmes and Cobbs nod their heads.

"So who was the rebel?" Ms. Headley finally asks.

Ivan slowly raises his hand.

Ms. Headley then smiles at him.

"You certainly have a lot of guts these days Ivan."

"That's good and I don't blame you."

"Yeah, he's one of our most outspoken students." Mrs. Cobbs adds.

"He's the only one." Mrs. Holmes reminds her.
"In all my years of teaching, I never knew anyone like him." She continues.

Mrs. Cobbs, and Headley both chuckles.

"There are a lot of rumors going on about him." Says Mrs. Headley.

"All of which are good." She then looks over at the star student.

"Growing more than just skin it seems like."

"But hey, I love the new you." Mrs. Headley then smiles at Ivan.

"All of it." She then briefly studies his physique as he stands up to stretch.

"And you're looking rather cute these days aren't you?"

"Ooooooh!" The rest of the class responds.

"Anyway, you shouldn't let anyone make a wimp out of you." Mrs. Cobbs also point out. "Regardless of whether its one of you're fellow peers, or even a teacher.

"And regardless of whatever the consequences are, always stick to your guns."

"Especially if you know you're in the right." Mrs. Holmes reminds Ivan as well as the rest of the class. "Obviously, Mrs. Headley here has an announcement."

"The floor is yours."

"Thank you maam." Mrs. Headley now walks toward the board.

"How are you guys doing this afternoon?" She first asks the students.

"Good." They all reply in unison.

"Well, I'd just like to let you guys know that there will be a Spelling competition down in the auditorium on the twenty first."

Many of the students now exchange satisfying looks.

Nikki, whose seat currently faces that of Ivan's now gives him a rather "friendly" stare. In response, Ivan returns the favor. He smiles back.

As they both remain in-tuned to Mrs. Headley's announcement, Ivan and Nikki suddenly find themselves staring into each other's eyes.

Underneath their desks, they now appear to be playing what is obviously a game of foot tag. Slowly planting her size six on top of his size nine, Nikki grins at him mischievously. As Ivan now plants his sneakers on top of hers, she quietly snatches away her feet and then blushes. Appearing as though he is trying to focus on Headley's comments to the rest of the class, Nikki now touches away at Ivan's shins with her left foot. He too blushes. The rest of the class is completely unaware of this.

"If you're interested, please see me in my office." "You know where to find me." Mrs. Headley now concludes. "Enjoy the rest of your day."

The former Miss Illinois beauty queen now leaves the room.

Walking down the blacktop-paved alley towards the end of his block, Ivan now reaches the corner of St. Louis Avenue.

Sanders Residence

Stepping up to the porch of the tan brick cottage, Ivan rings the bell twice.

There is still no answer.

Now passing through a freshly paved gangway which also shares that of a common boundary between Nikki's house and that of a boarded up apartment structure which is now being refurbished and restored, Ivan quietly takes a stroll around the back.

Having entered the rear of the house, he spots Nikki herself.

Working diligently and tirelessly on her footwork while dribbling and thus reviewing her jump shots as she literally takes her Wilson to the hole, Nicole turns to Ivan and waves. "Well if it isn't Kermit the Frogwoman here." He teases her.

Nikki's caramel complexion, which bares Dutch features, is already turning red.

As she continues to play, she laughs.

"Nobody's thinking about you frogman!" Nikki snaps.

Flinging the ball at him, she sticks out her tongue.

Nikki misses by one inch. "Ha, ha!" Ivan points and laughs.

Picking up the ball, he hands it back to her.

"You're looking good." Ivan begins.
"Thanks." Says Nikki. She makes another shot.
"Is your mom still at work?" Ivan asks.
"Yeah." Nikki responds as she bounces her ball.
She acts as though she is actually on the court.
"You wanna join me?" The sweaty young lady asks.

Despite being sweaty, the sweet scent of what appears to be cinnamon grows.

"Don't play with me like that girl, you know I do."

He now takes his defenses to her.

Ivan quickly parries the ball away from her and instantly, he takes it to the hole.

"No you didn't!" Says Nikki. The acting young hostess is smiling.

"How dare you dunk on me in my own house?" "Get out!" Nikki says jokingly.

"I do what I want here, killing or dunking." Ivan grins.

"Oh, we'll see about mister!" Nikki punches his arm.

Initiating a defense move of her own, she therefore pays him back. In the backyard of what is currently the Sanders, lies a newly resurfaced foundation of what used to be a garage. A gazebo that was recently built by Nikki's grandfather (her mother's father) now sits in its place. Surrounded by a large body of sod which acts more as a buffer between the gazebo and the open porch, which corresponds to that of the building, is a concrete island. A lone gas grill and two swings occupy the latter.

Just as a tall, but wooden picket fence covers the entire property from the outside, exterior tier lights (mainly at dusk) illuminates the yard from within.

Nikki along with her friend and neighbor are playing on what appears to be a glass rim facing the building. At this point, they are both sweaty and charged up.

As they both hustle for the ball, Ivan finally gets the upper hand and attempts to make his shot from the right of the building.

He shoots, the ball circles the rim once.

However, this time it doesn't go in. "Time, let's take a break." Nikki calls out.

Despite all of the noise that surrounds them, Nikki and her favorite guest are well relaxed as they rest on the swings. "Man, that was fun." The hostess herself begins.

She sighs and looks up at the seemingly less polluted sky.

"It certainly was." Ivan looks over at her.

"I'd never though you'd me a run for my money like that." Nikki then faces him.

"No more kid gloves for you!" She teases.

"You're quite the competitor yourself Ms. Frog lady." Ivan pushes back.

"Without me sounding politically incorrect or in simple English, sexist."

"You're actually the first girl, that I know so far who is really good."

"I was actually more of a tomboy anyway before I moved up here." Nikki explains.

"For some reason, I was never surprised." Ivan happily responds.

"Many of the other girls just didn't like me when I lived back in Atlanta Ivan."

"I was forever getting into fights." Nikki continues to share her revelation.

"What was their beef with me?" She then chuckles.

"Only God knew." Ivan happily nods his head word for word.

"I always made the grade down there in school, as I do up here."

"Had a few friends, my mom was always among them."

"I enjoyed the same hobbies as I do today, and for the most part I never bothered anybody." Her hazel eyes still remains glued to that of Ivan's almond brown.

"I should have known that when we first met." Ivan smiles.

"When it came to me fighting, sometimes I won." Nikki begins.

As she still sits on her swing, the young hostess now plays with her hair.

“Others I didn’t.” “My mom didn’t whoop me or anything because she knew that I was trying to defend myself.” “Despite the fact that I still ended up in detention.”

“As you know.” Nikki goes on.
“I have no brothers nor sisters on my mom’s side.”
“And with me being the only child, I at some point had to create more alliances.”
“Mainly with the boys.” Ivan nods.
“Spent a lot of time around some of my male cousins, and they really taught me some things.” “I even learned how to fight a little bit better too.”

“At the same time, I still remained lady-like.” Nikki then smiles.
“That’s cool.” Ivan says with the uttermost of satisfaction.
“Not too many girls wanted to challenge me after awhile either.”
“Just like that song by the DOC Nikki.” Ivan begins.
He playfully slaps her across her left thigh. She smiles.
She is clad in a T-shirt, maroon sweat pants as well as a pair of designer cross trainers.
“You’re beautiful but deadly.” Ivan’s tone is rather smooth.
His compliment is sincere, honest and yet a pleasant one.
Nikki blushes and then smiles for the fourth time.
“You really are sweet Ivan.” She softly replies.
It sounds almost as though she is whispering.

Although she is only eleven, Nicole who lineage descends from freed slaves, Dutch traders, a defected Confederate-turned Union soldier, and two known native groups: The Seminole and the Choctaw, her body has already began rapidly developing.

It appears as though she is now sixteen.

Getting up from his swing, Ivan begins to assist his friend.

He pushes her as she now takes a hold of her swing.

With her eyes closed for the moment, it feels as though the weight of the world has vanished. She disperses a sigh of relief. Ivan pushes her higher and higher.

After achieving her half hour long natural high with her swing, she now briefly retreats to the inside of her home. Twenty minutes later, Nikki now returns with a tray of freshly made brownies and two glasses of lemonade.

Ivan feels even more at home as he happily accepts her treat.

Nikki's attire has also changed since her brief retreat.

Now clad in a midnight blue body shirt revealing her blossoming bosoms and well-toned, but gutless stomach, she now also sports a pair of tight black jeans as well as a pair of strapped sandals. The latter of course employs a single strap at the heel displaying only one toe. Ivan is even further impressed. "Thank you." He says.

He happily accepts his refreshments.

"There's nothing like a little southern hospitality in the Windy City." Ivan then says.

He abruptly goes to work on his first brownie.

"You're welcome." Nikki softly replies.

They both head over to the gazebo.

"It was about time that somebody handed Wentworth her ass back to her." Nikki begins. She slowly sips her lemonade and then bites into a brownie.

"Never thought it would be you Ivan."

"Maybe those within our own age group, I'd expect for you tell off."

"Go toe to toe, literally get physical and you have."

"But adults, elders especially those with some, significant authority."

"You're taking the fight to them now."

"Where I'm from----------."
"I know Nikki." Ivan rubs her hand.
"Southerners whether they're black, white or whatever…."
"Atleast many of them remain firm believers in good old fashioned manners."
"They're honest, respectful, straightforward, and quite humble." Ivan breaks it down.
Nikki's most outspoken guest proceeds to make his case. She smiles.

"And even if they don't think highly of you, the southerners will let you know immediately!" "Northerners, sadly many will do the exact opposite."

"Yeah, I noticed that on my first day of school here." Says Nikki.

She has already polished up first brownie and has already done away with her lemonade. Ivan also follows suit. "I can't lie to you Ivan." Nikki begins.

"Even though I am surprised, I don't blame you."

"I knew that you had another reason too, as to why you went off on Wentworth."

"I'm through playing games with our fellow peers, these mean spirited, ignorant, so called teachers." Ivan further breaks it down.

"To a lesser extent Nikki, my family members."

"And last but not least, these bible-thumping elders."

"Unless I'm really out of line and rebellious, then that's a different story."

"But otherwise, step off."

Ivan chuckles just as Nikki happily listens.

"Whether its verbally or physically, at all cost I'm prepared to defend myself."

"Damned the old school traditions, sharecropping days are over."

"I'm not taking any more prisoners, and in conclusion." Ivan smiles at Nikki once more. "Regardless of the consequences."

"I hear you." Nikki then pours him another glass of lemonade.

"So you're a big time rapper now huh?" She punches his arm once more.

"That was really impressive how you roasted Mrs. Wentworth."

"Anyway, how are you gonna roast the music teacher?"

"You really had me thinking that you were going to sing something positive."

"But yet, you really did tell Wentworth something about herself."

"It was warranted Nicole, just like when I whooped my cousin's ass months earlier."

"And he ain't never come back either." Says Nikki.

"Didn't he?" "Hell naw." Chuckles Ivan. "I exiled him."

Nikki giggles. "You're funny."

Ivan playfully shrugs. "What?" "I was just thinking about something." Nikki insists.

"Well it seems like Curtis and Malik are friends with me again." Ivan begins.

“I never really understood as to why they went rogue in the first place.” Says Nikki.

“Especially Curt.” Ivan responds with a shrug. “Anyway, its still a good thing.”

Having finished their snack, Nikki and Ivan now head inside.

Thompson Residence

After completing his homework, Ivan joins his family in the dining room where they are now playing a game of chest. Prior to his entrance, his parents have literally taken turns as they play back to back, thus defeating one another.

Mr. Thompson takes his plug at least four paces before strategically jumping cleaning his wife’s clock. “Checkmate sister.” He says. Mrs. Thompson chuckles.

“Yeah, so what!” She then grins.

“You may have won yourself another victory, but yet you haven’t won the war.”

“Assured Mutual Destruction baby.” Mr. Thompson roasts.

“Me and Kryptonite are close.” “Ha!” ha!”

“Ha!” Ha!” Hell!” Chuckles Mrs. Thompson.

“The south will rise again!”

“Okay Stonewall Jackson!” Her husband cracks.

“Forget you Ike.” Mrs. Thompson sighs jokingly.

“What the problem is Tina?” Mr. Thompson begins.

He now begins imitating the long embattled singer.

Ivan’s mom then tosses one of her Bishop plugs over at his dad.

She misses. “How you like me now heifer?” Mr. Thompson grins.

“Whatever, no desert for you young man.” His wife teases.

“Well, in that case no car for you then.” Mr. Thompson now holds up a set of keys.

Twenty years and yet they still have a strong sense of humor as well as the love.

Walking into the room, as he looks in on his family (including his brother Simon), Ivan then smiles as he now takes a seat. "Are you finished with your homework man?" Asks his father. "Yes, I am." Ivan responds. "Good, you might as well pull up a chair then." Ivan quickly takes a seat. "If you able to snatch the pebble, then you can go."

"You won't need a teacher no more."

"I'll play you first." Simon begins.
He takes a seat directly across from his younger brother.
Their parents are now situated along the sidelines at this point.

Simon's best friend D.J. Killer watt otherwise simply known as Ken or Kenneth Davis, and Ms. Cartier, his grandmother from downstairs is also in attendance.

"Ivan appears to be quite the thrill seekers these days." Simon points out to Ken.

"Always looking for more challenges, hardly ever backing down, becoming quite the problem solver, more aggressive, and last but not least he's got a heck of a lot more heart than our arch enemy around the corner does." Ken and the others nod their heads.

"Yeah, that's a lot of heart man." Says Ken. He smiles.

"But then, everybody's got more heart than he does."

Mr. and Mrs. Thompson laughs. "Hannibal is a punk all the way." Ivan adds.

"Well, it's the ugly truth." Mr. Thompson happily begins.

"And the reason why he is, is that you guys have to understand this."

"Henry, Isaac, and Michael unlike you three don't have a father."

"Whoever had a hand in raising them never really taught right from wrong, and how to be the productive and respectful young men they should be."

Mrs. Cartier and his Mrs. Thompson nod their heads.

"They're under this bullshit notion that they can take whatever they want, someone always owes them something, and they strongly feel that they can terrorize anybody."

"Henry especially was never really taught to how value anything, and he doesn't even know what it means to be a true leader."

"He runs his little punk assed set, sell his drugs, and he thinks he's La Costa Nostra."

"Just the black version." Adds his wife.

"And if they keep it up, sooner or later he along with Michael, and Isaac are either gonna wind up in prison, dead or to a lesser extent crippled."

"You three Ken, Simon, and Mr. Ivan here are nothing like them." Mr. Thompson then pats all three young men on the shoulder. "And Charles."

"Douglas, although he didn't become a statistic still had to learn the hard way."

"What happened to him sir?" Ken asks. "If I may ask."

"He got his ass whooped and got sent home." Chuckles Mr. Thompson.

"Literally." Simon tells his friend.
"Doug moved up to Wisconsin and hasn't been seen since."
"We haven't even heard from him either."

"But despite Doug's rude awakening, he was still the lucky one." Adds Mrs. Thompson. "I bet he is." Says Ken. "Even though I know for certain that none of you will follow the path that Henry and his friends have long chosen, you Simon, Ivan, Ken and Charlie just continue being yourselves."

“We plan on it.” Says both Simon and Ken.

“Good, that’s the answer I was looking for.” Says the elder Thompson.

“Unless Henry continue to pose a threat to your immediate safety and you know for certain that he doesn’t have a gun, you know the drill.” Mr. Thompson concludes.

All the while their father was giving them the much-needed advice in terms of surviving and thus co-existing among their opposition, both Ivan and his older brother continue their game. Ivan, who has often endured countless defeats against his more advanced sibling, has in recent months pulled even.

Simon, who is eighteen, participates in tournaments at least once a year.

Many have likened him to being that of the next Bobby Fisher.

Simon, like that of Ivan also has many talents and is also quite handsome.

Despite being his brother’s senior by four years, a few inches taller, and a shade darker, their resemblance remains comparable.

It has been well over an hour since the Thompson brothers began.

The two are now more focused than ever as they carefully dispatch their plugs.

Patiently waiting out the other, quietly adding and subtracting.

Both Ivan and Simon already have already collected a substantial amount of plugs from one another. Ivan, who is sweating mainly on the account of the room temperature, wipes his forehead. He still awaits his next move. The rest of the family along with their guest happily looks on. “You don’t want to take too long son.” His dad suggests.

“They’re both actually good.” Ken begins.

“If it came down to them playing as a team, they would actually fair well.” Says Mrs. Thompson. Her mom, Ms. Cartier seems to agree. She nods.

“Especially if they played globally.” Ms. Cartier adds.

“They would literally have the world by the balls, I think.”

“And what made Ivan decide to take an interest in this game so suddenly, I like it.”

“He’s definitely my boy alright.” Mr. Thompson adds.

“Checkmate!” Ivan announces.

Jumping around Simon three more times, Ivan clears the board.

Feeling only mildly disgusted, Simon smiles and then shakes his head.

“Good game man.” Simon tells his brother. The two shake hands.

“Thanks.” Ivan responds. “Let’s make a deal.” He begins.

“Why don’t we take a little break, and then we’ll play again.”

“Sounds good.” Simon responds.

“I’m looking for a rematch anyway.”

“Do you feel like going to grab a pizza?” Mr. Thompson asks.

“Yes, I do.” Ivan abruptly replies.

“I called Willie already, he said it’ll be ready in about fifth teen minutes.”

“Thanks, and for going you can keep the change.” Mr. Thompson announces.

“Thanks Dad.” Ivan responds.

Upon collecting the money from his father, Ivan takes off.

Willie Johnson’s Pizza

Situated along south Kedzie Avenue, a corridor surrounded by blighted commercial buildings (most of which are still in use) and crumbling sidewalks is the local pizzeria.

Formerly known as Don's, which was short for Donatello's Pizza, decades earlier sometimes during the early 1970's, a young California businessman named Willie R. Johnson purchased the then recently mothballed parlor.

Just like that of his predecessor Donatello De Rossi whose restaurant was family owned and operated, Johnson (now forty-nine) continues to keep that tradition alive.

With the exception of the three employees who are now seen taking orders, sweeping and preparing the food; all of those who are not seen are of course family members.

The building that houses the restaurant was just recently renovated.

While many of the commercial structures on this block correspond to live-in residences on the upper floors (given that each building ranges only two to three stories), this storefront is no exception. The latter unlike its neighbors is completely modernized.

A newly built wooden porch covers the back, while the front exterior corresponds to that of an English-style pub. Colorful neon signs complements the slightly tinted windows. Under the bright fluorescent banner displaying the name of its founder, is another sign saying that its black-owned.

As a beautiful red, black, and green flag hangs above the entrance, another flag, which of course represents the U.S., stands by its neighbor.

In what appears to be a strong gust of wind for the moment, both of the latter seems to blow freely. The sun now settles behind an empty and boarded up storefront. Located just beyond the adjacent parking lot to the south of Flournoy Street, which services the Area Four Police Station on the opposite side, the scenery appears to mimic what looks like a third world setting. However, even the toughest neighborhoods located in places like the Middle East, and North Africa makes this west side neighborhood look like Wilmette.

Upon his entry into Willie's, Ivan spots several youths.

Hanging out in front of this otherwise prominent establishment, many of these youngsters who obviously knows him quickly greets him.

Shaking hands with them, Ivan now makes his way inside.

The interior lobby consists of a five coin-up machines (arcade games) a jukebox, and a recently added dining area. A large screen TV hangs in the center of the room as well as a see through partition where one can see their food being properly prepared.

At this time, Ivan is the only sole customer in line as he waits for his order to be taken.

"Hey, how ya doing?" Says the owner himself.

For almost as long as Ivan's family has been in the neighborhood, beginning with his parents, the Thompson's have been among Willie's loyal customers.

"Pretty good Willie." Ivan happily responds.

"How are your folks?"

"Comparable, we're all just spending the evening at home." Ivan begins.

"You know, my brother, grandmother from downstairs and Ken dropped in."

"That's good." Says Willie. He appears to be rather impressed.

"I already got your father's call."

"It'll be ready soon, for the time being you know what to do."

"And I see there are at least maybe one or two new games behind me that are just waiting to be played." Ivan says to the owner. He smiles.

Reaching into his jingling pockets, Ivan makes his move.

29

Having already played through six flawless rounds on Street Fighter, one of two recently installed consoles, Ivan now does battle with a character whose image is quite similar to that of Mike Tyson's. In the beginning, Ivan who has been playing as Ryu, a devoted master in the art of Shotokan Karate has succeeded over his P.C. controlled rival thus nearly achieving another perfect. However by the second round after a single reversal and three fierce combos from his opposition, it was now time to improvise.

So the buck stops here huh? He asks himself.

After the electronic ref announces what is the third and final round, Ivan prepares to engage in another battle. The group who has been initially hanging outside of the establishment now enters the lobby. Ivan meanwhile, maintains his focus.

But yet, as he continues on with his game, Ivan is far blind.

The leader of this rather small group is less than one inch shorter than Ivan and he appears to be quite heavy. He dons what appears to be a very thick chain around his neck and wears a designer silk shirt. Also clad in a pair of gray sweat pants (with one leg folded up) and a pair of custom designed snickers, the obese young man also don a matching Kangol that is seemingly tilted to the left.

"So what up Ivan man?" Says the not so obvious thugster.

"What's going on Tre?" Ivan responds.

Without looking back, Ivan still manages to give him a pound as he continues to work the console. The young man who is apparently impressed, smiles.

He then turns to his friends who are also pleased.

They too smile. The leader then chuckles.

"I've always liked this dude." The young man insists.

Ivan who was always less gullible, know when he's being patronized.

But yet, he still smiles back and plays it cool for the time being.

Tremaine "Tre" Gordon, also thirteen was formerly a student at Ivan's school. He was recently expelled for excessive fighting, profanity, theft and vandalism.

In and out the classroom, he is also known as Crazy "T."

To some of the elders in the community, he is better known as the Devil's Ambassador. Upon being expelled from his previous school, Tre ended up being sent to an alternative. His second in command and first cousin is Butch Holland.

Butch, who is about twelve, is a rather tall and lanky fellow.

The young man whose facial features coincides with that of a raccoon, is clad in a T-shirt that displays a more ghetto version of both Mickey and Minnie.

Donning what appears to be designer clothing (most notably Fila), Butch also sports a pair of baggy stonewashed jeans and recently polished white sneakers.

The apparel worn by the rest of the group is comparable.

At this time while Tre and Butch continue to watch Ivan conduct his business with the machine, the others begin filling the tables nearby.

Chatting amongst themselves, they pretend to browse through the menus.

Tre and Henry, who are both members of the 24th Mafia, are at this time rolling eight deep in members. Lounging in the dining area, while just chilling they finally decide to order something. While Ivan continues to put in work on the machine, Tre and Butch decide to have a rap. In other words, just talk to him.

While playing, Ivan himself begins to smile.

"So what's up Tre?" He begins.
"Are you sure don't wanna join me by any chance?"
"What about you Butch?"
Butch grins. "Ha, ha!" He responds.
"Nigga, you real funny."
Tre on the other hand laughs.
"Yo, straight up Butch." He says.
"For a nerd, you cool as hell Ivan."

Ivan chuckles as he remains focused on the screen.
"Thanks." He says. Once again he gives them a pound.
"How's Doug man?" Asks Tre.
"Doug is straight." Ivan assures them.
"As a matter of fact, he's coming back into town around June."
But of course Ivan himself knows the real answer.
At this point, he even finds himself grinning.
"He's looking forward to seeing you all too."
"I talked to em last night as a matter of fact."
"Straight up?" Asks Butch. "Word." Ivan lies.

Almost three rematches and another two dollars (in quarters) later, Ivan is still unable to defeat that very same fighter. He calls it quits
.

"Hey, can y'all do me a favor?" Ivan asks both Tre and Butch.
"Anything homey." They both reply.
"If Willie's looking for me, tell him that I had to run across the street for a minute."
"I'll be right back and shit."
"Aight cool Ivan." Butch assures him.
"We'll be looking out for you."
"Cool, I appreciate that."

Giving Tre and Butch a pound for the fourth time, Ivan briefly steps out.

Trevor's Cut Rate Liquors

Located directly across the street is Trevor's. Like that of Willie's Pizza, this business is also black-owned. Established sometime during the mid 1950's unlike many of the other liquor stores in this neighborhood, Trevor's is open twenty-four hours a day, three-hundred and sixty-five days out of a year and there's an armed guard situated inside.

Upon walking in, Ivan greets the guard the evening staff, as well as owner Trevor Gillespie himself. Snatching a three-liter of RC cola from one of the coolers, Ivan quickly pays the cashier. Before leaving the store, Ivan puts a quarter into the payphone located near the exit. He waits for a dial tone.

"Hello?"
"May I speak with Charles please?"
"Yeah, you're speaking to him what's up?"
"Ah, what's up Ivan?"
"I'm waiting for a pizza up at Willie's, and I had to stop at Trevor's here to get a pop."
"There is something really funny going on up here."

With the receiver still clutched into his left hand, Ivan catches a brief glimpse from the inside of the store. He peers over at Willie's as well the neighboring West Side Video.

Eight more youngsters who are now seen exiting the latter greet Tre and Butch.
Shaking hands, Tre himself welcomes them into Willie's.

Ivan is almost ready to laugh as he now shakes his head. He chuckles. Get the hell out of here! He says to himself. Come on. You have GOT to be shitting me!

This game is really getting old.

These bastards really need to get a life.

"Hey, you still there Ivan?" Charles asks.

"Yeah, my fault man."

"Tre and Butch call themselves trying to set me up that's all."

"They're pretending to be all nice to me, acting like we're all boys."

"Like its goddamned Leave to Beaver in the hood." Ivan chuckles on the line.

"Despite the fact that Crazy "T" and Butch probably didn't get that memo yet."

"But anyway, I step out and come into Trevor's here to get a pop."

"At first when I walked in, it was just Tre, Butch and a few of their other homeys."

"I follow my instincts, even though I had to stop in here anyway."

"Just to size them up, I step out for a second." Charles nods on the other end.

"So I buy my pop, and now I'm looking out the window."

"Behold, it is now sixteen of them."

"This bullshit ends right here, right now Charles!"

"Of course you know, I can handle them now." Ivan continues on.

"But that's not my concern right now, my primary concern is this pizza."

"I just want to get it home in one peace without dropping it."

"And not to mention the possibility of having to wait almost another hour, because its getting busier right now." Ivan takes another peek outside.

"No problem Ivan, you know I've always got your back." Charles says happily.

"How long have we known each other?"

"A long time Charlie, but to sound less vague Kindergarten."

"I ain't gonna sell you out like Douglas did, you can chill on that."

"Me and Lazarus will be up there along with a few other people shortly."

"But for the time being, just act natural, go back in and get your pizza."

"I've got you man." Charles reassures his lifelong friend.

"Thanks." Says Ivan. "That's what friends are for."

"Alright, piece." Ivan hangs up.

Willie Johnson's Pizza

"What are you all doing in here?" Willie himself questions Tre and his friends. The graying but still physically fit owner summons a rather serious and no nonsense stare.

He was initially watching the group from a network of monitors in his office upon their arrival. "Whatever you're selling namely wolf tickets, y'all gonna have to take it outside." Tre and his fellow thugs are all seated. Eating their meals which consist of individual slices, a bag of fries and their choice of drinks, they all exchange puzzling looks as though they have no idea as to what the owner is saying.

Both Tre and Butch dispatch their shrugs of sarcasm.

"We're paying customers here too." Butch vaguely replies.

"We're all eating sir, of course you can plainly see."

"Remember, I'm watching you." Willie begins.

And despite the smirks that both Tre and Butch especially bear as well as those of their friends, Willie on the other hand is not laughing. "You'll end up dining out on the choke specials next door if you're not careful." He warns. "You know how I run things in here, act like you know." "Man, he's trying to sound all cool." Says one of the others in the group. "Well he is fool!" Another young man pops him in the back of the head.

"You heard the man, chill." Tre calmly demands.

The two unidentified youths both comply.

Nodding his head in agreement, Willie returns to his office.

The young man who implied that Willie wasn't "cool" pretends to shoot the owner the moment he turns his back. "What are you retarded?" Tre thunders.

Surprisingly, both Tre and Butch in unison smack the young man in the back of his head. The others all laugh, point, and then whistles.

Not too long after returning to pick up his food, Ivan once again takes off.

Meanwhile, Tre and his friends who are now done eating themselves quietly gets up from their table. Having done away with their garbage, the large group slowly disperses. At this point, they proceed to follow Ivan. Shaking his head without even looking back, Ivan himself (obviously annoyed) sighs.

At this point while the original party of eight (including Tre and Butch) heads across the street while maintaining their visual, the newest group continues to follow Ivan. They walk side by side as though they're attempting to surround him.

Tre and Butch who lead the others although they're on the opposite side of the street continues (from a distance) stalking a seemingly unsuspecting Ivan.

They at first pretend to laugh and joke amongst themselves.

"So what we gonna do for the rest of this evening G-Man?" Asks one of the hoods.

"Shit, I don't know Eight Ball." Answers another group member.

The black hooded youth then shrugs.

"Damn, I guess we can see what they got in the video store."

Another youngster pretends to look at his watch while another yawns.

At least four others slowly attempt to walk up on the already mindful Ivan Thompson.

As sneaky and cunning as they appear to be, these hoods are still no match.

Ivan quickly snaps two solid jabs knocking out the first two (who immediately falls to the ground), before giving his third opponent a palm strike to the face.

As a result of the latter, a loud grotesque sound of what appears to be a broken bone is heard. Blood gushes almost uncontrollably from the young man's nose.

He screams in agony.

Tossing the pizza carton into the air, Ivan quickly parries away multiple punches from a fourth opponent before turning and then twisting his right hand.

As his bones began to crack, he too howls.

To finish him off, Ivan who still has control over his hand then snaps a roundhouse.

Now looking as though he is constipated, the young man passes out.

Ivan gives his fifth opponent a double sidekick while enemy number six catches a powerful (right) hook kick across the face.

Quickly returning to his stance, he still manages to catch the pizza.

Mysteriously, it still remains just as it was as to when he first bought it.

Meanwhile, back in Willie's business begins to pick up. As more customers began awaiting their orders, and more employees manning the kitchen, the owner's wife Irene is also seen assisting the phone operator. The few patrons who are seen now occupy the tables, just as a congregation of youths works the video games nearby.

The smell of garlic and other spices blends in with what appears to be the smell of hickory smoke. To a lesser extent on the account that fried foods are also being prepared, cooking oil. De La Soul's newest song "Saturday" works the jukebox.

Ivan who is unscathed, but mildly sweaty returns to the lobby with his pizza.

"Is everything okay baby?" Asks Mrs. Johnson.

"Actually, the pizza is fine Irene." Ivan assures her.

Wiping the sweat from his forehead he hands her the pizza.

"My only problem remains among certain elements at this time."

"Oh, I get it." Says the petite bronze complexioned woman.

"We'll keep it warm for you then."

"Thanks." Ivan responds. Will returns from his office shortly thereafter.

"Damn, I dropped my pop!" Ivan sighs.

"We'll give you another one man." The owner assures him.

"Its Tre and Butch isn't?" Willie begins to ask.

"Don't they have anything better else to do?" Says Mrs. Johnson.

"Apparently not." Willie tells his wife.

"I warned them as to what was going to eventually happen to them."

"They were going to end up messing with the wrong person one day."

"Do what you gotta you gotta do Ivan."

Willie shakes Ivan's hand as he heads back out.

"Just to teach them a lesson Irene, I hope that Ivan beats the hell outta them."

"Tre, Butch and his hoods are forever hard headed." The owner continues on.

"What part of fat meaning greasy don't they understand?"

"From the looks of it, I think they're going to find out." Mrs. Johnson says happily.

"Are you all stupid or what?" Storms Ivan.

The first five youngsters that he initially dispatched are still unconscious and still moaning in pain as others attempt to surround him.

Unfazed and well focused, Ivan is still in his fighting stance.

"Mothafucka, you tell us." Smirks one of the other youths.

"Fake assed Bruce Lee Roy."

"Why you keep comin up here anyway?" Asks another.

Ivan chuckles. "Well, let me see." He begins.

"Like you, because I feel like it."

"Oooooooh!!" Replies his opposition.

"You're gonna continue to mess with me every time you see me huh?" Ivan questions.

"Well, uh yeah." Another youth in the group snarls.

Ivan immediately snaps a punch into his larynx, followed by another to the sternum.

The last and final blow summons his opponent's abdomen.

A single motion employs all three punches; the face of the trash talker first turns red, and then purple and then back to his normal fudge brown. He also falls to the crumbling pavement. Grinning and pointing another attempts to attack Ivan from behind, but instead catches an elbow. He drops to his knees. Without actually looking back Ivan kicks his left leg high above his head and knocks out his ninth man.

As another attempts to charge in like a bull, Ivan summons all of his weight, steps in and delivers a double palm strike utilizing both hands.

The latter resembles that of a relaxing Taichi-like motion as both hands collides directly across his opponent's chest cavity.

The young man is instantly stopped in his tracks.

Spitting out a wad of saliva, the now incapacitated hood first drops to his knees and then rolls over. Attempting to catch his breath as clutches away at his chest, he now lies sideways. Returning to his stance, Ivan who is only mildly disgusted shakes his head.

Upon furiously parrying away at another opponent's would be punches, the Kung Fu Kid turns and then twists his right hand.

Despite déjà vu with one of his earlier opponents, Ivan instead sticks out his right foot and sweeps him off balance.

Upon running briefly, Ivan jumps up and then lands on to a parked Chevy Suburban. Flipping into the air, he comes down with two roundhouses for two more hoods, while another catches a clean axe kick to the head.

Giving another opponent a spinning hook kick, spinning crescent kicks is summoned to two others within Ivan's reach.

Dancing on the balls of his feet, Ivan changes his stance.

With his rear left leg (acting as his rear) behind his right, Ivan snaps out the sole of his latter dead across the face of an even heavier youth. As he loses his balance and begins to stagger, the seemingly "little big man" crashes directly into the storefront of what is now Kedzie Beepers. Glass shatters immediately upon impact.

Hip tossing another and then drop kicking what appears to his twelfth opponent, Ivan distributes his left backfist to a young man, who suddenly spits out three of his teeth.

"Ah, fuck!" His voice is grotesquely strained as a string of blood and saliva hangs from the corner of his mouth. "My mothafuckin teeth man!"

Two of the hoodlums even have the audacity to flash gang signs.

This time Ivan laughs.

What used to be symbols of power have now become symbols of one who is handicapped. Pressing away at their nerves, the youth's hands quickly grew numb.

Instantly petrified, both now drop to their knees. They whimper.

"Are we done here?" Ivan says to his remaining opposition.

"You heard the man." Says an unknown voice.

"Yeah, answer his question." Another young man replies.

As many as forty young men many in street clothes (others in designer gear), are now spotted in both directions. These would be troublemakers are completely surrounded. They are now dumfounded, distraught and feeling perhaps somewhat ill.

The not so obvious much needed help that Ivan requested each carries a wooden as well as a metal baseball bat. The few who are well dressed each employs a machete.

This group now awaits further instructions.

"Are we done?" Ivan now asks his already broken down opposition for the second time. "Let's go y'all." Says a now acting leader. He goes only by the name of King.

Tre and Butch are suddenly nowhere to be found.

Ivan bows his head just as King and the remaining 24's scoop up their friends.

Many of the spectators on this block (most notably the residents, pedestrians going to and from and even some business leaders) all began to clap.

"Y'all have a nice evening." Charles says to the outgoing hoodlums.

"Thank you, come again." Lazarus responds with a mock Middle Eastern accent.

Charles and Lazarus now embrace Ivan.

"Nice work dog." Lazarus gives Ivan a pound.

"Thanks, you know I'm always practicing." Says Ivan.

"Hey, thanks for coming through."

"I'm going back into Willie's and get my pizza." Ivan announces.

The other young men, who assisted Charles and Lazarus, also embrace Ivan.

"For the time being, I've got to head back to the house."

"We have like a family moment right now, but I'm still coming through later on."

"By the way, what happened to Tre and Butch Ivan?" Charles asks.

"Your guess is just as good as mine Charlie."

"They broke, that's what the fuck they did." Says Lazarus.

"Butch and Tre for once are scared, and they should be."

"They knew they fucked up this time." Ivan says with authority.

"But we can talk about all of this later."

"Alright. Cool." Both Charles and Lazarus respond.

Shaking hands, the three young men part their separate ways.

Thompson Residence

As Mr. Thompson briefly takes a smoke out back, Simon and Ken who are now in the basement continue on with their game of pool. They eventually enter the dining room just as Mrs. Thompson sets the table. Mrs. Cartier, her mom assists her.

It is now a quarter to seven. "Where is in the world is Ivan?" Asks Mrs. Thompson.

Shortly thereafter, Ivan comes in through the front door.

Returning with the large family size pizza and drink that his father ordered, the family prepares to eat. Upon opening the box, everyone begins carving their own slices.

"What happened to you out there man?" Asks Mr. Thompson.
"Well, actually Dad, I was somewhat held up." Ivan explains.
"Atleast, you finally made it back." Says his grandmother.
Anyway, let's eat." Says Mr. Thompson. Dinner is served.

The Villa Historic District (Irving Park)
Wednesday May 5, 1989

Located just off the John F. Kennedy Expressway (Interstate 90/94) within the city's greater Irving Park neighborhood just northwest of downtown (about roughly six miles), this community is best defined by its award winning parkway streets, stone planters and last but not least: Its award winning residential homes.

All of which has been around for more than likely the first part of the century.

A triangle of a hundred and twenty-six homes, bordered by Addison Street, Pulaski Road, Avondale Avenue and Hamlin Avenue was established in 1907.

Many Victorians, Craftsman-style bungalows, Prairies, Colonial Tudors and not to mention Chicago's signature bungalows aligns each of the latter corridors.

For the past three years, residents have been working diligently to replace at least over a hundred and twenty of their trees, which had been casualties of a Dutch elm outbreak (sometimes during the 1960's). Surprisingly, they even employ their own snow equipment to clean their streets and the area is also classified as a national historical district. In conclusion, the not so obvious uniqueness of this community is that this area offers a quiet suburban-like setting.

In what is now a peak period for both motorists on the Kennedy and its West Northwest riders awaiting trains to O'Hare Airport, the Loop and its far west side terminals at the Harlem transit center in the Norwood Park neighborhood, Cedric Holt is among them. Boarding a south bound O'Hare Douglas "B" train he begins his trip.

Traveling in the median of the now congested highway, Cedric takes note of all the historic architecture along the way, some industrial sites, and what appears to be Lorado Taft High School. After leaving another major transit center at the Jefferson Park station (formerly the end of the line), his train bypasses Montrose which is a designated "A" station. One "AB" Station later, Cedric reaches a "B" station, which is lies at Addison Street. He exits the train here.

Dubois Residence, The Villa

Having finished her homework, Hannah Dubois heads out. But however before doing so, she summons her gym bag. "I'm heading over to the park." She announces to her mother. Her mom who is now seen in the living room doing her aerobics, smiles and waves while at the same time, maintaining her pace.

Walking out of what almost resembles a subdivision, Hannah heads east along Addison. Walking alongside this still quiet residential corridor, which employs mostly apartment dwellings as well the contemporary bungalow, some two flats (both plain brick and greystone in between): she greets some of her fellow residents.

Born to a Caucasian French-Canadian mother and a black Haitian father, twelve-year-old Hannah Dubois is indeed like a diamond to those who are closest and dearest to her.

As an only child to Jean Luc and Sophie Dubois despite her recently adopted bad company, Hannah also despite the fact that she is rather stuck up and perhaps vein may not be the "vampire princess" as she is often perceived.

Her parents, who were happily married from the time of her birth up until her dad's untimely demise provides a more legitimate explanation.

Mr. Dubois, once a prominent lawyer and a pillar in the community was a loving father to Hannah and was literally in her corner every step of the way.

Well, at least until last year.

On his way home from working late, as he was driving Mr. Dubois was unfortunately killed by a drunk driver.

He was only thirty-six.

Prior to her father's death, Hannah was the exact opposite.

Less conceited, more caring, considerate or just plain down to earth.

For a time even before Nicole Sander's arrival, Hannah even adored a once pudgy and timid Ivan Thompson. For her mother, despite her late husband's top dollar life insurance Ms. Dubois unlike her daughter grieves in silence.

Ms. Dubois, who is thirty-three works as a flight attendant for American Airlines.

She currently pays the mortgage for their Victorian located on north Hamlin.

Hannah, who bares her mother's features is every bit as beautiful.

Often mistaken as a full-blooded Caucasian girl, many on all sides not just black and white alone liken her to a human chameleon.

Some of the boys at her school as a complement, calls her "white chocolate."

Crossing the overpass above the Kennedy Expressway and the O'Hare branches Addison Station, another Skidmore-designed relic (circa 1970), as well as the rest of this line, Hannah with caution watches out for the oncoming traffic.

Mindful of the ramp to her left where many vehicles began their decent, she safely crosses the street.

Athletic Field Park

Located directly on the opposite side near the corner of north Drake Street, Hannah enters the field house. Named for recreation facilities that it provides with the employment of a Spanish Revival style field house, perhaps one of its most popular programs as of this moment would be the Ceramics class.

At this time, Hannah now clad in her swimsuit that reveals her already well-blossomed figure (shiny red toenails and all), steps onto the diving board.

Peering down at the rippling water, which in part, complements the smell of chlorine; the obviously skilled swimmer takes her position.

Now in her form, Hannah begins her dive.

Even without her frame bending back as the momentum and the velocity increases, Hannah still succeeds. Without the excessive splashing, Hannah executes the perfect dive. Now swimming towards the shallow end as though her life depends on it, Hannah kicks, flaps, and turns her head repetitiously. As the oxygen rapidly increases with every stroke, Hannah whose father trained her early on makes it to the shallow end within seconds. Her long brown hair is now stringy just as her facial features (most notably her nose and cheeks) turns red. With a consistent rhythm, and without stopping of course from the deep end that corresponds to at least nine and a half feet, to the shallow end and back, this is apparently her primary sport.

Well, this along with volleyball.

Among her friends who are situated in the right corner of what is the shallow end, is Sarah Barscz, Jessica Lubinski, Heidi Pierog, and Elizabeth Torres.

Her only male friend from the neighborhood (also seen with the girls) is Roger Cooper. And last but not least, there is of course her bad boy: Cedric Holt.

Glen Reed, twenty-seven is assigned here as the Lifeguard now on duty.

"You broke a new record Hannah." He says clicking his stopwatch.

Emerging from the pool-soaking wet, Hannah briefly sucks in some wind.

Taking a deep breath, she slowly exhales.

It has been only two minutes and yet, Hannah has already completed ten laps.

"I was born for this sport." She chuckles.

"We know." Says the others.

Joining her friends for the next few minutes, they all continue to mingle and share laughs. Hannah and Cedric depart shortly thereafter.

Dubois Residence

As the song "Moments in Love" by the Art of Noise echoes from the entertainment center in the living room, Hannah and Cedric (now on the couch), slowly makes out.

After awhile of open mouth French kissing, sucking on each other's neck, with Cedric catching a dark red hickey, Cedric himself tries to return the favor.

Upon sucking and biting away at his girlfriend's creamy neck, she suddenly clears her throat. "We'll have to try something else." She whispers in Cedric's ear.

"You won't be too disappointed." Hannah grins.

"Neither will you." Cedric smiles back.

Lying on her back with Cedric on top, Hannah's eyes looks up at his.

She then closes them as he sucks on her neck, and then her ears.

Hannah quietly moans.

With her legs wrapped around his waist, she slowly lifts up the back of his shirt.

At this point, her nails begin to travel up and down Cedric's spine.

He is equally aroused. Both are still fully clad.

While Hannah's nails explores his entire back, Cedric on the other hand slowly lifts up her shirt. He begins to lick circles around her navel.

Hannah continues to moan quietly.

Cedric slowly continues lifting up her shirt.

Hannah at this point is running her fingers through his hair.

She moans. Finally, Cedric reaches her bra.

Hannah then takes his hand and places one on her breast.

"I told you that you wouldn't be disappointed." She smiles once more.

Lifting up her bra, Cedric discovers that it isn't stuffed.

He slowly begins sucking away at her breasts.

While moaning, Hannah's face this time reddens.

Oh Cedric! She begins whispering his name.

Maxwell Street Market, Near West Side

The birthplace of Chicago's Blues and of course home of its signature hotdogs, not to mention the University of Illinois in its backyard; this area, literally functions like one gigantic flea market. One can buy almost anything here.

Whether it's legal or not.

And as for the old but still active 7th Police Precinct smacked in the middle…

Who gives a damn?

In need of a job, fast money fledging entrepreneurs, they all come here.

This area is perceived by many as the largest open-air market in the nation who chooses earn their living. From clothes, to produce, to cars, appliances, tools and virtually anything anyone might want, Maxwell Street offers discount items to consumers and is an economic hub for the poor seeking to get ahead.

Merchandise is often hijacked, or pirated from railcars/rail yards and transporter rigs for a rapid resale and a possible liquidation of other stock.

Sometimes if the price is right, some questions that are asked in reference to the origin of these products can actually be answered.

Many believe this market was set up in part to counter retail giants who choose to stand alone with their brutal unreasonable price structures.

This brand of commerce has recognized the availability and the influx of Asian and other global import markets that are priced dramatically lower than American manufactured goods. Wholesalers summons Roosevelt Road with goods from all over the world; these savvy vendors buys and then resells these "five finger products" at a profit thus corresponding at a one hundred percent markup.

Furthermore, this particular market responds to the spending power of mainly immigrants and minorities who will take their cash where they are welcomed, accepted and can shop. These merchants who are now seen as the evening begins, represent countries such as Ghana, Morocco, China, Japan, Mexico and so on.

As the sun slowly sets, many customers still takes it to the streets in search of a discount. Mainly along Halsted Street between Roosevelt Road and 16th Street.

The time is now 5:15 as Cedric and Hannah comes out of the Maxwell Street Polish stand. Holding hands while carrying what appear to be bags of clothing and accessories taken from other stores in the area, the Bonnie and Clyde-like minors now meets up with their friends who have assisted them on the recent flea market jobs further west.

As usual after spending at least a month or more studying their targets, even if it means having to buy some products to appear less suspicious, Cedric and his small network of thieves are ready to go to work. But before doing so Cedric quickly convenes a brief conference. They now stand at a nearby bus stop.

"Remember, a few simple ground rules." He begins.

"Don't mess with the street vendors out here."

"We're only interested in the small shoe stores, clothing stores for right now."

"The usual norms." The others nod their heads in agreement.

"Act natural, never draw any unwanted attention."

The others happily nod their heads once more.

"It's almost six." Cedric checks his watch.

"We can all chill after this, maybe see a movie down at Burnham Plaza."

"Aight, cool." Says Quentin. He claps his hands.

"Let's do this." Maxwell Hopkins responds.

Slowly but yet simultaneously, each member walks into their nearest clothing store.

Magnolia Park, North Lawndale

Located just west of Kedzie in the 3200 block of west Flournoy Street, a corridor complimented by Field's, a local mom and pops corner store, a lone vacant lot, a three-story apartment dwelling, a lone one flat with an assortment of two flats, two single family homes supported by well-manicured lawns and an even larger, but gorgeous courtyard structure (which even has two payphones) most notably near Spaulding Avenue the west corner, is where this park lies.

Also in the shadow of a skyscraper-sized billboard overlooking the nearby Eisenhower Expressway, this "park" is actually more than of a play lot as opposed to the latter.

Inside of this play lot, smaller children run and play in was appears to be the sprinklers.

Others with adult supervision does the swings and play on the slides, while four others play on what is obviously a wooden "teepee."

A modest basketball court, which is heavily occupied, rests at the north end.

Several porches and connecting garages in the adjoining alley parallel to west Harrison are also seen. A colorful gang slogan almost in the form of a mural is written on one of the garages. It bears: 2-4 MAFIA KINGDOM 4 LIFE. WILD WILD WEST!!!

Also seen is a well drawn set of fingers representing the numbers two and four as well what appears to be a cowboy hat. Another sketch bears what looks like a forty-five.

Although every player on the basketball court (with and without their shirts) all of whom are actually quite talented despite the elbows, the pushing and the occasional body slams; are very much unknown. However, the not so obvious rift raft some of whom are key spectators while others play craps are.

The young ladies presumably in their teens that are in attendance, idly cozy up to the latter. Fully clad in their top of the line designer gear (others scantily dressed), they appear to be having a good time. The time is now seven p.m.

Among the spectators are Michael "Mookie" Mitchell, Isaac "Ice Pick" Pittman, and Remington "Remy" James. Remy, thirteen years old is the youngest among them.

He tends to his pit bull "Two Eleven" along the side of the lot behind the existing one flat. Eleven viciously mauls away at a raw pork steak now thrown to him.

Another young man presumably seventeen or eighteen with a lean frame and somewhat handsome features, appears to be under the weather.

With two beautiful young ladies at his side who appears rather concerned about his ailing appearance, is quickly relieved when he summons his bottle of Maalox.

Sometimes known as the "Maalox Man" of course, otherwise he is known as Adam "Asteroid" Henson. For the moment, these toughs are minding their own business.

Ivan who is seen with his friends Charles, Lazarus and Nikki now enters the gate.

Tre and Butch who are at the water fountain suddenly find themselves looking up.

Appearing dumbfounded, appalled, and somewhat startled mainly by Ivan's entrance, the two obvious cowards then scoffs. "What the fuck?" Butch sighs.

Paying them no mind, it maybe possible that Ivan and his friends come in peace.

They proceed to the basketball court.

Other eyes are already watching as Ivan and his friends approach the crowded court.

As what is seemingly a gesture of friendship on behalf of the local hoodlums, is really a hint of sarcasm as Ivan, Charles, Laz and Nikki now watches the ongoing game.

Once again Mookie, Ice Pick, and Remy began to applaud.

"Well, well, well." Remy begins chuckling.

“If it ain’t the Last Dragon in the Hood and his fake assed disciples to be.”

While the rest of the group laughs, their little lady friends on the other hand shares giggles. However, most of them are actually attracted to Ivan’s physique as they now began undressing him. With their eyes of course.

“You know what, I’ve been really impressed with yo ass.” Remy continues on.

After briefly playing with eleven, he then orders him to sit. Eleven obeys.

“And I’ve always been don’t get me wrong and shit.”

“Funny.” Ivan begins. “I’m actually flattered Remy.”

“I have to say, damn!” Remy once again chuckles.

“You’ve been quite the busy boy this year.”

“Word, showin’ initiative.” Says Asteroid.

“He sho ain’t the same mothafucka either.” The others whisper among themselves.

“He’s really cute.” Says one young lady. Nikki smiles.

“So Ice, how’s the bladder?” Charles cracks.

Both sides begin to laugh. “Fuck you man!” Ice Pick softly replies.

“Trying to come up in the world huh Ivan?” Asks Mookie.

“Just last week, you really served some of our boys back there at Willie’s.”

“You served up some mo of our soldiers up at the Y earlier this year.”

“We don’t know too many niggas who can actually pull that shit off around here.”

“Let alone just one mothafucka.” Says Ice Pick.

“I even hear rumors that it was yo ass that started that riot down by California.”

“That’s some bullshit.” Butch shakes his head.

Tre’s bronze complexion turns green.

“So you think you the black Chinese super ninja or some shit?” Asks Remy.

“You think you’re that hard?”

Ivan clears his throat and smiles.

"I'll do." He replies. Charlie and the rest of his friends laugh.
"You're funny, not the punk ass I though you was and actually a smart mothafucka."
"Even better than yo cousin Doughboy."
"That's why you should join us." Ice Pick claps his hands.
"It'll really be yo time to come up."
"Hey yo, any friend of yo cousin or even a family member is a friend of ours."

The youngsters who were just playing basketball a moment ago has suddenly stopped. They slowly began to surround a would- be unsuspecting Ivan and his friends. The southernmost youth who bares a gut and what appears to be "male tities" attempts to move in on Ivan's space. Slowly. The rest of this unknown group follows his lead.

Meanwhile, Ivan who is further turned off by the gang's proposal/ ultimatum appears to be mildly disgusted. "Once again you all." Ivan begins with growing disdain.

"Thanks, but no thanks."

"Nikki, Charles, and Lazarus."
"Let's go."

Just barely looking behind him just as the lard ass attempts to strike him, Ivan who is already in his fighting stance, snaps a rather powerful back kick. The big boy spits out tiny molecules of saliva as he struggles to breathe. The youth drops to his knees.

With the employment of his best footwork and signature rhythm, Ivan changes his stance and snaps a double sidekick into the head of another.

Following up with a combined hook kick which reverses to a roundhouse, this young man falls to the pavement. For the next ten minutes, his world becomes black.

A third angry hood that attempts to throw a punch is quickly knocked on his ass as Ivan's rear leg hook kick aligns to the back of his head.

Although far from knocked out, the husky young man is seated on the ground.

Shaking as though he is hemorrhaging, this hood is apparently in a daze, disoriented, and quite confused as to what has just happened.

Maintaining his rhythm as he does his breathing, Ivan with his guards up spins and snaps multiple crescent kicks. As each blow makes contact with the bodies of his opposition, some of their common fluids began to spill.

Mainly sweat, saliva, some of their funk even their blood.

A much taller youth who appears roughly five-eight whose punches are parried and quickly blocked by Ivan catches a flying crescent kick.

Just like a ton of bricks (literally), this young man collapses.

Delivering two axe kicks, which already cause two more hoodlums to fall back, Ivan then spins before executing a double sidekick to what is already his ninth enemy.

Coming cross with another spinning hook kick which causes his tenth to see a brief flash before passing out, this furious young fighter sweeps more of his enemies in one circular motion with his foot.

They simultaneously fall to the ground.

Dancing on the balls of his feet, Ivan snaps a left jab into the face of one individual while punching another in the throat. At this time, more youth's storm into to this now crowded play lot. Charles, Nikki, and Lazarus look on happily.

Taking control of the wrist of the first incoming combatant, Ivan snaps a knee into his abdomen and turns his body counterclockwise. With that, he rolls him onto the pavement. Sticking his foot out for the next one, Ivan grabs his wrist, summons his left foot behind the back of his calf and sweeps him to the ground.

As his last opponent, throws multiple punches, Ivan catches, blocks and parries every single one of them. Utilizing this young man's body as though he's his own personal Wing Chun dummy, Ivan educates him.

While deflecting and blocking, Ivan summons his fists targeting all of his vital organs. But however, Ivan spares him.

"You all might want to consider working on your jump shot." Ivan dribbles the ball of his now laid out opposition. "It really stinks."

Upon handing the ball to the one youngster who is managed to escape Ivan's wrath, Ivan himself bows his head. "You all have a nice evening."

Stepping around the bodies of those who are both limping, crawling, and to a lesser extent still unconscious, Ivan summons his own basketball who then throws it over to Charles. "Let's go." After shaking hands with Charles and Lazarus, Nikki surprisingly takes Ivan's hand. They now began to leave.

Looking on as though they have witnessed a national tragedy, Remy and the others now appear gravely ill. Reaching into his pocket, Asteroid summons his bottle of Maalox and takes a swig. Only their girlfriends appear to be pleased as they as they bid Ivan farewell. "Bye Ivan." They all reply in unison.

"Tre!" Remy barks. Eleven at first growls and then whimpers.

The entire group appears as though they are nauseated.

The park suddenly smells like human feces.

"Mothafucka, go change yo pants."

"Goddamn!" Mookie holds his nose.

A dark brown spot suddenly makes it presence known in the back of Tre's jeans.

Tre Gordon has indeed become thc shit.

30

SALAZAR RESIDENCE, SOUTH LAWNDALE
THURSDAY 4:00PM

"Como estas son los su padres Ivan?" Asks Mr. Salazar.

Seated in the dining room, Diego who is a friend as well as a fellow up and coming young martial artist is now having dinner.

Among all of those who are present other than the younger Diego, there are his parents as well as his two other siblings.

His slightly older brother Marco, who is fifteen, is a sophomore at Whitney Young high school. His resemblance between he and Diego is relatively strong.

Irma, Diego's youngest sister is eleven and like her brother, she too is in the same grade. Both are enrolled in the same elementary school and enjoy reading.

They both attend Andrew Jackson Language Academy, which is also on the near west side. Both Diego and his sister, are both straight "A" students.

Marco, an Art major is also an honor's student.

The siblings three are also athletically inclined and have not only the bodies, but also they even have the awards, the trophies, and the certificates to prove it.

The entire family appears to be extremely photogenic as many photos and portraits hang throughout the house. Even earlier photos of a then newly wedded Mr. and Mrs. Salazar is seen, as well as toddler versions of Diego and his siblings.

Diego Sr. who is thirty-nine and his wife Raquel, thirty-seven has been married happily for about nineteen years.

Diego's father, like that of Ivan's is also ex-military and has also served in Vietnam, has a degree in business management and works as a field supervisor at the Brach's candy factory. His mother, an assistant bank manager works at Talman Home Federal Savings downtown. Both parents have held their posts for over a number of years. The current family dwelling consists of a two-story brick structure located here on Pulaski Road. Surrounded by mostly like homes covered by trees and well-kept lawns, a modest network of businesses corresponding to industrial just off the Stevenson Expressway and some commercial venues are seen near and around west thirty-first Street. The Sanitary Canal flows directly along a now congested Stevenson Expressway.

The Salazar's like the Thompson's, and the Wang's have dwelled in this city for generations. And they too have the tastes, as well as the opinions and the credentials to prove it. With both languages greatly welcomed, with English being the most dominant, Diego's family has taken great pride, the liberty, or simply just made it their business to further Ivan's pre-existing knowledge of their great grandparents native customs as well as the Spanish language itself.

Even Ivan has shared some ideas regarding his own culture to both Diego as well as his friend Tommy Wang. Mr. and Mrs. Thompson has likened their son as well as his friends as being "a young united nations."

Despite the fact that Chicago still remains not by far, one of the most racially and ethnically divided cities. But yet compared to the turbulent sixties and before, she has also come a long way. Like the Reverend Jesse Jackson once said "Keep hope Alive."

"Son los muy bien Mr. Salazar." Ivan responds. "Como estas su trabajo?" Asks Mrs. Salazar. "Esta la todavia que divertido." Ivan begins. Diego and his friends nod their heads in agreement. "Tal vez que, no lo tengo trabajo esta noche."

Their meal for the evening consist of a traditional American steak, refried beans with melted cheese, southwestern-style spicy cornbread, and some traditional Spanish rice. For dessert: homemade chocolate ice cream and fried bananas.

Ivan, who ventures from beyond his adjoining neighborhood almost on a regular basis with his parent's consent, is already enjoying his meal here.

"Ello's siempre que hambre?" Says Diego's sister. She smiles at Ivan.

"Si Irma, esta la verdad." Ivan responds. "Esta cierto."

Diego laughs. "Ivan aqui, el come que todo." He says about his friend.

"No me digas!" Marco chuckles.

"Ellos que fuerte como ti Diego." Marco adds.

"Estamos que muy feliz con tu muchachos." Mr. Salazar says to both his son as well as his guest. "Por que, de dos de ti estas con los artes de los martiales."

"Muy bien, por su seguridad, y por divertido." Mrs. Salazar adds.

"Boxeo de oeste tambien." Marco adds. "Exactamente!" Says his dad.

"Como estas su hermano?" Marco asks Ivan.

"He's alright, Simon's doing fine." Ivan responds.

"For a time, mainly during his freshman and sophomore years." He begins.

"He's a senior at Curie now, by the way."

Mr. and Mrs. Salazar both happily nod their heads.

"Simon and his friends from near us were always being jumped on by the Conquistadors on the corner out there." Ivan points toward the windows.

"Until Simon improved his fighting skills." Marco steps in.

"One of his friends who was with him I think, although Simon managed to tear Enrique's set apart literally, not to mention another eight who tried to rush in."

"Ran off and got on a bus." Ivan chuckles.

"Simon paid Sheldon back on that very same evening too."

"And since that fight, every other non-Hispanic black has gotten a free pass."

" Not to mention, that the Conquistadors has quite a working relationship with the 24's back in my neighborhood as well." Ivan concludes.

"It's been that way since the late 70's." The senior Diego adds.

"There was like this gang summit in the county, and every gang ever known was in attendance." "Kind of a Warriors style meeting."

"My brother was a corrections officer working there at the time."

"And two different factions were created, the Alphas and the Betas."

"The Conquistadors, the 24's, the Ravens, and the Latin Knights all coincide with the Alphas." "And their rivals, like Los Locos, the Fifth City Family, and the Six Corner Crew all fall under the Betas." Mr. Salazar concludes.

"The original purpose of all these gangs especially when we were coming up." Mrs. Salazar begins. "Was specifically to protect our communities and fight racism."

"Now they've become the true internal bloodsuckers."

At this point the entire family and their lone guest are very much done with their meal.

"Marco and me had our own fair share of problems with the gangs early on around here." The younger Diego tells Ivan. "Just like you and your brother."

"I was among the ranks myself when I was younger." Says Diego's father.

"But I got out because I was bored, joined the service did one tour in Vietnam, went to UIC, met Mrs. Salazar here and started the empire."

The others laugh. "There's really nothing that you get for joining a gang nowadays anyway." "They represent nothing but cultural shams." Says the younger Diego.

"They rip off the very neighborhoods they've been sworn to protect, terrorizing its own residents and even those within their sets just because they feel like it."

"If you're fortunate enough and you don't get arrested, don't become a cripple, or get yourself killed, and you just get out for whatever reason, they want to mark you for death." "Or another case of scenario, as a part of their initiations you'd have to take a beating to get in as well as another to get out."

"That's why I love being a neutron." Chuckles Marco.

"Someone should have told my cousin Doug that." Says Ivan.

"What happened to your cousin Ivan?" Asks Irma.

"I ended up beating him silly and practically drove him out of town." Ivan tells her.

Irma and her mom are appalled.

"Just to get a promotion within the 24's, my own cousin used me as his own sacrificial lamb." "He literally betrayed me." Ivan breaks it all down.

"He's in Wisconsin now, living with his mother."

"Blood is supposed to be thicker than water." The younger Diego sighs.

"It is Diego." Ivan assures him.

"My parents had me under house arrest for at least a week."

"I ended up destroying some furniture in the process." Ivan explains.

Mr. and Mrs. Salazar nod their heads in agreement.

"It was warranted, given that I had already endured so much prior to that."

"But things are really starting to look up now."

"That's always a good thing." Says Mrs. Salazar.

"So how's school on your end?" Asks her husband.

"Fine as usual." Ivan replies.

"Also right now, I'm in a citywide spelling competition with my school."

"That's nice." Both of Diego's parents reply.

Irma, who briefly leaves the room, returns with dessert.

As she returns to her seat, everyone from this point on began serving themselves.

The mealtime conversations with Ivan and the Salazar's continue.

Little Village (South Lawndale)

Located just five miles southwest of downtown and just off the Stevenson Expressway the Little Village also known as "La Villita" is also where Diego Salazar and his family resides. La Villita which is the Spanish pronunciation for "The Village" is also a part of the greater South Lawndale area. A well crafted arch along west Twenty-sixth Street stretching from California Avenue to the east to Chicago's western border, a border also shared by the town of Cicero, a visitor can easily discover that he, she, or even they have entered what is today a Mexican as well as a Mexican-American enclave.

This neighborhood is also less than one mile from Ivan's adjoining North Lawndale.

Cermak Road another commercial thoroughfare acts as a dividing line, although a small but growing black population (within South Lawndale) exists.

Farrugut, a high school named for a Spanish-American Civil War General here on south Christiana houses a student body that caters to both ethnicities.

Since the late 1960's to possibly the early 70's, both of the latter has at times found themselves at odds with one another. But yet, they still manage to get along.

Many believe that this rift is more about gang territory as opposed to race.

Three flags: One of Mexico, the African continent, and United States are seen flapping at full staff just outside of the campus building.

Like its next-door neighbor to the north, South Lawndale was founded after the Great 1871 Fire. During that period Germans and Czechs (Bohemians) were among the dominants groups. The Poles who eventually succeeded them later joined.

By the early 1970's the Hispanic population consisting of mainly Mexicans began arriving. During this period they only accounted for four percent.

After the 1980 census was recorded, following the exodus of white ethnics, Hispanics now accounted for almost fifty percent. Today their numbers rapidly continues to climb.

Since the last census, it is also believed that half of the population as opposed to aging is actually getting younger. And with that, it is believed that at some point that many of the public schools and some parochial in this neighborhood can or will be overcrowding.

Namely in the coming years.

Despite the loss of some of its industrial hubs such as International Harvest and Western Electric in the nearby suburban town of Cicero, this community even though its not middle class, still holds its own and remains affordable.

Along Twenty-Sixth, which is now, vibrant with locals and outsiders alike roaming about, countless restaurants, shops, banking institutions, even a few flag ship stores like Goldblatts, and even Ames are seen. A few vendors in between are also spotted as they too get their hustles on. Another day, plus another dollar, equals a better life.

An existing 1970's GMC-made bus employs a lakefront-bound Blue Island/26 now stopping at the corner of 26th near Kedzie. A more modern MAN series: 4022 working a Roscoe-bound Kedzie&California mingles with the latter as it shares passengers.

While the older series bears its "roller curtain" destinations signs on the front and right sides, the more recently delivered fleet bears a digitized marker.

At some point, a driver on the Kedzie route is seen ending his shift while another begins his. A supervisor who sits in a nearby booth looks on.

Having greeted his passengers, the driver (a seasoned veteran) begins his trips.

The supervisor, a graying but petite woman looks at her employee and smiles.

Stepping out of his family residence, both Diego and Ivan began their journey north along Pulaski. Some youths, who dwell on the corner in front of Dukes, a local greasy spoon near Thirty-First all acknowledges both Diego as well as Ivan (who can actually blend in), with a friendly nod as they idly walk by. Ivan appears to be every bit as welcomed as other residents also greets him. They continue west along Thirty-First.

Piotrowski Park

Formerly known for its surrounding namesake community "Lawndale Park", this site was renamed fifth teen years ago to honor a Ms. Lillian Piotrowski, a lifelong neighborhood resident. Piotrowski, up until her death in 1974 devoted much of her life to politics and public service while living in the community.

It was believed that she even worked as a member on Cook County board of Commissioners as well.

Situated on the corner near Karlov Avenue and Thirty-First Street facing the world famous Home Run Inn, a long time pizza joint, surrounded by other modest businesses, a church, and many two and three story flats structures, with multiple bungalows and limited greystones in the shadows, Diego and Ivan are already here at the field house.

Practicing on their fighting techniques, both young men utilizes the same power as they repetitiously exchange kicks and punches.

Clad in their respective gear, they dance, bob and then weave.

Shuffling up, both boys considering they have just eaten changes stances almost back to back. Exchanging hits under a coach, the two now began to grapple.

Sweating profusely, Ivan and Diego literally takes turns slamming, and flipping one another to the cushioned floor before exchanging submissions and then reversing them.

Among the spectators is none other than Diego's friends.

Many of whom he has known since the first grade.

Upon drinking some water at the fountain, the two summon their Kali sticks and take their stances. "Remember, this is almost like using our swords in class." Diego begins.

Ivan happily nods. One of Diego's friends Violet pops a tape in to a radio as the two begin was is believed to be their last drill of the evening.

The two have been training for at least a good hour.

It is now close to 6pm.

As a warm up, the two start off relatively slow as they feed each other different angles in what is known as a "six count."

Now walking across the room while maintaining their stances, both boys are still able to summon their strikes. After alternating for the first fifth teen minutes, Ivan and Diego now focuses on their momentum. As the duo trains, the Simian Remix of Inner City's "Big Fun" featuring Kevin Saunderson thumps throughout the room.

Riding cross-town onboard the number seventy-four Fullerton bus, Cedric Holt who is actually without his mate slash sidekick travels from his quiet middle class neighborhood of Montclare to what is now a more upscale Lincoln Park.

Just to the east of Halsted Street where the bus turns around, the area's namesake park, its zoo and not to mention the beach and Lake Michigan are all within reach.

The historic DePaul University has roughly thirty-six acres encompassing Fullerton and Sheffield Avenues followed by the west side of north Halsted.

Just to the north of Halsted and Fullerton, is where Lincoln Avenue begins.

Among the many shops, restaurants, and some banks that are seen along the latter there are at least two existing movie theaters. Located to the right in the middle of the block lies the historic Biograph. Still airing first run performances after nearly eight decades, this was also where FBI agents shot the infamous bank robber John Dillinger after watching a gangster movie. Almost funny, but yet still ironic.

Its marquee displays the titles: MAJOR LEAGUE, HOW I GOT INTO COLLEGE, and ROAD HOUSE. Cineplex Odeon is now the dominant franchise.

Directly across the street is the Three Penny Cinema, which is just as old, but shows mostly foreign, classic and independent films.

Along Fullerton many pedestrians who represent all walks (most notably college students) are as usual out and about here. It is of course rush hour as countless automobiles and buses supplement the latter. Trains continue to roar and stop at the recently spruced up station, (another turn of the century relic) as they summon multiple passengers.

The McCormick-designed row houses along Fullerton encompassed by trees are also supplemented by a combination of brownstones as well as two lone Victorians.

Avery Residence

Despite decades of urban renewal, gentrification, the ongoing exodus of poor working class families as well the current influx both students and childless couples, the Avery's represent a small number of upper-middle class families.

Scattered throughout the neighborhood, they are lawyers, CEO's, doctors, teachers, real estate agents, bankers and so on.

To namely those who live outside the community (most notably their working class friends, family members, and some others), they often refer to the Avery's as the real life Huxtable's. Abbott Avery, forty-one a Harvard Graduate is a prominent judge.

Born in the south, and raised on the south side most of Mr. Avery's cases are either civil or criminal. In his courtroom when it comes to trials pertaining to a shady corporation, a common criminal, or one whose rights have been infringed upon, not to mention the lawyer or better yet the relentless D.A. who fights to plead the others case, nothing goes through unless this man okays it.

Because of his heavy clout and political might, some actually call Mr. Avery "The Juice man." Prior to his current seat, Avery was not only a defense lawyer, but he was also a prosecutor. He now has the ultimate prize.

Ellen, who is thirty-nine and his wife of twenty-one years is actually a Speech Professor at the local university. A very attractive couple, down to earth and far from bourgeois the Avery's is still committed to the very communities in which they came.

Mrs. Avery, who also grew up poor and aided her mom in raising her siblings, besides waiting on tables to pay her tuition, good ol' Ms. Ellen Henry even swung the poles.

Among her customers was none other than a fresh out of college Abbott Avery.

Among their children, there's Alice, she's nineteen and attends school in Hawaii.

Rebecca, who is their middle child, is fifteen.

She is currently a junior at Jones Magnet Career.

And last but not least, their youngest son.

Abbott Junior, or just simply known as "A.J.", is thirteen.

A seventh grader at Schiller Academy in the heart of the neighborhood, A.J. like his siblings is academically inclined, sometimes travels with his cousin (considering that he has no brothers) enjoys sports, hanging out at the mall, enjoys reading, and like that of any other normal youngster, A.J. enjoys talking to girls.

The current family residence consists of a lone Victorian located here Fullerton Avenue. A mixed "L" train of Pullman 2000's and Budd 2600's is seen in the distance.

These units , which employs a Linden-bound Evanston Express now stops at its namesake station. Located directly to the right of the grade level stationhouse, lies the Lincoln Park Branch of the Chicago Public Library.

A.J. who is seen with his friends as they now exit the building, with the exception of one, the other four takes off. The lone young man, who now joins A.J. as they head east, is his most recent acquaintance: Cedric Holt.

Upon entering the family residence just five doors down, A.J. and Cedric makes it to the front porch and discovers Rebecca chatting with a male friend.

Greeting them both, A. J. and Cedric goes inside.

Upon greeting his mom who is in the kitchen cooking, A.J. and his guest head upstairs. His father, who is not present, remains at work.

After playing several games on his Nintendo, the two now browse through multiple magazines most notably Mad, some Hustlers, a few Playboys, and a stack of Penthouses.

"Where's that fine white chocolate girlfriend of yours man?" Asks A.J.

"Oh, she's chilling with some of her girls right now." Cedric smiles.

"You'll get a chance to meet her." He begins. "Is that who I think it is A.J?"

"Yep, that's ol' girl from Bay watch." "Erika Eleniak."

"Be sure to check for Jasmine Guy from a Different World, page thirty-four.

"Word, Whitley really is fly." Cedric now turns his magazine upside down.

"Anyway, as I was saying." He resumes.

"At the Brickyard, you might wanna consider trying to get with Yolanda."

"Yeah, she seems decent." A.J. agrees.

"Damn, I've got to head to the john man give me a minute." The junior host gets up.

"No problem man, take your time." Cedric insists.

"Be right back." A.J. then runs off.

Making sure that the coast is clear, just as he heads off to the bathroom, Cedric studies the hall in both directions. And with that, he now makes his move.

Upon going through his friend's dresser, Cedric finally comes across a Hershey's can, which is actually a makeshift piggy bank. Opening the can Cedric discovers a wad of money consisting of multiple unmarked bills.

As he hears the sound of the toilet now flushing, Cedric quickly grabs the money and puts the can back. A.J. re-enters the room shortly thereafter.

Cedric, at this point resumes reading his magazine.

With the risk comes the reward.

Thompson Residence, North Lawndale
Friday, 7:00am

After having her morning coffee, Marie Florence Thompson now fully clad summons her keys and her briefcase before heading out.

It has been at least a full hour since her husband Frank left with the Blazer to go to his own job. The latter is located only a mile and a half from where they live.

Mrs. Thompson, who has a longer commute further north, is driving the BMW still parked in the garage. As the sun continues to rise above the downtown skyline, Ivan her youngest son returns from his early morning jog.

Smelling like that of baby powder as he enters the house, he kisses his mom who is now seen leaving. Simon, at this time is already at school.

He began first period. The only other occupant in the entire building besides Ivan himself is his grandmother downstairs.

"Have a good one." Says Mrs. Thompson.

"Don't burn down the house, and tell Nikki and the others I said hi."

"No problem mom." Ivan briefly kisses her.

Mrs. Thompson heads out.

Forty-five minutes after freshening up and changing his clothes, Ivan prepares breakfast. The doorbell rings shortly thereafter.

Sitting at the dining room table is Nikki, Andrea DuPont, Denise Wilson and Arthur Amos. Arthur, who is twelve, is also another longtime friend of Ivan.

Originally from the neighborhood, he and his parents have long moved to the Rogers Park area. Located on the city's northeast side.

Arthur Terrell Amos, better known as Art is also a handsome young man.

Having experienced a recent growth spurt, Art is now rather tall.

About five foot seven and quite lean, the often-mellow youth has a smooth brown complexion and, can be sometimes rather charming.

With a tall fade similar to that of Kid the rapper, Art is every bit as down to earth as the acting head and his fellow guests before him.

Art, along with Ivan and Charles who still lives in the neighborhood have all known each other since kindergarten. Currently, he and Charles succeed Ivan by one grade.

Listening to the college-run WCRX 88.1 on the FM dial, a station that plays House, Rap, Freestyle, but mostly dance music, Ivan is now serving his friends some scrambled eggs, bacon, as well as French Toast. Donning a neon apron, jokingly it reads: "Kiss the Cook" with what was intended to be "kill" in the middle. The latter is scratched out.

As his friends pour their own juice, Ivan finally joins them.

He even takes the liberty of fixing a plate for his grandmother.

"I'll pick Ivan's cooking over the that of the school's anytime." Art begins.

Everybody now digs in. "Okay?" Says Denise. "You have some really ugly gifts." Andrea responds as she drinks her milk. Art looks at her and smiles.

She briefly wears a white mustache.

"With that nice chocolate complexion of yours, along with that milk mustache, you actually look sexy." "Ooooooh." Reply both Denise and Nikki.

"Thank you." Andrea says quietly. She almost blushes.

She then licks her lips before ingesting some eggs.

"Get a room already." Ivan swallows a piece of his toast.

He chuckles. "Shut up!" Andrea snaps.

"What?" Shrugs Arthur. He tries not to laugh.

"D.J. Dirty Ass." Andrea roasts. "Whatever." Art nods.

Art, who loves to hoop, play soccer, and play football, is also a young talented D.J. who enjoys mixing on his tables. "I'll help you with the dishes Ivan." Nikki responds.

"Thanks." Says Ivan. He smiles.

"And besides, I don't want us all to be late for school anyway." She then adds.

Once Again, her eyes are glassy.

"Um hm." Andrea shakes her head.

Everyone in the room is now facing them.

They smile. "Maybe you too should get a room." Andrea grins.

"Whatever." Says both Ivan and Nikki.

"Ooooh, I knew it!" Denise claps and then points at them.

"Get outta here." Ivan laughs.

"Anyway, I can't believe Cedric actually ripped my cousin off yesterday."

He now finishes his last strip of bacon.

"What happened?" Asks Arthur.

"A.J. who like recently made friends with Cedric out by the Brickyard, invited Cedric over to his house, and they were like just chilling, so I'm guessing."

"I knew who A.J. was talking about for two reasons that from time to time, Rizzo and me would hang out at the Boys and Girls Club over by Washington and Sacramento."

"This was long before I found out that he was actually a thief."

Art and the others all nod their heads as they listen.

"I would recall actually seeing both Ced and Hannah." Ivan continues.

He is the first to clean his plate.

"They would hang out there too."

"He probably didn't know that you guys were related." Says Andrea.

"I wish that A.J would have told me about him a lot sooner, he's one of my two favorite cousins." Ivan scoffs. "Cedric ganked him out of at least four hundred dollars."

"That was like his petty cash."

"My cousin, and his family are practically rich."

"His dad is a judge, and his mother is a college professor."

"They live in Lincoln Park, just four blocks from the Lake."

Art and the others whistle. "And A.J.'s father is a judge?" Says Denise.

"Cedric might be finished either way on this one Ivan man."

"I really owe this guy big, he's gone too far this time."

"Cedric and his mother used to live over here too didn't they?" Asks Denise.

"Yeah, he did." Ivan responds.

"In what had been the Busy Bee Lounge, across from the school, on the second floor." "Cedric and his boys were among the countless others who picked on me almost every day." "They were a bunch of ignorant, pathetic, cowards who had nothing better else to do." "But I already paid his friends back, plus interest, when they tried bum rush me ." "I'm surprised that he didn't bring Hannah with him this time."

"She was probably out with her girlfriends or something, who knows?" Says Nikki.

"Cedric probably wanted her to come along, but he couldn't find her."

Nodding his head, Ivan begins to speak.

"You know, I think its time that Cedric and me had a talk."

Art and the others nod their heads in agreement.

Jensen Scholastic Academy, West Playground.
12:30pm.

As usual around this time while most of the teachers are enjoying their breaks on the inside, their students immediately after lunch, will enjoy what is now their recess.

It now appears to be rather gloomy as the sky becomes somewhat dark.

Oddly enough, some of the streetlights along Harrison Street suddenly come on.

The forecasters sometime earlier this morning predicted that at some point in the day, the entire Chicago area has at least a fifty percent chance of getting some rain.

But yet despite the ominous-like clouds, the children continue to play.

Cedric Holt, who is seen taking some of his fellow classmates to the hole most notably on the basketball court while Hannah happily looks on, is suddenly distracted as Ivan who is joined by Nikki, Andrea, Denise and Art now approaches them.

Donnie Nicholson along with Curtis Hawkins and Malik Allen also follows the latter. They all appear to be rather calm, relaxed and at ease.

Ivan, with his hands folded behind his back leads the group.

Mr. Dunn, the security guard closely monitors them from a distance.

Some of Cedric's friends who are already startled and reluctant to step forward stays put. Others pretend to look tough, but slowly they still back away.

"Ah ha!" Chuckles Curtis.

Donnie on the other hand points and whistles while Malik snickers.

"You're a bully man!" Curtis teases Ivan.

"That's their prerogative if they choose to fear me." Ivan shrugs.

"You know what?" Donnie begins.

"That's what y'all get for fuckin with people."

"I kept telling y'all dumb Asses."

Nikki, Andrea, and Denise all turn to a now pale Hannah.

"You're not so stuck up now are you?" Asks Andrea.

Only Cedric who now buttons up his shirt, smiles.

Ivan who is also smiling, motions for everyone to settle down.

"So how's the new neighborhood Ced?" Asks Ivan.

"Its fine now, I just had to give some of the boys a lesson on diversity." Cedric says.

"Did some male bonding, and bought em a slice of pizza."

Ivan smiles and nods his head. He then claps.

"Despite the two of us being at odds with one another." Ivan begins.

"We're not really so different after all."

"Nowadays, you actually impress me more." Cedric cuts in.

"Maybe I was wrong about you throughout the years."

"You have really come a long way, especially from a year ago Ivan."

Both groups all nod their heads in agreement.

"You know whatever you all did, especially you Cedric early on."

"I think that we can let it all go for now."

"What do you all think?" Ivan questions his fellow classmates.

"Yeah, straight up, word." Says the others.

"So what do you have in mind?" Cedric finally asks.

Many of his friends are already uneasy about Ivan's forthcoming proposal.

"Well since you are now a fellow artist like myself." Ivan begins.

"How about a good challenge?" Only a handful of Cedric's friends cheer.

For Ivan's group, the support is unanimous. They also cheer.

"Now I'm really starting to like you." Cedric tells Ivan.

"That's cool, so what is the only rule if I win?"

"Well for example, there's my cousin A.J." Ivan breaks the news to him.

"Wait, A.J.'s your cousin?" Asks Hannah.

Both she and Cedric are both appalled.

"You fucked up homey." Art chuckles. "His pops a judge."

"But I spoke with my uncle, and he'll probably give you a break Ced."

"Ivan's actually got a little juice." Says Dean Kensington.

"He's got my respect." Willie Garrison adds. He gives Ivan a pound.

Although Cedric manages to keep smiling, he suddenly feels cold.

"Hey, that's good to know thanks." He also gives Ivan a pound.

"You're scared now aren't you?" "Why are you shivering?" Donnie busts him out.

"Maybe you've got me mixed up with somebody else." Cedric insists.

"But anyway, If I win." Ivan continues on.

"You will pay back every dollar that you took from my cousin."

"Nothing more, nothing less." Both sides once more nod their heads in agreement.

"And if I win?" Cedric finally asks. "Then you owe him nothing, you walk."

For the third time, both groups nod their heads in agreement.

"That was your friend, your homeboy, your ace boon coon." Ivan shakes his head.

All of Cedric's friends including Hannah are now facing him with the uttermost of disdain. Scoffing repeatedly, they sigh and continue shaking their heads.

Despite the not so obvious new strain in their relationship, Cedric still manages to save face. "Alright bet." He finally replies. As the two shake hands, Ivan bows.

"How's Garfield Park?" Ivan suggests.

“Monday after school at the Golden Dome.”

“Cool, see you there.” Cedric says.

“And I know we have to talk by the way.” He says to his friends.

“Alright Ivan, see you Monday.” Cedric’s group responds.

As the teachers return for their students, the bell rings.

Following the sound of thunder comes the rain.

Just before beginning his evening with his friends after school, Ivan despite the fact that its still raining begins running several laps around the block.

Clad in a gray hooded sweat suit, he continues pacing himself.

Briefing in through his diaphragm (in through the nose and out the mouth) combined with the smell of the rain, grass, and earth, all that Ivan can really taste is life.

And it is this life that further fuels his lungs, sustains him.

While running continuously in this early evening shower, Ivan shadowboxes in between just as his increase in oxygen coincides with his momentum.

Upon the completion of his twentieth lap, he then cools down and begins to walk.

Thompson Residence

With his hand wraps supporting his knuckles Ivan dances on the balls of his feet. As he employs his footwork, Ivan viciously punches away at the bag.

His combined speed and power as he snaps relentlessly echoes throughout the entire basement. Now kicking away at some bags held by Rizzo, and Charles who has already been knocked down several times, Ivan then goes to work on his Wing Chun dummy.

Executing his multiple blocks as well as parries at an alarming pace with rhythm well beyond one's imagination, Ivan then kicks away at it knees as he steps around while maintaining his stance. Attacking multiple pressure points throughout the dummy's wooden body, Alfred Miller, Rizzo Harrison's friend who is also present, chuckles.

"You're like the fighting equivalency of Benny Hill." He cracks.

"You ain't right man." Says Charles.

As Alfred mocks Ivan's movements mainly his attacks, the others began laughing.

"But you're a bad boy Ivan, don't get me wrong."

"He's a quick learner." Charlie adds. "I see, straight up." Alfred responds.

Alfred himself, who now lends a hand, summons two pads.

Ivan now snaps his knees continuously into the latter and then his elbows.

Having done some pushups and sit ups, supplemented by crunches, Ivan then works his newly bought weight set. Meanwhile, his three guests all exchange satisfied looks.

Enter the Golden Cub.

"Ivan didn't hurt you too bad, did he?" Mrs. Thompson asks Ivan's guests.

They are now in the living room located on the second floor.

"Nah, he's actually really good Mrs. Thompson." Charles happily answers.

"That boy has every bit of a strong spirit as he does a heart." Says Mrs. Cartier.

Ivan's grandmother who is also Mrs. Thompson's mother briefly joins them.

Sitting directly across from Alfred, Charles and Rizzo, she sips her coffee.

Ivan rejoins them shortly thereafter just as his mother returns with her own cup.

The woman otherwise known as the second head here in the Thompson household now summons the recliner. Mr. Thompson, her husband now watches TV, in their bedroom. Meanwhile the outside view behind her has long improved.

The skies are now clearing up just as the sun although descending slowly, makes one final stand. It is now 6pm. Realizing that the rain has finally let up, Ivan and his friends gets up and then leaves. "Be sure to be back here by nine-thirty at least." Mr. Thompson calls out to his youngest son. "No problem." Ivan acknowledges

"Thanks son, and you all stay out of trouble."

"If you decide to venture beyond the neighborhood, don't hesitate find a phone."

"Now get on out of here."

"Thanks a lot Mr. Thompson." Charlie and the others respond.

"Bye Mrs. Thompson, Ms. Cartier."

The boys all head out.

Atgeld Park

"I don't believe it man." Leon Young begins.
"Believe it." Charles insists.

At this time, these two youngsters along with the Powell's: Craig, Brian, and Jason, Thomas Moore as well as Ahmad Carr and William Kent are all situated in the field house. After nearly five hours of heavy rain, with a few flooded basements, some partially flooded side streets, and some hydroplaning motorists navigating the visibly flooded viaducts as evidence, life in this park slowly but surely returns to normal.

Only the outdoor swimming pool remains closed until further notice.

The latter remains deserted and cordoned off.

"Believe it homey." Charles tells Leon.
"Ivan and me have known each other since kindergarten."
"He wasn't playing about challenging Cedric."
"We were just at his crib, helping the guy train." Alfred adds.

Alfred himself, who has lost at least twenty pounds in just over three months, is also in attendance. "He damned near killed us when we were holding the shields and pads for him." Adds Charlie. "This guys has more speed and power than all of us in this room."

"Even Ready Rock." Adds Thomas.
"Ivan, was the one who saved our asses from those dudes they found out south."

"Although he wasn't the one who killed them, or even left them in the woods, Ivan really made them the laughing stock when he knocked their guns out of their hands, and beat the shit out of them." Adds the Powell's. "They tried to jack us." Says Alfred.

"We couldn't say exactly, that he had done it with such ease."

"We still had some involvement in that." Alfred tells William and the others.

"It smelled like his signature alright." Charles nods.

"It was said to really be hot down here."

"But he got a lot of help from our friend Ernest and his boys too." Says Thomas.

"After the failed two-eleven, those same two fools tried to sick a mob on us."

"That was when the posse came through, and Ivan ended up fighting the boss."

"I'm telling y'all and you too Charles, it was a clean and healthy fight."

"Ivan beat Mack Truck, made him bleed, and dislocated some limbs."

"But in the end, Ivan fixed him up, snapped those same limbs back into place and sent him on his way." "Yeah, that's him." Charles shakes his head. He smiles.

"Lately, at least recently when some 24's tried to take his pizza up on Kedzie, and some more tried to jump on us at Magnolia." Charles sighs, and then chuckles.

"The remaining thugs who was still standing, he didn't want to fight em."

"He was probably trying to show a little mercy and maybe have some compassion." Alfred tries to explain. "Yeah, word Al." Charlie Praises.

"You all have to understand that Ivan here ain't no thug, he's a warrior more than anything." Alfred reminds them. The others all nod their heads in agreement.

"Shit, I think that was a really noble assed gesture that Ivan made to this Cedric dude." Alfred further responds. "An honest, one on one traditional ol' school fight."

"No guns, no bottles, no knives."

"Limited ground rules, something that probably hasn't been heard of since our parents were children." Says Leon. "Or better yet, since WE were born." Adds Thomas.

"Those 24's actually like Ivan now." Charles begins.

"The only reason as to why they've been stepping up their attacks is because they want to swear him in." The Powell's and the others nod their heads in agreement.

"The leader especially wants Ivan because, he can fight now, he's book smart, and most of all Ivan's a cultural intellect, he's universal."

"That means an expansion of the gang beyond the traditional hood." Alfred finishes.

"He's tri-lingual, and ol' Ivan here loves to travel." Charles reminds them.

"His cousin Doughboy was a part of the gang, and tried to use Ivan to boost his status."

"And Ivan whooped his ass, and drove him out of town right?" Asks Thomas.

"Yep, you hit it right on the money Tom." Charlie confirms.

"Ivan ain't playing with mothafuckas any more, that goes for the rest of his family too."

"And its about time that, Cedric gets a taste of his medicine." Cedric continues on.

He smashes his left fist into his right palm.

"Historically, Cedric was always picking fights with people twice his size."

"He targeted Ivan at first because he knew that Ivan didn't like to fight."

"So for a time, Cedric took great pleasure in always bullying Ivan."

"Another reason as to why Ivan didn't want to fight him was because he was little."

"And I'm guessing that at the time, was that Ivan, didn't want to seem as though he was a bully and shit." "You couldn't blame him for that, but I was still pissed off with Ivan."

"We were all in the same school then."

"Cedric and Hannah shared a classroom with me, before I got transferred to Jackson."

"Ivan eventually started standing up for himself after I left, but by then, it was still an uphill battle for him, and he was still forever getting his ass whooped."

"Almost two weeks ago when they tried to take his pizza, although I knew that Ivan could now handle himself, as his friend I still had to have his back."

The others nod their heads in agreement. "So I had some people I knew, look out for him." Charles further breaks it down. "Hey, that's what homeys do."

"Word." Says the others. They all shake hands.

Meanwhile, speaking of Ivan, both he and Rizzo are seen in this very same room just as Charlie and the others continue to observe. Playing a game of one on one basketball, both youngsters appear to be neck in neck in terms of points.

Both of them have so far taken turns in sticking very tight defense, joint fouling (not to mention Ivan sweating up a storm), and now both Ivan and Riz are like glue.

As Rizzo dribbles and tries to fake Ivan by going left, Ivan remains almost unshakable. Riz, who is light on his feet as he ducks and dodges now gives Ivan the slip, and goes left. Dribbling the ball as he runs with it, Rizzo executes a lay-up.

The game is tied with six up.

Ivan who responds with the same play although slightly faster at this point takes flight and dunks! Six to eight. "Its not the size of the dog that in this fight." Ivan tells him.

"You're good." Rizzo grins. He now has the ball.

Dribbling and dancing, Rizzo goes right.

Attempting to hit a three pointer, Rizzo jumps up.

Ivan smacks the ball out of his hand.

"Yeah right!" Ivan chuckles. Attempting to score his own three pointer from the sidelines within, Ivan tries but he too fails. "Ah ha!" Rizzo points. Both youngsters continue to hustle. Despite their no so obvious love for this game, it remains all in good fun. Ivan, for the first time in this game actually scores a three pointer.

In response, Rizzo flies over Ivan and delivers his first dunk.

"That's the spirit!" Ivan claps.

"Its Eleven to eight." Rizzo announces.

"We're just playing up to twenty.

"Aight, bet." Says Ivan

They both continue to play.

Saturday

After a few hours of working at his Uncle Joseph's photography studio on the north side and attending his regularly scheduled martial arts class on the south side, Ivan showers briefly at his school before heading back north.

Upon meeting his cousin A.J. at the Fullerton "L" stop near his Lincoln Park home, the two began their ascension onto the platform.

They immediately board a northbound Englewood –Howard "All stops" on the inside track. Not too long thereafter, solid four-car trains of St. Louis 6000's summons a Kimball-bound Ravenswood onto the outer track.

Rogers Park

Exiting the recently renovated Loyola Station, Ivan and A.J. began their descent onto the street below. Strolling along north Sheridan Road, a corridor surrounded by a diverse network of restaurants, a few banks, trendy shops, coffee houses, as well as a core of residential high-rises, apartment dwellings (both historic and modern), one strip mall and a lone bar, Ivan and his cousin now reaches the corner of west Columbia Street.

Situated along the latter lies an existing movie theater.

Originally known as the Regent Theater in 1912, today it is known as the 400.

Currently still functioning as a single screen theater seating roughly 700, and unlike many theatres (minus the Music Box in Lincoln Park), the 400 even show double feature films. The admission is at least 2.75 daily.

Also housed in the same building is a White Hen Pantry, and a small art gallery.

Just to the right in the opposite direction where Ivan and A.J. now turns, are more apartment houses, a few single family homes and even more high rises overlooking the lake. A private beach corresponds to the northeastern most complex.

This neighborhood that lies nearly ten miles north of downtown, accounts for one of Chicago's most densely populated and diverse areas.

Between the late 1830's and his death in 1856, Irishman Phillip Rogers acquired roughly 1600 acres of government land, part of which became the nucleus of Rogers Park. In 1872 Roger's son-in-law, Patrick

Touhy, subdivided the land near the present day intersection of what is now Lunt and Ridge Avenues.

Around 1878 enough settlers had moved into the area to incorporate this then village. The number of residents outpaced its West Ridge neighbor and aided Rogers Park annexation to Chicago in 1893. The 1915 annexation of the area north of Howard Street, east of the present day North-South “L” tracks, and south of the Calvary Cemetery, previously known as Germania and South Evanston brought about a new northern boundary. Large houses on sizable lots during the end of the nineteenth century sprung up along Green view and Ridge Avenues and then north along Touhy to Sheridan Road. When the Northwestern Elevated Railroad opened the still existing Howard Station in 1908, the population jumped dramatically, almost overnight.

The construction of single-family homes slowed as sub dividers built multiunit dwellings and the neighborhood’s suburban qualities just died.

Many of the large apartment buildings now seen here today accounted for the most intense construction ever north of Howard Street.

Also along the “L” tracks in the eastern portion of the neighborhood.

Rogers park almost since its birth was and still is a largely rental community.

The intensive construction of apartments consumed almost every piece of available land there was. The housing shortage during World War II was no laughing matter.

Population density especially north of Howard invited lower rents, followed by more transient populations. Concerns about poverty, crime, and congestion were at the forefront. The situation with neighboring Uptown was comparable.

Private-Public partnerships surfaced in reference to upgrading the housing stock, and a variety of social services were later employed as a means of stabilizing the community. New construction here, most notably for the last three decades consisted of moderately sized apartment dwellings, townhouses, and nursing homes.

Some of the latter are seen further north along Sheridan Road.

Business activities in the neighborhood, entertainment spots and religious institutions are clustered along other main streets and at transportation centers.

Especially along Clark Street, and Devon Avenue.

The community's four "L" Stations also accounts for a lot of the continuous foot traffic. Up until recently entertainment venues were considered to be an important part of these districts. Elaborate movie palaces seen here such as the Howard on its namesake street has closed its doors. The Granada that sits on Sheridan Road recently lowered it curtain leaving the Adelphi (now North Shore Theater) on Clark to pick up whatever patrons its predecessors lost. Throughout the years, this neighborhood has been the home to many things from a ballpark to a country club.

As of now a flourishing live-theater community is growing.

Other religious faiths now co-exist besides the traditionally Jewish and Roman Catholics, although historically the neighborhood has always been open. Loyola also employs a Rogers Park Campus just to the south of its namesake "L" stop. In fact, the college campus actually faces the mothballed Granada.

Over time even since its beginning, Rogers Park has always been socially diverse.

The Irish, Germans, and the Luxemburgers represented the major ethnic groups during the earlier years of development. By the late 1960's, the neighborhood welcomed Russians and East Europeans, as well as immigrants from Asia in the 1970's.

Also during the latter period, African-Americans, African immigrants, and others from the Americas were also encouraged. Its an endless melting pot.

The total number of all current residents both local and foreign-born stands at almost 60,000. Despite the overall density with some rough areas in between in terms of crime, drugs, and gang activity, a large portion of the neighborhood (primarily in the shadow of Loyola University) remains relatively stable.

As Ivan and A.J. now takes a stroll further west on Columbia, a tree-lined residential street dominated by mostly single family homes as well as a few apartment houses thrown in the mix, the two discover some youths, socializing and eating on the porch of a graystone. The latter sits in the middle of the block.

Amos Residence

Originally from the west side, this graystone here on the fifth teen-hundred block of west Columbia has been considered home to Arthur Amos and his immediate family for at least five years. Art, who also has a slightly younger sister named Alexia, like Ivan, his cousin, and Charles also lives with both of his parents.

His mother, a caterer has her own business near the university, while his father oversees a franchise of auto repair shops, now blossoming across the city.

At this time, the entire house is filled with mostly young people primarily adolescents as well as a few preteens. Of course they laugh, they talk, some dance. Others eat.

A more modest congregation lounges in the back, while the rest continues to chill out front. Lake Michigan, which is seen in the distance, summons a breeze to the west.

Such a party is of course, not without adult supervision.

Upstairs Art, a very young but talented D.J., a protégé of Kenneth Davis (D.J. Killer watt), is now seen mixing it up in the living room.

Scratching away on one table while Ice T's "Power" plays on another now comes the song "Life is Too Short." Most of the partygoers hail Art with showers of cheers as they continue to jam. The hardwood floor under them continues to creak.

Although Art himself is not the birthday host, one of his best friends from the neighborhood, Veronica Nunez is.

Veronica, who is now dancing with A.J., has just turned thirteen.

The daughter of a Dominican mother and a Belizean-born father, she was also among the first of Art's new friends upon moving in, and was actually born here in the city.

Her parents, along with Art's and a few other adults remain present inside the house.

It is about 7:00 in the evening.

In what is now the second full hour, things are going as well as planned. The beautiful and semi-exotic birthday girl is still smiling.

Veronica, who silently makes a wish, now summons her gifts.

Upon receiving them, she embraces all of those responsible before joining them downstairs. Ivan and A.J., who now stands with Art behind the table, all enjoys a plate of barbeque. Art, whose equipment now runs on auto, joins them.

"Ken has taught you well." Ivan begins.

"Just like I told the birthday girl down there, this is a dope party." Adds A.J.

"Thanks man." Art responds.

"And your mother can really throw down on the food here too." Ivan stuffs his face.

"Do you ever get full?" A.J. asks his cousin.
"Give your cousin some slack." Art suggests.
"The man trains almost twenty-four-seven."
"Yeah, that's right." Chuckles A.J.

Suddenly, the boys as well as some of the guests hear a loud commotion, brewing beneath them. They all head downstairs.

Upon entering the dining room on the first floor that remains occupied with other guests, Ivan and the others discovers an argument between a young lady and her young male friend. On the account of his presumed lifestyle given in part to his attire and his not so obvious thuggish demeanor, the young lady at this point informs him that their relationship is over. Apparently in a state of disbelief, the young man appears to be mostly distraught as opposed to being crushed.

The adults who were already at the forefront on this matter closely observe them.

Veronica, at this time was out back.

As the young lady attempts to leave, her now former boyfriend yanks her.

In response, the young lady stings him with a jab that only leaves him stunned.

The young man turned punk actually slaps her.

An enraged adult male attempts to tackle him, but the youth pulls out a real 38.

Despite backing off, the obviously embarrassed youngster still points the barrel.

The guests are now overcome with fear.

An older neighbor tries to talk the youngster down.

The young man, who now cocks the barrel, faces another dilemma.

While his gun is still pointed at the man who attempted to stop him.

Ivan, who has quietly advanced snaps a powerful left drop kick.

The now dumbfounded youth loses his sidearm. Ivan, who is beyond furious, stares into the eyes of a now startled Daniel Webber.

Meanwhile, Art's parents are now helping up the young lady. Just outside of the Amos House, many of the guests including the adults who think there is a lesson to be learned, now watches Ivan as he sticks it to Webber.

The gun that was procured by Art is now in his father's possession.

Executing a jab-cross-backfist across Webber's battered face, this is perhaps the first time since he exiled his cousin, that Ivan has become merciless.

A handful of residents also look on.

A bone within Webber's nose is now broken as Ivan delivers a palm strike.

It bleeds. Ivan follows up with a right jab into his abdomen.

Webber, who is now in a dazed-like state, catches a knee to the stomach.

Ivan turns him counter clockwise, and rolls him to the pavement.

Staggering to his feet, Webber appears completely out of it.

Upon snapping two left sidekicks, and then coming around with a spinning crescent Webber falls to the ground for the fourth time.

This time lying face down, he doesn't get up.

Retrieving a garbage can from a nearby alley, Ivan empties the contents onto a now laid out Webber. "Real warriors don't use guns, nor do they hit on females."

"Be sure to scoop up your ego before you leave, asshole."

He bows. "I'm sorry Mr. and Mrs. Amos."

"That's alright Ivan, actually you did nothing wrong man." Says Art's dad.

"The little punk actually had it coming." Art, his mother and A.J. happily nods.

"Had the nerve to think that he owned some body, and bring a gun into my house."

"Then he smacks his little girlfriend like she owed him money."

"Then he had the nerve to try to shoot somebody."

"You actually kept the peace, and you saved someone's life Ivan." Adds Mrs. Amos.

"You were always a sweet young man." She kisses his cheek.

"And thank you for taking it outside by the way."

Ivan happily shakes his head. "Are you alright?" He finally asks the young lady.

She bares no bruises. "Samantha." She introduces herself. "And yes, thanks."

"The police will be here shortly to pick up Ike Junior." Says Art.

"For the time being our neighbors will watch him."

"Now let's go back inside." Veronica suggests. She smiles once again.

"It might be my house and all, but its still your party girl." Art pats her on the back.

"You all heard her." He claps her hands. "Let's go!"

Cheering and clapping, everyone goes back inside.

The party continues.

Thompson Residence, North Lawndale
Monday, 4:30am

As the alarm sounds, Ivan rises from his slumber. Experiencing only mild fatigue, he immediate becomes alert and well focused.

Throwing on some sweats and a T-shirt along with his cross training sneakers, Ivan heads out to the backyard. Although the sky, most notably toward downtown has become increasingly bright over the past fifth teen minutes thus setting the stage for daybreak, its other half that faces Oak Park, Forest Park, and other suburbs further west remains in the dark. Although many of the streets and the alleys throughout the neighborhood remains lit, even the birds are out. Their chirps are heard just as Ivan begins to stretch.

Beginning the first half hour with some Taichi, he then procures a bag of charcoal and dumps several briquettes into the grill.

Upon striking a match, come the crackling flames.

At this time just as the fountain continues flow and the landscape lights proceeds to burn for the next hour, Ivan trains himself by quickly gripping, even holding, and not to mention sifting through the warm and fiery briquettes using both hands.

Even as some of the latter is reduced to ashes, he continues to sift.

Simultaneously putting one hand into the burning mixture of charcoal and ashes and then the other as he rotates consistently and quickly, Ivan now gets into a horse stance.

With both hands in their chamber positions, Ivan quickly places one fist after the other as he now punches down into the grill.

Now situated in the basement, Ivan works with his Wing Chun dummy for at another half hour, before kicking and punching the bags.

After shadowboxing with his knees and elbows, Ivan jumps rope before finally curling some weights. By the time he completes his training the sun has already risen.

The Golden Dome (Garfield Park)

Situated across the lagoon as well as within the shadows of its world's famous conservatory, this facility employs an indoor gym, a fitness center, and a swimming pool.

On the second floor facing the Lake Street "L" lies a special arena.

As two Lake-Dan Ryan trains roar past, rattling the windows as well as the hardwood surface below, scores of youths most notably all of Ivan's friends from school and beyond has already began filling the bleachers.

The same can be said about others who have come to support Cedric.

Others in between are just simply passing through as they too enter the auditorium. Playing in the background appears to be a blend of mellow rap songs ranging from Special Ed's "I've Got it made", De La Soul's "Jenifa and "Buddy", "The Luck of Lucien" courtesy of a Tribe Called Quest, and Tone Loc's "Wild Thang."

Several park district employees are also seen keeping the peace while another serves as a referee. Ivan, who is now clad in the traditional Chinese apparel sits alone in the locker room. He meditates. However, it is not Lord Buddha for whom he prays upon.

Nor is it the Confucius.

Just the traditional, but yet timeless: Lord God Jesus Christ.

Just as Ivan meditates, he also performs a split

Stretched across two chairs, he remains focused.

Meanwhile, Cedric who is already out in the makeshift ring performs a demonstration in what appears to be the art of Tae Kwan do. Hannah who is seated in the opposite corner looks on. Cedric is clad in an orange neon Korean-Japanese style fighting ghee.

Both camps at this time remain at peace.

Another mixed train of colorful Boeing 2400's and Budd 2600's roars on the outside.

Locker Room

Just as Ivan prepares to head out to the auditorium, Rizzo and Charles along with Lazarus and Alfred comes in. "Well, this is it Billy Lo." Riz pats him on the back.

"This is the moment you've been waiting for." Adds Charlie.

"You've been training yo ass off all year man." Lazarus punches away at his arm.

"Along with retaining your family's honor especially your cousin's, even your own."

"I trust that you know what else you're going to get if you win."

"Anyway, we have to tell you this because you're our boy man." Alfred begins.

"Stay focused." They all reply in unison. Ivan and his boys head out.

Shortly after Cedric completes his demo and bows before his audience, spectators on both sides respond by giving him a brief round of applause.

Upon entering the ring, Ivan also bows.

The applauding is almost continuous as he briefly demonstrates what has taken him three months to somewhat master.

Although he still has a very long way to go, Ivan has at least acquired the simple basics. Zui Quan, better known as the "Drunken Fist Style", this technique is not by far the most difficult in which one can ever learn.

Consisting of a category employing various techniques, forms and fighting philosophies this skill enables its practitioner to imitate the movements characterized by one who is intoxicated. The postures are created by momentum and weight carried out by the body as to what Ivan is now demonstrating. In slow motion.

Staggering and wobbling as though he is indeed drunk, Ivan whose balancing act remains on a "medium novice level" sways, and pretends to fall.

Blocking and striking his phantom while at the same time pretending to hold a cup, he then executes a series of modest acrobats.

Spinning, wobbling and punching, Ivan then sips from his imaginary cup before kicking out his feet. Returning to his stance, he bows once more.

Cedric happily nods his head in agreement while audience clap once more.

A park employee, and a not so obvious fifth degree Dan given his belt and black ghee, acts a the ref between them. "Among the rules and the guidelines pertaining to this match is this." He begins. "There are no elbows or striking below the belt."

"Obey my commands at all times." Both fighters nod their heads.

"Fight for as long as you can, while at the time make it a clean one."

"Otherwise boys, shake hands, bow and come out fighting."

Shaking hands, both Ivan and Cedric bows.

In the background, Fast Eddie's "Let's Get Funky", now blows out the speakers.

"Come on Ivan!" Shouts Nikki and the girls. The rest of his friends clap.

"Go ahead Cedric!" Cheers Hannah. The rest of the group whistles and claps.

Both combatants began exchanging strikes only to block and to parry off the other's attacks. Dancing and rocking away, Cedric executes multiple kicks just as Ivan himself continues to slap them away. Throwing even faster punches, Ivan slaps and parries away. Five minutes into the first round, neither fighter has been successful in landing not one single kick, not one punch or even a signature strike.

Upon stealing the other person's stance, Ivan successfully summons Cedric's wrist and flings him to the mat. Getting up on his palms and feet, Cedric returns to his stance and snaps multiple kicks, punches and then spins around once.

Ivan, at this point employs his Wing Chun blocks just as Cedric spins and summons rapid sidekicks, hook kicks (both left and right), spinning crescents and one axe.

As Ivan smoothly works his way through blocking Cedric's equally aggressive would be hits , Ivan successfully dispatches a series of punches while using his feet to block his kicks. Ivan delivers one punch to almost every major pressure point.

Minus the groin. Ivan, who then snaps a right spinning back kick, sends it dead into Cedric's stomach. Cedric's ass slides across the mat.

Half of the crowd cheers.

Cedric, who is already bruised, also sweats.

Shaking it off, he quickly rises to his feet for the second time.

With his guards up, Cedric attempts summon multiple front kicks just as Ivan continues to block, catch and parry.

Now taking flight, Cedric then attempts to hit Ivan up with a flying crescent.

In mid air, Ivan this time stops him with a left spinning back kick.

Cedric falls to the mat for a third time.

"Come on Ced." Willie Garrison claps. "Don't let em get this round."

Cedric rises and returns to his stance.

Despite his left jaw being bruised, Cedric still holds his own.
Ivan nods his head in agreement and smiles.

It is presumed that Ivan for the first time has met with someone who can be almost just as competitive. Cedric himself is also smiling.

Ivan this time becomes the aggressor.

Executing non-stop consistent snake hands, Cedric responds by parrying them off.

Ivan manages to thwart off Cedric's own attacks, and snaps the sole of his right foot into Cedric's now unprotected shin. Upon experiencing a brief sting, Cedric then catches Ivan's rear left sole despite his back being turned. Ivan himself who only jumps up slightly snaps the rear of his right sole dead across Cedric's face.

He staggers just as Ivan continues to snap his own multiple kicks.

Although Cedric successfully blocks nearly all of the latter, he yet still fails to catch a flying crescent that sends him falling a fourth time.

The bell sounds.

Rizzo, Charles, Lazarus, and Alfred all rushes to Ivan's corner.

"You're really looking good out there man." Charles pats Ivan on the back.

"Although Cedric's kicks are every bit as fancy as they are solid, he's still wearing himself out somewhat." "You never want to give your opponent everything you've while at the same time giving him everything you've got so soon." Alfred adds.

Just as he massages Ivan's shoulders, Lazarus hands him a bottle of water from out of a portable cooler nearby. Nikki hands him a towel.

"You've got to fight smart just as you have been doing." Rizzo further suggests.

Both Ivan and Cedric, return from their corners.

Despite wearing a mouth guard, Cedric still tastes blood. Well at least within the inner wall of his right jaw. Briefly turning his head, he spits .

Returning to his stance, Cedric continues to dance around the ring with Ivan.

Attempting to close in on Ivan with circular spinning crescents and then several sidekicks (at lightning speed) before trying to hook his rear right leg, Ivan sweeps him off balance. Cedric takes his first fall in what is now the second round.

As a gesture of sportsmanship, Ivan this time helps him up.

The two young warriors continue.

Ivan who attempts to initiate a jab-cross combo, for the first time is stopped as Cedric catches it and snaps a combined hook-roundhouse kick.

Coming around with a rear spinning hook kick, Cedric snaps a left jab-cross, summons a double (stomach to face) back kick, and then snaps a spinning inside crescent in mid air. Cedric's left foot smashes directly across Ivan's face.

Losing multiple molecules of sweat, Ivan for the first time falls to the mat.

Just like the well-skilled practitioner that he is, Ivan with unspeakable rhythm bounces back on his feet. Although stunned, he remains un-bruised.

Shaking it off, Ivan remains in his stance.

Now as Cedric attempts to deliver multiple punching combinations, Ivan abruptly smacks away at every one, charges in, jumps up as though he's doing a back flip and snaps both soles clean across Cedric's chin. He spits out saliva.

Cedric falls for the second time.

Getting up, Cedric tries to deliver a chop, but Ivan instead intercepts Cedric's palm, turns and then twists. Cedric howls just as the sound of cracking bones are heard.

Ivan follows up by snapping a roundhouse kick into his abdomen, and then snaps a left hook kick across Cedric's head. Ivan's friends all cheer as he continues to strike away at his opponent. Upon delivering his left hook kick, Ivan summons a dropkick and delivers a one, two, three backfist employing both hands.

The latter corresponds to what appears to be Jeet Kune Doe.

Cedric is bruised once more.

The bell sounds.

Maurice Mosley, the ref motion for the boys to continue.

Changing stances, Ivan penetrates Cedric's defenses, executes a double sidekick smacking across both his abdomen and face, comes around with a spinning hook kick, and begins blocking, parrying and catching whatever punches Cedric can deliver.

This is now the third round.

Ivan extends his left leg and snaps his sole into Cedric's abdomen, snaps the right side of his foot into his shin, jumps up with his back slightly turned while maintaining his stance and snaps the rear of his left sole into Cedric's face.

With what now appears to be a cut over his left eye that is actually dripping with blood and sweat, Cedric also loses his mouth guard.

As the bell sounds, both fighters return to their corners.

While all of Ivan's friends, most notably Rizzo, and Alfred along with Lazarus and Nikki who now massages his shoulders assist him. An unknown hand places an additional bottle of water into the cooler. Rizzo hands Ivan this bottle. The bell sounds.

In what has become the fourth round, Cedric who was briefly treated for his wounds and reclaims his mouth guard, dances with Ivan.

Ivan snaps a spinning hook kick immediately across Cedric's face and summons three consistent axe kicks to his head. Cedric gives Ivan a clean hip toss who does fall to the mat, but quickly gets out of the way just as Cedric's knee descends.

Ced misses and catches a foot sweep by Ivan, but quickly emerges.

Ivan succeeds by executing two “She Xings” (snake hands) to Cedric’s throat followed by a stinging one-inch punch to the chest.

Cedric who now appears as though the wind has been knocked out of him still soldiers on. Ivan who is quite focused and yet far from exhausted, is now suddenly in a daze. He appears confused and disoriented. All visual images have become blurred.

Despite feeling light headed, Ivan still manages to block Cedric’s now aggressive attacks. However, Ivan still grows weaker. His momentum crashes.

Although everyone in his camp has now become gravely concerned, a sizable number of those who support Cedric are also shaking heads.

In a seemingly slow motion, Ivan who is completely dazed and literally helpless endures his opponent’s powerful kicks.

Dancing and spinning with his hands up, and thus rocking on the balls of his feet, Cedric jumps up and snaps a powerful inside crescent across Ivan’s temple.

As the sweat pours, comes a red bruise.

Ivan falls instantly.

Getting up while yet still dazed, Ivan attempts to hang in there. Even the ref is growing concerned. The look on his face appears to be rather grim as though he suspects something. Despite maintaining his stance as he rises, Ivan is barely able to stand.

The bell sounds.

"What's wrong with you man?" Charles frantically asks his best friend.

"I don't know." Says a now beat up Ivan. His voice is strained.

What had been a red bruise on the side of his face now turns purple.

"I just suddenly feel tired." Ivan struggles.

"My head is killing mc, and the right side of my face hurts like hell."

"Did you eat too much before the fight or something?" Asks Rizzo.

Ivan who is almost slumped over in his chair responds with a painful nod.

Nikki, whose left eye becomes teary, treats him with Vaseline.

"He ate light." Explains Alfred. He pours a cup of ice onto Ivan's head.

Lazarus towels him dry while Rizzo rubs his shoulders.

The rare and mysterious water suddenly disappears from the cooler.

"You know, even though I can't put a finger on it entirely." Lazarus begins.

"But something is up with this fight." Alfred, Rizzo, and Charles nod their heads.

"You're ok Ivan, we know you ain't giving it up."

The bell sounds.

Despite the ice and the water, even a bottle of Gatorade donated by Art, Ivan is still unable to recover. However, he emerges from his corner still in his stance and with his hands up. This is no Zui Quan. Ivan really is out of it. It appears as though he's been drugged. But yet, this does not stop Cedric as he continues to own it up.

Executing what appears to be a "Tornado Kick" followed by a right front backfist, Cedric summons Ivan's hands as he himself lands on the mat.

With his back against the latter (while lying down), Cedric kicks out his left leg and throws him over. Ivan, although he breaks his own fall feels sick.

As soon as he is able to rise again, Cedric surprises Ivan with a continuous jab-cross-jab while mixing it up with an ongoing left sidekick.

While executing the latter technique, to his opposition Cedric is still able to skip on his right leg, while causing Ivan to stagger back towards the middle of the ring.

Jumping up, Cedric comes around with another inside crescent.

As he continues to mix it up with two axe kicks, one left and one right, he finishes off Ivan by snapping a flying right back kick to the face.

As the sole of his opposition stings him comes a brief flash. In slow motion once again, Ivan sees himself falling back before ultimately crashing onto the mat. Now tasting his own blood within the walls of his mouth as well as that of a warm swelling across his jaw, Ivan for the first time struggles to get back on his feet. The voices of his friends and others sound as though they've been disguised. The room spins.

As far Ivan is concerned, despite his first loss, it isn't over until the fat lady sings.

Northwestern Memorial Hospital, Streeterville (Near North Side)

Located just several blocks east of the luxurious magnificent mile commercial center, most notably Michigan Avenue, this particular hospital with a namesake university employing multiple buildings and dorms in the shadows of upscale residential high rises, historical mansions, and vine covered row houses with Lake Shore Drive acting as the easternmost boundary (Lake Michigan flowing along the latter), is indeed among the best in the country, possibly the world in terms of Science as well as modern medicine.

Some two decades earlier, Ivan's mother even gave birth to his eldest sibling, Jennifer here. Jennifer who bares her mom's maiden name is now attending college out of state.

It is about 5:15 as Ivan himself leaves the emergency room.

Upon receiving a thorough examination including a blood and urine test, the tough youngster despite his loss remains in high spirits , he remains alert, and is very humorous.

His tests revealed that Ivan only tested positive for what appeared to be animal tranquilizers. The latter was detected in his urine.

Now joined by only his father, the two pulls out of an adjoining parking garage in his recently washed and newly polished Chevy Blazer.

Mr. Thompson is every bit as relieved as he is impressed.

His youngest son has received a band-aid directly above his left eye, where a cut had been; the swelling that still occupies his jaw remains visible, but yet still treatable, and the body aches, most notably in the head region is no more.

The two now heads west on what is now Ontario Street.

Many professional office centers, restaurants, and cultural venues are also seen as they venture toward what now becomes a feeder ramp just beyond north Orleans Street.

This particular ramp, which is at least a mile long, provides, access to the nearby Kennedy Expressway, which appears to be running smoothly.

"You know, you're a good son." The elder Thompson begins. "And I love all of my children, by the way."

"But out of the three of you, you've actually been less of a pain."
Riding shotgun on the passenger side, Ivan only listens.
"I had a talk with your uncle Abbott and A.J."
"A.J. had told me about the money that this Cedric cat had stolen from him."

"I understand that you tried to win his money back by challenging Cedric to a Kumate." Chuckles Mr. Thompson. "And for you to look out for your cousin like that by trying to get his money back, and defend his honor, I likes that in you."

"On top." With one hand on the steering wheel, Ivan's dad gives him a high five.
"That was actually rather noble of you, despite of you getting yo ass whooped."
"So what it was foolish, but at least you've got some damned courage."
"Looking out for your family and your friends, even well to do strangers."
"You are just like me man." "You care about people!"
"You have good judgment of character for a thirteen-year-old."
"And then A.J. told me about the fight outside of Arthur's Saturday."
"He just told me that you actually kept the peace." Mr. Thompson smiles.
"A.J. said that you beat the shit out of this other boy who had a gun."

"It was like this domestic fight between this other party guest and her boyfriend." Ivan begins to break it down. "Art, A.J. and myself were eating upstairs, when we heard all of this racket under us." "So we all go down to find out what's going on."

Mr. Thompson nods his head while changing lanes on what is now the Kennedy.

"We see this girl and her friend, he looked like he was a thug or something."
"The girl announces that its over and she tries to leave."

"He grabs her, and the girl hits him."

"The boy literally slaps her, and this one man, I think he was one of Art's neighbors, became enraged." Mr. Thompson continues to nod.

"I bet he did." Says his father.

"I think he was going to box that kid silly." Ivan tells his dad.

"But before the man could grab him, the boy actually pulls out a gun!"

"He points it at the man." Mr. Thompson shakes his head.

"Nearly everybody is terrified, and this old woman tries to talk him down."

"Meanwhile, the boy still has the gun pointed at the man."

"While the old woman was talking to him, I slowly made my way toward him."

"I knew that it may have been reckless and stupid, but somebody had to do it."

"But I ended up kicking the gun out of his hand, and asked him to step outside."

"Yeah you could have been dead, but keep talking." Mr. Thompson advises.

"Although he ended up petrified when I disarmed him, he still accepted my challenge."

"You beat the shit out of him." Mr. Thompson finishes. "Didn't you?" Ivan nods.

"This guy had me heated up Dad." "Yeah, I bet he did."

"I beat him silly, took a trashcan and dumped it on him."

Mr. Thompson begins laughing almost insanely. "You are definitely my son alright!"

"While he was laid out, I reminded him to pick up his ego before he left."

"Damn, he sounded like a real asshole and a pussy for that matter." Says Mr. Thompson.

"Couldn't fight, hit a female, tried to shoot somebody, and got his ass whooped."

"That nigga really had a bad day didn't he?" Mr. Thompson chuckles.

Ivan laughs. "He definitely did." "I ended up apologizing to Art's parents."

"You know, I have to agree with Art's father on this one." Mr. Thompson begins.

"You did nothing wrong, and at least you took it outside."

"Art's house remained intact, nothing was torn up, and you kept the party going."

"One of Art's neighbors called the police, and they cuffed him and took him away."

"I couldn't blame you for whooping Doug's ass." Mr. Thompson continues.

"That boy really did lose his mind, and he got what was coming to him."

They are now passing through what is known as the West Side Medical District along the Eisenhower Expressway. While traffic in the eastbound lanes drag, the west remains on a roll. Among some of the prominent medical facilities there's Presbyterian St. Luke's Hospital, its adjoining research buildings, Cook County Hospital, The University of Illinois Hospital, and the County Veteran's Hospital.

Malcolm X College formerly Crane College sits to the left along Van Buren Street.

Dozens of commuters occupy the Medical Center Station on what is the Congress line in the median. Two trains of like equipment (mainly Budd 2600's and Budd 2200's) summons passengers here. It is still rush hour.

"The only problem that I had, was when you started tearing things up."

"I think I was aware of that." Ivan smiles.

"And then there was that high assed medical bill."

"Your mother and I thought that you at least deserve a week to think about it."

"Well, nothing ever comes cheap." Ivan happily responds.

"Yeah, you've got that right." His dad gives him a pound.

"I think your fight was fixed by the way son."

"That explained the tranquillizers in your piss."

"But it doesn't matter, in my book you still won."

"And I'm still proud of you Ivan." Mr. Thompson shakes his son's hand once more.

"Thanks." Ivan finally responds.

Having crossed the Sacramento underpass and then another at Kedzie Avenue, Mr. Thompson and Ivan eventually reaches Homan Avenue.

Just to make sure that their son was okay in the wake of his injuries from his fight the day before, Mr. and Mrs. Thompson allows Ivan to sit this day out in terms his school, his job, and to a lesser extent his martial arts class.

For the time being he rests at home.

Tuesday May 11, 1989 (The next day)

Although there are already rumors circulating throughout the neighborhood that Ivan deliberately threw the fight, many others beg to differ.

Among them besides his closest of friends, family members and even his teachers (most notably Mrs. Holmes) who suspects that it was "some bullshit", Ivan's brother Simon, his friend Ken and many others confront his long time adversary Hannibal up at Magnolia Play lot Park. As usual, the prominent local gang leader joined by his girlfriend Katherine "Kat" Waters and his lieutenants Ice Pick, and Mookie who also have their own companions are just lounging and chilling out.

On the basketball court, presumed regular foot soldiers are seen mixing it up amongst themselves as non-member residents (those with families) enjoy the mid afternoon sun. Upon seeing Simon and his friends who enters the park, the foot soldiers suddenly stopped playing. Just as they prepare to assemble, Hannibal throws up his left hand. Obeying their leader, they return to the court.

Before Ice Pick can respond Ken verbally cuts him off.

"Yeah, yeah, yeah, fake assed Frank Nitti, we know who you are!"

"Apparently, you know why we're here then." Simon begins.

"Because you would have BEEN summoned your boys over there."

"You've always been one of my most respected enemies and shit." Says Hannibal.

"I'd have to give that to all of y'all. Adds Mookie.

"You might not be gangsters like us, but y'all still some real mothafuckas."

"Thank you." Ken replies with sarcasm.

"Well first I gotta tell you Simon, that both you and yo brother's got heart."

"And I'm just as fucked up as you are." Hannibal resumes the floor.

"He ain't bullshittin, we wanna know who gave em the shit too." Says Ice Pick.

"On my momma, we don't fix fights like that around here."

"Hey Si, man I don't think they're bullshitting us." Ken insists to his friend.

"You might be right Ken, after all they do like Ivan now anyway."

"Ivan whooped Doug's ass, Doug is gone and they still need a replacement."

Simon nods his head in agreement. "Let's step."

"Aight y'all." Says Simon. He, Ken, and the rest of their group begin to leave.

"I may not be one time, but I'm always watching yo ass." Simon points to Hannibal.

"Word, he's a funny ass mothafucka." Hannibal says to his friends as his rivals depart.

Kat, along with Mookie, Ice Pick and the others all nod their heads.

New Skool Café, 4pm

The presumed winner Cedric Holt, although he wasn't drugged still sustained similar injuries from his bout with Ivan. At this time, he is now here with Hannah as well as his usual entourage as they dine out and work the video games.

"I actually underestimated Ivan all these years." Cedric begins. He now sits at a table with Hannah, Scotty Winfield, Dean Kensington, and Mustafa Henson.

Unknowingly, among the others (most notably under their table) Hannah's foot canvasses Cedric's leg as they all continue to mingle.

"He really is far from a punk now."

"We were certain that he had you in that third round." Adds Scotty.

"He made you really work for yours Cedric."

"Just as you gave him a good run here and there." Dean takes the floor.

Hannah then slowly fondles Cedric.

"Ivan could have either outscored you by a few more hits , or possibly you guys would have slugged it out to a draw, but for some reason in those last two rounds it was like he got distracted or something." Mustafa shrugs. "Or maybe something was on his mind."

Rizzo Harrison who is joined by Charles Davis, Lazarus Dent, and Alfred Miller all bursts into the establishment like gang busters.

"You know, you've reached a new low Cedric!" Rizzo says with disdain.

Some of the other patrons are startled. Cedric and his friends are clueless.

"Isn't Ivan okay?" Asks Hannah. "Yeah, he's fine." Says Charles.

"And why do you care about him anyway?" Asks Alfred.

"What are you talking about Rizzo?" Cedric interrupts.

"It was a fair fight, your boy just lost focus." Mustafa insists.

"Did you really think that is was a fair fight Ced?" Charles drills him.

Cedric and his friends are all puzzled.

"As long as I have known you Cedric, I have never suspected you as being a cheater."

"What the hell do you mean Charles?" Cedric scuffs.

"Ivan was drugged." Lazarus says quietly.

Cedric and all of his friends (including those sitting with him) are appalled.

"He was what?" Cedric shouts. He quickly apologizes to the other patrons.

While Cedric now gets an account from Ivan's friends as to what really happened, several of his other friends in the restaurant most notably, a weasel-looking Lance Crews quietly sneaks out. Cedric although blind as to who really drugged Ivan, is furious.

He storms out of the restaurant shortly thereafter.

31

MAYFAIR THEATER, DOWNTOWN
THURSDAY JUNE 13, 1989

Located in the luxurious Bismarck Hotel on the corner of Randolph and Wells Streets in the shadow of the Loop elevated where other various points such as City Hall, the Daley Center, a recently built atrium complex, a Greyhound bus terminal and remnants of a fading theater district corresponding to the east, hundreds, possibly thousands of people are seated as they watch some of the brightest young men and women in the country complete in what appears to be, an annual spelling contest.

The youngsters, between the ages of eleven to fourteen appear to represent various backgrounds and demographics.

Ivan, who has just recently won the city and state finals, is now among them.

Among the finalists besides Chicago's very own Ivan Thompson, there's Carmen Hernandez, who is twelve. She resides in Newark, New Jersey. Next, there's Kellogg Silverman, who is eleven. He is a native of Providence, Rhode Island.

Melissa Oh, thirteen is a resident of San Francisco, California. Brian O' Neal, last but not least lives in Boston Massachusetts. He is fourteen years old.

At least all of Ivan's immediate family is in the audience, including his eldest sister Jennifer who has flown in from Montreal.

A former alumni and a recent graduate at Lakeview High School here in the city, Jennifer Lucy Cartier, age twenty current attends the University of Montreal.

Named valedictorian among her peers when she attended Lakeview, Jennifer was not only at the top of her class, but she was also the youngest.

Upon receiving her diploma on the day of her graduation, Jennifer was only sixteen. When arriving in Canada in August (the same year she graduated), Jennifer instead chose to live off campus and moved in with her Aunt Daisy and her Uncle Chris.

Majoring in Law, she is now a senior and has her own apartment. Sitting alongside her parents, Jennifer whose complexion bears a yellowish crème closely resembles her mother as opposed to her father. Her long natural red hair, stretches beyond her shoulders and appears quite curly. Her eyes are just as brown as the rest of the family's.

Her figure, which corresponds to mostly curves, firm hips, and an upper body that can even give sight to a blind man, Jennifer is every bit as attractive on the inside as she is outside. For the time being, she remains single.

Among Ivan's friends Nikki, Charles, Rizzo and Lazarus are also in attendance.

"Spell astounding Mr. Silverman." Says a male voice.
The latter is heard from a gentleman on a nearby balcony.
Seated among several judges, he employs a rather loud microphone.
"Astounding." Kellogg begins. "A s t o u n d in g."
"Very good." Says the ref. The audience cheers.
"Mr. Thompson, would you please spell Inevitable."
Clearing his throat, Ivan goes to work. "Inevitable."
"I n e vi t a b l e." "That is correct." Responds the ref.
"Ms. Hernandez, would you kindly spell the word Irreversible?"
"Irreversible." "I r r e v e r si b l e." "Excellent."

"Our next finalist…Ms. Oh."

"Our next word will be evolution."

Taking a cue from Ivan, Melissa clears her throat and pours herself a glass of water.

"Evolution." "E v o l u ti o n." Outstanding." The audience continues to clap.

"Mr. O'Neal, can you please spell the word compliant."

"Compliant." C o m p l ia n t." "Well done." The audience claps.

"And that concludes the second round ladies and gentleman."

Now in the main lobby of the building which is consists of vintage chandeliers, leather cushioned furniture, priceless artifacts and endless wall to wall carpeting, Rizzo, Charles, Nikki, and Lazarus are all seated near what appears to be a statue of Jean Baptiste DuSable located near the elevators. "You're really looking good in there."

Says Charles. "Thanks, but these words appear to be too easy." Says Ivan.

"Consider it a warm up." Nikki smiles. She playfully ruffles his hair and smacks him across the cheek. "Well for what its worth, I didn't expect to make it this far."

Says Ivan. "You're perfume smells good." He tells Nikki. "Thank you." She tells him quietly. "Ok, I go against my fellow peers at school, I think nothing of it."

"I compete on a citywide level, I'm still asleep, but yet I keep winning."

"Now I'm competing on a national level, its time to get up."

"You've come a long way this year, period Ivan." Charles shakes his hand.

"Yes, he has." Adds Mrs. Thompson.

She joins her husband and her oldest daughter.

"How long have you been doing these?" Asks Mr. Thompson.

"Since third grade, at least." Answers Ivan.

"You were always good at this." Says Jennifer.

Simon and Kenneth who are also present, now combs the lobby for girls.

"You know we believe in you man." Says Ivan's father.

"Even if you don't finish first, we'll still love you."
"That's always good to know." Ivan now hugs them.

They all return to the auditorium.

As the contest further progresses, the number of its finalists slowly decreases. It is now down to two contestants: Ivan Thompson himself, and Melissa Oh.

It is now the fifth and final round as the two mentally continue to slug it out.

"Can you spell Articulate Mr. Thompson?" Says the well-clad ref.
"Yes, I can sir." Ivan happily responds.
"Articulate." "A r ti c u l a t e." "Very good sir."
"Ms. Oh, would you please spell the word incapacitate?"
Ivan pours himself another glass of water.
"Incapacitate." I n c a p s i t a t e."

"Its either this word or the next one following, should end this contest." Says Mrs. Thompson. Brandishing her Polaroid, she snaps a picture." I think so too." Jennifer whispers." Both Ivan and Melissa has been neck and neck for over a good hour now." Says Simon. "Whoever doesn't get the next one, its over." Charles insists.

The others nod their heads in agreement. "Are you certain ma'am, that you have the correct answer?" Asks the ref. For the next five seconds the room remains silent.

"Yes sir." Melissa confidently responds. The judges engage in a brief conference before rendering their verdicts. After briefly consulting with the ref, he returns to the stage. "I'm sorry Ms. Oh, but that is incorrect." "And this concludes the final round!"

Thrusting his left fist as to acknowledge his imminent victory, Ivan then looks up at the ceiling. Commending his maker, he then shakes hands with his fellow contestants. Now shaking hands with

Governor Thompson, no relation, his first lady, as well as Senator Harrison, Ivan now accepts his reward.

For Ivan Thompson, earning the respect of his peers in his neighborhood and even beyond supplemented by the power to ensure his survival on the street, is just another beginning…

THE GOLDEN CUB COMMETH
BY FURIOUS

Saturday, January 27, 1990
Washington-Dearborn subway station, Downtown
West-Northwest (Dearborn Subway)

Seated before four uniformed Chicago Police Officers within their own office situated on the recently renovated mezzanine level of the station, a mezzanine that employs two stainless steel agents booths as well multiple automated turnstiles, an existing concession stand as well as two pedestrian walkways which connects to Daley Center, City Hall, and the traffic court building to the left and the North-South (State Street Subway) to the right, Ivan and his friends Charles Davis, Rizzo Harrison, and Lazarus Dent tries to cooperate. It is about two in the afternoon.

And yet, they have no idea as to why they're here.

The air quality in the room as opposed to the rest of the tunnel bears more of a faint stale odor, just as the trains roar and screech.

Countless pedestrians carry out heavy foot traffic as well as riders moving to and from, alongside this well illuminated corridor.

The overall façade that covers the entire mezzanine employs a marble, stainless steel as well as a tan brick combination. Outside the office, the heavy smell of buttery popcorn and pretzels seeping in from the concession stand somewhat improves the air.

"Perhaps, one of you gentlemen or maybe the lone female before you who is present, can explain to me as well as my friends as to why we're here?" Ivan begins.

He appears rather calm, focused, and quite reserved for one who is coming of age.

Three of the four cops are appalled by his response.

"I believed that my friend asked you a question officers." Rizzo backs Ivan.

"Why did you stop us?"

He, along with Charles and Lazarus face the officers with much greater disdain.

"Ah, we just received a report from one of the ticket agents outside, that four youths fitting your descriptions jumped some turnstiles." A younger female cop explains.

The freckly-faced but not so bad looking red head for a moment turns pale.

She obviously appears to feel some guilt.

"It never fails." Rizzo quietly thunders." Define descriptions Officer Maloney."

"In other words, you've just picked up the first black youths that you saw."

"That's smart!" "So tell me, is this what they teach you guys at the academy?"

"What else can you say Riz?" Charlie shrugs. "They're the blue mafia."

He chuckles and shakes his head. Ivan, and two other male cops begin to smile.

"This is bullshit!" Lazarus sighs. "Its not bullshit." Growls a third male officer.

The Veteran officer's face has gone from a medium pink to a brighter red.

Officer Dawson gives Lazarus a rather menacing stare.

Lazarus, on the other hand is unfazed. He instead chuckles and shakes his head.

You don't scare me! He thinks to himself. You can take me to the station.

You can shock me with a cattle prod, or even drop me off in Canaryville.

Hate will get you nothing more, but a one-way ticket to hell you fat bastard!

And there will still be more of us. “Are you certain Officer Maloney?”

Ivan peers at the female officer’s nametag as well as other credentials.

“Yes we are you little smartass.” Dawson snarls.

“We’re detectives!” “This is what we do.” “ Some detective work.” Sighs Rizzo.

“What did you say boy?” Ivan is furious by Dawson’s remark.

“I would advise for you not to call him that again.” The young leader says with authority. Ivan yet still maintains his noble tone. “And furthermore if I may add sir, I think that you’re being very rude.” Once more the other cops are stunned.

“I think we’ve made mistake here Will.” A younger male cop says with disdain.

“Wait a minute, where are you guys from?” He then asks.

“Well, actually we all live in the North Lawndale area just off the Ike.” Ivan replies.

“You don’t seem as though you’re from the hood.” Says the rookie-like officer.

“Well, you don’t appear as though you’re from Edison Park yourself.” Ivan smiles.

Officers Rizzoli, Maloney, and a burly looking gentleman all began laughing.

Charles, Rizzo, and Lazarus who are also laughing all share a handshake.

“Alright, everybody quiet down.” Says Dawson, the presumed senior officer.

Unlike those who are under his command here, Dawson is clad in plain clothes.

“And who do you think you are you uppity little shit?” Dawson quietly snarls.

“Perhaps, you may want ask yourself that question Officer Dawson.” Ivan responds.

"I'm not sure if you or your colleagues are aware, but this is a high traffic station."

"Not to mention that you are, after all downtown."

The other three officers all nod their heads in agreement.

"There are at least maybe a hundred and fifty to possibly three hundred thousand people who uses this station daily." Ivan begins to make his case.

"Let alone even beyond weekends, holidays and of course during rush periods."

"Countless riders arriving and thus departing."

Even Charles, Rizzo, and Lazarus nod their heads in agreement.

"I would actually have no doubt whatsoever, that there maybe was some youths who actually jumped the turnstiles out there." Ivan points toward the door.

Sergeant Dawson begins to sweat. He appears rather nonchalant and quite arrogant.

"Of course you can look on the table and plainly see that we have our transfers and our tokens stating that we've paid our fares."

"Who the fuck are you to question our authority?" Sergeant Dawson fires back.

He smashes his fist down on the table. "We ask the questions!"

Ivan remains cool and yet, he still unfazed.

"You know what gentleman." Ivan now faces his friends.

"This interview is over." "Let's go."

Procuring their wallets along with their transfers, tokens along with some loose monies, Ivan and his friends began to leave. "You sit your ass back down."

Ivan ignores the sergeant's order and continues to walk out.

The now disgruntled sergeant attempts to run after Ivan, but is quickly held back by his officers. Officer Maloney happily summons the door for them.

"Try to have a nice day sir." Ivan smiles.

Leading his friends out of the office and back unto the platform, Ivan and his group boards the next train heading west.

Now glancing at the monitors back in his office, Dawson curses himself silly.

That little punk! Punching the two-way mirror once, he summons a carton of smokes and steps out. Heading up to the surface in the seemingly not so dead of winter as the streets and sidewalks remain free of the falling snow which is somewhat ignored by both vehicles and pedestrians alike, the head transit cop summons one of his Marlboros. Lighting a fresh butt, Sergeant Dawson takes one long drag and then exhales.

Maybe that little son of a bitch was telling the truth. He thinks to himself.

That kid really had some balls!

Maybe there's hope for America's youth after all.

Yep, that boy is definitely going places. He takes another drag.

Printed by BoD™ in Norderstedt, Germany